Emily was born in London to a Welsh mother and Spanish father, but spent her teenage years in Barcelona.

Her debut book Shop Girl Diaries began as a blog about working in her Mum's eccentric chandelier shop. It won the CompletelyNovel Author Blog Awards at the London Book Fair and inspired her script for Shop Girl blog, which was shown at the London Short Film Festival.

Her second book, a romantic comedy called The Temp, also began its life online, as a serialised novel on Wattpad and racked up two million hits under its original title Spray Painted Bananas.

Emily has contributed articles on social media to guidebooks and magazines including Publishing Talk, Blogging for Writers, Writers and Artists and Mslexia. She also runs Get Blogging Workshops.

She now lives in Mallorca with her husband. If she's not writing or thinking about writing, it's probably because she's up a mountain, in the sea or fast asleep.

http://emilybenet.blogspot.co.uk/

@EmilyBenet

#PleaseRetweet

EMILY BENET

Harper
impulse
we've got the love

Harper*Impulse* an imprint of
HarperCollins*Publishers* Ltd
1 London Bridge Street
London SE1 9GF

www.harpercollins.co.uk

A Paperback Original 2015

First published in Great Britain in ebook format by Harper*Impulse* 2015

A catalogue record for this book is
available from the British Library

ISBN: 9780008158071

Automatically produced by Atomik ePublisher from Easypress

Printed and bound in Great Britain

*For my brilliant father, who has never
tweeted in his life.*

Prologue

SPARKYMAY @SPARKYMAY
Woman loses phone, almost starves to death. Says didn't see point in eating if she couldn't share her #nomnomnom pictures on Instagram.

I don't usually tweet pictures of my food, but Clare Willis has outdone herself this time. We're used to her unveiling sophisticated tarts and rich chocolate cakes with dustings of cinnamon and crushed hazelnut. Never have we seen her make anything this bright. The icing is the perfect Twitter blue and as smooth as plastic. I don't know how she's managed to get the shape so accurate; the bird's breast curving into an apostrophe, its wings clipped into three, a delicate beak open to tweet *#OMG May Sparks has a job!* in a speech bubble of white icing. A Twitter brand manager would have been proud to witness such attention to detail.

Emma puts her arm around me and gives me a squeeze. Clare finally loosens the cork on the Prosecco, the celebratory pop accompanying the reappearance of Anna, who has been breast-feeding three-month-old Hughie.

"Hit me!" she says, reaching out for one of Clare's frosted champagne flutes. "It's now or never."

Hughie is the reason we're at Anna's flat rather than some noisy bar on nearby Clapham High Street. I'm glad of it now. I feel this warm glow spread over me as I look around at my lovely friends. They are so pleased for me.

And me? Am I pleased for me? Right now, my main feeling is of relief that those six months working as an unpaid intern for the freshly bankrupted fashion magazine, *Belle Femme*, weren't a complete waste of time. I could have ended up like the other staff, unemployed once again, but instead I got singled out by Craig Brown to be a founding member of his new PR startup. It was the award that swung it. Despite dire sales, we won *The Reader Engagement on Social Media Award*. Bit of a mouthful, but an award is an award, whether celebrated at Claridges with Veuve Clicquot, or in a drafty community centre with Tesco's finest.

Everyone knew it was down to me, because there hadn't been any social media engagement until I turned up and gave *Belle Femme* a Twitter account. Craig wanted me because, being Twitter-savvy, Facebook-fluent, Pinterest-proficient, Insta-sightful and Blogger-herant makes me the perfect candidate to help celebrities with their social media marketing.

"You've got to promise us you'll never talk in hashtags," Anna says.

If she followed me on Twitter, she'd be aware of my view on unnecessary hashtags.

SPARKYMAY @SPARKYMAY

#Hashtagging #every #word #makes #you #look #like #an #idiot...

"I would never talk in hashtags," I say, and wait a beat, "hashtag-never-say-never!"

Anna groans. "It's begun."

I laugh, enjoying myself. I still can't quite believe I'm going to be paid so much money for doing something that comes second nature to me. I've been tweeting since Twitter was born and have managed to attract 8,000 followers just by poking fun at life and sharing my way of seeing things 140 characters at a time.

Craig is starting me on thirty grand and assures me my income will double by the end of the year. Double! It feels a bit like winning the lottery, to be honest. A good salary hasn't exactly run in the family. There's not one banker or broker on our family tree. There are a lot of volunteers, though, including a cousin on my mum's side who was shot in Rwanda while working as a nurse.

Financial freedom is something I've read about in self-helps. It's the dream and my desire for it is, no doubt, a consequence of growing up in a household on a tight budget. At the moment I'm way off target with £10,000 worth of credit-card debt to pay off on top of a hefty student loan. I just cannot wait to feel that burden slip off my shoulders.

Tweeting PR news for C-listers, many of whom will be famous for being famous, is not my ideal job. I don't follow reality TV shows, I'm the type who complains that if everyone keeps watching them, the TV channels won't be motivated to commission anything decent. Only when I'm really tired, I'll watch an episode and just from that one episode I'll usually work out everything that's happened in the whole series and everyone involved. However, I'm a practical girl, and right now it's the only job that's going to liberate me from my debts and get me on track to be more financially free than my parents ever were.

"We should go on holiday together," Emma says, suddenly. "When's everyone free?"

"When Hughie finishes school," Anna sighs, "so, 18 years from now?"

I don't believe the self-pity in her voice for one minute. Anna's besotted with her new son and doesn't really want to consider anything else but him right now, especially not a trip away with a bunch of single girls who won't be watching their alcohol intake or worrying about nap time. She just worries we'll think less of her if she admits she's very happy staying at home with a crying, weeing, pooing machine.

"Give me a few months," I say. "I can hardly start a new job by asking for a holiday."

"But you can tweet from anywhere," Emma argues. "Your boss won't even know you're gone!"

"That's true," I laugh.

It's not true. I will have to show up at an office every day. At least for now, Craig said, hinting at flexible hours in the future. I'm determined to be really organized, use my time efficiently and schedule all my tweets for the evening so when I leave work, I really leave work. Not like in *Belle Femme*, where even though I was an unpaid intern, I was doing ridiculous amounts of overtime. The boss must have loved me. I was such a pushover.

"Wait!" I say, as Clare holds a knife above the blue surface of the spectacular Twitter cake. "One more photo. Let's try to get us all in."

I'm really not one of those people who documents every second of their life, but this does feel like a special moment. A few more glasses of Prosecco and I can see myself having a happy cry with these girls, and reflecting on how grown up we've all become.

There's a faint but distinct murmur of a baby waking up.

"Quick!" Anna says.

"We have to be quick because I'm running out of battery," I say.

We all squeeze in behind the cake and I hold out my phone as far as I can to take the picture. The image wobbles as I try to fit us all in. I get the giggles. Hughie starts to cry. Emma tells everyone to keep their eyes open.

"Hang on..." I say.

Emma turns her head to one side to get her best angle, her blonde hair draping over one shoulder. Chubby-cheeked Clare breaks out in dimples. Anna's nostrils tense as she smiles, her sharp green eyes daring the camera to take a bad photo.

"Hurry!" Anna growls through gritted teeth.

I push forward a few more of my red curls, tip my head up and to the side because it's working for Emma and beam at the screen.

But just as I'm about to take the snap, my phone starts vibrating, and in place of our picture Craig Brown's name appears on the screen. There's a collective groan of disappointment and Anna immediately breaks ranks to fetch Hughie.

Why is my new boss ringing me on a Saturday afternoon? I feel a little tug in my stomach. Could he possibly have changed his mind?

"Hello?" I answer tentatively.

No one bothers being quiet, so I step out of the kitchen-cum-living room into the corridor.

"May! How are you doing?" he says, in his very well-spoken and quite abrupt voice.

"I'm fine, but I haven't got much battery."

"Rule number one, never run out of battery. In our line of work, running out of battery is like a hospital running out of electricity. We can't perform essential operations without it."

"Okay..." I say, not sure whether to laugh or not.

"Rule two is always have your notification alerts switched on so you know when your clients have big news."

Couldn't this have waited until Monday? They're going to cut the cake without me in a minute.

"Even on the weekend?" I say, forcing the cheer in my voice.

"Which brings me to rule three, the internet doesn't stop for the weekend. The internet is NOW... That's not actually a rule, just a fact."

Anna slips past me with Hughie over her shoulder, dribbling onto a flimsy white tea towel. Emma calls for me to hurry up.

Craig's tone softens a little. "You don't mind me ringing you on a Saturday, do you?"

To say yes would seem rude. In the end, I don't get to say anything because my phone dies. I head back into the kitchen feeling disconcerted. What if he thinks I hung up on him?

"Oh no! What's wrong?" Emma cries. "What did he want?"

I quickly rearrange my face back into a carefree smile. "Nothing, nothing... He was just checking I was alright."

"Congrats! You have a caring boss!"

"That's weird," Anna says, always the cynic.

Clare is looking guilty. There's telltale sponge crumbs on the cake knife. I look down and see that she's gone ahead and cut into it, and the tweet has now been split in two.

"I was hungry," she says. "We'll get a post-cake picture."

I laugh, but I'm a little bit disappointed. It would have made a good memento. Never mind, there'll be more good times. Right now I've got a slightly more pressing matter on my hands, which is assuring my new boss I didn't just hang up on him.

"Has anyone got a phone charger?"

"I'll get you one after I've had my cake," Anna says, heading over to the sofa with her baby and plate of cake.

"Just tell me where it is and I'll get it."

"Relax. Have your cake. I'll get it in a minute. "

I feel a ripple of anger. How hard is it to direct me to a charger? It's probably in a plug socket somewhere. Will she get annoyed with me if I start looking?

I catch myself getting agitated and make an effort to let go of the feeling. Craig knew I was running out of battery.

Clare hands me a plate with a fat chunk of blue-topped cake and I sit down in the recliner. I'm still thinking of the charger when I swallow my first bite.

"Can you taste it?" Clare says, winking at me.

Taste what? I take another quick bite, realising I was completely disconnected from my taste buds.

"Yum! Vanilla!" Emma says.

Of course, vanilla, my favourite!

"It's delicious. Thank you Clare."

I'll finish my cake and then I'll ring Craig. In that order. It's Saturday. He can't possibly expect me to be switched on all the time, can he?

I do have a life...

Chapter 1

My job is to show the world the best side of a person. I'm specifically talking about the kind of person who, given half a chance (or half a drink), will show the world their worst side. C – and D – list celebrities mainly; the loose cannons of the group. The ones who lash out, fall apart, reveal their prejudices at the slightest provocation and spew their guts across the Twittersphere.

Is it their fault? Are they particularly weak? Or are they just normal people being abnormally scrutinised? I don't have time to answer these questions because it turns out it's a very busy line of work.

Six months ago I took on my first five clients. They were, and remain, a mix of low-profile soap stars and one-hit wonders. My task is to keep their fans updated with their news. I use the word "news" lightly. Mostly I'm tweeting about what shoes they're lusting over or what they're having for breakfast. I spent the first month cringing a lot and telling my friends I'd sold my soul to the devil. It's getting easier, though. I no longer wince when I bang out five exclamation marks in a row or churn out a line of emojis. In fact, sometimes I even catch myself adding xxx on automatic to my @SparkyMay tweets. Luckily I'm quick on the draw, hitting the delete button within seconds of release. My personal followers aren't into cute.

A steady stream of emails from my clients means I'm always informed about the minutiae of their lives. Why don't they just share stuff themselves? Friends ask. Well, like I said, they're loose cannons. Once they start tweeting they can't stop themselves, and it doesn't take long before they've either managed to embarrass themselves or offend half their following.

Up until now it has always been clear when it's a PR person tweeting for them (me), and when it's the client. That's about to change. After much talk, we have launched the Platinum Package, which is for clients who want their fans to think it's them being active online. That it's *them* tweeting and retweeting and responding, when really it will be me.

I've had some sleepless nights over it. I mean, it's highly deceitful. When Craig first outlined the plan, my exact words were: "Are you asking me to be a professional liar?"

He argued that it was not lying, but "repackaging". We were just helping decent people who had flawed communication skills. We wouldn't be hurting anyone. Alone with my thoughts, I reasoned that tweeting on behalf of a few needy stars was probably a lot less misleading than most of the advertising on telly. Meanwhile, my growing credit-card debt told me it didn't matter whether I agreed or not with what we were about to do. I was simply not going to find another job this well paid in a hurry.

My phone is buzzing and I hold up a finger to Craig, who has called the meeting.

"May Sparks speaking."

It's DJ Buzzya's agent, Malia. She's concerned about a rumour going around on Twitter that her client was seen snorting coke at a charity fundraiser for young offenders. She hasn't been able to get hold of him. I'm guessing because the rumour is true and he's in a comatose state somewhere. To sum it up in hashtags: #fail #idiot #whoinvitedhim?

Buzzya, real name Emmanuel, was my second-ever client and despite being on our silver package, expects premium treatment.

I'll have to send a firmly worded email later. For now, I reassure his agent, get off the phone and log into my social media manager from my tablet.

Craig is used to these interruptions and turns to the Nespresso machine to top up on Caramelito. He has a sweet tooth and punishes himself for it with an hour on the treadmill every morning. Behind their backs he laughs at them, but the way he keeps his tan topped up and his suits sharp, it's obvious my boss fancies himself as a bit of a celebrity himself.

It takes me seconds to compose a tweet for DJ Buzzya. It helps that he's not a complex character. For true authenticity, I should probably misspell more words, but I have my limits.

DJBUZZYA @DJBUZZYA
Feelin #inspired after last night's gala! Those kidz killed it!
Donate money to #yesplus and change lives! Please Retweet!

The tweet gets instantly retweeted by five obedient fans. I'll need to do better than that if I want my salary doubled. It's a promise that hasn't been mentioned again since my informal job interview and I'll need to make a significant difference to my clients' reputations before I work up the guts to remind Craig about it.

"I'm with you," I say, sliding my tablet away from me. My phone is bleeping with a dozen different alerts, but I ignore it.

Craig's focus returns to me. There's very little time when we are offline and able to pay each other full attention. Some of our workload will be lightened now with the help of our new receptionist, Abigail, who I was introduced to five minutes ago. She doesn't know everything we do here, just enough to answer calls and make appointments in the diary. Craig says she's on trial, that he doesn't know if he can trust her yet.

There's also Gabe, who looks after our sports personalities. He's thirty-three years old, a devoted gamer and proud owner of the first-ever Panini football-sticker album (Mexico 1970). He wears bright comic t-shirts under his work shirts as if he needs to remind himself that he has a life outside the office.

Gabe's the Photoshop king. He has the skills I'll be needing more of if I want to impress my future Platinum clients. It's a make-believe world, but I'm still going to try to be as authentic as I can. My aim is to make my clients a source of inspiration, not envy.

DJBUZZYA @DJBUZZYA
Think Big. Believe Big. Act Big. And the results will be BIG.

Gabe's missing the meeting today because he's shadowing a second-division goal keeper who wants to be a TV star and is considering signing up to the Platinum Package.

"Bernard Thompson-Skinner," Craig says, passing me the file he's compiled of our newest client.

"The drunk TV presenter?"

Craig smiles. "We prefer 'misunderstood'."

"Misunderstood because he was so drunk on his show he was slurring his words!"

I open the file and a sheet of paper falls onto my lap. It's the printout showing why Bernard shouldn't be allowed access to the password to his own Twitter account. It's the interaction with book reviewer Sandy Hubert aka @sanhubreview, which took place six months ago. It's fair to say she didn't think much of his misery memoir *Backstage*.

I scan it briefly.

SANDYHUBERT @SANHUBREVIEW
Clumsy metaphors, unrealistic sex scenes & a character with less depth than a contact lens. #Backstage #bookreview

BTHOMSKINNER @BTHOMSKINNER
I doubt @sanhubreview would know what a realistic sex scene was if it hit her in the face. Would someone like to volunteer?

PS not to have sex with her, just to hit her in the face.

Cue: uproar from Hubert's following.

SANDYHUBERT @SANHUBREVIEW
@bthomskinner's misogyny as convincing on paper as it is on TV show. Clearly from the 'write what you know' school.

BTHOMSKINNER @BTHOMSKINNER
@sanhubreview Shut up you pompous old dyke. Don't you have some carpet to munch?

I breathe in deeply. In 20 minutes I'll be meeting this man and I've got a feeling he's not going to be happy about handing over control of his online identity to a woman half his age.

"He's going to hate me," I say.

"Why? It's only women he can't have that he doesn't get along with," Craig says, with a little laugh. "If he thinks he's in with a chance he'll turn on the charm."

I turn the page and scan his details. Sixty-six years old and married.

"It says married, but his wife walked out on him a month ago, caught him with a young model," Craig says. "It's a miracle it didn't get more attention in the media."

I try to control my initial expression of disgust. One thing I believe is that there's never just one side to a story. People muck up. It doesn't mean they're evil. It just means they're human and they probably shouldn't be allowed on the internet.

"You can handle him, can't you?"

I shut the file and stand up. "Of course I can handle him."

I've already downloaded his memoir in preparation for the job. It has 82 five-star reviews on Amazon, so it can't be all bad, although one of the one-star reviews has summed it up in those exact words: *"It's all bad"*.

I used to love reading, but I can't seem to find the time at the moment. Most of the books I've bought recently have been to remedy the situation of not having enough time, which is ironic, I suppose. Currently on my bedside table are:

1. *How to Stop Time*
2. *The Ultimate Guide to Time Management*
3. *Get Everything Done and Still Have Time to Play*

So far I've failed to unlock the secrets within their pages. I seem to have increasingly more to do and less time to play. It hasn't skipped the notice of my friends, who have been getting irritated with my uncharacteristic flakiness.

"May..."

"Yes?"

Craig is looking serious. "There are three other clients in the pipeline who I'd love you to take on."

"Great," I say, hiding my rising anxiety behind a confident smile. There must be a way of getting everything done and keeping your social life. I've just not found the right self-help yet.

"I need you to nail this one," Craig says.

"Of course I'll nail it."

He looks relieved. I shoot him another reassuring look before heading back to my office to prepare for this new skin I'll soon be stepping into.

Chapter 2

Growing up, I was definitely the more sensitive sister. While Katie used Barbie's hot-pink convertible to pummel ladybirds into the carpet, I built hospitals out of match boxes to deal with her victims. A fly with reduced wing capacity spent six weeks swaddled in tissue in the ICU unit. Everyone said it was dead, but how could they be sure it wasn't in a coma?

I wanted something cuddlier than a disabled housefly, but Katie was allergic to cats so a kitten was out of the question. We didn't have much space either. After a lot of begging my parents finally caved in and bought me the smallest dog they could find in Battersea Dog's Home, a Jack Russell called Sid. Poor Sid. I'd only had him six weeks before he ran into the road and got run over by a learner driver. The woman panicked and stamped down on the accelerator instead of the brake. It was a tragedy. My parents blame that day for everything that happened afterwards.

What did happen? My memory is that I recovered pretty well after the funeral, once I'd lapped up the story about doggy heaven from my atheist parents. But when I grew up they needed an explanation as to why I hadn't become a teacher, or a doctor, or a social worker, or some other noble profession that would better suit their socialist ideologies. Why, instead, had I become an ambitious, money-chasing media type?

That's what they assume from the location of my office (Soho), my manicured nails (£10 at my local Vietnamese nail salon), my glam outfits (eBay), and my preference for sparkling water over natural (it really is more refreshing). "*Lah-di-dah*", they'll say, forgetting all the anxiety the modest incomes from their noble jobs (as recycling officer and part-time social worker) had caused them.

Is it so wrong to seize a chance to make some money? It might not be the most worthy of jobs, but it could be worse. I could be an arms dealer or drug trafficker or a poacher of rhino horns...

At least I've got a job. Wouldn't it be worse to be still living at home, relying on my parents for handouts? Don't they want me to have security? Don't they want me to own my own place? With a job like mine, that's actually a possibility. Don't parents usually want for their children what they didn't quite manage to achieve themselves?

If *I* had a daughter I'd be really proud if she managed to put a deposit down on a flat in one of the most expensive capitals in the world. I'd toast her independence, commend her for her hard graft.

I suppose my parents' main issue is that they feel I should be using my own voice, not mimicking the voices of people I've expressed very little admiration for in the past. I don't blame them for not understanding it. Every day I experience an acute moment of self-loathing, which paralyses me for a moment, but soon passes.

The problem is, no one is going to pay to hear my voice. Not now at least. I'm always scribbling down ideas, but if I'm going to add my voice to the millions of other established vloggers and bloggers, then I want to make sure it has a strong identity and that it's adding something useful to the world. Until then, I'm going to get on with my job of being the voice of Bernard Thompson-Skinner.

He definitely has a lot to say. I know I don't have enough words to fill that doorstopper of a memoir with leftovers for a sequel. I don't blame Bernard for getting annoyed with Sandy Hubert. It's harsh having someone dismiss two years of work in less than

140 characters. The least Hubert could have done is dedicate a full blog post to ripping it apart. If not a blog post, then a long Facebook status with the appropriate emoticon attached – *feeling blah after reading the worst book ever...* The emoticon for "blah" being the one with eyes squeezed shut and tongue out. Obviously.

I know what it's like to be criticised. When I was thirteen I started a blog called *May's Maze*. It didn't last longer than a month because some nasty person starting hounding me, posting foul-mouthed comments anonymously. *Shut up you fucking bitch you're so boring and annoying and no one cares...* the words punctured through my teenage heart and I believed every one of them. I deleted the blog and didn't tell anyone the real reason. I was so ashamed. If anything, it's that experience that changed me, not the tragic death of poor Sid.

I'm not saying Bernard was justified in insulting Sandy Hubert in public. Of course he wasn't. He should have dealt with his emotions in private and like a grown-up. In other words, switched his Wi-Fi off, given his phone to a friend, and only once incommunicado allowed himself to get drunk and throw darts at a picture of Sandy's face.

We always advise our clients not to engage on their social networks when they're in a heightened emotional state, and if they receive abuse not to engage at all. But if they had that sort of self control they wouldn't need us. So here we are. Bernard has come to the conclusion he can't keep his temper on a leash. Or rather, he's been warned that if he doesn't clean up his act and ingratiate himself with the general public, he will be replaced as the host of *Bring on the Bad News*, a ranty show with guests as opinionated as himself.

It's obvious as soon as he walks into my slick office that he feels he has been bullied into this meeting.

"Please come in. It's lovely to meet you," I gush.

He ignores my outstretched hand, eyes my Scandinavian ergonomic fjord phoenix vanity chair with suspicion, before lowering himself into its snow-leather embrace.

In my spare minutes I've devoured as many facts about him as possible. Originally from Norfolk, he moved to London when he was sixteen. A Libra. Started his broadcasting life on a hospital radio station. Moved to television and hosted *Good Morning, What's in the Post?* for two years, before ratings dropped so low it must have only been the crew watching in the end. A flat near Hampstead and a sprawling house in the south of France. One dead father, a mother with dementia and a brother in China. He hates reality TV, celebrity chefs, *Downton Abbey*, Oxford Circus, the Labour Party leader, football, football fans, Russians, the Americans, inexplicably the Canadians (who doesn't like Canadians?) and anyone with a name that sounds made up. His second memoir *Stage Door: the Exits and Entrances of Bernard Thompson-Skinner* is due for release next month.

"You must be May," he says. "How old are you? Eighteen?"

I laugh good-humouredly. "Thank you, I'll take that as a compliment."

"You can, but it isn't one."

Good start.

"Actually I'm quite a bit older than that."

His brown eyes narrow, the thick folds of his eyelids sagging around them. Being in the spotlight has clearly not motivated him to invest in expensive face creams. He has the skin of a fisherman.

"Quite a bit older are you... 40?"

I catch the laughter in his eyes and realise he's teasing me. Getting his sense of humour right online is going to be tricky.

"Twenty-eight," I say. I've got a lot to do and I'm eager to push on "So, I've been looking at your file."

"I sound like a criminal."

"Well, I'm sure a few people would love to lock you up."

He has the throaty laugh of a smoker. I sense I might have just earned a point for honesty. He needs *me*, that's what I've got to remember here. On his own he's capable of pissing the whole world off. If he does that, then who will watch his show? Who will buy his books?

"Have you thought about what kind of impression you'd like to give?"

His expression changes immediately. He looks scornful.

"I haven't got a problem with myself, you know. It's other people who've got a problem with me."

"Unfortunately you're in an industry where public opinion matters."

"The public love my show. It's only a few humourless lefties getting their knickers in a twist about my honest approach to life... do I have to please everyone?"

I want to point out that "a few" is a gross understatement for the amount of people who are annoyed with him. His tweets have been scrutinised in newspapers and debated over. Freedom of speech versus hate speech. Where do you draw the line? There are people who think he should be in jail rather than on television. Instead of pointing this out, I nibble a layer of skin off my bottom lip.

"You know, it doesn't have to be personal..." I say, and I'm aware of the irony of this statement. If your online personal profile isn't personal, then what is it? "Being on Twitter and Facebook is just another side of show business. Away from your audience, you can be whoever you want."

His gaze is steely and I become aware of how fast my heart is beating. I'm supposed to be proving to him that I, despite my younger years and lack of showbiz experience, could imitate him. What is Craig going to say when our first Platinum client changes his mind because he thinks I'm rude and incompetent? Maybe he'll just tweet me.

CRAIGBROWN @CRAIGBROWN
@SparkyMay You're fired. LOL. #packyourthings #thatsnoty-ourlaptop #givebackthelaptop

"Go on," Bernard says.

I let go of my breath, relieved to see he's not going to storm out just yet.

"I've got quite a long questionnaire for you to fill out. You don't have to do it now."

"I *am* going to have to do it now, aren't I? My book's coming out in less than four weeks and I need to have wooed the nation with my wit and charm by then, so they get off their arses and go to the shops to buy it. Isn't that why I need you?"

He's right, of course. Shame he has to be such an arsehole about it.

"They don't even need to get off their arses these days, they just need to click a button... " he continues, his face darkening.

I rest the questionnaire on the desk in front of him and swallow. "Obviously the sooner you complete the questionnaire, the better."

For the Platinum service to be successful, I need to know as much about my client as possible. There are questions about music, food, politics, religion, films, family history, habits. There are also questions about abbreviations and text speak. Some are obvious. Bernard is unlikely to approve of BAMF (Bad Ass Mother Fucker) and seeing as he's so bad-tempered I doubt he'll ROFL (Roll On The Floor Laughing). In fact *I* will ROFL if he wants to use BAMF.

Other things are less obvious. I have one client who is strongly against me using LOL in his updates and another who feels a tweet is naked without a kiss at the end. For some people text speak is absolutely fine, others feel it is a curse on the English language and predict that in 20 years we'll just be spitting at each other because we'll have forgotten how to use vowels. I imagine Bernard is in this latter category. He would not be happy if I mixed up "your" and "you're" unlike DJ Buzzya, who would be shocked to know "ur" isn't actually the correct spelling.

As Bernard reads through the questionnaire, I make nonsensical notes in my pad.

I haven't got what I want yet. I don't know what my first

tweet would be as Bernard and that worries me. *Day in the Life*, I scribble. That's what I need to get, a sense of the man's life from the moment he wakes up to the time he goes to sleep.

"Can we go through your average day?"

He looks up, one bushy eyebrow raised. I get the sense he's pleased to be asked.

"If you like," he says, leaning back in his chair.

"I think it would help."

"Alright." He squints up at the ceiling. "At 4am I get woken up by my wife's bloody cat."

Aha! A feline friend. #Perrrrrfect.

"What's its name?"

Pets get a lot of love on social media and often that love is transferred to the owner.

"Baxter."

#Loveit.

"I know what you're thinking," he says. "That it's a bit of a dog's name. That's because I wanted a dog."

"But your wife won?"

His face sours. "My wife left me."

"I'm sorry."

Dare I ask the gory details? He might never stop talking.

I try not to think about my inbox, which must be full to the brim by now. I've scheduled updates to go out for my five original clients and it's hard to let go of the feeling of wanting to check up on how they all went down with the different fan bases.

Out of all the notifications, Retweets and Facebook "likes" are my crack. They were long before I ever got this job. It's approval, isn't it? People liking what you post is them thinking you're cool or funny or clever, and that gives you a boost. The problem is the boost lasts about a second and as soon as it's gone, you want another. So you post something else. You keep chasing that little high, even though it's essentially meaningless.

I know it's not just me who feels like this. My bet is that it's

19

most of us on Twitter and Facebook. When I open my Facebook account and don't see that little red flag, or when I tweet something and don't get any response whatsoever, it makes me feel flat and restless. It's an addiction. The difference is instead of waking up in old age to lung cancer or liver failure, one day you wake up to the awful realisation that you've lived half your life through an odourless, tasteless, texture-limited screen. That, and you have severe arthritis in your scrolling finger.

The job has increased the number of highs and lows in my day. It's like I'm on some robotic seesaw that's going up and down so fast I can't jump off. What I find amazing is just how many likes and retweets these minor celebs get for content which, I have to admit, is pretty damn average. For instance, I posted a Photoshopped picture of a rabbit wearing headphones yesterday on DJ Buzzya's Facebook page. It got 300 likes and it didn't even have a caption! In fact, I asked people for a caption, and over 200 people submitted their suggestions. Twenty-two people thought "hello, I'm a funky rabbit" was worthy of some serious LOLs. I managed a smile at *music so bad, only rabbits will listen to it* and then hid the comment so DJ Buzzya wouldn't stumble on it and then ring me up at one in the morning crying about how mean everyone was. I should turn off my phone at night, but Craig must be a Jedi, because every time I'm about to turn it off, I think of him and his rules, and just can't bring myself to do it.

These days, anything over 50 Likes or Retweets gives me a high. Anything lower than ten and I start to feel twitchy. I'll delete content after half an hour if it gets a poor approval rate and then I'll hunt for new content to get my good feeling back.

The five original clients I'm referring to still have access to their social media accounts. What I'm about to take on for Bernard is much more hardcore. From the moment he signs the contract, I'm effectively going to *be* Bernard.

If I think about it too much, I start to feel a bit sick. The key is to just get started.

First tweet as Bernard?

BTHOMSKINNER @BTHOMSKINNER
Awaiting delivery of #StageDoor proofs. Pondering whether to talk to postman about weather or state of Middle East. Both catastrophic.

"I think you should take some pictures of Baxter for me... 'the writer's cat'... people love that sort of thing."

I envisage an overweight Garfield-lookalike lounging across Bernard's keyboard #WritersBlock.

"You can't offend anyone with a picture of a cat," I say, feeling a burst of optimism.

"I bet you can," Bernard grunts.

"Well, you can't please everyone."

"Then why am I bothering with all this?"

The thought comes in before I can stop it, that I'm not surprised his wife left him. I ignore his question and look down at my scribbles.

"We also need to give the impression that you respect women."

"I do respect women."

A few knots start to unwind.

"*You* know that and *I* know that," I say. "Now we've got to show that side of you. Respectful, egalitarian... People are bound to be thinking you're homophobic after what you said to Sandy Hubert, so we'll need to work on reversing that."

He rolls his eyes. I know it's because he's irritated he has to prove himself, but the tiniest gesture can easily be misinterpreted and made a meal of in the media. Perhaps Bernard has been misunderstood. Perhaps his bad temper is due to the changing world around him and not being able to keep up.

"Are you writing anything at the moment?"

"Yes. I'm taking advantage while the show's on a break. I'm writing a novel set in the Second World War. It's not going well.

In fact, at the rate I'm going it'll coincide with its centenary."

"Do you mainly write in London?"

I'm thinking stunning views of the city to illustrate the walks Bernard will take between writing sessions. Does he write in the morning or late at night? I glance at his paunch and wonder if he walks at all. Does the reality matter? Walking is such a wholesome activity. If people decide to go for a walk because they think Bernard is walking, how can that be a bad thing?

"I am at the moment, against my will," he says. "I hate it. I hate even more that phrase, *'if you're bored of London, you're bored of life'*... what utter bullshit. It's perfectly legitimate to be bored of a stinking, pox-ridden city."

After a week of being jostled on the Tube in rush hour I've said the same sort of thing myself, just without the description of the city circa 1500.

"Best to keep your dislike of London a secret, I think. There's a lot of publicity to be got from it."

"You're probably right. The problem is my wife is in our South of France home and until we sort things out, I'm stuck here. I'll send you a picture of the place. It's beautiful... a small corner of paradise." He looks up at the ceiling and sighs. "God, I've been an idiot..."

I feel the little hairs on my arms stand on end. Is Bernard Thompson-Skinner about to open up to me?

"I'm hopeless without her."

My expression softens.

"You should see my botched lunches! They're quite depressing."

Ah. Not so romantic after all. On the up side, I bet I could make his bachelor meals look gourmet with an Instagram filter.

Bernard is looking at me strangely now, a frown deepening across his forehead.

"You can get her back for me..."

"I'm sorry?"

"If you're so good at your job, surely you can create a Bernard

Thompson-Skinner so appealing that Joyce will realise she's made a mistake leaving me."

Alarm bells ping in my head like a 100 Twitter notifications. I'm trying my best not to jump to negative conclusions here. It's just the way he's phrased it makes it sound like a man who just wants his wife back so he can be allowed back in his holiday home and be cooked a decent lunch.

"Well? I know it sounds bad, May, but as I told you, I'm lost without her."

"Couldn't you just go on a cookery course?"

He snorts, surprised and amused. I'm guessing he wasn't expecting me to be so candid. Nor was I, until I opened my mouth.

"It's not about the cooking."

I feel myself melt a little.

"I mean, she's not exactly Nigella Lawson," he adds, ruining it.

"What about the... you know..."

"What?"

"Your affair..."

I stop myself saying "with a younger woman".

"It was a mistake! I was an idiot. My ego couldn't resist the adoration of a beautiful woman. It's happened to a lot of men before me, you know."

Does he feel remorseful? Is he upset he got caught or upset he did it?

His face has grown quite red. And then he snaps.

"For God's sake! How are you going to pretend to be me when you think I'm such a monster? How can you possibly paint me in a sympathetic light when you're so unsympathetic? Sitting there, judging me, like you've never done anything wrong in your entire life! Well, maybe you haven't! But I tell you, make it to my age and then tell me how perfect you are!"

It's horrible to be shouted at by a client at such close proximity. I'm much more used to being yelled at over the phone. I was prepared for some disagreement, just not at this volume. But this is why Bernard is here. He shouts, he rants, he speaks his mind, he rubs people up the wrong way.

There's a knock on the door. Craig pops his head around it, a smile clashing with the tension in his jaw.

"Everything alright? I was just about to send Abigail out for coffees."

We really are experts in lying in this company. Abigail is not going out for coffee because we've got it on tap. Craig has obviously overheard the shouting and is gagging to know what's going on. He was *Belle Femme's* gossip columnist in our former life together.

I look at Bernard, who is trying to compose himself, and I smile warmly to show I've taken no offence.

"Not for me, thanks," he says, and looks at me warily, "I suppose I'd better be getting on with this bible of a questionnaire if we're alright to go ahead?"

"Of course. I'm very happy to proceed."

I can feel Craig's relief lifting up the room. He winks at me, "I'll leave you to it, then."

Bernard gathers his things together; his battered leather shoulder bag and the bent umbrella with the one exposed spoke. Away from the camera, he really doesn't look like much. I feel suddenly sorry for him.

"What will help me is if you let me know more about her."

Shit. Did I really just say that?

He looks at me, a sparkle of hope in his eyes. "Yes, of course, anything... what do you want to know?"

I swallow. It's not like I'm going to pretend to be Bernard and talk to her. I'm not going to send her messages. I'm just going to tweet with her in mind. It would be something Bernard might do if he were better on Twitter.

"Well, what she likes, I suppose. Poets I can quote from, her favourite flowers, her way of thinking, authors she likes, authors she detests..."

"Me? There, that's one author she can't stand."

"Well, hopefully we can change that."

I'll do my best to present to the world a balanced, thoughtful, intelligent man. A man who everyone knows is fallible, but who can show remorse. My parents don't need to worry about me. I *do* have good ethics and moral principles. It's easy to help the lovable. It takes much more compassion to help the ones who have trouble being loved.

"Good, I'm glad we've sorted that out, the sooner I'm back in France the better."

My sympathy evaporates. "You mean, the sooner you're back with your wife the better."

He beams. "Exactly."

After he leaves, I feel an urge to lie on the floor of my office and reflect on the meeting, and on the man I've just agreed to be. But I don't have time. There are hundreds of notifications to deal with. During the day I act; night-time is for plotting and planning. It's lucky I can function on so little sleep.

It suddenly occurs to me that my flatmate might be home now. Louisa has been on holiday in Greece, and I vaguely remember her complaining about the early flight home when she booked the tickets. That'll be good for my diet since she's a great cook and it will mean eating properly each night, less good for work. When I'm alone I don't have to hide the fact I am failing at any sense of work-life balance. With a flatmate watching, I really do.

Chapter 3

I open the front door to a delicious smell of coriander and spices.
I breathe it in and feel some of the tension slip from my shoulders.
Louisa's suitcase is lying open in the corridor, colourful chiffon
spilling over onto the parquet. I have trained myself to ignore her
mess. When it gets too much I escape to my own room. I wasn't
always tidy, but the busyness of my online life has made me crave
order everywhere else.

In the kitchen I find her leaning over a steaming frying pan,
stirring a creamy yellow concoction with a wooden spatula. It's
some sort of delicious Thai curry. She looks up, her eyes clearing
before letting out a shriek of delight.

"Yes! You're here! I was worried you'd be working late."

She swings her non-spatula arm around me and squeezes. She
smells of coco butter and sunshine. I pull back to get a look at
her post-holiday glow. Her skin is golden-brown and her blonde
hair has white lights bleached into it.

"You look gorgeous."

'Thanks! I feel it!"

She's wearing a turquoise t-shirt and chunky wooden beads,
which rest on the swell of her cleavage. Louisa is very proud of
her cleavage. I've heard her say a million times she would never
go on a diet in case it shrank. These announcements are usually

followed by a sympathetic glance at *my* chest, which, if pushed between the right kind of wrench could also manage a perfectly decent cleavage.

Louisa is the only one who calls me "Legs". Not *long* legs or *white* legs or *skinny* legs (which they are), just *Legs*. My slim physique is part genes and part due to the fact that when I'm busy or worried I don't have much of an appetite. Because I've been anticipating the launch of the Platinum Package, I've been busier and more worried than usual. It's not something I've admitted to my flatmate, although she's obviously noticed. Next time I'm working late I'll make an excuse. I'll tell her I'm having a drink with friends.

Louisa doesn't want my legs, and neither does she drool over my long red hair like Clare does. Not even now that I've finally nailed the bouncy-curls-at-the-ends look. I tried curling tongs first, then normal rollers, heated rollers. Now I just leave hairbrushes hanging from my hair in the morning. *Blondes have more fun!* says the sign above Louisa's mirror. She believes it as if it were a scientific fact. But redheads know that while blondes may *have* more fun, we *are* more fun. At least, I used to be more fun, and will be more fun again, once I've got on top of my workload.

"If you'd told me it was so sunny here I wouldn't have been so depressed about coming back," she says.

Has it been sunny? I hadn't even noticed. Craig had dropped in another client file as I'd been considering taking my cafeteria-bought sandwich outside. In the end I'd stayed at my desk, dropping crumbs over the bullet points. Only now I notice how warm the weather is. The watery evening light filters in through the kitchen window, summoning memories of past summers.

"We have to organise some picnics," she says, turning back to the curry. "And barbecues and we've got to go to Brighton and actually swim this time, even if it's freezing."

"Yeah, definitely. I can't wait."

This isn't entirely true. I wouldn't mind putting summer on hold for just one more month. I just need a bit more time to research my new clients so their voices come naturally to me and I'm not over-thinking everything I do.

"I think we're going to have a brilliant summer this year," Louisa says brightly. "We deserve it after all that pissing rain."

She throws a few chopped peppers into the mix and I spot an opportunity and take out my phone.

"Hold that a sec..."

She rolls her eyes, but keeps the spatula steady so I can take a shot. I haven't updated Libby Loherty's profile today. The actress was one of my first clients. She handed herself in to me after tweeting that all Hollywood directors were prostitutes. Yes, *all* of them.

She later tweeted an apology, of sorts:

LIBBYLOHERTY @LIBBYLO
I apologise to all the prostitutes I may have offended with that tweet.

Libby is on the copper package, so I only need to update once a day. Now she can have a simple what-I'm-eating-for-dinner-tonight tweet. Except, nothing that comes out of Libby's (daughter of an earl, owner of two ponies) mouth is ever straightforward.

"I need a pretentious quote about food."

"Virginia Woolf," Louisa says.

"You're so good at this. I wish I could hire you as my assistant."

"And spend my life on the phone? No thank you."

"It pays well."

"So you keep telling me. What are you going to do if you ever go on holiday?" she says. "Does your phone even have an 'off' function or did Craig customise it so it only turns off when your clients die?"

I laugh. "Of course I'll switch off if I go on holiday."

"*If* you go, not *when* you go? That means you're never going."

"Actually I was looking at flights to Ibiza only yesterday."

I never used to lie to Louisa, but now I find I'm telling her little white lies all the time. I did look at pictures of the party island yesterday, but it was only because one of my clients had just found out they would be filming there soon and wanted a "See you soon!" tweet to rouse excitement from their fans. Ibiza would not be my first choice, even though I've heard it's not all drunk Brits and used condoms on the beaches – although, why risk it? I'd choose Sardinia... or Malta... apparently Croatia is beautiful too.

"Oh yeah? When are you thinking of going?"

I push away the treacherous image of a beach.

"I'm not sure yet. This new project is only just taking off."

"It's been taking off ever since you started."

"No, this is the real take-off. You're going to laugh when you hear who my newest client is."

Louisa is one of the few people outside work who knows about our latest premium service. I had to sign a confidentiality agreement promising I wouldn't tell anyone so word doesn't spread. Fans would be angry if they found out their idol, who they'd been loyally following and interacting with, was just a paid stand-in. Of course people know that VIPs have their publicity people sharing information for them, but they still expect the personal messages to be genuine. The president of America signs off with his initials when the tweet is from him. Is it from him really? I don't know. More likely someone is running it past him. I doubt he actually types it out with his own presidential fingers.

"I'll give you a clue. He launched his career showing off on a reality TV show."

"Well, that's pretty much every celebrity since 2000, isn't it?"

"Fair point. Okay, he was in one of the first *Big Brothers* and had to leave early because of an injury."

Her eyes widen. "Not the broken penis guy?"

I shrug suggestively and she lets out a whoop of delight. My reaction was quite the opposite when that file landed on my desk. Me? Working to promote some so-called star from my least-favourite show in the whole world? Destiny was obviously taking the piss.

"Damian Dance!" she cries.

"The one and only... Thank God."

"Didn't he do it trying to break-dance from one sofa to another?"

"Lucky for him there was no Twitter in those days."

A world without Twitter? It must have been a much quieter place. I mean, I was there, but I can barely remember it. There must have been so much more time. Time to stare into space. Time to consider things a little longer. Or maybe my nostalgia is misplaced and we were just as distracted, playing Tetris and looking after our Tamagotchis. But I definitely don't remember this urge to document and comment on everything I was doing.

It occurs to me I was going to post a tweet for DJ Buzzya and I log into his account.

"Put your phone away," Louisa scolds. "We're eating now."

I do as I'm told. I know how annoying she finds it. When I'm alone I can eat a whole plate of food without moving my finger off a screen. I hate myself for doing it because I know it's disrespectful to my food. A little voice, which sounds a lot like my mother's, will whisper, *think of how long that potato took to grow, think of the water it needed and the sunshine, think of the farmer who had to dig it up...* Worse if I'm eating meat. *That creature died for you, are you not even going to acknowledge its sacrifice?* That usually makes me push my phone away, feeling disgusted with myself.

The problem is if I slack, my clients notice and start emailing me whiney messages about how they think I could be doing more. If posting a few extra pointless tweets gets them off my back for a day, then I'm probably going to keep doing it.

Louisa spoons out the rice then drowns it in curry. We move over to the small table by the window and tuck in. The flavour catches me off-guard and I forget everything for a moment as I savour it.

#Bestmealever

It would be embarrassing if people knew how many hashtags

pop into my head every day. They pretty much come at me constantly, like fruit flies hovering around a bowl of fruit. At least I don't talk in hashtags like Craig does. He answered the phone the other day with "Hashtag-OMG where have you been?" If I ever do that, I hope I'll have the integrity to jump off a bridge.

I haven't posted very much on my personal social networks recently. After a long day writing on everyone else's accounts, I don't want to write another mundane sentence. Sometimes I even feel tempted to delete my Facebook account to lessen the overall noise of my online life. But I don't, because it keeps me connected with my friends. I check it a couple of times a day to get an overview of what they're all up to, which is a variation on the following:

Clare Willis: *I've just baked my third cheesecake this month!!!!!! Maybe I should open a bakery? LOL :) xox*

Anna Jamison: *Baby poo and vomit down my top AGAIN. Thanks bubba, you know how to make mummy's day!*

Rob Bennett: *Has anyone got a van I can borrow?*

Joe Mathers: *BLOOD THIRSTY BASTARDS! LEAVE THE DOLPHINS ALONE! Sign the petition (link to campaign).*

Emma Priestly: *I don't even want to talk about it.*

NB Emma *does* want to talk about it and probably already has to all the people who have commented with hearts and kisses. The people asking "what happened?" and "are you alright?" will have to suffer the suspense a little longer. I'll get the full story when I meet her later on in the week. She said if I cancelled one more time, our friendship was over. The emoticon at the end of her Whatsapp message had steam coming out of its nose, so I knew she was serious.

"So what are you going to say, then?" Louisa says. "I mean, what would a Damian Dance Facebook page update look like?"

I've been asking myself the same question.

"I don't know yet. I'm meeting him tomorrow."

"That's so hilarious." Her eyes wander. "I wonder what he looks like these days."

We've probably got the same image of him in our heads. Back when he was in *Big Brother*, which was over ten years ago. Sandy blonde hair in greasy curtains, one eyebrow pierced, the other with two shaved lines through it. Trying to be a bad boy, while admitting his mum did everything for him, including tying his laces, which is why he only wore slip-ons during the show because he wasn't confident doing "the bow bit". He had his tongue pierced, too, was always playing with it. Big chin. He tried to grow a box beard in the second week #fail

"He thought Hong Kong was the capital of Japan..." I say, casting my mind back. "...and that paediatrics was the study of paedophiles."

She narrows her eyes, trying to remember something. "Didn't he have a big tattoo?"

"You mean to say you've forgotten the guinea-bear-tiger?"

She claps her hand over her mouth and crumples over her curry, laughing.

Damian had only ever worn vest tops during the TV show to parade his tribal bands. It wasn't until a couple of days in did he show the world his masterpiece; a leaping tiger, which spanned his entire back. It had the face of a rodent, the arms of a bear. He was hoping for admiration, but his fellow contestants and most of the watching world either doubled up laughing or just stared with open mouths in shock at the premature ruin of such a young, handsome body.

"Oh my God, what an idiot," she says, catching her breath.

It crosses my mind that Louisa has a pretty awful tattoo herself.

It's a blurred green mermaid on the small of her back. She did it as an act of rebellion after her mum wouldn't let her go to Glastonbury with a group of twenty-year-olds. She was fifteen and burst into tears straight after she did it. She spent so many summers devising ways of avoiding exposing it to her posh family. In the end *she* was the one who got the shock when her mum revealed the cupid inked on her bum cheek that she'd had done in the sixties.

"He might have got it lasered off, I suppose. You'll have to ask him to show you," she says. "How can you possibly *be* Damian Dance if you don't know the state of his body art?"

"Yeah right. What am I going to say? Can you strip off, Mr Dance, so I can get a good look at what I'm working with?"

"Yes. That's exactly what you should do."

I feel the familiar anxious twist in my stomach. I can't believe the meeting is tomorrow. For a while it had felt as if this Platinum package idea was only that, an idea. Now it all feels as though it's happening too fast.

Do I know enough to pull this off? Should I have downloaded the *Big Brother* series he was in? As worried as I am, I don't think I could put myself through all those hours of people lounging on sun beds talking bollocks.

"I'm going to have to tell him I loved the show, aren't I?"

Louisa laughs. "Yes."

God, I'm completely the wrong person to work for him.

"Shit. I'm nervous now."

"About meeting Damian Dance?" Louisa scoffs.

Does he expect me to know everything about him? Ten minutes after I'd got his file, I'd listened to the songs that had made him a hit in Russia. A few hours later and I've already forgotten them.

"Don't be silly, May, you're much cleverer than him," Louisa says, waving her hand dismissively.

"It's not about that. It's about sounding authentic."

"Imagine if you had to tweet for the prime minister, though.

You'd have to know about policy and have a clear opinion on everything wrong with society and be able to explain why it's the other parties' fault. With Damian, you just need to know what he likes and doesn't like."

"It's a bit more than that."

"Just don't make him sound too clever."

There's a knock on the door, which is unusual. Sometimes delivery men buzz from downstairs, but it's a bit late for that.

"I'm not expecting anyone," Louisa says, and shovels another spoonful of curry into her mouth, a signal that she's not getting up.

I head down the passage and slide away the doormat so I can open the door properly. It's supposed to be *outside* the door, but Louisa keeps kicking it in as if she's worried someone might want to steal a second-hand Garfield doormat.

The man standing on the other side of door breaks into a warm smile when he sees me. He's good looking with tussled brown hair, designer glasses with thick black frames, and a pair of bright-blue eyes looking out from behind them. He's nailed the smart-casual look in a grey v-neck, dark-blue jeans and suede lace-ups.

"Hey," he says, with a friendly smile.

He looks familiar. I know that angular nose, those neat picket-fence teeth.

"Hi..."

His eyes widen. "Wow. You don't recognise me, do you? It's me, Alex."

"Oh my God!" I cry. "The beard!"

What a transformation! It's our neighbour, Alex Hunter, but like I've never seen him before. He rubs a hand over his clean-shaven jaw and laughs. He has thin ribbon lips and a dimple in his chin.

"I feel so naked," he says. "It's so nice."

Louisa appears by my side, gasping like an aerosol spray.

"Oh my God," she cries. "You've done it! You've cut off the Osama beard!"

I can't believe she's just blurted that out.

He looks taken aback. "Is that what you called it?"

"Not always," Louisa laughs, "sometimes we called it the hipster terrorist beard."

"That bad?"

Down to his chest and looking like it had the texture of pubic hair? Yes it had been very bad. We had talked about the food that must get lost in it, what it would be like to wash it, whether he combed it and what it would be like to kiss him.

"You look so different, so sexy... I don't remember you wearing those glasses..." She leans forward to gently touch his cheek. "Ooh! So smooth!"

She's such a flirt.

Alex cheeks have turned a light shade of pink. If it wasn't for his olive skin he'd be a tomato.

"Yeah, I usually wear contacts. The beard was for a part in a film."

I sense Louisa straightening up like a fox that's caught a scent.

"Don't tell me you're an actor?"

His eyes dart from mine to hers.

"I do a bit of acting, but mainly I direct."

We've been sharing the building with Alex for at least three months and up until now we've only talked about the weather and the runaway recycling box.

"Oh my God," Louisa says, the excitement building in her voice. "That's so crazy!"

"It's not *that* crazy," I say.

She sounds like one of my clients' fans.

"*I* think it is. That's so typical London. Everyone keeping themselves to themselves..." Louisa gushes, "such a shame we've wasted all this time! Because you'll never guess what I do!"

She raises her eyebrows coquettishly. *Such* a flirt. Alex holds up the magazine. It's a copy of *The Stage* and it's got Louisa's name and address printed on the plastic jacket.

"I think I might be able to guess," he says, grinning. "Are you in theatre?"

She snatches the magazine, "Yes! It arrived! I needed this!"

"You know they have a website too," Alex says, looking bemused.

"Oh I hate all that, computers, clickety buttons, screens..." she says, waving a hand at me. "May is online enough for both of us."

He turns his attention to me. "Oh yeah? What do you do?"

I have a line I use for moments like this.

"She pretends to be celebrities and tweets for them and stuff," Louisa says.

I stare at her in horror. How many people has she told? Has she told them the names of the clients too? Am I going to have to stop telling her things? All this runs through my head in the space of a few seconds.

"Oh sorry," she says hurriedly. "That's *not* what she does at all."

"You live together and you don't know what you each do for a living?" Alex says, laughing.

She grimaces at me, "What was it you do again?"

"Social media marketing," I say, returning her tight smile. "It's really not that interesting."

"No, it's really not," Louisa says, and I catch the significant look that she throws at him.

I feel stung. Just before Alex knocked she seemed very interested in my job. If this was a Buzzfeed quiz of "whose job is more boring" she would win hands down. She might say she's an actor but she spends four days a week making coffee.

"Social media marketing..." he echoes. "Like tweeting and stuff?"

"Yeah... I mean it's more than that... it's um..."

He's looking at me with his intense blue eyes and I feel this urge to make my job sound cool.

"It's all about helping people communicate their vision."

Louisa snorts with laughter and I feel my cheeks redden.

"What?" I say, glaring at her. "It is."

Alex looks unsure. He's delivered the magazine and now we're just standing awkwardly at the door.

"Do you want to come in for a drink?" Louisa says. "May's a

workaholic, but I've just come back from Greece and as far as I'm concerned I'm still on holiday."

"I'm not a workaholic!" I protest. "I just have a busy week ahead of me."

If he was thinking of coming in, he's just changed his mind.

"Thanks, but maybe another time," he says, and he glances at me, "when you don't have loads of work."

"Yeah, any day that's not a Monday," I say, with an apologetic smile. So much for red-heads being the fun ones.

"Boring!" Louisa chimes.

He laughs and heads up the stairs, calling back half way, "Enjoy your magazine!"

I close the door. Louisa stomps passed me, back to the kitchen.

"I can't believe you just blurted that out about my job. Do you tell everyone?" I call after her.

"Oh come on, I was so vague."

"If you'd had half a minute more you would have given him all the details. I told you it has to be secret."

"You're making such a big deal out of nothing," she says. "Sometimes you're so selfish, May."

I can't believe she's just said that. I'm not selfish. I'm actually very generous, which is why I offer to pay her rent when she's behind, and why I don't nag her about her mess even though I risk a broken neck every time I go to the toilet in the middle of the night.

"You know how hard it's been for me to get acting jobs, don't you?" she says, banging her spoon against her bowl as she stirs her now-cold curry. "Didn't you hear him? He's a director! He's the kind of person I need to be friends with!"

"It's not my fault he didn't come in."

"You didn't encourage him, did you? You said you had a busy week ahead... another way of saying, don't come in, I'm too busy!"

I feel a pinch of guilt. I hadn't clicked that's why she'd invited him in. I thought she was just flirting. She gets up, leaves her bowl on the table. I wish she would at least put it in the sink. But she's done the cooking and that means absolutely everything else is down to me now.

"You really need to chill out more, May," she says. "You should never get so busy making a living that you forget to make a life!"

Warning! High risk of #InspirationalQuoteInducedNausea.

I want to reach out and unfollow her by clicking on her nose or something. But I don't have to. She's got no more quotes up her sleeve, unlike me who has amassed hundreds over these last six months. Me, who used to unfollow people for emptying their tweets of wisdom onto my feed. She heads up the corridor to get her suitcase and drags it into her room like a lion dragging home a mauled gazelle.

In half an hour her mood will have cleared and she'll be offering to make tea as if we'd never said a cross word. But she always manages to put too much milk in the tea, so I'll say no, and then she'll think I'm still angry... so maybe I'll say yes and then tip it down the sink. God, she's a pain in the arse sometimes.

I reach for the rubber gloves and start to wash up, my mind quickly wandering away from the dishes. I compose tweets in my head for people who aren't me.

DJBUZZYA @DJBUZZYA
OMG. 2 hours to cook. 2 mins to eat. I'm not loving that ratio boyz n girls. LOL

BTHOMSKINNER @BTHOMSKINNER
Baxter has brought home a friend to play with. Friend less eager to play. Friend is a sparrow. Friend is dead. Friend not a friend.

DAMIANDANCE @DAMIANDANCE
I'M BACK! AND YES, MY PENIS IS PROPER FIXED! #back-inthegame

I squeeze my eyes shut to blot out the noise in my head. Thinking about Damian has made my stomach lurch. For a moment I wish I could just quit. I would be within my rights. Craig said we would help people market themselves, not take over their lives so we could do a better job.

There must be other companies needing an award-winning, digital marketing graduate with a natural ability to bullshit. The thought of getting a CV together and hunting down a new job makes me feel tired. If only I could work for myself. If only I could set the rules.

As I plunge my gloved hands into the boiling water, I let myself imagine what it would be like to drop all this responsibility and walk away. Of course it would involve even more work, going it alone, but at least I'd be doing what I loved. What is it I want to do, though? I can conjure up my desk in a shared office of young entrepreneurs. Steel rafters running across the ceiling, walls of exposed brick. I'm at my Mac clicking away, selecting content for my award-winning website. What's it about? Is it a resource hub for people wanting to learn about marketing? Or is it something closer to my heart? A collaborative platform showcasing lifestyles from around the world?

The more I try to pinpoint what I want to do, the faster it fades into nothing.

Then my mind snaps back to them. All those people who have sat in my office, desperate to be presented in their best light to a world so eager to criticise. They need me.

Isn't a little bit of fear healthy?

Life begins at the end of your comfort zone...

A comfort zone is a beautiful place but nothing ever grows there...

Know your limitations and then defy them...

#SHUTUP

All I need to do is make a list and systematically go through it, completing one task at a time.

But even as I'm trying to convince myself of that, a part of me knows that pretending to be a person is nothing like a normal chore. In ten minutes, I'll have finished washing the dishes. But being Damian Dance, or Bernard Thompson-Skinner, or whoever else Craig appoints me... when does that end? Will there ever be a good moment to walk away?

Chapter 4

Instead of taking a moment to collect my thoughts, I decide that 7am on the morning of a very important meeting is a good time to try on all the expensive mistakes I've ever made. I'm nervous and wanting to make the right impression, and for some stupid reason I think the right impression might exist in the bag of clothes I've been meaning to take to a charity shop.

Once again, I fail to unearth a gem. The tweed waistcoat feels like sandpaper, the sequined trousers still belong to the circus and the *"Oh but it's Vivienne Westwood so I have to buy them"* trousers have got enough room in the crotch to smuggle a kilo of marijuana and a family of rare monkeys through customs.

In the end I opt for my initial choice of olive-green blouse with capped sleeves and a figure-hugging pencil skirt. The doubt sets in as soon as I get on the Tube and see someone else wearing the same outfit. The only difference is that their blouse needs an iron. It dawns on me that Damian Dance isn't going to be impressed by my office-angel look. It's just going to make him wonder if I'm up for the job of impersonating him. I can just imagine it. He'll call his agent and tell him in a low voice, but loud enough for me to hear, that the young girl in the office clothes might be good at spreadsheets, but clearly doesn't have a clue about his music or fashion sense; and that quite frankly if his mum knew how to tweet she would do a better job. But short of buying a new wardrobe on the way to work, there's not much I can do about it now.

Abigail is early and clearly trying to make a good impression while she's on her three-month trial period. With her Lego earrings and streaky purple highlights, it's obvious to me that her real calling lies beyond sitting on reception. She's a creative who needs to pay her rent. My guess is she's in a band and plays gigs in pubs with sticky floors and broken toilets. The band could probably benefit from some social media marketing.

"Can I make you a coffee?" she asks, eager to please.

I like the routine of making it myself so I politely decline. For the best, really, as the phone starts ringing.

"Good Morning, SMCB, how may I help?"

I hover nearby, curious to know how she'll be able to handle enquiries when Craig has been so vague with her. She thinks we're a straightforward PR company specialising in social media. We were, until recently.

"I'm sorry, can you spell that?" Abigail says, sounding flustered. "T.H.I.... J? Okay... S? T.H.I.J.S..."

Abigail is not an experienced receptionist, but she wrote "quick learner" on her CV and out of the thousands of people who've written the same, there's got to be one who actually means it.

I make myself a coffee and settle down in my office to deal with the barrage of emails. Bernard's agent has sent through the itinerary for his book tour so I tweet details about that. The replies come in at once. It's 9am and everyone's looking for an excuse to delay starting work just another tweet longer.

PAGETURNERBOOKSHOP @WINPAGETURNERS
@bthomskinner We're looking forward to having you! Your books should be arriving in a couple of weeks!

I favourite the tweet, it's the easiest way to show my appreciation without having to reply.

READERDUDE @DUDE3611
@bthomskinner Can't wait to read Stage Door. I was also brought up in deepest, darkest Norfolk!

I can imagine Bernard tweeting back that that's where the similarities between himself and a man who calls himself "*Reader Dude*" end.

JANBOOKISH @JANBOOKISH12
@bthomskinner isn't it unusual for you to be up this early?

I tense. Who is this @janbookish12? And how well does she know him?

I can't ignore her. The new Bernard needs to be engaging and show he's got time for people.

BTHOMSKINNER @BTHOMSKINNER
@janbookish12 You know me, I like to be unpredictable! That or my watch has broken. Isn't it noon?

My cursor hovers over the tweet button. Is it too abrupt? Judging from the first chapter of *Backstage*, Bernard favours long-winding sentences. Twitter, however, does not.

"Shit..."

I simply can't take this long over one little tweet. I've just got to go for it. I delete the exclamation mark and tweet it.

The knock on the door makes me jump. Craig opens it before I've asked him to come in. I pop my nerves in a drawer and switch on a confident smile.

"You're looking very chic this morning," he says. "Have you got a date?"

I'm surprised he's asking about my personal life a few minutes before our big new client is about to sail through the door.

"Very funny."

43

It's not that funny. Three months ago I was sharing a fish platter with James, an engineer from Plymouth. We'd met at Louisa's birthday. Somewhere between squirting lemon in my eye and wiping his nose with a fishy wet wipe he'd told me he wasn't looking for anything serious.

"We'll have to start you on online dating. I'll ask Abigail to do it for you."

His little cheeky wink isn't convincing anybody. The last thing Craig wants is me getting distracted by a boyfriend.

"You do know Damian is going to be here any second, don't you?"

He cocks his head towards the door. "I think I've just heard him"

"Fuck."

It comes out before I can stop myself. We have a casual relationship, but still, I don't like Craig to see my doubts.

"What's the matter?"

"Nothing, nothing."

"You've got to relax, May. Have a little flirt with him."

"I'm not flirting with him. I'm a professional."

"Have a professional flirt, then. He'll be eating out of your hand."

I feel another wave of frustration at myself for not having taken a quiet moment to collect my thoughts this morning.

"I'd better greet him," he says. "Good luck."

I run over the facts in my head while I wait for Craig to reappear with my new client.

Damian Dance. Middle name: Thomas. Thirty-five years old. Born on 11th April. Aries. One sister: Amy. Spent five weeks in the Big Brother house before having to leave due to a groin injury. His single *The Rhythm of Her Hair* reached number eight in the UK charts, was number one for a month in Russia. A show-off by nature. Quick to lose temper. Arrogant.

The door opens and I feel my nerves float to my throat. I'm expecting to feel the ripple of his ego before he's even stepped into the room.

"In here, is it?"

His voice is soft, unsure. I hear Craig replying to go on in. Then there he is. Damian Dance is in my office. He's shorter than he seemed on television, which suddenly makes him seem less intimidating.

Our eyes meet and his face cracks into a friendly, sheepish smile, causing a ripple of little lines around his mouth like speech marks. I feel my corset of nerves give a little.

He reaches for my hand, "Hi, I'm Damian."

It strikes me as sweet of him to say so.

"May Sparks. Please, have a seat."

His eyes are muddy green.

"So this is where the magic happens," he says.

"Yes. My drawers are full of white rabbits."

He's generous enough to smile at that. His eyebrows rise up under the flop of sandy-blonde hair, layered and styled low across his forehead. There's a scar left by the past piercing on his right eyebrow.

Damian has ditched the vest and tracksuit bottoms. He's wearing a white t-shirt with fluorescent paint strokes splattered across it, and baggy stone-washed jeans with rips at the knee. Instead of the clunky silver chain around his wrist, there's just one pale- blue plastic band for a testicular cancer-awareness project, which has "FEEL MY BALLS" on it in big white letters.

Seeing him in the flesh has stopped me in my tracks. I just want to stare at every inch of him, to familiarise myself with him. He looks so different. He looks good.

We start talking at exactly the same time, then break off, laughing.

"Please," I say, "you first."

"I just wanted to say... Well... I'm a bit embarrassed..." He runs a hand through his hair and my confidence grows as I realise *he's* the one who's nervous. "About not being very good at this."

His honesty is endearing. The preconceived ideas I had about him start to crumble.

"Don't be," I say. "Lots of celebrities need help with their online profiles."

"Am I a celebrity? I was just in one little show."

I'm slightly thrown. I had assumed that in his head he shared a podium with Brad Pitt and David Guetta.

"I don't think you can call *Big Brother* a 'little show'."

He grins. "No, but it's not Hollywood. Still, crazy it's gone on so long."

"Tell me about it," I say, instantly regretting my tone.

He frowns. "You didn't think it would do well?"

"I doubt anyone expected it to do as well as it did."

"You hate it, don't you?"

My heart starts racing. "No, of course not. I didn't say that."

"You didn't need to." He leans back in his chair. "Wow. I don't know. Maybe this..." he gestures between us, "isn't going to work out after all."

"No, no, no! You've completely misunderstood me. From the beginning I thought it was a really interesting social experiment. I just didn't think the public would be as open to listening to other people having discussions and..."

I stop. There's laughter in his eyes.

"Wait... are you?"

"Kidding? Yes," he says. "I don't care what you think of *Big Brother*. That was ten fucking years ago."

I breathe out. He grins.

"You look cute when you're trying to dig yourself out of a hole."

Did he just say *cute*? Wow. This meeting has gone downhill fast.

"Let's start again," I say.

"Why? I was enjoying myself."

I make a renewed stab at professionalism." Right... first off... Twitter."

"What have you got there?" he says, wincing.

I cast my eyes down at the file in front of me, the contents of which are to blame for my tossing and turning last night.

"That's not my Twitter performance is it?"

"Performance" is one way to put it.

Assmonkey, dumbfuck, dickwad, jerkoff, fuck you, fuck your mum, mother fucker are all on the list in front of me.

"Getting emotional online is very common," I say.

"What a twat."

"That's about the only word you haven't called someone."

"It was only a matter of time."

I fail to suppress a smile. It feels like having a meeting with a friend, not a big, important client.

"When you're on Twitter, you forget loads of people can see what you've written," he says. "I know I should rise above it. It's just I get so pissed off. Why are people such dicks to people they don't even know? They don't know anything about me, so why are they making judgments and criticising me?"

"People who can't create criticise," I say, automatically.

Quotes on criticism? Oh I've got tons.

To escape criticism – do nothing, say nothing, be nothing...

Criticism comes to those who stand out...

Don't be distracted by criticism. Remember: The only taste of success some people have is when they take a bite out of you...

"It's not criticism, it's abuse," he says.

My eyes float back over the page in front of me. It looks like he's given as good as he's got. But the problem is you can't fight abuse with abuse, you've got to ignore and block. Responding to the haters is how you feed them.

"I know I probably shouldn't have reacted," he says, reading my thoughts. "But I can't help it. I feel I've got to stand up for myself, otherwise people will think I'm a wimp."

"That's what they want. They want you to react. It's a sport to them."

"They must be sad little people, sitting at their computers all day sending nasty messages to people."

"They get pleasure out of it, apparently. I read a study on trolls. They tend to have narcissistic, psychopathic or sadistic personality traits."

"A shit personality, then," he says. "What did the trolls do before Twitter?"

"They hid under bridges and scared goats."

"Those good old days," he says.

His laugh feels like a little reward. This is going to be alright. I already like him a lot better than Bernard. He's definitely a lot cuter than Bernard. If he wasn't a client and I saw him in a bar...

"Anyway, the good news is you won't have to deal with them any more because you've got me."

"You must be wondering why I want back in to the celebrity circus," he says.

It's not that difficult to guess why. He wants to feel special. He's tasted the high of fame and wants to feel it again. It's like going from the kick of a thousand little red flags on Facebook each day to none.

He narrows his eyes. "No, you can see right through me, can't you? You think I'm dying for the attention."

"No, of course not."

Can he see through *me*?

"It's not like that, though," he says. He leans forward in his chair as if he's going to share a secret. "To be honest, I've enjoyed being out of the spotlight."

I fight the urge to raise a sceptical eyebrow at this.

"I know you don't believe me."

I squirm. "It's not that, it's just..."

"What?"

"You're a reality TV star," I say. I edit the words that are about to come out of my mouth and settle for, "I didn't expect you to be an introvert."

He bursts out laughing. "I'm not an introvert! I just like being left alone sometimes. At the same time I want to sing. I *need* to sing. But the industry only lets people in if the public is making a load of noise about them already. So if getting into the limelight again can help me make it big in music then I'm ready."

"Good. Getting people into the limelight is what we specialise in."

Good? Snorts my inner voice. *How is that good for the shy, talented musicians? What about the artists who care more about making music than parading in front of the cameras?*

"What I need from you is as much information as possible so I can do a great job of showing you in your best light. While I sort out your online profile, you can get on with what you love most, the singing."

I listened to *The Rhythm of Her Hair* again last night. It *is* catchy. It also sounds like every other dance tune played across holiday resorts throughout the summer. He sang it through a vocoder.

"So you think you can pull it off?" he says. "I mean, obviously that's what you do but... we're so different... you're a woman, I'm a bloke... you're a bit posh, I'm about as posh as a Mars bar... you haven't been on TV, my career began because of TV... Do you sing?"

It's like listening to all my own fears. I had them on repeat last night, which is why I couldn't sleep.

"I'm not doubting you," he says, before I can answer. "I'm just a bit of a worrier and want to get it right."

"It's normal to be worried. But as you say, this is what I do."

I remove the questionnaire from my top drawer, thinking, not for the first time, how much I'd hate to have to fill one in for myself.

"This is our client questionnaire."

He pretends to buckle under the weight of it. "All this? Can't we just have a chat?"

"We can do that too."

How much time do I have? The odd thing is, I'm not feeling my usual urge to charge through the meeting so I can get on with all my jobs. I've got this fluttery feeling in my stomach.

"Okay...right," I say, more to focus myself than to get Damian's attention. He's looking at me, waiting for instructions. "Day in the life?"

"What do you mean?"

"Your average day."

He rubs the top of his arm, pushing up the sleeve of his t-shirt so I catch a glimpse of his dark tribal bands. Did they always look like that? Why do I think they make him look so hot now? Like he actually *is* in a tribe and could throttle a jaguar with his bare hands...

#PullYourselfTogether

I summon the guinea-tiger-bear to get things back into perspective.

"We're just going to do this here?" he says.

I glance around my office, unsure of the problem. It's a stylish, comfortable office, west-facing so it doesn't get much sun, but sun isn't much good when you're working on a screen all day.

"It's a really beautiful morning," he says. "Why don't we go out for a coffee?"

Because by the time we get to the café, order coffee, drink it, get to the crux of Damian Dance, half the day will have gone.

Then again, won't it be nice to escape the office for a bit? I feel a ripple of anticipation.

"Or aren't you allowed out?" he says.

"Of course I'm allowed out... I'm just thinking where the best place to go is."

"Soho House is only down the road. Are you a member?"

Of a private member's club in the centre of London?

"Um, no..."

"That's alright. I am. I'll get you in. I just hate being cooped up in an office," he says, getting to his feet. "I could never do an office job... no offence..."

"None taken," I say breezily.

I wish Louisa was a fly on the wall now and could see me stepping out for a coffee with this handsome celebrity to an exclusive club. In fact, I wish all the girls were flies on the wall. See girls, I'm not a workaholic! I can escape my desk whenever I want to!

Damian holds the door open for me, waiting for me to shove my tablet into my handbag. I push away the thought that, in actual fact, I'm taking my desk with me wherever I go.

"So you're outdoorsy?" I say.

"Outdoorsy sounds like I get up at five in the morning for walks in my waterproof trousers and my pro walking sticks."

I laugh.

"Alright, then. What are your favourite sports?"

His hand brushes against my back, steers me ahead. I feel a tingle of electricity. It must be the new carpet giving off static.

"Come on, May," he says, his smile playful. "Let's get a coffee before you start the interrogation."

No, it's not the new carpet. Hearing him say my name so casually has just delivered another little shiver down my back.

Am I to call him Damian? Or Mr Dance? It makes him crack up when I ask him. His eyes sparkle as if I've told him a wicked joke.

"You're going to find out everything about me," he says. "We're going to get close."

The lift doors ping open at that moment and we join three other people going to the ground floor. *We're going to get close.* We're so close we're touching right now. I feel my heart racing. He leans into me, so close I can feel his breath on my neck.

"Call me Damian. And I'll call you May."

I nod but don't reply. There are other people listening. I don't know if they recognise my client or not, but they are definitely listening. The lift reaches its destinations and we step out into the reception hall, and on out into the sunshine.

51

Chapter 5

"Madame, may I take your coat?"

It's not a question you usually get asked when you go for a coffee. I let out a little "oh" of surprise and instantly wish I was more subtle about not being used to this kind of treatment.

The French host smiles knowingly. His slick hair is shaved at the sides, long on top and gelled in the style of a 1920s soldier. His suit is tailored; his tie a skinny slither of black. I think of him turning his nose up at the high street label inside my jacket, and decline the offer with an apologetic smile and mumbled excuse about always being cold. I think how I should have worn the Vivienne Westwood trousers with the baggy crotch and make a mental note to rescue them from the bag for charity when I get home.

"Shall we go to the roof terrace?" Damian asks.

He seems completely at ease, whereas I'm secretly bubbling with excitement, and holding myself taller in an attempt to look richer and more sophisticated.

"Why not?" I say, with a shrug of faux nonchalance.

In the lift I think how my parents would label this place elitist and therefore wrong. They'd have turned Damian's offer down in favour of a sticky pub with wobbly seats and no table service. They'd have felt all self-righteous about it, while secretly wishing they hadn't ordered the cheapest wine on the menu. I don't have a problem with enjoying the finer things in life when the finer things present themselves free of charge!

What I don't like is obscene extravagance or wastefulness, but being whisked off the bustling London streets to enjoy a coffee in a beautiful setting and being treated like a VIP is something I totally approve of.

The lift pings open and we step out into a scene from a Mediterranean holiday brochure. Smart white parasols shade rows of square marble tables and grey rattan armchairs. We choose a table and I sink into the grey and white-striped cushion. There's only one other couple, who are in the far corner, engrossed in conversation; delicate espresso cups between them. I was going to order a coffee, but my beautiful surroundings have made me crave something with a little more sparkle. I check my watch. It's way too early.

"Are you in a rush?" Damian says.

I let out a little laugh. "No. I was just double-checking the time. Not noon yet, so coffee it is."

I need to remind myself that this is not a social meeting, this is a business meeting.

"We *are* celebrating," Damian says, with a wink.

"We are?"

"Yes. A new beginning. No more Damian Dance cocking up online!"

I smile. *He* said it.

The waiter comes over to take our orders. He's another handsome, well-groomed young man, who has eyes for Damian, not me.

"May I take your order, sir?"

Damian opts for a carrot-and-ginger juice, which surprises me. I was expecting him to order something horrible, like a vodka and red bull.

If he's not going to be naughty, there's no way I can be.

"A latte," I say.

Damian shakes his head. "No, she'll have a glass of champagne."

I let out a little giggle of surprise. "Oh, will she?"

"I like ordering for other people."

"Well it's lucky I like champagne, then!"

If the waiter is judging my breakfast beverage, he's too well-trained to show it. Champagne for breakfast! My job suddenly doesn't seem quite so bad.

"This is why I don't leave my office for meetings," I say. "Look at me, acting like I'm on holiday."

"Fuck it," Damian says. "Life is short."

"It'll be shorter if I drink champagne every morning."

"It's not heroin."

I laugh. "No, but it's a slippery slope."

His juice comes in an impressive glass with half a herb garden in it and I automatically reach for my phone.

"Twitter photo?" I say.

His smile is too forced, lips drawn up to reveal his gums.

"Take it again," he says, "I can tell by your face it was shit."

"Look natural, then."

He pulls silly faces, which make me laugh. Last night I barely slept because I was worried about meeting him and now here we are, relaxed in each other's company.

I was expecting the restless, arrogant young man I'd seen on the television. Looking at Damian's grinning face it's hard to believe he's the same person who was so quick to temper, whose language unravelled at the slightest provocation and had to be censored with an ear-splitting *beeeeeeeeeeeeep*. Not that I doubt he's a potty mouth, or hot-headed, but just that I can see there's more to him than that.

I should have known it was partly an act, that reality TV is edited to manipulate our emotions. He was probably paid to be obnoxious. There must have been a script and stage directions and instructions about what he had to wear. Perhaps that awful tattoo was just a transfer... My eyes undress him. I saw proof of his good body years ago. Now I'm thinking how delicious and how liberating it would be to not care whether a guy is intellectually and emotionally compatible, but to fuck purely because their body is smoking hot.

Damian stops fooling around, and his face settles into a smouldering smile, his teasing green eyes looking right into mine. There's a fizzle of chemistry between us that makes my cheeks burn.

I take the picture. He leans in to see it.

"Do I look gorgeous?" he says.

"Don't worry, I'm good at Photoshop."

"Oi! Don't say that," he says, his weak smile hiding genuine concern. "Take another one."

There it is. His ego has finally made an appearance. I take another photo but he doesn't like that one either. He fusses with his hair and rearranges himself in his seat. I snap away until, finally, he's satisfied.

"My agent, Andy, said you're going to change all my passwords."

"It removes the temptation of saying something you'll regret."

He frowns, plucks a mint leaf out of his drink and rubs it between his fingers.

"It's not that I can't control myself. I just hate Twitter. It's like loads of mosquitoes buzzing in your ear. I don't know how you do it."

I don't know how you do it. I wish it sounded like he was impressed I can do it, rather than baffled why I would want to.

"I suppose I'm good at filtering." I take a sip of my chilled champagne. "Plus I'm good at managing my time."

Well, I'm evidently not quite nailing it today. While I'm basking in rare sunshine, the notifications are piling up for me to answer. But how can I tweet like a celebrity if I don't know how they live? This is a perk of the job, and as long as I don't forget I'm supposed to be doing a job...

"So, have you thought about the impression you'd like to give to the public?"

"I suppose I just want to be seen as a normal, nice guy," he says, "and not some arrogant twat who broke their cock."

"Ouch," I wince, "how is your..."

I stop, horrified at what I was about to say. He bursts out laughing so loudly the couple in the far corner break off mid-conversation to turn and stare. It crosses my mind that Damian probably isn't the classiest member of this club.

"I wasn't going to say what you think I was."

"And I thought northern girls were forward!"

I reach out and give him a playful punch on the arm. If it's inappropriate then I blame Craig for telling me to flirt.

"I was just going to ask how's your health... in general," I say, not convincing anyone.

"Do you need a picture of it to show the world it's healed up nicely?" he says. "Are you even allowed to tweet a live penis on Twitter?"

"I wouldn't do that!" I hiss, embarrassed because he's talking so loudly and I'm sure the other couple can hear every word.

"Why? You haven't even seen it. It's got a lot of character."

"Stop, please!"

I don't know why I didn't think Damian was good-looking before. His jaw's a bit wide and square, but compared to how I remember him it's as if he's grown into his face. He gets dimples when he smiles and his nostrils flare as though he's holding back a laugh, as if he needs to hear yours first. Maybe I would have found him cute back then if I'd pressed mute. A bit like now, too. It was funny at the beginning, but now he's starting to repeat himself.

It must have been his waxy curtains that hung limply over his face. Now his hair has a style. Short at the back, dishevelled at the front and without the gluey hair products. It's a bit boy band. The kind of floppy fringe you see fashion-conscious guys stroking like a pet weasel. They always seem to be pushing it out of their eyes only to push it back in exactly the same place. A bit like what Damian's doing now...

What's wrong with me? Am I looking for reasons not to fancy

56

him? Because there's one that's pretty obvious. He's my client. He's also a showman; a player. He gets inside people's knickers, knickers he shouldn't be inside. People's girlfriends. That hooker. I'd almost forgotten about Diamond Daneesha and her double-page confession in a tabloid newspaper.

#SHUTUP

I just need to get all the relevant facts so I can do my job well.

"Do you still have that tattoo on your back?"

I can tell I've touched a nerve. The laughter vanishes from his eyes.

"Thanks for bringing up the two things I don't want to talk about for the rest of my life. I thought I was doing this to get away from Twitter. Feels like I'm still on it."

He looks away, his lips pursed together in a pout.

I feel like such an idiot. I should have waited for him to bring it up.

"I'm sorry, Damian," I say. "That was insensitive. Perhaps we should rewind a bit."

I reach for my tablet. I'm going to take notes, just so I don't have to meet his gaze.

"It was so humiliating," he says, letting out a deep breath. "I'm laughing now, but I was crying for years. I didn't realise how bad it was until it was all over the telly. After *Big Brother* I didn't want to take my top off ever again... Not to swim, not even to fuck..."

I feel his eyes on me, but I can't meet them. I scratch at the back of my neck and glance at my screen, trying not to imagine him doing aforementioned activities.

"Couldn't you have got someone to work on it?" I say.

He looks away, his eyes misting over. "I had someone work on it but they messed it up."

How could they have made it even worse? I'm dying to know what it looks like now.

"I've just found someone in Italy," he continues. "It's going to cost me eight grand to turn it into something good."

"Is it a secret?"

He shrugs. "Whatever you think."

I'm thinking of it going viral. "Send me a picture when it's done."

"Anyway... I don't think that's true, what I said before, about wanting to be seen as just normal and nice."

"No," I agree, before quickly pushing my fingertips against my lips. I'm always butting in. It's a terrible habit.

He frowns. "You don't think I should either?"

"Well, relatable is good."

"But I need to stand out."

"You can't be boring."

#StopTalking.

I'm just putting more pressure on myself. Now he's going to have these huge expectations and he'll be so underwhelmed when he reads my mediocre tweets. I swallow, my throat feels dry.

"I want people to know I'm happy now," he says. "I'm not the same angry guy I was back then. My mind has opened up. I've read some books that have really changed my view on life. I'm even doing yoga, for fuck's sake. I never thought I'd do yoga. It's great, though. Do you do it?"

"Yoga?"

"Yeah."

"Uh, not any more."

"You should."

"I've got a mat."

There was one short week in my life when I did yoga every day with Louisa.

"I'm also having a go at visualisation..."

It sounds very much like the cliché of the recovering celebrity.

"That all sounds great," I say. I should stop there, but I can't resist. "So what diet are you on? Paleo?"

Or are we back to Juicing? Didn't Atkins kill off a few celebrities?

"Yeah, yeah, laugh away, I know what you're thinking," he says.

I'm thinking I should play it safer. If I continue to offend him, I might lose his business.

"I'm just trying to get a better idea of your lifestyle for all your fans," I say.

He likes the sound of that. He looks thoughtful now.

"I'm learning to cook..." he says, after a pause.

I can imagine him in an apron.

An apron and nothing else.

"Everyone loves a man who can cook," I say, unable to stop the blushing.

"I'm still on the scrambled eggs stage, so don't tweet something really fancy yet, okay?"

I add *food tweets* to my list.

"You've got to send me a list of artists you like," I say. "Your favourite songs, gigs you're getting excited about... that sort of thing..."

"Maybe we should go to some clubs together?"

The suggestion gives me a thrill. I'm not big into night clubs, but then again I'm guessing with Damian there would be no queues, no dancing around handbags and getting crushed, and no night buses. I'm thinking cordoned-off VIP area, champagne in the ice bucket and a driver to take you home.

Of course the last thing I should be doing is drawing attention to myself with Damian and have the media speculating whether I'm his girlfriend. They'd have a field day if they then discovered that I was the voice behind his online profile.

"Or not," he says, leaving it open.

"Probably better not..." I say, and feel disappointed.

I can barely assert my professionalism on a sun-lit rooftop, let alone in a dimly lit club with alcohol flowing and music playing.

"So, tell me about your comeback plan," I say.

"Oi, don't call it that! It's a progression!"

I let out a burst of laughter. "God, I'm being so offensive this

59

morning."

"Yes, you are. Are you sure you're not one of my Twitter trolls?"

"Not that I know of... what's your Twitter handle again?"

He shakes his head and I realise it's probably time to end the flirting and get down to business.

"Seriously, what *is* the plan? What are you working on?"

He slurps up the dregs of his carrot and ginger and pushes the glass away.

"I'll let you know as soon as I know a bit more. Anxious Andy has some ideas up his sleeves."

He's ending the meeting and I feel like we were only getting started. I was worried about it going on forever and now I'm sorry it's ending so soon. I have a feeling I may not have used our time together very effectively.

"Let's have lunch some time," he says.

I feel relieved. I also feel I should be encouraging him just to email me instead. Although it seems a shame, what with him being a member of this fancy place.

"Yes, definitely. Give Abigail a call to schedule something in."

"I have to call Abigail now? Are you playing hard to get?"

What goes red and white, red and white a dozen times in the space of half an hour? Someone who shouldn't have a crush on a C-list celebrity she previously thought (and still suspects) might be a bit of a vain idiot.

"Of course not," I say, trying to sound smooth. "Use my direct line."

Next time we're meeting in the office. Another of these escapades with Damian Dance and things might get out of hand. If he were to see the tweets I'm composing in my head right now, he'd run a mile...

DAMIANDANCE @DAMIANDANCE
My next song is going to be about making love to a sexy redhead I just met on a rooftop. #LoveAtFirstSight #NotEvenJoking

Or to sum it up in hashtags: *#Mayisabithorny #NoMoreAlcohol ForMay*

Chapter 6

Emma cuts through my excuses. "How long are you going to be?"

I grimace at the impatience in her voice.

"Five minutes," I say.

"If you aren't here in five minutes, we're going to order food. Clare is starving and we've already eaten two baskets of bread."

"I'm literally around the corner."

Emma huffs into the receiver and then hangs up on me. The problem is I've been literally around the corner for over half an hour. I emerged at Clapham High Street to five missed calls from Craig, so I had to ring him back. He wanted to run some ideas past me about sponsored tweets. I kept wanting to say, "Why can't we talk about this tomorrow?" But I just couldn't do it. It's my stupid ego. I want him to think I'm amazing, that I have the attitude and stamina of a high flyer. He could have chosen so many other people to join his new company, but he chose me; the intern who was being paid in soggy cheese sandwiches. I should have set some boundaries at the very beginning. Now it feels impossible to change them.

My high heels were a mistake and my toes are burning by the time I make it to the restaurant. I've got plasters in my bag, but there's no way I could have stopped and taken another five minutes to unwrap them. Perhaps a raw open blister will soften my friends' hearts towards me.

"We've ordered," Emma snaps.

I catch Clare's eye, hoping to find some sympathy there, but she looks away, concentrates on the bottle of wine they've nearly finished in my absence.

"I'm sorry," I say, my shoulders sagging. "I'm just rubbish at saying no."

"You're good at saying no to us," Emma says.

"I'm here, aren't I?"

"An hour late. You've missed the interesting stuff."

I want to point out that at least they were waiting together. It wasn't like I left one person waiting for me outside in a storm. But I sense it's best to be contrite and promise I'll do better. I haven't seen either of them for weeks and I just want to get my being in trouble over with so we can all catch up.

"What interesting stuff?"

"Oh, you know, Anna's Phil being offered a job with Qantus, Mira being pregnant, Clare moving..."

"What?! Slow down. Where are you moving?"

"You should order," Clare says. She slides a menu across the table. "Or our food won't come at the same time."

My phone is ringing. I can feel its vibration before anyone can even hear it. I swear internally as the tune picks up volume.

"Oh for God's sake," Emma mutters.

Who is it now? Craig again? There's no way I'm going to check it. I'll let it ring, even though the not knowing is making my stomach hurt. I'm not going to check it precisely *because* it's making my stomach hurt. I shouldn't let my phone control me like this. It's a quarter to nine on a Friday evening and I have a right to be switched off. Who does Craig think we work for? The government?

"I'm switching it off!" I say. "Look, watch me."

With great ceremony I remove my phone from my handbag and press the off button.

"There. Impressed?"

"No," Emma says. "I'd be impressed if you threw it under a car."

"Oh, come on! I'm not that bad!"

Neither of them answers. Am I that bad?

"Fine," I say, resigned to the cold shoulders. I pick up the menu.

"They do really good lamb here," Emma says.

An olive branch?

Clare pours the last of the red wine into my glass. I suddenly feel quite moved.

"Look, I'm really sorry about being so flaky lately," I say. "It's not on. I'm going to change."

"You have been really flaky," Emma grunts. "How could you miss Anna's birthday?"

"*I* missed Anna's birthday," Clare says quietly.

Emma frowns at her. "You were at a funeral."

"I'd only ever met the woman once, though," Clare says. "It was my grandmother's friend."

I cough and raise my glass. "Look, let's toast to me being a better friend in the future?"

Emma rolls her eyes, but there's also a trace of a smile. She leans against me, gives me a friendly nudge then kisses my shoulder.

"We just miss you," she says.

"And we worry about you," Clare adds. "We don't want Craig taking advantage of your ridiculous work ethic."

"I know, I just always feel like I have to justify being the one he chose. Then there's the salary... I still can't get my head around the fact he's paying me to tweet rubbish all day."

"You don't tweet ru..."

"I do," I interrupt Clare. "We all know it."

"Look, you've got to stop thinking like this," Emma says. "What you don't realise is that you're doing something that other people find very difficult."

"Really? I tweeted a video of a puppy on a skateboard today."

"And you made the world a happier place because of it."

"Mmm..."

"You completely deserve your salary. You also deserve and are entitled to a social life. "

"And a love life," Clare adds.

"Really? I wish you'd told me that earlier! I wouldn't have said no to all those perfect men that keep asking me out."

"If you put your phone down for five minutes, you'd probably land someone quite quickly," Emma says.

I think of how I lusted over Damian on the rooftop this morning. Then I think of the champagne and feel pleased I've got something to share that isn't negative about my job.

"You all think I spend my life cooped up in an office on my phone but that's not true..."

"Isn't it?"

I raise an eyebrow. "Nope. This morning I escaped to meet a gorgeous man on a rooftop in a very glamorous establishment and drank champagne..."

Clare's eyes widen in surprise. It does sound good, doesn't it?

Emma looks suspicious. "What? Who? Tell us everything."

I feel a trickle of regret that I can't be completely honest. On the other hand, I've just made them forget how disappointed they are in me. It feels like it always used to, when the three of us would meet up every other Thursday in the Falcon.

"Go on!" Emma says, tugging at my arm.

So I tell them a different version of the story, omitting Damian's name and the fact he's my client, changing his status from ex-reality TV star to "someone in the media". I focus on how gorgeous he was, how spontaneous his invitation when we bumped into each other near my office, and how I could get used to being taken to fancy places.

"Are you going to meet again?" Clare wants to know.

"I think so..."

Ah, my moment of self-loathing. Two moments in a day. Or possibly an hour. I never used to lie before this stupid job. I just want to prove to everyone I'm fine, my life is balanced, but if I'm lying that means it's not, doesn't it?

Can I backtrack? No, I can't backtrack. For starters, I can't reveal that Damian Dance is my client... and if I did, they would just laugh at me, because I've spent half my life ranting about how shit *Big Brother* is.

"What was your Facebook status about?" I say, turning to Emma.

She frowns. "Which one?"

"You said you 'didn't want to talk about it'."

"Oh..." she blushes. "I had a rubbish day."

"There was a tiny delay on the Tube," Clare scoffs. "She got home a whole half an hour later."

"Twenty minutes, actually," she says, with a sheepish grin.

"Meanwhile half of Facebook thinks something awful has happened to you," I say, shaking my head.

"You didn't ring me to find out, though, did you?" she says pointedly.

"Because I know you. I knew it was going to be something like that."

She laughs. "True."

"That's not your worst update either..." Clare says.

"Not by far," I agree. I'm just relieved the focus has left me. "You've written some really great ones over the years."

"Don't!" Emma protests.

But we can't resist bringing them all up. We order another bottle of wine and get stuck in. Our laughter grows as we tease each other.

"You can't talk anyway," Emma says. "What about @SparkyMay? She used to be all cynical but funny cynical, and yesterday you were all like, LOL this, listen to this banging tune, come to this gig yo... it was so weird!"

I stop laughing.

"What?"

Her laughter falters. She senses there's something wrong.

"Yesterday," she says. "You went all gangster rapper on us."

66

I feel a cold prickle of sweat at my neck as I realise what must have happened. I reach for my handbag and grab my phone.

"What's wrong?" Clare says.

"Oh shit, I shouldn't have said anything," Emma says. "It doesn't matter! No, don't turn that bloody thing back on! It was ages ago. Who cares?"

I did it. I did that thing that I'm always so anxious to avoid. I tweeted for DJ Buzzya from my own personal account. No wonder I'm losing followers.

"It's so weird no one said anything..." I murmur, as my phone loads.

Maybe because my followers are losing interest in me. I feel this pressure to tweet something brilliant...

"May, it's no big deal," Clare says, reaching for my hand.

@SparkyMay is my voice. My real voice. If that becomes just another marketing tool, then what have I got left of me?

Clare's wrong. It is a big deal. I've got to be more careful. I've got stay focused. I drop my phone back in my bag, but this time I leave it switched on.

Chapter 7

I'm about to push my keys into the lock when the door springs opens. Alex Hunter is standing in the doorway. He looks as surprised to see me as I do him and for a split second I think I must have walked up an extra flight of stairs, and that this is in fact his flat not mine. But then I spot the Picasso print on the wall and Louisa's knackered beige ballet pumps on the floor.

I smile uncertainly while my brain whips up a scandal.

"Another magazine delivery?"

"No, I was just checking out your flat for a, uh, scene..."

"A scene?"

I'm a bit tipsy and almost blurt out, *A sex scene?* Then again he doesn't look crumpled enough to have had a passionate encounter with my flatmate. If his grey-and- white check shirt was ever off, it's now very much on, and buttoned down.

"Is that Legs?" Louisa calls from the kitchen. She's not huge by any means, but she walks like an elephant, stomping down the corridor.

Alex moves to the side, "Sorry, I'm stopping you coming in."

As I step past him, I catch a scent of his cologne; a mixture of musk and leather. There's something very arousing about it and I linger in the corridor, breathing it in.

"A scene for a film?" I ask.

"Yes, I can tell you all about it," Louisa cuts in. "Alex has to rush off to a birthday."

She sounds like his girlfriend, like she knows everything about his life. Up until yesterday he was just the man with the awful beard.

He shoots me an apologetic smile, "Yes, for my short film, but if you're not happy with anything, just let me know, there's no pressure."

"Of course she won't mind," Louisa says. "She won't even be here. She'll be at work."

"I wasn't at work just now," I grumble. "I was with friends."

"I should hope so, it's gone eleven-thirty on a Friday night," Louisa says.

"Sorry not to have more time to explain..." Alex says, catching my eye.

I shoot him an enthusiastic smile and tell him not to worry. I don't want Louisa convincing him that I'm the difficult one. Once he's gone I follow Louisa into the kitchen. I've had enough wine, so I switch on the kettle. I notice the clock and think about Alex's visit.

"Isn't it very late for him to be popping in? You could have been asleep."

"We met on the landing. I was coming in and we started talking about his film."

I notice she doesn't meet my eye. I'm guessing the meeting wasn't as serendipitous as Alex thinks it might have been.

"You look tired," she observes.

"Thanks."

I study my face in the living-room mirror. My eyeliner has left grey smudges beneath my eyes, giving the impression I've pulled an all-nighter. My red lipstick has faded to an outline and my concealer has worn so thin I can see the little red spots on the side of my nose. Now she's said it, I do feel tired. The encounter with Damian had given me an adrenalin rush that had kept me going through the morning, while meeting the girls had given me

69

a second wind in the evening. Now, my adrenalin is low, and I feel like stretching out on the sofa and falling asleep.

"It's such a coincidence, really," she says, flicking the switch on the kettle. "Alex is directing this short film he wrote himself and our flat is exactly how he imagined one of the character's flats."

"Even your bedroom?"

She ignores me. "He's really excited about it because it's his own project for a change. He's co-written it with his friend, Jacob."

The kettle boils and I get to the milk first. Once I've stirred in the right amount, I feel I can relax. I settle onto the sofa. It dawns on me I could take advantage of my steaming mug and tweet a #welldeservedcuppa moment for one of my clients. Craig would love that. I rest my mug on the coffee table and take the snap. Now to add a filter and make it look groovy. God, I'm tired.

"I'm assuming there's a part for you in this film, though."

Louisa looks uncomfortable. "I don't know yet."

"You haven't asked?"

"Not yet. I didn't want to seem pushy."

"Just ask when the auditions are."

Louisa looks thoughtful, "yeah, I hadn't thought of that..."

When it comes to her career, she has this annoying habit of becoming shy. She's fine to flirt, bold as brass when it comes to telling other people what to do with their lives, but if anyone gives her suggestions about her own career, she'll bat them away, insisting that the acting world is different, that it doesn't work like that.

"So how long will they be shooting in the flat?"

"Not long. A day or two."

Louisa's right. I won't be here, so it doesn't matter. It will mean tidying up and hiding anything personal, though. I close my eyes and lean back into the cushy embrace of the sofa.

"Maybe I'll invite them over for dinner? Alex and the other writer... What do you think?"

I open my eyes again. Louisa is perched on a kitchen chair, a plan hatching behind her eyes. The idea of dinner doesn't appeal hugely. I've eaten with Louisa and her fellow artists plenty of times and it always gets so deep; or at least, they think they're being deep, but to me they just sound pretentious. I bet the conversation will be 100 per cent film – and theatre – related, and granted, Alex is very easy on the eye, but I think Louisa has made it pretty clear he's hers, so... what's the point of dinner?

"Won't they be busy planning the film?" I say.

"It's just dinner," she says, her lip curling. She's heard the reluctance in my voice.

"I'm just saying he might be busy."

"No, you're saying *you* might be busy."

"I'm not. I'd love to have dinner with them!"

She looks out of the window, her mind still plotting. "I'll ask him. I think it'll be good if we can share a bottle of wine, get to know each other..."

In her head, I bet she imagines Alex offering her the part at the end of the evening because she's proved she's got a connection with the story. Well, if it helps her, I'll do dinner. But I can't be drinking so much mid-week. It makes me feel so sluggish in the mornings and I can't afford to be off my game.

I should start doing yoga. Not just for the physical exercise but for the spiritual element. My life is definitely missing something deeper. An anchor. I was speeding towards Tottenham Court Road station last week, panicking because my Twitter app had crashed and the email marked "important" from Craig wasn't opening. Then someone thrust this leaflet into my hands and it said: *Peace comes from within. Do not seek it without.* I slowed down to read it, stunned because it felt like the universe was speaking directly to me. Then someone bumped into the back of me, swore loudly in my face, and I almost burst into tears. The fact is, I feel like I've been renting my "space within" to a hoarder for the last six months. I just can't face going inside.

Yoga might help me get through the door of my inner sanctum. It might quieten some of the buzz in my head too. On a less

meaningful note, it will also give me some cheesy photo opportunities. All my clients can be doing yoga without moving off the
sofa. I'll just take pictures of my mat and some Photoshopped feet.
Do they all have a full set of toes?

Oh God, it's going to take a lot of yoga to silence some of these
stupid thoughts. That or a new job. But I can't think about the
latter now. Instead I picture Damian doing a warrior pose without
a shirt on. Does he have a personal trainer? Or does he attend a
top gym? I wonder if he can get me in for a session. Again, purely
to see how my VIP clients live so my tweets can be more authentic.
Or maybe we should just do some yoga together. Naked yoga.

#ShutupMay.

He's my client and he's totally out of bounds. Plus he's not my
type. I can't even chat with him normally because all the time I'm
aware I'm going to have to replicate his voice later on Twitter. It's
not just the content, it's the Mancunian slang. I've got a few sites
bookmarked for research and am halfway through a Buzzfeed post,
which translates some of the more common vocab:

1. *"Us" = Me*
2. *"Dinner" = Lunch*
3. *"Tea" = Supper*
4. *"Supper" = A bit of toast before bed*
5. *"Dead" = Really*
6. *"Pop" = Fizzy drink*
7. *"Lamp" = To hit someone*
8. *"Clear Skies" = Mythical weather*

Louisa's good at accents, maybe she can help.

"So, I met him," I say, suddenly.

"Who?"

"Damian Dance!"

She's curious, but not as enthusiastic as she'd been the previous
day. "How did it go?"

"Yeah, he was nice, actually. I'd expected him to be really arrogant, but he wasn't. He was easy to talk to."

If she was showing a bit more interest I'd admit to getting butterflies.

"Did you see his tattoo?" she asks.

"No. We were on a rooftop at Soho House."

She's not impressed by private members' clubs. Half her family are signed up to one or other.

"Shame," she says. "I wonder if it's still as bad."

It's like getting a tiny taster of what Damian must have had to put up with for all these years. No one caring much about what he's working on, just wanting to know about his tattoo. Am I feeling defensive on his behalf? Shit, I must be more drunk than I thought. Next, I'll be mouthing off on Twitter!

"He's cute, you know."

That gets her attention. "Really?"

I shrug, backtracking a bit, "Yeah, he looks much better than he used to."

If she asked, I'd show her the pictures I took. She'd laugh at his posing, and his boy-band hair, but really she'd think he was cute.

She turns back to the window, her eyes glazing over, her mind already elsewhere.

"I'll have to check if they're allergic to anything."

I should probably be relieved she doesn't care. Yesterday I promised myself I wouldn't tell her anything about my new clients after she blew her mouth off to Alex.

I turn to my phone and scroll absently through my Facebook account.

Emma Priestly: *Out with the girls for a much-needed drink!*
– feeling emotional

I click 'like', pleased I'm still one of the girls. Now I just need to stay in their good books while keeping Craig happy at the same

73

time. A thought occurs to me that I don't have to get up early tomorrow, that I could schedule some tweets now and be ahead of the game over the weekend. Although it might sound a bit like something a workaholic would do, it's not like I haven't had my fair share of fun in my twenty-eight years on earth. I take another gulp of tea and feel my resolve strengthen. If I power through into the early hours today, then I'll reap the benefits all week.

Chapter 8

Blurry-eyed on Monday morning after a weekend with hardly a break from the screen, I'm scanning through Bernard's direct messages on Twitter. It catches my eye because it doesn't start with the irritatingly chirpy, *Thanks for the Follow!* like all the other automatically generated message.

MISSINKYTOES @MISSINKYTOES
@bthomskinner what do I have to do to you to get into your next book? ;)

It's just a fan. If I'm going to panic every time someone gets a little personal with my clients on social media I'm going to have a heart attack by the time I'm thirty.

Who is this @missinkytoes? The fact she's been able to send a private message means that Bernard is following her too. Perhaps her profile picture seduced him. It's a cartoon of a sexy superhero; a woman with big green eyes, flicky-up hair, a big pink cleavage spilling out of a tight blue leotard and a red superhero cape. Did he really fall for that? Did he not consider that in concealing herself, she might be hiding less-appealing superpowers, like the ability to cross her twenty-stone thighs or French plait her chin whiskers?

Her biog reads: *book-lover writing her own pages.*

So she's a writer who likes books. But is she Bernard's fan or Bernard's friend? And then another thought strikes me. What if she's the lover?

My office phone starts ringing and I tear myself away from the screen.

"Hi, May, I've got Ta...Tai..Tice's manager on the phone for you," Abigail says uncertainly.

"Who?"

"From the band Five Oars."

I do a quick Google search. Of course I'm aware of them. They're the band reportedly headed on the same trajectory of fame and fortune as One Direction. Jake Helms is the main singer. It's his picture that comes up when I type in the band's name. Voluminous blonde hair styled across his eyes so he can't see anything, a leather jacket to identify him as faux dangerous, twinkly blue eyes to show he's soft inside.

"What's his name again?"

"Tice?"

"How do you spell it?"

"Oh it's impossible."

It's not what you want to hear from your receptionist. Now I feel irritated because I'm going to have to pretend to his manager that I know who he is. Thanks, Abigail.

"It's Dutch, I think..."

"Okay, put him through," I say, googling *Dutch member of Five Oars.*

"The manager is a 'she'... Maria Hu... Hubal? ... sorry..."

"It's really important you get people's names right. Just put her through, please."

I feel a stab of guilt at being so curt with Abigail when I locate a picture of him with his name written in full in the caption. Thijs Vandroogenbroek is a pale-faced teenager with round cheeks and no discernible chin. I don't know how his name rolls off a tongue in Holland, but there's no rolling happening off mine.

"Good morning, May Sparks," I say, accepting the transfer.

"Good morning, my name's Maria Kuebler, I'm Thijs Vandroogenbroek's agent from the band Five Oars."

Tice. Like Dice. That's how she's just pronounced it.

"Oh hello!" I gush. "How can I help you?"

"Well, let me put it like this..." Her accent is clipped, faintly foreign and gives the impression of someone efficient. She's the kind of woman you feel you need to prove yourself to. "Have you heard of Jake Helms?"

"Absolutely."

"And Andrew Donahue?"

The Irish one. Dark hair. Pink cheeks.

"Yes."

"Andrew Lancaster?"

The boy next door. Slightly chubby, cute features.

"Yep..."

"Eddie Ex?"

I scroll down my Google search. I'm pretty sure I could pick him out of a line up. He's supposed to be the clown of the group.

"The comedian, right?"

"Very good," she says. "And what about Thijs Vandroogenbroek?"

I've heard of him *now*, does that count?

"Exactly," she says.

I scratch the back of my flushed neck with the end of my pen. "I mean, I know what he looks like."

Because I've just seen his picture.

"They've only really started getting big media coverage recently, haven't they?"

"Please," Maria cuts in. "There's no need for justifications. I've proved my point, I think."

I notice there's been a new interaction on Bernard Thompson-Skinner's Twitter account and click onto it. I feel a little jolt in my stomach when I see @missinkytoes has moved from private message to open feed.

@bthomskinner stop pretending you're too busy to answer your DMs ;)

The power the winky face has to make a message sound flirty is astounding. Just imagine the tweet without it:

@bthomskinner stop pretending you're too busy to answer your DMs

It would sound threatening, like there's an implied "or else" at the end.

"Craig told me about you," Maria says. "He was very secretive at first, but I'm good at making people talk."

She laughs, but I can tell she's being serious. I push away the tablet, sensing where this conversation is going. Craig didn't warn me about this call. Is it another Platinum Package? Am I ready to adopt another voice so soon after taking on Bernard and Damian?

"What did he say?" I'm trying to sound bright and eager, but I'm concerned about my growing workload.

"Oh, you know, that you're award-winning, attracted a million followers in six months by the power of your wit and charm."

A million? I think he inflates that figure a little bit each week.

"He also said you could help my client," she says, getting to the point.

"Thijs?"

I click back onto his picture. He can't be more than eighteen. He's from the social media generation. How much help does he need?

"The problem with my client is that he has no personality."

I lean back in my seat, fighting the urge to breathe out my surprise into the receiver. That's a pretty crappy thing for your own manager to say.

"He doesn't have the *right* personality," Maria corrects herself. "Not for a pop star in a boy band."

"Is he an introvert?"

"Not really. He just doesn't care."

I frown, waiting for her to go on. I'm surprised he's managed to get so far if he doesn't care.

"He's not engaging with the public. He's not putting himself out there. He needs to establish his own group of fans like the others are doing. He'll miss out on lucrative advertising opportunities because he stubbornly kept himself to himself."

There must be a reason he's in the band, though.

"How's his singing?"

There's a pause and then, "His *singing*? What's that got to do with anything?"

I feel my eyes widen and I have to restrain myself from being rude. "Well, the band. What's his role in the band? Is he a key member?"

He's not good-looking like Jake, but that might mean he can sing. If he can't sing either then I might be able to understand why Maria is so anxious to secure some public support. It's because he's in danger of being replaced.

"He writes the songs," Maria says, sounding grumpy.

I'm impressed. I'd assumed a band like Five Oars were just given their songs on a plate.

"That's brilliant, then."

"It's not enough."

"Well I think when people find out he's the talented one, he'll get so much respect."

"He's like an old man," she says, ignoring me. "He's 18 and he's not even on Facebook. There's something wrong with him."

My instinct is to run to his defence and I press my fingers to my lips to stop the words spilling out. Do I really want to be dissuading her from using our services? I've got a salary to think about. Now I've entertained the thought I might be able to own my own place, I can't give it up that easily.

"Will you meet him?" she says. "You'll see what I'm talking

about then."

"Yes, of course."

"Next week?"

I don't feel like I've got a choice. "Perfect."

Maria hangs up and I'm drawn back to the image on the screen in front of me. Can this young lad really be so dull?

Before I know it, half an hour has gone by and all I know is that he was born in Holland to an English mother, a Dutch father and moved to England when he was seven. He joined Five Oars last year. Not having a Twitter or Facebook page really does wonders for retaining some anonymity.

When I see the time, I feel slightly ill. I turn back to Bernard's Twitter account and finally reply to @missinkytoes.

BTHOMSKINNER @BTHOMSKINNER
@missinkytoes that's a dangerous request. If you become a character in my book, the plot might command me to kill you off.

I feel a little rush of excitement after I've sent it. Irritation, too, that I can't be more detached.

The plot might command me to kill you off?

Is it me or does that suddenly sound like the ominous words of a serial killer?

I couldn't have added a smiley face at the end because Bernard doesn't do emoticons. He doesn't do *cute*. Even his cat is ugly, a bit like the grumpy cat that's still doing the rounds on Facebook.

It's just one tweet. Soon it will get buried by a million other tweets. I have to move on. I've got so much content to invent, share, allocate, schedule, comment on... my stomach constricts as I hear the ping of another email landing in my inbox.

I'll get sucked in if I take a look now, but I can't resist.

It's from Damian Dance. I push down the excitement that's bubbled up. He's used the subject line very efficiently:

Lunch?

A chat would be good, I think, grinning as I open the email. Better still if the lunch is rustled up in a Michelin-starred kitchen.

I scroll down. Nothing. The email is blank.

The phone starts ringing and I let out a groan. I wanted to salivate a little longer over the thought of a six-course tasting menu at Dinner by Heston Blumenthal. My taste buds would probably explode at the unusual combinations.

"May?" Abigail sounds apologetic.

"Yes?"

"It's Damian on the phone."

I bite back the smile, a fancy meal back on the cards.

"I'm really sorry, I didn't get his surname," she continues, sounding close to tears. "Do you want me to go back and ask him?"

"Don't worry, Abi, really, it's fine. Just put him through, thank you."

The dialling tone sounds in my ear and I pick up.

"Good morning, May Sparks."

"Hi, May, it's me... Damian Dance." I love the way he introduces himself, like I won't recognise his voice. "I just sent you a blank email."

"Yes, I've just read it, well, the subject line."

"So, how about this Friday night?"

I can feel my face being drawn into a smile and a frown at the same time. "Is Friday night when you usually have lunch?"

His laugh is loud and easy. "Yes. So are you in?"

Am I in? This doesn't feel like he's setting up a work meeting at all. I feel a duty to steer things in a more business-like direction.

"I think lunch in the day would suit me better."

Would it, though? If I meet him in the evening I won't miss a day's work.

"I just don't think I'm going to be able to do next week."

My attention is momentarily distracted by a flirty reply from @missinkytoes on Bernard's Twitter feed. I twist away from the screen, feeling ruffled. It's nothing. It's a flirting fan. Get a bloody grip.

"Let's go ahead and do the Friday evening," I say.

He sounds surprised. "Yeah?"

"Yes, I think better sooner than later."

I'm glad he's not in the office to witness me blushing.

"Exactly. That's what I thought."

"Good."

"I'll think of a place and send you an email with words in it next time."

"Great. I look forward to it."

After I hang up I turn back to my screen and faff about until I come across an article about authors and their writing sheds. I tweet the link from Bernard's account and wait with baited breath for the retweets.

Please retweet! Feeling impatient, I log in to my own account and retweet as @SparkyMay to my 8,000 followers. It's a bit lame after two days of silence, but any content is better than those mistaken-identity ones for DJ Buzzya.

I become aware of the tense muscles in my neck and knead them. Only when the tweet has reached 15 retweets do I start to relax a little. Posting something neutral was a good move. It'll show @missinkytoes that Bernard is not interested in flirting with cartoon superheroes. He has a wife to win back and, ridiculous as it sounds, that means I do too.

Chapter 9

Craig pokes his head around my office door the next morning.

"I just thought I'd check how things are going."

I stifle a yawn and tear myself away from Bernard's Facebook page, where I've instigated a lively discussion about the best war movies of all time. If I'd wanted a job pretending to be a 66-year-old TV presenter with a chip on his shoulder, then I'd say things were going very well. The trouble is, I didn't.

"I'm good," I reply.

Craig takes a seat. "It looks to me like you've been doing a great job, very engaging, people-pleasing stuff."

He's come in to boost my morale. Perhaps he heard my soul scratching at the door, trying to exit the building.

"You didn't mention the Five Oars band member," I say. "Thijs Van Wotsit."

I feel another yawn coming on and swallow. Anna Jamison's Facebook statuses aren't helping.

Anna Jamison: *Spent the night dealing with Bubba's pooathon. Slept one hour. So exhausted I put my phone in the fridge and fish fingers in my handbag. :(*

Maybe the NHS could package her updates in some way and use

them as a cheap contraceptive. She's definitely making *me* reconsider ever having children.

The main reason I'm so knackered, though, is that I was up till 2.30am watching YouTube clips of Bernard's show *Bring on the Bad News*. I thought if I saw every episode I might stop worrying about getting his tweets wrong. I watched with a pen and paper, jotted down anything I thought important. His thoughts on every subject, his slang and mannerisms, the jokes he laughed at, the guests he liked, the guests who were obviously chosen by the channel. Some people think I'm a winger who gets through life with a bit of common sense and bags of confidence. The reality is I've always been a swot. I've never turned up at an exam unprepared and this job is basically that, a test I can only pass if I've done the research.

"What do you think?" Craig says.

"About Thijs? ... He's so young."

Craig rubs his chin and looks towards the window. "Yeah, I know. Shocking he's not a fluent social media user, isn't it?"

"Maybe he just doesn't like it."

He frowns, like he doesn't understand the concept. That's where we're different. I have a love-hate relationship with social media. I respect people who aren't on Facebook, or those who are, but don't feel a need to update five times a day. I also respect and admire people who are on it all the time, but who are using it to their advantage. I'm talking about those entrepreneurial spirits who build audiences so large and influential they can fund projects on Kickstarter.

My boss feels that not being on social media makes you a loser. To him it's all about showing off your lifestyle, and the more money you make from documenting your life, the better.

"Damian was telling me he hates it," I say.

Craig snorts. "Damian doesn't like social media because he can't control himself."

"Well, he won't be able to log in once I've changed the

passwords."

"Online you've got control, but I'm not so sure about offline. You know what he's like."

"I think he's changed a lot from his *Big Brother* days, if that's what you mean."

My mind flits to our scheduled meeting. I think I'm on my way to knowing him a lot better than Craig.

"Let's hope so."

Craig breathes out and stretches his legs. I wonder if he's so relaxed this morning because he's passed me all the new clients. Who is he looking after now?

"When are you meeting Thijs?"

"Next week. That'll take it up to three new Platinum clients. It'll be full on."

"What about four?"

I look at him, feeling wary. "Four?"

"Angel Butler," he says. "She's out on her own. No agent. She needs us."

Angel Butler gained fame two years ago after flashing her boobs to the judges of *X-factor* when they said she couldn't sing. *Does it really matter when I've got these puppies?* she'd said. *We all know that's what the music industry really wants.*

The clip went viral. There was outrage. There was laughter. The press loved it, the women argued, the men either drooled or shuddered and the feminists cried themselves to sleep. One high-profile male journalist decided she was making a poignant critique about the state of the industry. Angel's own mother was supportive. She told reporters, *I always told her, if you got it, flaunt it.* Sadly she didn't stop there. *All my girls have always had good tits, even when they were little,* she continued, causing an outpouring of anger and ridicule about bad parenting and lack of strong female role models in the world. Angel's boobs were successful and got her onto a few chat shows. If only her boobs could have done the talking too because the stuff that came out of her mouth made even the most sympathetic person want to gag her.

"Really?" I say, feeling a wave of dread. "Don't you think we should hold out for someone a little bit more..." The word "worthy" is on the tip of my tongue.

"Angel Butler is our ideal client. The public thinks she's stupid, talentless, drunk and a bad mother."

I'd forgotten about her baby with the footballer. *It was just a drunken shag*, Angel had said. Poor child, she'll have to read about that one day.

"Our mission is to take control of the reigns these people keep dropping and turn the cart around..."

I think Craig fancies himself a bit of an orator. People are always telling him he looks like Peter O' Toole in *Lawrence of Arabia*, and it's gone to his head.

"But what does she do? How can she afford to pay us?"

"Oh, she's got money left," Craig says, confidently. "She just needs to get back out there."

"And do what?"

Bernard is an obnoxious but experienced broadcaster, Damian is a singer, vocoder or not. Thijs is a songwriter who just needs a little help with his public persona... but Angel? She's just relying on her boobs to carry her into stardom. It's not sitting well with me right now.

"You'll think of something," he says. "Create a new identity for her, opinions that won't offend everyone, and who knows? She could end up with a column in one of the tabloids."

"Can she write?"

Craig shrugs. "Maybe you'll have to do that too."

I feel my eyes grow wide. He laughs. "I'm joking! You wouldn't write it... unless she paid you a fortune. Anyway to make it more manageable, I'm going to get you a couple more phones. If you let Abigail know your ideal model I'll get them in for you by next week, alright?"

"I don't know, Craig, I don't think I want to take on Angel

Butler."

Neither do I want to carry around more than two phones. What will bouncers think of me when they shine a torch in my bag? Either that I'm a fraudster or that I've just nicked them.

"Well, it's not really an option, May," he says, wincing as he says it. "It's the job."

He gives my desk two knocks and gets up. Up until now he's spoken to me like a partner rather than a boss. Maybe that's why I feel a bit put out that there's not going to be any more discussion. The decision has been made. He leans on the door and looks back at me, his gaze intense.

"I know it's a lot of work, but if you pull this off you'll be getting that pay rise we talked about," he says. "You'll be buying your own place in no time."

He's finally mentioned the pay rise. The hope makes my heart beat quicker.

I give him a measured smile.

"I'm sure Angel has lots of good qualities."

What have I always said? There's never just one side to a story. Angel just hasn't had the education to deal with the spotlight. She's raw, open, honest. A-list celebrities have worked with life coaches, therapists, personal trainers. They've learned what to say and how to say it.

"And if she doesn't have any redeeming qualities, you can always give her some!" Craig says, cheerfully.

I shake my head and tut in mock disapproval at his cynicism. "She *will* have some, I know it."

But I don't go looking for these good qualities as soon as Craig's out the door. I'm not ready to type Angel Butler into Google search and be inundated with reports and opinions. Everyone on social media has an opinion. You have to wade through them all, avoiding the sewage that comes pouring in from all the haters. Some of it is so violent and so angry it makes me curl up inside myself and ponder the impossibility of world peace.

Another yawn and this time I don't bother to cover my mouth. *An incessant, noisy and vacuous stream of self-indulgent crap,* is how my mum once described social media. We were arguing about what I was doing with my life. I told her that, actually, social media had been an incredible force of good in the world. It had united the oppressed, raised awareness of numerous cases of cruelty to man and mammal and been key to the success of very worthy petitions across the globe. *But that's not what you're using it for, is it?* my mum had retorted.

I could argue that I'm helping the victims of a hypercritical society. My clients have faced harsh judgement and derision. I'm offering them a chance to put on a new skin and go out into the Coliseum once again to face the bloodthirsty public. This time to win.

Who am I kidding? I cried watching *Gladiator*, but that's because he was being forced into the Coliseum against his will. He was a slave! All the victims were slaves. They didn't choose to fight. These celebs *want* to perform in front of the public.

The phone is ringing and I snap out of my reverie.

"Bernard Thompson-Skinner on the line," Abigail says. She sounds proud of herself. It must be because she's got his name right. It's all about the little things when you're doing a job you don't really like.

"Thank you. Put him through."

Considering it has only been a couple of weeks since Bernard signed up I feel like I've done a good job on his profile already. I'm expecting some respect, not the abuse that pours out of his mouth as soon I answer.

"What the fuck do you think you're doing sharing that pretentious shite of a fucking excuse for an article?"

My heart starts pounding. I race to open Bernard's Twitter account and run down his feed to find the article.

"Don't you know that fucking Oliver Ricketts annihilated my book? Don't you do any research? For God's sake, get it off now!"

He catches his breath and I click open the link. It's not even an article, it's a photo gallery of authors' sheds. There's a brief introduction by Oliver Ricketts. I was going to hurriedly delete the tweet, but seeing what it is stops me in my tracks. Bernard is completely overreacting. My job isn't to do whatever he wants, because what he wants is usually the wrong thing. I'm being paid to run his social media accounts because I'm the expert and I'm not going to be bullied.

"Have you finished?"

I wouldn't have had the guts to say that if he'd been standing in front of me. I listen to him moving around his flat, heavy footsteps, doors banging. He's muttering under his breath, words I don't need to hear.

"Have you removed it?"

"Have you read the article?" I counter.

"And give him the satisfaction of another fucking hit?" he snarls. "I knew you'd be fucking useless! Have you even read my book?"

The awful feeling that I'd made a mistake has been replaced with a wave of anger. I may be useless, but at least I can keep my temper!

"Yes, I have in fact."

"Well, that's not the point. The point is that I'm paying you and I'm telling you to get that article off now."

"I think you'll find it's a very inoffensive photo gallery of places where famous writers have worked." It is my prerogative to keep calm. By keeping calm I'll show up how rude and irrational he is being. I check the stats. "Fifty-seven of your followers retweeted it, which is more than I can say for any of your tweets over the previous month."

I don't know if this is true, but I don't care. I'm guessing he doesn't know any better.

"Yes, well, but still, Oliver Ricketts rubbished my book!"

The anger in his voice has subsided. Now he sounds like he's whining.

"That's why it's good to share something neutral of his, and show there are no hard feelings."

"But there are hard feelings!"

I roll my eyes up at the ceiling and wait a moment for him to calm down.

"It shows you're a bigger man."

No answer. I hear the squeak of a chair. Clicking. He's on his computer. He's checking the link now. I can almost smell his doubt. He knows he's overreacted.

"While you're online..." I say, seeing an opportunity to clarify an issue. "I wondered if you had any idea who Miss Inky Toes is, following you on Twitter?"

"No."

"Are you sure?"

"Why?"

"She just seemed a bit flirty, wanted you to write her into your novel."

"Fucking women," he mutters.

I hold my breath and count to five, by which point he's mumbled a half-hearted apology. I don't say it's alright, I just wait for a resolution.

"Alright, you can leave Oliver Ricketts this time," he says.

"Good. I think it would be good if you shared from different sources. It gives the impression you're balanced."

When clearly you're not, I think.

"Yes. You're right. I'm sorry for shouting. I just saw red when I saw his name."

"Alright," I say, with a note of finality. I need to wrap this up. I have work to do.

"While I've got you, when are you going to start on the... you know..."

I wait, because I don't know.

"About my wife."

Right now I want to send her a warning message: *Save yourself!*

Don't even think about getting back with this horrible man!

"When I get your questionnaire back."

"I'll get to it. I'll also get the pictures of Baxter you wanted. I think you'll like them a lot. He's a funny cat."

Now he's trying to be friendly, to make up for swearing at me. His temper is his weakness. He knows it. We know it. I've got to forgive him and move on.

"Great," I say. "I look forward to seeing them."

After I hang up, I lean back in my chair, my head aching. I take a couple of aspirins and swallow them down with the cold dregs of my coffee. I used to moan how taking pills for every symptom was not sorting out the problem. We should be asking, why have I got this infection rather than popping antibiotics at the first chance. I should listen to my body, but listening requires being quiet, and I feel like I'm drowning in noise.

Back on my computer I review the likes and shares and comments. My week's input has increased numbers and followers across my client base. A voice in my head smirks, *So fucking what?*

I stand up abruptly and stretch my arms above my head. I hate negativity. I hate its ugly claws. Am I going to be one of those people who complain all day but does nothing about it? Or am I going to accept the job at hand and get on with it?

I shake my hands, take some deep breaths.

This is why I need to start yoga. I need access to my well of inner peace. Right now, I don't even have a bucket.

My phone buzzes and I let out an involuntary sigh. It's a text message from Louisa informing me that supper has been set for Friday. That's the evening I'm meeting Damian. We're going to Babylon at the Roof Gardens in Kensington, Richard Branson's very own restaurant. Apparently there are flamingos living on the rooftop. There are also water features. In fact I've already had a little fantasy about us getting it on by the flamingo pond. I don't know what's wrong with me lately. Maybe it's some survival instinct kicking in after two years of celibacy. I need to sleep with someone or my race will be wiped out, that sort of thing. Except it's just a business meeting so I won't be sleeping with Damian, or anyone else in the restaurant for that matter.

The only question is, if it's just a normal business meeting, why have I avoided telling Craig about it?

Chapter 10

I've got less than an hour until my meeting with Damian and I'm in the toilets reapplying my makeup. Louisa is still annoyed with me about dinner, but she should have asked me if I had plans rather than assuming I hadn't. Alex voted for postponing it, which makes me wonder what our neighbour really thinks about Louisa's sudden interest in him. Is the feeling mutual? Or is he regretting opening his mouth and telling her what he does for a living? She can be so intense sometimes.

Gabe's door is open and I pop my head in on the way back to my office. I haven't seen my colleague in ages and wonder if the goalkeeper signed the contract in the end. Gabe glances up.

"Oh hi, May."

"Hi, I thought I'd see how you are."

Judging by his sallow skin, he needs to be laid out in the sun for a while. His eyes are bloodshot and he's got bags under them. He needs a Louisa in his life to remind him to eat and sleep. At the moment his only flatmate is a Mexican redleg tarantula called José. I notice the bottle of beer open at the side of his computer. I'm about to ask him if he's in for a late night, but he starts talking first.

"I've got some great content for you," he says. His fingers dance over the keys. "I'll send you over the album. I've got food, fashion, lifestyle stuff, great views and a guarantee that no one is going to pop up and say, hey I took these photos."

He's great at this job, but I know in his heart he'd rather be designing computer games than working as an online ventriloquist.

"Anything you want Photoshopped in, just ask me."

I think of my yoga mat. "I might need help with some feet."

"Sure. Just let me know."

"Just need to do a toe count first."

He laughs. "Any time... You're looking hot, by the way. Where are you going?"

He's such a confidence booster.

"Just a meeting."

"Who with?"

I shouldn't have said anything. Now I can feel the blush coming on.

"A client. Yep, on a Friday night, what a pain!"

"Anyone I know?"

I try to look nonchalant. "Damian Dance?"

Gabe frowns. "Really? You're meeting Damian Dance on a Friday night? Is that safe?"

"It won't be a late one."

"From what I've heard, he'll be in and out of the toilet all night."

"Because of his groin injury?"

"Ah, lovely innocent May. Good luck."

I realise, too late, that he's implying Damian is a cokehead. I've already read that opinion online. I've also read that he's living in Monaco with a wife and two kids. You can't believe everything you read.

"It's just a meeting."

"Remember, he's a client," he calls after me. "Don't let him get you drunk and try to sleep with you."

"Shut up!"

"You're very attractive, May. He's bound to try it on."

I just laugh it off and head to my office to collect my handbag. In the lift, I think I probably needed to hear it. Yesterday I kept

94

catching myself thinking about what I was going to wear. I've opted for a figure-hugging sea-green dress that always gets compliments. The colour goes well with my red hair, which, after much effort, is falling in big curls over my shoulders. The dress is smart, sophisticated and down to the knee, which cancels out the rather low, round neck. That's how I work it out, anyway. A short skirt is fine if you're not showing your cleavage as well. One or the other.

Seriously, what am I doing? Why am I wearing my favourite bra? The one that boosts my B cups to the next level. I can't lie to myself. I want Damian to find me attractive. I am still enjoying the little idea of being kissed by the flamingo pond, even though I'm not going to let it happen in a million years. Imagine if we were snapped and it was plastered on the front page of the tabloids. *Big Brother Star Snogs the Woman Faking His Tweets! #AWKS*. Craig would fall over and die.

We're not meeting at the restaurant but at a little pop-up gallery nearby. Damian isn't someone you meet outside the Tube. I'm ten minutes late by the time I've found it. The mild evening has lured everyone outside, including tourists, who love to stand in the middle of the pavement to take in the view. Between the gaps of limbs and heads I catch a glimpse of him in a green-and-white trucker hat; wooden rosary beads dangle around his neck. His outfit is not the only thing that stops me in my tracks. He's also in conversation with a woman. I told him that I couldn't reveal my identity to his friends.

"Hi, May!" Damian greets me, cancelling my option to invent a new name. He kisses me on the cheek and I'm acutely aware of the touch of his lips on my skin.

He looks like he's been styled for *Backpackers Gazette* in his v-neck coral t-shirt, torn jeans and lime-green Havaianas. A model of a backpacker, that is, as he's too scrubbed to convince anyone he's actually one. I'd feel completely overdressed if it wasn't for the statuesque woman he's talking to who's wearing a striking orange-and- black maxi dress accessorised with chunky bronze jewellery.

"This is Ola," Damian says.

"I love your dress."

She smiles, her full lips parting to reveal a diamante sparkle on one of her teeth.

"Thank you. It's my own design."

"Ola's started this new fashion brand. She gets all her materials from artisans around the world," Damian says. He looks proud of himself, possibly for his attentive listening. "She's working with people who could turn a broken car into a mini skirt."

Ola laughs and flaps a hand at him, "not cars, I said *cans*," she leans into me, "I work with people who make beautiful jewellery out of scrap. This bracelet..." she holds up her hand and the sun dances across it, "is made from old tins and my earrings are recycled paper."

"They're beautiful," I say, meaning it. I want to reach out and touch the scrolls of tightly rolled paper hanging from her ears in a glossy fan.

I'm getting the impression that they've just met, which is a relief. She probably doesn't know who Damian is and, if she did, I doubt she'd be impressed.

"We also work with independent weavers and dressmakers," Ola continues. "What matters to me is that everyone is treated with respect and paid a decent wage. I think if people saw how most of their clothes were made, they would be ashamed to wear them. But no one wants to know. They don't want that responsibility."

I nod, feeling like a hypocrite. What did I do when that Bangladeshi clothing factory collapsed and all those people were killed? What stand did I take? I just stopped shopping for a week or two because I felt guilty. Like that's going to help anyone. The high-street retailers signed some agreement a few months after the tragedy. What did they agree on? To pay workers two pence more an hour? Or that they should have fire extinguishers on every floor?

Someone is calling to Ola from inside the gallery.

"I better go, it's my friend's exhibition," she says, and holds out her hand. "My brand is HappyHeart. I hope you like it. Tell your friends! I need all the support I can get. It's so difficult trying to do something good and make a living at the same time."

"I can imagine!" I say cheerfully.

Imagine is all I can do since my job doesn't require any such battles for justice. The thought catches me off-guard that, compared to hers, my job is meaningless.

Damian turns to me, his eyebrows raised as he looks me up and down, "Well, *I* feel under-dressed. You look amazing."

"I've come straight from work," I say, trying to brush the compliment away as fast as possible. "So... shall we go?"

I don't want to engage with people and have to give an explanation of who I am and what my connection is. At least with Twitter you can Google before you reply to someone. Face to face is a much trickier operation.

"Do you like the hat?"

He takes it off and brushes a hand through his hair, sweeps his fringe to one side and turns to me. His hopeful eyes search my face, eager for my opinion.

"Or should I ditch it?"

"It's very relaxed... you look good without it too."

He should totally ditch it.

There are girls who would be so envious of me right now. I'm about to go for dinner in a swanky restaurant with Damian Dance on a Friday night and he wants *my* advice on his outfit.

SPARKMAY @SPARKYMAY
I have a strong urge to take a selfie. Who have I become?

"You don't like it, do you?" He folds it up and stuffs the hat into his back pocket. "You prefer the smarter look. I bet you like a man in a suit?"

"It depends on the occasion."

His frown deepens. "Fuck. Should I go buy a suit to change into?"

"What? *Now?*"

"They're going to think I look like an idiot, aren't they?"

"Who? The waiters? No! They aren't going to care what you're wearing as long as you tip them."

"Not the waiters," he says, looking restless. "Everyone else."

He's actually serious.

There's no way I'm going to traipse around High Street Kensington looking for a suit. Especially not in six-inch heels. And not when I have a reservation to eat food that, according to their website, is going to *thrill* my taste buds.

"You're a DJ, a TV star, you're not supposed to wear what other people wear!" I say. "You're supposed to show your personality."

Could I ask him to lose the rosary?

"Yeah, well, I feel like a bit of an idiot now. It's just the sun was shining and I thought I'm going to pretend I live in LA and wear flip flops."

I decide to redirect the conversation. "Would you like to live in LA?"

"Yeah. If a good opportunity was offered to me. I'm up for anything."

Up for anything. Some people would say it smacked of desperation. But isn't it adventurous? Doesn't it make him more in sync with life than the rest of us? He's heading through one open door after another...

If I ask him to lose the rosary he'll get really offended, won't he? Then he'll want to go searching for a suit again. I better not risk it.

"Don't look so worried," he says. "I'm not likely to move anywhere any time soon."

I squirm. "I'm not worried. I was just thinking."

"You'd have to come with me if I move," he says.

I laugh. "I don't know about that."

He slows down as we reach the restaurant's entrance and places his hand on my back.

"In here," he says.

I don't know why his touch feels so intimate. It's just my back, and it's just his hand. Perhaps because it lingers so long, and it's my lower back. Very low, in fact. Any lower and...

"Good evening," the receptionist greets us with a big smile.

It's like stepping into a hotel lobby. Chrome and white, crisp and clean. She shows us where the lift is and a moment later we enter a tasteful dining area. I straighten my back, wanting to fit in with all the other elegant guests that have come here tonight.

The maître d' is speaking to someone, giving me a moment to get a good look around me. It's light and airy. Playful dashes of lime green in the curtains and chairs complement the black-and-white flock wallpaper. Beyond the glass patio doors, there's a decked terrace. That's where most of the diners have chosen to eat tonight. The sun is setting over a stunning view of London and waiters are lighting candles on the tables.

"May I take you to your table?" the maître d' says.

It's been a long week and I'm looking forward to a drink. I'm thinking a fresh gin and tonic in a crystal glass with a slither of cucumber.

"Can you get us two tequila shots?" Damian says, before the waiter has even handed us the menus.

I let out a surprised burst of laughter.

"Just to get us going," Damian says with a shrug.

The waiter nods, "Of course. What tequila would you like?"

I feel my cheeks reddening. "I think I'd prefer a gin and tonic."

"No, have a tequila with me. Then you can have a gin and tonic."

I exchange a baffled look with the waiter. "Okay. I'll have a Patron."

The waiter nods. "And you sir?"

"Yeah, same."

I have a feeling the waiter could have brought him a shot of nail-varnish remover and he wouldn't have been able to tell the difference.

"Sorry, I'm a bit bossy, aren't I?" he says.

I smile. "I'll translate it as 'assertive'."

That's my job description. I repackage and resell.

He looks at me with his muddy green eyes and I find myself softening. I'm being a snob. He's being who he is, doing what he wants to do. I'm play-acting, sitting here stiffly in my high-street dress hoping it looks like something else. I spend my whole day playing at make-believe, at least when the client is in front of me I should try to be myself. I should also focus on the job, while being myself. I hadn't really considered the implications of dinner, specifically the eating part. How exactly am I supposed to conduct a successful data-collecting mission and eat attractively at the same time?

The waiter sets down our tequilas in elegant frosted shot glasses.

"This is just to get you talking," I say, raising my glass.

"Didn't you see me on *Big Brother*? I didn't shut up."

My mind flips back to him with his greasy curtains and white vest, prancing up and down in the *Big Brother* living room, ranting about the injustice of not being allowed to phone his Nan on her birthday.

"I can't tell if you like remembering your time on it or not."

Damian shrugs. "It changed my life. It's not like I can forget." He raises his glass, a mischievous twinkle in his eye. "What are we toasting? To finding out the real May?"

I narrow my eyes in mock warning. "No. That's not the mission at all. As far as you're concerned I don't exist."

If that were true I wouldn't have wriggled into this dress or faffed about so long with my hair. Even that silly rosary hasn't stopped me wanting him to find me attractive. I sip my tequila. He downs his.

"Oh, come on," he says, licking a droplet off his lip. "I should know a little bit about the person who's pretending to be me."

I glance around, nervous that he's speaking too loudly. It seems to be a trait.

"Oh, sorry, do you think there's someone from MI5 here?"

"Probably," I say. "They're more likely to be eating here than at a Wimpy."

He laughs. "I grew up on Wimpy."

"It's not funny," I say, "you do have to be quiet about this. It's your reputation at stake."

"I know, I'm just teasing."

His smile is apologetic, his eyes search mine and seek out forgiveness. It's not hard to get. It's been a while since I felt an irrational crush like this. The coral is good on him, it picks up his golden tan. I should get a picture.

The waiter comes over to tell us the specials. Damian asks him to explain every word he doesn't understand. There are quite a lot of words he doesn't understand. I don't know what a carrot *raita* is either, or an *espelette* pepper, but I would have guessed rather than admitted it. By the time he's finished his lesson in deciphering posh menus, we are ready to order. The buccleuch beef for me, the braised pork cheek for him. Red wine for me. Vodka and Redbull for him.

"We could start by going through some of the questionnaire questions..." I say. If this bill ends up on Craig's plate, I'm going to need something to show for it. With a bit of luck, Damian won't think twice about paying. If he's hired me to tweet for him, he can't be short of money. "What football team do you support?"

"Man City."

"Okay."

I rest my tablet by the side of my plate. It feels wrong to have it out, but I need to take notes before the wine sets in. I write down Manchester City and make a note to ask Gabe for football updates.

"Have you always been?"

"Yeah, my dad was and I wanted him to like me."

I feel like there's a story in that statement, but I'm not sure what to ask. "Are you close to your dad?"

"We're better now. He was a right cock before, but he's calmed down a bit since he's become a granddad."

"Amy's kids?"

"Someone's done their homework."

"Do you see them often?"

"I would if my sister wasn't such a bitch."

He catches me wincing before I can stop myself. For a moment he sounded like he did when he was in *Big Brother*. A bit ugly. I'm not exactly close to my sister, but I'd never call her that. Neither would I call my dad a cock.

"She cashed in on me back when I was all over the papers," he explains. "She talked to the tabloids, told them anything they wanted to know. Family shouldn't do that. They should be the ones you trust."

"God, that's horrible..." Actually I probably would call Katie a bitch too if she ever did that to me. I'm still not sure I'd call my dad a cock, though. "Sounds like it's been a rough ride."

He frowns and scratches the back of his neck. "I don't want to complain about my life. I'm lucky, I know I am."

"You must have some close friends you can trust, right?"

I'll need to find out if they're on Twitter, set up a list of them so I don't start replying to them as if they were strangers.

"I feel like I know lots of people, but I'm not close to them. Not *close* close. I want to be but... I don't know. I just want to work, so it's probably my own fault. You must know what I mean, you're out with me on a Friday night instead of your friends!"

His observation doesn't sit comfortably with me. I want to point out that I wouldn't have agreed to a meeting on a Friday night with any of my other clients. But maybe that's not true. I might have agreed to meet Bernard if I'd thought it would make my job easier.

"It's understandable," I say, blinking away my thoughts. "So much of your life is spent at work so you've got to strive to get a job that you love. As long as you're happy."

He nods in agreement. "Exactly."

"But I guess you've got to enjoy the journey too..." It's something

Louisa keeps going on about. I'm living for the future, she says, and the future never comes.

"So do you love your job, then?" he says, brightly.

"Me?" I don't like lying even if I'm good at it. "Yeah, yeah I do." It's not like I could give him a different answer.

"Alright, your go. Ask me a question," he says.

I say the first thing that comes into my head. "What's your exercise regime?"

He fake yawns.

"Sorry. I just need to know some basics," I say, feeling a blush start up again.

I want him to know that if we were on a date I wouldn't be asking such wooden questions.

"Let me think... weights, yoga... a lot of sex."

He laughs at my attempt to hide my surprise.

"I'm kidding... I haven't had sex in ages," he says.

#KeepCalm. Go away naked image of client holding weights!

"You're not seeing anyone at the moment, then?"

"Nope. No distractions."

I think about Diamond Daneesha. "Nothing casual?"

"I know I'm supposed to be this big player, but I'm really not."

"I'm not going to tweet about your relationships. If someone accuses you of something, I'll consult with you."

"Accuses me?" he says, frowning. "You're thinking about that hooker, aren't you? That was such a load of bollocks."

I lower my voice, hoping he'll do the same. "Was it?"

"Yes."

Do I believe him?

"I mean, I did sleep with her, but she didn't tell me she was a hooker until afterwards."

I hope he used a condom.

"She wasn't even a hooker. She just wanted to screw me for my money."

"I'd say that's a pretty accurate job description of a hooker, or

103

did you think she was doing it for the cuddles?"

We're both laughing now. Borderline flirting?

He narrows his eyes at me, "I mean, she wasn't a hooker until we'd slept together, smartarse, and then she demanded a grand off me."

"Was it worth it?"

"I didn't pay. It was false advertising."

"You've got to be careful."

"I didn't go looking for it, you know, I'm not the person people think I am," Damian says. His voice is low and filled with emotion. He's looking at me like he really wants me to know he's serious. "I just have trouble showing the real me."

"That's why I'm here... To help."

His grateful smile tugs at my insides. Where is the arrogant, cokehead player now?

The arrival of our drinks breaks the moment. Damian sits up, his eyes clearing.

"Well, I think that's enough painful stuff out of the way," he says. "What's next?"

Me and you.... down by the flamingo pond. Is it going to happen?

"Um... musical influences?"

He visibly brightens. "Great, this is good."

I force myself to concentrate as he starts ticking off the people who inspired him. It's easier when I'm not looking at him. He has sexy lips, the bottom one a little heavier, a cupid's bow on top. He smiles easily.

"I've been thinking," he says, breaking off mid-sentence. "I'd like to keep my passwords for now, if that's okay."

The request makes me snap out of the dreamy little moment I was having.

"Really? Why? "

It's not like I can deny him access to his own accounts, but I feel worried now.

"Is everything alright?" he says.

"Fine."

My tablet has just died and I'm going to have to ask the waiter for a pen and paper.

"Are you sure?"

I was already feeling overwhelmed by the task of being Damian Dance. The only thing keeping me from panicking was thinking his aversion to social media would keep him from monitoring my online activity.

"Yeah, I'm absolutely fine," I lie. "Just thinking how awesome your online profile is going to be."

He smiles. "I've got a good feeling about it too. I wasn't sure about it at first, but now I've met you I know you're going to do a brilliant job."

I smile and swallow the remains of my tequila. Suddenly one shot doesn't seem nearly enough.

Chapter 11

I open my eyes and the dream I was having frays and fades until all I can see is the shadows on my ceiling. I listen out. Except for the hum of electrics, the flat is quiet. Louisa will still be asleep. She was pretty drunk last night when I came in. As dinner had been cancelled she'd spent the evening with her old drama-school friend, Henrietta, drinking wine and watching old films on Netflix.

I close my eyes and go back to my dream, where instead of taking the Tube home, I've gone back to Damian's. My body still tingles with desire and I slip a hand inside my pyjama shorts. I conjure a penthouse with a city horizon twinkling in the distance. Patio doors slide open onto a terrace of wooden decking, where there's an infinity pool glowing with underwater lighting. The warm water laps at our thighs. Damian is behind me. He slips off my silk shirt and I can feel his skin against mine.

"LEGS! Are you awake?"

I open my eyes, my hand sliding back up to rest on my stomach. "NO!"

I hear her faint giggle.

What if I had a real man in my bed? Would she respect our privacy? Or would she walk straight in, plonk herself down at the end of the bed and ask, *How was it, guys?*

I haven't had a chance to find out. I haven't had anyone in

my bed for two years. The thought makes me want to throw the covers over my head and sleep for the rest of the day. It's not even that I'm ridiculously fussy. It's just I never seem to meet anyone new. It's always friends of friends who I've shared a moan with about not finding anyone. And all the other men I meet are either paired up or gay, or they're wearing their singledom a little too desperately and we have no chemistry.

Damian Dance is not my idea of *the one*, but there is this fizz of chemistry between us. The way he looks at me makes me aware of my body, my sensuality. I bet if we slept with each other just once I would get all this pent-up lust out of my system.

That's not going to happen, though. Ever. He was flirty last night and may have opened up to me, but he didn't suggest going for another drink after our meal. He had a party to go to and I couldn't have gone along even if he had invited me.

All those questions, all that note-taking. I was so boring. If I hadn't been doing a job, it might have gone down differently. I suppose I should be relieved nothing did happen. But I'm tired of going home alone. I want to wake up with someone's arms wrapped around me.

"We're going on a picnic today!" Louisa calls out.

My eyes move to the window. A path of sunshine is streaming through the curtains. I love the sun. Who doesn't love it after six months of grey skies? Yet today I wish it was raining.

I hear Louisa in the kitchen, her big fluffy rabbit slippers rustling against the floor because she doesn't pick up her feet. Why doesn't she ever get hangovers? It's unfair. Pots bang, the tap runs at full blast and the boiling kettle sounds like a rocket about to take off. I soften when she knocks tentatively on my door and comes in bringing a cup of tea.

"Bonjour mademoiselle," she says, handing it over to me. "I think I've even got the right amount of milk this time."

I don't tell her that the tea is now too strong. She looks too happy.

"So we're going on a picnic today, me, you, Alex, Jacob and maybe some others, depending if they text back..."

"Does Alex know he's going on a picnic?"

"Of course he knows! It was his idea."

So he's not trying to avoid her. That's a surprise, and good, obviously. But then Louisa has never had a problem attracting men – it's just keeping them.

"We're going to go early," she says, cheerfully. "Noon has a good ring to it."

"So does three o'clock."

She glares at me. "Remember, this is my career we're talking about! I need these people."

I glance up at the ceiling. "He can probably hear you."

Louisa looks momentarily alarmed and then changes her mind, "No, he can't. We never hear *him* do we?"

"Because he spends his evenings lying on the floor with a glass against the floorboards listening to us."

"I doubt it. If he was that nosy, he would have found out I was an actor ages ago and we'd be making films together by now... Right, I'm going for a shower."

Alone again I rest my tea on the bedside table and try to get back to where I was. I close my eyes and call back the images of Damian kissing me. Nothing. My body doesn't respond. The mood has passed. I throw off my covers and lean over the bed to unplug my tablet. There has been some activity on Bernard's Twitter account.

MISSINKYTOES @MISSINKYTOES

@bthomskinner Looking forward to a memorable night in Winchester ;)

It's only a book reading, but she manages to make everything sound naughty. If I was Bernard's wife I'd be suspicious. Once you've been cheated on, how can you not be suspicious of every winky face?

MISSINKYTOES @MISSINKYTOES
@bthomskinner You're a very enjoyable author ;)

Enjoyable author? Half the book is about how miserable he was growing up in Norwich. I scanned most of it because I found it so repetitive. Bad weather and an uncle that looked at him "funny" wasn't enough to pull at my heartstrings.

Her winky faces are getting on my nerves. I'm tempted to ask her if she's got something in her eye. Should I ignore her? What would Bernard do? I think he'd flirt outrageously and then wonder what the fuss was about when some journalist pulled him up on it. That's the problem. That's why Bernard has handed me over his passwords. If he wants his wife back then he's got to be considerate and responsible.

I pull up my notes on Bernard's wife's favourite things. She loves the war poets: TS Eliot and Siegfried Sassoon. How am I going to weave them coherently into Twitter on a sunny day like today?

"Only those who will risk going too far can possibly find out how far one can go."

Oh God. No, no, no. It sounds like he's justifying the errors of his ways, that he was seeing how far he could push his wife before she left him. I hear the boiler switch off. Louisa will be out of the shower in a minute. She'll get annoyed if she sees me on my tablet. I'm on edge now. I must tweet *something*

A quote grabs me and I copy and paste.

"Success is relative. It is what we make of the mess we have made of things" – *TS Eliot.*

I hear Louisa singing in the bathroom. She's got a tan to moisturise, so that might take a while. Good. I'll need time to respond to any replies the tweet inspires.

....

Nothing? Is it going to be ignored by every one of his 10,934 followers? Is an ignored tweet really any better than a tweet provoking a negative reaction?

I think of another bloody quote: *there's no such thing as bad publicity.*

But of course there is, otherwise I wouldn't be doing this job.

One notification!

I click on it, feeling tentative.

It has been favourited by a Twitter user called @merlottijoie. So not a complete and utter failure, unless you're paying £995 a month for my service, which Bernard is. My shoulders sag when I see @merlottijoie has only one follower and her profile picture is of the default Twitter egg. If your profile picture is of an egg, then you're either:

a) a bot
b) shit at Twitter

Getting a favourite from someone like @merlottijoie is a very low-grade D/grade E in the Twitter grading system, which goes:

A* Retweet plus reply
A Retweet
B Modified Retweet
C Reply
D Favourite
E Favourite by bot
F Ignore

"Shower's free!" Louisa calls.

I tear myself away from Bernard's Twitter notifications and grab my dressing gown.

The key to success is simply increasing content. The more content I post online, the more opportunity for engagement. The more engagement, the more follows, the more follows the bigger the fan base, the greater chances of engagement... and on and on. It's exhausting. But it's also fascinating how quickly an audience can build through persistence. People think there's some big mystery behind it, but there isn't. Not really. I suppose I do get a kick out of playing the game well, even though it makes me feel a bit nauseous at the same time.

I'm certainly not proud of the content I post for my clients. It was never my intention to join the *I share, therefore I am* brigade. But now I've become one of those people, stopping to take a photo every time I eat or drink or notice the view or see something that could look #urban with the right filter. Does it make it any better that it's not for me but for someone else? Or is it worse because instead of cherishing the moment and wanting to share it with my friends, every moment has become a marketing opportunity?

These banal updates are what the fans want, though. If they didn't care, they wouldn't share it. Doesn't that make me a good business-woman?

The problem is, I don't want to just make money, I want to feel like I'm doing something worthwhile. Just because people love trashy TV doesn't mean they won't watch something of quality if it was on offer. Shouldn't I strive to educate these fans, rather than choose this easy route of satisfying them with fluff?

I guess my parents have instilled some values in me that I can't ignore.

Or maybe I shouldn't over-think things. When I start questioning my choice to go along with the controversial Platinum Package I feel depressed. Better to focus on the positive stuff. It's not a job that's going to enrich my soul, but it does give me financial security, and that does help with my inner peace, whatever the yoga leaflets say.

I rub tangerine scrub into my temples, wanting the lush smell to dissolve the remainder of a headache. At least the pictures of the picnic today are going to be useful for my clients. Is Damian a picnic kind of guy? I think he's more of a barbecue man. I'll have to order ribs next time I'm out just to be able to take a snap, even though I'm not a massive fan of ribs, so maybe I need to invite someone out with me who does so I can take a picture of their food...

There I go again! Shsssh brain, shsss...

Back in my bedroom, I go straight to my tablet. I haven't dried myself properly and drops of water fall onto the screen making rainbow bubbles.

I can't believe it. Not one of Bernard's followers considered the tweet worthy of a response. Now I feel like I have to tweet something else much better or that'll be the first thing anyone sees.

I refresh his Twitter page hoping to find new interactions. Instead I notice he has one less follower than before. #Fail.

"What are you wearing?" Louisa calls.

"Clothes!"

Humour is the most retweeted thing on Twitter #Funfact. What I need is a one-liner...

I used to be indecisive. Now I'm not sure.

Thank God for bloggers and their compulsion to compile random lists.

Nostalgia isn't what it used to be.

He'd probably like that one. But now I've got a dilemma. I've just tweeted a serious quote by a war poet. How can I follow it up with a joke? Maybe I need a tweet in between... or I could add, *On a lighter note...*

Louisa knocks on the door and pushes it open in the same action. She's holding up a bright-yellow halter-neck dress against herself.

"What do you think?" Before I can answer, her gaze falls to the tablet in my hands and I see her eyes fill with dismay. "No, May! It's Saturday! You're not allowed on that!"

She lunges for it and I move to intervene and accidentally catch my elbow against her cheek. She yelps in pain, and the hanger of her dress clatters to the floor as she lets go of it to cover her face with her hands. My elbow is tingling so I can only imagine that it must have really hurt.

"God, I'm sorry," I say, reaching for her shoulder. "Are you okay? I thought you were going to break it."

She lowers her hand. There's a small patch of pink beneath her eye. It doesn't look like much, but it's not like I can tell her to get over it.

"Does it hurt? Do you want some ice?"

Louisa picks up my tablet from the bed where I've just placed it. I have to restrain myself from grabbing it from her. It puts me on edge knowing how easily she could send something off under the guise of one of my clients.

"Can you please switch this off just for one day?" she says. "I think it would be really good for you."

It occurs to me, with sudden clarity, that I need to find her a boyfriend. With a boyfriend in her life, her focus would move away from me and she wouldn't care that I was working on a Saturday morning because she'd be too busy poaching eggs for her man.

"Well, I wasn't going to take it out on the picnic!"

Why would I when I've got a phone that does the same thing and is much smaller?

"Good. I wish it wasn't such a sacrifice to you."

"It's not a sacrifice," I say. "I'm really looking forward to this picnic."

She looks sceptical, "Really?"

I nod and she smiles with relief.

I don't tell her that what I'm really looking forward to is her getting together with Alex Hunter so she'll be off my case.

Chapter 12

At the last minute, Louisa has a change of heart about her outfit and runs to her bedroom, leaving me to answer the knock at the door. Alex smiles back at me, his lips turning up at one side. His hair is tussled and slightly wet.

"Hi, are you guys ready?"

"Yeah, I think so."

I still can't believe he's the bearded man. Behind his black frames, laughter lines fan out from the corners of striking sapphire eyes. Deep and sparkling, rimmed with grey. They make me think of huskies. The kind of eyes that start to make you feel self-conscious if you look too long.

He's older than us. I'm guessing mid-thirties. He's got an air of intelligence about him. Perhaps it's just the air of a morning person; alert, bright-eyed. I don't think for a minute that Louisa has gone to all this effort to meet up like this just because of her acting career. Alex isn't her usual type, but he *is* handsome. Louisa tends to go for men dressed like scrapbooks, the messier and more random the better. Alex's nautical outfit of striped t-shirt, navy chinos and espadrilles is probably a little too smart for her. I think it's cute, though. The thought passes through my head that if I had kept up my subscription to *Private Eye*, he might have delivered that instead of *The Stage*, and I would have called dibs on our handsome neighbour.

There's a drum of footsteps on the stairs above us and another man appears behind Alex. He's short and stocky, his tight khaki-green t-shirt highlighting an ongoing battle between a paunch and a six-pack. He's got a round face, small features and a head of frizzy afro hair.

"Jacob, May... May, Jacob..." Alex introduces us.

Jacob offers me a hand and I can feel callouses on his palms. His small brown eyes explore my face and his smile is a little hesitant. I've got this horrible feeling that I've been tricked into a double date. While I was wondering how I might get Louisa a boyfriend, my flatmate has been plotting a twist in my own love life.

Louisa steps into the corridor in a floppy pink t-shirt and denim shorts so tiny the linings of the pockets are visible at her thighs.

"I'm coming!" she calls, rushing off to collect her basket from the kitchen. "I've got hummus, olive spread, boiled eggs..."

When did she do all this? I feel guilty for not helping at all.

"I've brought some homemade beer," Jacob says.

I look at him in surprise. Who has time to make their own beer?

"It's really good," Alex adds.

Is Alex Louisa's accomplice? Have they spoken about getting their two single friends together?

Louisa returns, her eyes all big and Disney.

"Did you say homemade beer? That's amazing!"

"I made wine once too, but it wasn't very good," he says.

Louisa hands me a hemp bag, hoists the basket over her shoulder and closes the door behind us. Then she links her arm in Jacob's as if they'd been friends for life.

"You have to tell me all about it," she says.

Getting all pally with Jacob must be a strategic move. She's either trying to make me see what a prize he is or trying to make Alex jealous. Jacob would be more of a prize if his eyes weren't so close together, if he were a few inches taller, and if he didn't have such a handsome friend.

Alex and I are left behind to follow them out of the building. For the first time in ages I find I'm in the company of someone I don't have to find out everything about for work purposes. I feel a bit blank.

"Busy week?" he asks, as we stroll in a leisurely fashion down the road.

"Yeah. Then again it's always busy because of the nature of social media, the internet doesn't sleep."

I feel as if Craig has hijacked my brain.

"Is all your work on social media?"

"Pretty much. I also get to answer a hundred emails a day, but usually the emails are just instructions for what I need to do on social media."

"So you're on Twitter and Facebook most of the day?"

Some people think it's #awesome.

I shrug. "Yep, pretty much."

"Wow. It must be hard to feel like you've actually achieved anything."

Ouch. I open my mouth to defend myself, but he gets in first.

"No offence, I just get really annoyed with myself when I've been faffing about on Facebook all day, so I'd feel really frustrated if I had to do it for a job."

"You know, saying 'no offence' before an insult doesn't cancel it out," I say. "For instance, 'no offence, but I think your job is shit' is still offensive."

He bites down on a smile. "I'm sorry. That's so true. I hate it when people say 'no offence', it's almost as bad as the misuse of 'literally'."

"Nothing is as bad as the misuse of 'literally'," I say, enjoying myself. "I overheard someone on the Tube the other day say, *I literally ate a cow.* I really wanted to say, no, you did not literally eat a cow."

"That's nothing. On the bus, I overheard someone *literally piss their pants*, and her friend *literally die of laugher*."

"I'm guessing it was a night bus."

He laughs. "You know what's worse, though, don't you?"

"Air quotation marks?"

"Worse."

"Talking in hashtags?"

"Oh shit. I hadn't even thought of that."

"What were you going to say?"

"The misuse of 'literally' sandwiched by unnecessary 'likes'."

I wince theatrically. "Ah, yes, that's pretty bad."

"I *like literally like* offended you a minute ago."

"And I'm like literally so offended I'm like literally going to kill you."

"I just want to pin people to the floor and edit their speech bubbles, you know what I mean?"

"I definitely do."

We both grin at each other and then I remember what he said before we found ourselves agreeing on the misuse of "literally".

"Anyway I'm not 'faffing' about on Facebook all day!"

"Oh, yeah, you also said you faff about on Twitter too."

His cheekiness is outrageous, but I kind of like it.

"You're so rude! It's not like I spend my day telling everyone what I'm doing, eating, thinking..."

Nope, smirks my inner voice, *you're telling everyone what someone else is doing, eating, thinking...*

"You're not?" he says.

"No!"

"You spend your day on Twitter and Facebook, but you're NOT documenting every thought, every meal, every passing emotion and every time you go to the toilet?"

"Please... I am not one of those people."

"So what do you do all day?"

"Marketing for my clients."

He looks sceptical.

"I can measure the results of everything I do!"

Well, not everything. As the saying goes: *50 percent of marketing works, but no one knows which half...*

"It's rewarding, actually," I say. I'm not having him thinking I spend my day posting pictures of kittens and trying to see how many LOLs I can squeeze out of the public. Even if that is partly the truth. "I like it. It's interesting."

"I thought people hated being marketed to on their social networks."

"They hate traditional marketing, but they don't mind content marketing."

He's going to make me explain that now.

"That's where you're tricked into reading a blog post by a snappy headline but really it's just a subtle advert leading you to a link to buy something, right?"

I'm surprised. It's not how I'd put it, but it's not a million miles from the truth either.

"Good blogs deliver on their headlines and offer worthwhile content..."

His look of amusement shuts me up.

"Anyway," I say, with a note of finality, "it's not like you have to buy anything. You can just read it, make use of the advice and then log off."

He smiles. "Do you write those blogs, then?"

I feel my cheeks reddening.

"No, but I'll retweet them if they're good... Anyway, what about you? Have *you* finished the week with a great sense of achievement?"

My pointed question makes him laugh. His face lights up as if he's remembered some happy news.

"Well, I'm really excited about getting a couple of weeks off and working on my film. The day job has been starting to really suck me dry."

"The acting?"

"No, the directing. That's my main job, directing music videos and adverts. Twelve-to 14-hour days means I don't have much time to work on my own stuff."

"Did you say adverts?" I can't help grinning. "Adverts to sell stuff to people?"

He shoots me a quizzical look. "Yeah, so?"

"Well, that's marketing, isn't it?"

"The key word is directing. I'm not doing any selling. At the end of the job I've created a piece of work I can put on my show reel and show to investors of future projects I care about."

I can sense him bristling. I think I've proven my point, even if he's unwilling to concede it. We are both engaged in influencing consumers and he has no right to act all superior.

My phone buzzes and I check the notification. Someone has tweeted a picture of a beard they have knitted for Bernard's cat. Well, that wasn't a waste of time... that's exactly what the world is missing, knitted facial hair for cats. God, what's wrong with people?

Click. Favourite.

"I planted those," Alex says suddenly.

I tear myself reluctantly away from the screen. "What?"

He's pointing to the base of a tree, where purple and white pansies are in full bloom. I look at him, wondering if I've missed the joke.

"Yup," he says, looking proud of himself. "I did it at night. Chucked a few seeds in, water them now and then... pretty good, right?"

"Why?"

I don't know why I ask that because... Why not?

"I thought it would be uplifting."

It is. The splash of colour is very pretty. It's really brought the square base to life.

"It's called guerrilla gardening," he says. "Loads of people do it. They try and brighten up dead areas and wastelands by planting flowers and even vegetables."

#Loveit.

"Can I take a picture?"

I'm already on my camera, centring the image.

"There are some great photos on their website," he says. "Someone grew asparagus in a ditch outside a disused railway station."

Suddenly there's a shriek from up ahead. I glance over my shoulder to see Louisa stopped at the zebra crossing, pointing a finger towards us. Jacob is standing beside her, looking confused.

"Confiscate it, Alex!" she shouts.

I swear under my breath and take the picture.

"What's that about?" Alex says.

"She doesn't like me being on my phone."

"Does she take away your pocket money if she sees you on it?"

I laugh, glad of the solidarity. "She thinks I'm an addict."

"Oh..." he says, as if it all makes sense now. His tone is teasing. "*Are* you? Do you by any chance bring your work home with you, May?"

I slide the phone back into the pocket of my silky green palazzo trousers and straighten my t-shirt. "I could be on it less..." I admit. "But she also could be less dramatic."

We catch up with them at the zebra crossing. Louisa scowls at me and holds out her hand.

"Give," she says.

I feel a bubble of anger rise up my throat. "No, Louisa, you can't confiscate my phone. I'm not your child."

"She was taking a picture of some flowers I grew," Alex says.

She looks suspicious. "What flowers?"

"Jacob makes beer, I plant flowers... that's how we roll."

Jacob laughs, but Louisa is still holding out her hand. "Give it to me."

I walk on ahead. "No. It was just a photo. I'm allowed to take a photo."

"But it wasn't for you, was it? It was for your job."

"Who cares?"

121

"It's why everyone gets so pissed off with you!"

The only person who gets pissed off with me is *her*! And that's because she can't stand not being the centre of attention for one second!

Doesn't she feel embarrassed making a scene like this? We hardly know these guys! I thought she wanted to make a good impression on Mr Director. Having a go at me and making me out to be a phone-addict loser is a weird way of doing it.

"She's going to pretend one of her clients grew your flowers."

Louisa talks like she walks, loudly. I feel my cheeks flush with heat. If she thought she was whispering then she needs an ear test. I should ignore her, but I can't help it.

"That's rubbish, Louisa."

"You know it's not."

"What do you mean?" Alex says.

"It's top secret," Louisa says drily. "But basically..."

"Louisa!"

"Alright, alright. I'm not going to say anything more about it."

She shrugs and I catch her rolling her eyes at him. Now I've become the drama queen. Touché. I feel a little ripple of jealousy. Me and Alex Hunter had been getting on fine until she'd butted in.

"So what do you mean you grow flowers?" she asks.

The next minute she's making over-enthusiastic noises as Alex explains it to her. Bunch of hippies, I think irritably, but really I can't fault the idea and find myself agreeing how ridiculous it is that guerrilla gardeners face fines for being caught. My green-fingered mum would love the sound of this. Once they've finished talking about weeds and wild garlic, I ask the guys how they met.

"Primary school," Jacob says. "We've been writing together ever since."

"We began with Superman sequels," Alex says.

Their laughter seems to sum up a childhood of fun. It's a heart-warming sound that makes me feel nostalgic for all the good times I've shared with my own friends, moments that have been few and far between just lately.

It turns out Jacob works as a kitchen assistant at a French restaurant when he's not writing, which explains his rough hands. Snatching moments to work on it between their jobs, it's taken them three years to write their new script, *Shadow Man*. It's about a swimmer destined for the Olympics, who falls into a coma after a tragic accident. I feel my mind wander. Hasn't this story been done before?

"Jacob wanted it to be a diving accident, but footage of a traffic accident is much easier to get," Alex says, before continuing the explanation.

While in the coma, the swimmer falls into this wonderful dream where he becomes fully aware of himself and is faced with a choice to stay in the dream forever or return to grim reality.

Jacob glances at me, hoping to witness my excitement at the idea, but my mind is attacking the practical side of it.

"Have you got money?"

"The script won a competition," Jacob says.

"That's so cool," Louisa says dreamily, as though she's already heard all this before.

The fact that he doesn't say how much money makes me think it wasn't mega millions.

"It's not even enough to hire a camera," Alex admits, "but we'll make it happen." The park is filling up fast. A group of young mothers have conquered a large area with prams and coolers and we move away from them and their screaming offspring. We avoid the Frisbee players too and the teens using their mobile phones as screechy little ghetto blasters.

We choose a sunny spot just beyond the leafy shadows of a plane tree. I find myself wondering if Louisa did invite anyone else, or if this encounter has been tailored for us to match up like this.

It's uncomfortable sitting cross-legged with my phone in my pocket, so I take it out and lay it on the grass in front of me. I've turned the notification ring off, but it still buzzes loudly. Luckily

Louisa is rummaging through her basket and doesn't hear it.

It's from Damian's Twitter account.

ELEANORMELDROOP @ELLIEMELLIE
@DamianDance omg is it true ur goin to b on sing me out of the jungle?

She's referring to a new reality show, which is basically a singing contest with the twist of being in a jungle. It was only a matter of time before they gave up on new ideas altogether.

"Beer?"

I look up to find Alex holding out a brown glass bottle.

"Thanks."

Louisa is still busy taking out the contents of her basket. I wonder how I can escape to check out this tweet. Damian should have told me if he was considering doing the show. I try to be discrete as I slide my fingers over the screen and take a look at @ elliemellie's profile, simultaneously taking a slug of beer.

Her profile picture shows a teen with pink hair and a t-shirt emblazoned with the word Ibiza in purple sequins. According to her profile she's a *crazy rebel* and *on* #teamfollowback. It's a team that irritates some, inspires love in others.

"I thought you said you weren't a phone addict," Alex murmurs.

I glance up, open-mouthed. "I'm not! I'm literally just checking one thing!"

"Yeah, yeah..."

"I'm serious!"

"What do you think of the beer?"

I've forgotten it was even in my hand. I take another swig. It's rich and hoppy.

I nod over at Jacob, smiling appreciatively, "It's really good."

I push away the phone. Fine. I'll follow it up when I'm not being spied on and when everyone's snoozing in the sun.

"So what were you going to do with that photo of my flowers?"

"Oh nothing," I groan.

Can't we drop this? It's not like his pansies are copyright. What does it matter?

"I don't mind what you use it for. I'm just curious."

Louisa holds out a pot of olives, she's already got one in her mouth. The bulge of it moves from one side to the other before she eggs me on.

"Just tell him. We're neighbours after all."

We've been neighbours for at least three months and he's never needed to know before.

"It's not a big deal," Louisa says. "She's just looking after some people's Facebook and Twitter accounts."

She looks over at me, her eyebrows raised, and I shrug, giving her my permission to carry on. If she doesn't tell him now, she'll only tell him behind my back.

"So she just shares things she thinks her clients would share if they were online and generally stands in for them."

It doesn't sound as challenging as it is in real life, but then it's not as if I'm a doctor working for *Medecins sans Frontieres* either.

Louisa breaks off the end of the baguette and passes it on to Jacob, who has been quietly studying an ant travelling up his bottle of beer. They reach forward for the hummus, talking about which kind they like best.

Alex is studying me with his intense blue eyes.

"So you're faking their accounts?"

"Faking" is such an accusatory word and I feel a bit taken aback.

"No, it's not like that. They hire me."

"But you're pretending to be them?"

"I'm looking after their profiles."

"Yes, by pretending to be them. Or is there a notice saying it's not actually them?"

"No, there's not a *notice* as such..."

I don't like the way Alex is staring at me like that, his eyebrows twitching between a frown. I feel under attack.

"It's not like I'm looking after people of great influence."

The frown solidifies. "Didn't you say they're celebrities?"

"Really minor ones! C list. D even."

"You can't say C-list celebrities aren't hugely influential to the masses. Think how many millions watch reality TV."

"He's going to guess who they are in a minute!" Louisa giggles, before clapping her hand over her mouth.

I glare at her.

"It's a pretty big deal faking their voices," Alex says, with an infuriating little shrug.

"Alright, calm down! I'm not going to use your flowers!" I say, losing my calm completely.

He laughs. "No, go ahead, you should. It will be good to have your famous clients showing their support for something other than designer shoes made by kids in sweat shops."

I open my mouth to protest, then close it again. I'm not going to rise to every taunt.

"Yes, give them some nice hipster hobbies," Louisa says, popping another olive in her mouth.

It gives me pleasure to see Alex grimace. "It's not a hipster hobby. If you have to call me something, call me an eco-warrior."

"You planted one pansy!" Jacob snorts. "Get over yourself."

"It's better than doing nothing. Haven't you heard about the bee crisis?"

"Yes," I say, feeling smug. "In fact, I signed an online petition."

"Ah yes, thank God for sofa activists," he says, with a bitter smile. "There's probably an app where you can grow some virtual flowers too."

The others laugh at that, but I feel furious.

"Online petitions work!"

I'm racking my brain for a good example. I can't remember which of the gazillion I've signed had a positive outcome. Was it the child brides in Afghanistan? Or the bear farms in China? Is the Amazon okay now? Are the Sri Lankan tigers safe? In fact, dying bees don't sound half as horrifying as most of the emails I get, so I must have been feeling very sensitive when I signed it.

"The bee population is dying out," he continues, ignoring me. "Seventy out of the top 100 food crops are pollinated by them. Basically without bees to spread seeds food crops will die off. How long before there's a food crisis?"

"We should get some window boxes," Louisa says.

"Yeah, you should."

There, that can be their first date, a day out at Home Base. Maybe they are right for each other after all.

"Go ahead," Alex says. "Use the flowers. You may as well promote something worthwhile while you've got their voices, because I'm guessing if they *are* reality TV stars they're attention-seekers and probably aren't going to think about anyone else but themselves."

"Wow. That's not judgmental at all."

"It is. But it's also probably true."

I take a gulp of beer to stop myself losing my temper.

"My clients are actually very good people."

"Well..." Louisa begins, but I cut her off.

"And I think it's disgusting they have to deal with so much ridicule and abuse and judgement from people who think they're entitled to an opinion on how they should live their lives. People who have no idea what they're really like. All I'm doing is giving them a break."

Alex throws back his head and laughs.

"What's so funny?" I snap.

"Oh come on, May! You make it sound like you're defending the weak and vulnerable!"

"Well, they are."

They are weak. Weak-willed. And as a result they are vulnerable.

"Why should anyone care about them? These celebrities do everything they can short of selling their mothers to be in the spotlight and then they cry when they discover the public is a bitch. So what?"

"I think we should change the subject!" Louisa says, her voice shrill. "I want to hear more about your film."

"I'm sorry, but it's something that really pisses me off," Alex says, serious again. "There's so many repressed people all over the world who have stories that really need to be heard and instead the stage is given to a bunch of self-obsessed idiots talking about what they had for breakfast."

"It's been like that since the beginning of time," Louisa says. "That's life."

"Yup," Jacob agrees.

I level my eyes at Alex, my smile forced. "Okay, so tell me one thing... What are you doing that's so great?"

"Can we please talk about something else?" Louisa moans. "Does anyone want a boiled egg?"

"Because your story about a fictional swimmer drifting off into a nice dream isn't really giving a platform to the repressed either, is it?"

Alex licks a drop of beer off his lips and stares back at me.

"No. That's what I thought," I say, unlocking myself from those mesmerising eyes.

Alex leans back on his elbows. "It's a lovely day for a picnic, isn't it?"

"It is," Louisa says, relieved we're moving on.

Have we moved on? It's obvious neither of us has anything left to say to each other. It comes as a bit of a shock. There was a moment when I thought we were really hitting it off.

Chapter 13

I take the train to my parents' on Sunday. It gives me an uninter-
rupted hour to send emails and address all the interactions that
have popped up on my clients' networks overnight. I shoot off
a message to Damian's agent asking whether the rumour about
him going on *Sing Me Out of the Jungle* has any substance to it.
I'm tempted to email Damian directly, but the idea behind him
hiring me is so that he doesn't have to mess around with this stuff.

The passenger sneaking glances over my shoulder gets off at
the next station and I log in to our business PayPal to buy 15,000
Twitter followers for Damian. The first time Craig suggested doing
this, I was horrified. But he makes a valid point. The key to success
with social media is giving a good impression. If you have loads
of followers people assume you're somebody. They think that if all
those people are following them, maybe they're worth following,
and so they follow them too. Eventually what was fake becomes
real. You've gone from being nobody to being somebody without
doing anything at all.

I find myself thinking of Alex. I'm sure he would have something to say about this method and the truth is, we'd be on the
same page. You can cheat your way to a big following, but if you
tweet rubbish, the real people aren't going to stick around long. It
works up to a point. The main thing is I'm not hurting anyone by

doing it. I feel a flicker of irritation as I imagine him disagreeing with me: *So you don't think lying to people is hurtful?*

I don't know how he can justify being on the moral high ground, though. Does Alex honestly think his clients are worthier than mine? The adverts he makes are for big greedy corporations that control and screw up the planet. He should think about that, put it into perspective. My clients offend people. His clients kill orangutans.

SPARKMAY @SPARKYMAY

Orangutans are sad their homes will be destroyed for #PalmOil based shampoos but relieved humans will keep their silky hair.

My parents made the move to suburbia a year ago. They've got a two-bedroom house on an interest-only mortgage that they'll be paying off for the rest of their lives. They prefer to focus on the positives, though, which is their own front door and a small back garden.

Mum doesn't believe in manicured gardens. Dirty blue hydrangeas have taken over the otherwise paved front yard, stopping some of the light coming in through the bay window. Dandelions have sprouted in between the paving slabs that lead the way to a red door with panes of stained glass. I tried to pull them up one weekend, but their roots were as thick as carrots and never fully came out.

Inside, I'm confronted with the familiar baggy blue sofa and mismatched wooden furniture of my childhood. The carpet, a brown diamond-patterned monstrosity, is the only remaining stamp from the previous owner, but it's a particularly overpowering one. Mum has a collection of carpet swatches on the bottom of the stairs, but she can't afford the one she wants, so decoration plans are on hold. The carpet shop will probably close down before she makes a decision. I wish I had the money to buy it for her. I've often imagined sending Mum and Dad out for lunch and getting people to come in to lay it. It would be like one of those

DIY shows, a miracle transformation done in sixty minutes, with tears at the end. Would Mum cry over a new carpet? She pretends she doesn't care about having lovely things, but I've seen her in John Lewis running her hand along rolls of fabric, a little smile of pleasure, followed by a hardening of the lips as she realises she won't be taking it home. I resolve there and then to buy her a carpet the day Craig gives me a pay rise.

"Is that you?" Mum calls from the kitchen.

You can only hear the doorbell if you've got your ear against the speaker, so I've used my old keys.

"No, it's a burglar!"

The kitchen is my favourite part of the house, being the room that's had the most love and money poured into it over the years. It's got natural slate tiles and solid oak cabinets with intricate antique brass knobs. The wrought-iron chandelier hanging over the table, the dried flowers on the windowsill and the wintry countryside landscape painting on the wall gives it a cottage feel that tricks me into thinking I've escaped the city.

Dad is at the table, the paper spread out in front of him, an overlap of tea rings at the corner where he keeps shifting his mug. Mum is on a chair reaching into a kitchen cabinet. She's dressed in her old favourites, three-quarter-length grey trousers that cut her legs in half and make her look short. Her top is new, a dark-purple slash neck that I imagine was an impulse buy from one of the market stalls on the way to Asda. It looks good. Now I just need to convince her to dye her roots again.

"How lovely, you're here! I'm not going to get down to kiss you or I'll never get back up again."

She seems to be having a spontaneous clear-out. Below her, an assortment of old mugs stand in a line on the worktop.

Dad's chair creaks as he pushes himself to his feet. He gives me a hug. His yellow polo shirt smells of soap and freshly cut grass. Over his shoulder, through the kitchen window, I can see the washing laid out to dry on the airer. I feel like going outside

131

and lying on the grass.

"We've missed you. How have you been?"

"I know, it's been ages. I'm good. Busy."

"Is busy good?"

"It's good financially! I've got four new clients."

"Four new clients," he echoes, nodding. I've explained what I do several times, but he still doesn't really get it. "You must be very good at the Twitter."

"It's not 'the' Twitter... it's just Twitter."

"Oh yes, I mix it up with the Facebook."

"Just Facebook."

"The YouTube?"

I laugh. "Nope."

He looks disappointed.

I don't want to mention it just yet, but I'm quite disconcerted by the lack of cooking going on. The oven is off and there's no sign of food preparation at all, nothing being chopped or marinated. I've got a million things to get on with and I was only really intending to come down for lunch.

"Katie called last night," Mum says, "she's coming to England in a month. Isn't that exciting?"

"For how long?"

One day my sister just quit her job at WH Smith, broke up with the weedy boyfriend she'd had for years and booked a ticket to Brazil to work in an orphanage in the middle of nowhere. My parents cried floods at the airport; they were so proud. Ever since then, my news has been relegated to second place.

"At least three weeks, I should think," she says, beaming. "And you know what else?"

I slide into a seat. "She's adopted three children?"

"No! She's bringing home Lucas! The boyfriend!"

Katie had mentioned him in a WhatsApp conversation a couple of months ago. I hadn't realised it was serious. I've been rubbish at replying to her messages lately. She always seems to write when

I'm knee-deep in emails and want to chuck my phone out of the window.

"Be a bit more excited, please!"

"I am, it's just sinking in. If it's serious that means she's not planning to move back."

I'm happy for her, and a little bit sad too. "They might move to London," Mum says brightly. "You never know."

"Why would they do that?"

In my mind I'm picturing a sandy white beach and a sparkling azure sea.

"The grass isn't always greener on the other side, is it?"

She lowers herself down from the chair, giving up on her job of clearing out the cupboard for now.

"Brazil is definitely greener than England. They've got the Amazon. What have we got?"

"The Lake District," my dad offers.

"Well, it's not about where you are," Mum says. "It's about being the change you want to see in the world *wherever* you are."

I roll my eyes. I feel an urge to reach out and press UNLIKE. If only that option existed on Facebook. Or better still, if there was a SLAP button. The problem is if UNLIKE and SLAP buttons did exist, they'd be used by trolls to bully vulnerable teens, who would then commit suicide because their selfie, which went viral, got a million SLAPS.

Oh God, the noise in my head. It just goes on and on. I wish I was on a beach in Brazil listening to the waves lapping against the shore.

"If you're not happy with your job, there's plenty of time for a career change."

I stare at my mum, wondering if I've spoken out loud. "When did I say I wasn't happy with my job?"

"You just look like you aren't."

"I haven't done anything. I've just come in and sat down."

"You can talk to Katie when she comes over. Ask her what her work is like."

"I don't want to work in an orphanage."

"I thought you liked children."

I think of Anna Jamison's latest Facebook status update.

Anna Jamison: *Bubba always waits until nappy change to pee in my face. I bet he'd cry if I did that to him too – feeling broken (emoticon face split in half)*

"Terrible, isn't it?" My dad mutters suddenly. He has sat back down in his place at the table and is shaking his head at the newspaper. "More girls aspiring to be glamour models than doctors and engineers."

I lean over to see what he's reading and my eyes widen as I spot a small picture of Angel Butler. The same picture was splashed all over the internet last year. It's the moment she pulled down her boob tube on X-factor. Her puffy pink lips are frozen mid-shout and she's wearing so much black eye makeup you could be forgiven for thinking she'd been punched in the face, twice. Angel is upstaged by three other popular pop singers. One picture is a poster I've seen on the Tube. The singer is posing naked, her limbs positioned carefully, the difference between something for public consumption and porn a matter of a few degrees. Her makeup is smeared and in her stare there's a mixture of anger and defiance. Junkie? Sex slave? Whatever it is, it's a pretty depressing look. What has getting naked got to do with making music anyway?

"Who are they?" Mum says. She has moved around the table to get a better look. She's squinting because she hasn't got her reading glasses on.

"I haven't got a clue," Dad says.

I prod my finger at each one and tell them who they are. I leave Angel Butler till last. It feels strange that she could be in my office next week. I keep my voice steady, not wanting to give anything away.

"That's Angel Butler, she was on a singing show and when the judges didn't put her through, she flashed everyone."

"And she's who girls are aspiring to be?"

I shrug. "I think it's fame in general."

"Well, I've never heard of her."

That's not really saying much. Mum's showbiz knowledge is so limited she probably thinks Sean Connery is still playing James Bond.

"Well, I think it's very sad that these women are using their influence to encourage girls to strip off instead of using their brains," Mum says. "With their high profiles they could really make a difference."

"It's not all their fault, Carol," Dad says. "They're surrounded by advisors telling them what they should be doing. They need role models too."

Mum fixes her eyes on me, "You're not working for one of these women, are you?"

I'm aware of my heart beating faster with the anticipation of the lie. "No."

"Good. You want to be helping people with real talent, who aren't getting a look in because everyone's being distracted by the ones taking their clothes off."

"I am," I say. "One of my clients is an 18-year-old singer-song writer."

Thijs isn't a client yet, but I've got a feeling he will be soon.

"Eighteen? Does he really have to bother with all this nonsense already?"

I shouldn't have mentioned his age.

"He won't be bothering with it because I will!"

"Surely if his songs are good enough they'll sell by themselves."

"You just said I should be helping the ones who have talent!"

"I know what I just said. But I can't help feeling that it's only the ones with dubious talent that need to make such a fuss about themselves."

My phone is ringing and I rummage through my handbag for it.

"No phones at the table," Mum says.

I let out a cry of exasperation. "We're not even eating!"

I'm about to ask what *are* we going to eat when I catch Gabe's name on my screen. I've known him to text me on a Sunday, but he rarely rings. I don't know if I should be worried or not, but since that's become my default state for work-related issues, the knot in my stomach twists. I get up and head into the living room.

"Hello? Gabe?"

"May, we've got a code pink."

Craig came up with a list of codes for different problems, but we've never used them. There's only one I'm clear on. Code red. That's for a client blowing our cover and admitting to using our services. I think it's ridiculous. We're not spies.

"Damian Dance has gone rogue," he clarifies.

"What?"

"He's shouting abuse at some kid on Twitter."

I hurry to get my tablet from my bag, ignoring my mum's questions as I head back to the sofa. I'd turned my notifications off so I wouldn't annoy anyone on the train. I flip to Damian's Twitter account and see the interactions are at double figures. I scan through them and my stomach turns.

ROONEYAZ @ROONAZ2467

Don't worry, folks, if @DamianDance starts singing in the jungle the animals will attack him just to shut him up.

SHAUN @SHOSHO

@roonaz2467 LOL. I reckon he'd get on with the monkeys @ DamianDance

TMEISTER @TREVSJ13

@shosho @roonaz I'm burning my telly if @DamianDance gets back on it!

At which point Damian jumps in and takes on @trevsj13

DAMIANDANCE @DAMIANDANCE
@trevsj13 I think I just saw you're mum in the jungle humping a gorilla.

I cover my mouth in shock. The 'you're' error makes it even more painful to read.

"Does he have his password?"

Gabe's voice startles me. I forgot he was still on the phone.

"Yeah, he insisted, just in case he needed it!"

"Oh God... that's like leaving an alcoholic with a bottle of wine to look after."

TMEISTER @TREVSJ13
@DamianDance my mum died of cancer

DAMIANDANCE @DAMIANDANCE
@trevsj13 well that's what happens when you shag gorillas.

How could Damian write that?! You can't make a crude joke about the death of someone's mum! How is that not obvious?

This is horrible. I feel sick. To make it worse a handful of cancer survivors and research campaigners, who have been alerted by the keyword in @trevsj13 tweet, start to voice their outrage.

I've got to get that tweet off now before it gets embedded into a thousand blogs and Damian's reputation is ripped to shreds once again. A part of me is thinking he deserves a public bollocking, the other part is employed by Craig and has a credit-card debt to pay off.

"I've got to go Gabe. I've got to sort this out."

Mum pokes her head in. "Everything alright?"

"Not really! I need to clear up someone's verbal diarrhoea! I can't believe how little self control people have!"

"They don't deserve you." She hovers nearby, which makes me feel agitated. "If it were me, I'd let them reveal themselves for who they are."

"I won't be long."

I click refresh and a sad face comes up. Connection lost.

"What's wrong with the internet?"

"I don't know," Mum says. "It's been doing funny things recently."

Is there anything more annoying than shit internet connection?

Yes, there probably is.

#Firstworldproblems

I swap tablet for phone and log into Damian's account. At least he hasn't changed the password. That's the first thing I'm going to do once I've deleted the increasingly ugly tweets. It'll be confusing for him on the other side, which is why I'm going to fire off an email to him. If only the internet was working properly, I could work from two devices.

"How's Louisa?" Mum says. "Has she got a boyfriend now?"

"One sec Mum, I really need to sort this out."

Come on, come on. Why is the offensive tweet not deleting? I feel like I can't breathe while it's out there exposed to the world.

The sound of the doorbell makes me feel even more tense.

"Is that the time!"

I glance at my Mum. "Who is it?"

"Didn't I tell you? It's John and Emmie from book club."

Shit. I don't have time for the ceremony of greeting my parents' friends right this minute. They'll want to know what I'm working on and whether I've been enjoying the lovely weather and whether I've heard from my sister lately and if I fancy living abroad for a while and have I cut my hair... I gather my things and head for the stairs. But it's too late. Mum has opened the door and Emmie, dressed in brightest fuchsia, bursts in, looking eager to smother us with her love. Emmie is the most interested person you could meet; she should have been a quiz-master.

"May!" she cries.

Oh God.

"So nice to see you!"

"Hello!" I cry, and hug her awkwardly because both my hands are full.

Next in, comes Jolly John with a bulging canvas bag. "I've got the meat," he says. "You should take a look at this meat."

"We haven't got the barbecue going yet!" Mum says.

"Hello, May, do you like meat?"

What sort of meat? I want to ask him, but I don't have time.

"May is dealing with a little crisis at work," Mum explains. She makes it sound like a photocopier has broken. They have no idea.

"On a Sunday?" Emmie says, looking very disapproving. "If I were you, May, I'd tell them to sod off. Excuse my French."

Their opinions on how unjust it is follows me up the stairs and I can still hear them going on about it even once I'm in my old room with the door shut. The internet connection is working again and I log onto my tablet.

I find the tweet.

DELETE.

A rush of relief runs through me as the odious tweet disappears forever, at least I hope so. And the next. DELETE. I delete all the ones that strike me as offensive. The problem isn't over, though. These tweets have been seen and shared already and I'm going to have to come up with an apology worth sharing too. I think I need something visual. A picture speaks a thousand words, which is a hell of a lot more than I can share on Twitter.

My phone makes me jump. I don't recognise the number on the screen.

"May? What's going on?"

It's Damian Dance. My first instinct is anger that he should dare ring me up to tell me to stop deleting his tweets.

"Did you just tell someone that their mum died of cancer because she shagged a gorilla?"

"No! Of course not! Did you?"

The realisation that his account has been hacked almost winds me.

"Shit. So you didn't tweet *'In the jungle, the mighty jungle, I'm a lion and you're a whining little piece of monkey turd'*?"

He makes a sound somewhere between a splutter and a laugh. "What sort of person do you think I am?"

For a moment, I'd completely doubted him. For a moment, I'd thought I'd made a huge error of judgement; that I'd been an utter fool to think he'd come so far from that angry, arrogant caricature from *Big Brother*.

"Sorry, it's just you still have your password," I say. "I've deleted the tweets now and changed your login details."

"Is that enough?"

"Don't worry. It will be okay."

My chest feels tight. Everything travels so quickly online. Who knows who could have seen those awful tweets? Someone could be slotting the screen shot of them into their blog now alongside an article on celebrity trolls.

"I'm not feeling good about this," Damian says. "Can you do something quickly to make me look less of a dickhead?"

"Yes, of course. I'll say your account has been hacked."

"Will they believe it?"

I feel a niggle of doubt. "Of course they will."

"Can you tweet something that makes me look like a good guy?"

"I'm on it."

I hear my mum calling me as she climbs the stairs. I cover the receiver and call out that I'm coming.

"So, you'll do something now?" he says, his tone understandably urgent.

"Yes. Of course."

I can't believe his account has been hacked in the first week that I've taken it over. In all the years of working with Twitter it's never happened to me before.

My mum pushes open the door and my heart sinks.

"I'll be one minute, Mum."

I feel my cheeks redden. I didn't mean to say "Mum" at the end.

"Everyone's waiting for you!" she says. "Come on! Don't you want to smell the barbecue!"

Of course I'd love to, but how can I?

Right now my priority is to find a picture of the cutest tiger cub in the whole world then Photoshop some endearing apology on it like *I'm sorry, it all got a bit WILD back there – my computer got hacked!*

"Look, I'll leave you to get on with it," Damian says.

"Yes, I'll do it now. I'm so sorry about this."

Mum is standing there, arms folded, waiting with open curiosity.

"He should be apologising to you," she says.

I glare at her, my heart drumming in my chest. Did he hear that?

"Oh, and May?" he says.

"Yes?"

"Send me my new login details. If it happens again I don't want to be powerless to do anything about it and you're obviously a bit busy."

He's annoyed with me and I feel wretched.

"It won't happen again. I'll be monitoring closely."

"I'd still like the new password."

I feel like it's *my* reputation that's in tatters.

"I'll text it to you. I'd better go and rectify the situation."

"Yes please."

We hang up and I breathe out heavily. "Shit."

Mum lets out a little laugh. "Well, that sounded a bit dramatic. Are you coming down now?"

"I just need 20 minutes... half an hour max..."

Mum looks disappointed. The smell of smoking fire-lighters is one of my favourite smells, which is why she came up to get me. I was always the first one out to help Dad with the barbecue, while Katie stayed glued to the television, only coming out when the food was ready. I wish I could go back to that carefree time.

"I'll be as quick as I can."

"If you feel it's that important."

I take another deep breath and type *cute tiger cub* into the search bar.

"It is," I say. "Really important."

I'm glad my screen is turned away from her so she can't see that it's full of pictures of tiger cubs yawning and flopping over each other. I sense it would undermine the importance I'm talking about.

Chapter 14

On Monday morning I discover Bernard has spent his weekend talking to my office voicemail.

I don't feel Project "Get My Wife Back" is moving fast enough. I imagine it's because you need to know more about her. So here goes. Have you got a pen?

I scrabble to find one in my top drawer and miss the dictation of five different French wines. He then mentions her favourite flower "gladioli" before moving on to works of art.

In his second message he remembers that she loves musicals and he should have taken her more often.

In his third message he sounds wistful describing how they met.

It was a terrible party full of pretentious students arguing about intertextuality and metafiction in post-modernist literature. I remember we escaped to a nearby fish and chip shop and argued about mushy peas versus meta peas...

By his fifth message, he's slurring his words and starting to get aggressive.

His sixth message is an apology for the fifth message.

I lean back in my chair and sigh up at the ceiling. How did I get myself into this? I don't want to be involved in some bad-tempered TV host's marital problems. Why can't he ring her directly like a normal person? How can he ask me to be his voice? Okay, so I'm an idiot for agreeing to help, but he's the one who should be really ashamed of himself.

Gabe pokes his head around the door, "Nice job on the tiger cub apology."

"Oh God, it was pathetic wasn't it?"

He laughs. "Yes, but it got a lot of love."

Damian's fans had embraced his apology with LOLs, XXX and even a hashtag #WeForgiveDamian, which unfortunately had failed to trend.

"Is he going to be on *Sing Me Out of the Jungle*?"

"According to his agent, it's very unlikely. Apparently the series producer has a grudge against him."

"He probably slept with her then never called."

"Ooh, bitchy!"

"Fancy a drink later?" Gabe says.

Abigail is ringing through from reception.

"On a Monday? I can't. I'm really behind."

It's not actually possible to be anything other than behind with this job.

I pick up the phone and Gabe gives me a wave, "Another time, then."

"Thijs is here," Abigail says.

I glance at my clock. He's half an hour early.

"He says he's very happy to wait."

There's a smile in her voice, which makes a change.

"His agent is on her way too."

I'm not looking forward to meeting Maria Kuebler. She sounds like the sort of person who reduces you to a bumbling version of yourself just with her presence. I run through the notes I've made about Five Oars. If she tests me again I want to pass this time with flying colours.

I've noted that the four other band members all have active Twitter accounts, the largest following predictably going to Jake Helm who runs with the cheesy biog *Just a boy singing his heart out*. Meanwhile, a number of his fans have opted for the biog *Just a girl wishing Jake Helm would sing his heart out to her* with little pink hearts dotted between each word.

How easily is Thijs going to go along with this? Is he making a stand by being offline or is he just not interested?

Abigail rings through ten minutes later to tell me Maria has arrived and I ask her to send them through. Whatever I'm going to learn from the internet won't be as good as what I'll get from talking to Thijs.

I stand holding the door open as they come around the corner.

"Hello, welcome, I hope you found us alright."

Thijs looks the same as in his photos. A round baby face with a tiny chin, pale- blue eyes, a ledge of stiff blonde hair sticking out at his forehead above a scattering of pink spots. You wouldn't guess he was a member of a boy band about to take the nation by storm. There's no sense of an image going on. He's wearing a plain-blue t-shirt and jeans too wide at the bottom, the hem shredded and trailing in a loop. Maria, in contrast, is highly groomed. She's wearing black stilettos, faux-leather leggings and a white shirt buttoned up to the top with a black bowtie. Her lips are bright red and her highlighted hair is combed back into a neat bun. In her forties, but not intending to age any further without a fight.

"A pleasure to meet you," she says, shaking my hand and then gesturing for Thijs to step forward, "this is Thijs Vandroogenbroek."

Thijs' handshake is weak, and the way he looks at me with a mixture of embarrassment and resignation makes me feel like a great auntie he can't place.

"Please have a seat, would you like me to start by explaining what we do here?"

"I've told him," Maria says dismissively. "What we need to

decide is who he is."

I feel uncomfortable talking as if he's not in the room.

"How are you feeling, Thijs?" I say, smiling at him. "I hear you don't like social media much."

"I think it can be very narcissistic," he says.

A laugh escapes me. Maria's face crumples into a scowl.

"It doesn't have to be, though," I say. "There are a lot of incredibly talented people on Twitter who are using it as another tool for self expression, art, creativity... and many people are making real poignant points, spreading worthwhile messages... and then there are the ones who are just plain hilarious..."

Maria gets to the point. "Don't you realise what a great opportunity you have been given? How many people would love to be where you are right now?"

"Yes," he says. "I started learning the guitar when I was five. I have worked very hard for this."

She sighs and fixes her eyes on me, "Help, please, because I can't make him see why it's so important."

"It's not going to make my music better, so what's the point?" he counters.

"No, it's not," I agree. "What an online presence will do is attract people *to* your music. You do want people to listen to your music, don't you?"

He hesitates and Maria rolls her eyes.

"I guess so."

"Great. Well, that's what it's about, bringing your music to people's attention."

He frowns at me, "But you don't know anything about my music so how can you help?"

Last night I spent two hours prepping for this meeting. I listened to every track Five Oars had ever played in their two-year history. After the fourth one they all started to sound the same. Cheesy ballads and predictable upbeat party tunes; not a patch on Take That.

"Yes I do... I love *Memory of You, That Holiday*... "

"*That Holiday*?" he says. "You don't think it was a rip-off of Floortje en Virenden's *Sunshine Sunshine*?"

I feel like he's just spoken to me in another language. In fact I'm sure he just switched into Dutch halfway through. I want to reach out to Google for help. If only this was a phone conversation and they weren't sitting right in front of me witnessing my face struggling to hide my confusion.

"She doesn't know who they are," Maria says, glaring at him. "No one does."

"Well I like them. They've influenced my music."

"I can listen to them," I say brightly, "I can listen to whoever you think I should."

"Can't you like someone people have heard of?" Maria says.

He smirks. "Like who? Take That?"

"Yes, exactly!" she says, throwing up her hands.

I look at him hopefully, wanting him very much to confess that Take That did, in fact, influence one of his last songs.

"No," he says.

#Shame. This is going to be a tricky one and I fear we're going to get a little stuck.

"Okay, let's leave music aside for a moment," I say, "I've got a whole questionnaire you can fill out about music."

He looks me in the eye. "What else have we got to talk about, then?"

He might be the youngest client we've got, but he's easily one of the most mature. An inner calm radiates from him. It must be because, unlike everyone else who has ever sat in front of my desk, he doesn't feel a desperate need to be liked. I admire him for that. In fact, if I'm honest, I feel a little envious. Not caring what other people think must give you an enormous sense of freedom.

I remind myself I should be pitching my services to him, not encouraging him to go it alone.

"Whether you like it or not, people are going to be interested

147

in you now," I say. "They're going to care about what you think, how you dress, where you go out."

"So?" he says, shrugging. "I don't have an obligation to tell them. I'm already giving them my music."

"Thijs!" Maria cries. "We've spoken about this. We agreed."

I know I can make him more likeable online. I can see why Maria is so frustrated. Thijs might be right, but right isn't fun, or fashionable, or seductive.

"I think what you need to do," I say, trying not to make it sound like I've said this a million times, "is treat it as just another side of the music business."

He looks at me, waiting to be convinced.

"Publicity is a necessary evil that artists never want to do but it needs to be done." The word "evil" jars with me, but I push on. "The good news is you don't have to do it. I'm going to do it for you."

He fills his cheeks with air and blows out slowly. He's doubtful. I get it. I've never been in a band, I don't know how to write music. I don't know what makes his foot starting tapping a beat, what tunes make him want to get up and dance and which ones fill him with teenage angst. I'm feeling pretty doubtful myself. In fact, if he could feel my fear right now, he'd be out of my office in a heartbeat.

"What would you do first?" Maria says. She pulls a shiny slither of a laptop out of her patent black satchel.

The pressure is on.

"The first problem is your name," I say.

"You want me to change my name?" Thijs splutters.

"No, of course not. I just want to make it easier for people."

"But without changing it? How do you do that?"

"I think we need to give you a Twitter handle which is shorter than your name and easy to say."

"Like what?"

I click on the list I'd started while listening to Five Oars. It looked more impressive yesterday.

"VanBroek?"

"That's my name with a chunk missing from the middle," he says.

"Yeah, I know, but... Vandroog?"

"A chunk missing at the end that time."

"VanDawg?"

"Like Snoop Dog?"

Maria shakes her head. "It's too hip hop for him."

I pursue, hoping I'm not betraying a sense of panic. "VanTune?"

"I don't like it at all," he says, looking confused.

"VanBro?" I offer, weakly.

To my surprise, he doesn't grimace. "What about Thijs VanBro altogether?"

I can feel Maria's eye boring into me.

"The problem is the 'Thijs' spelling," I begin, tentatively. Don't give them problems, give them solutions! "But we can just say something in your biog... *Thijs, like Nice...* you're going to get so big it will be a household name soon anyway!"

THIJSVANBRO @THIJSVANBRO
Hi guys, be nice to me, this is my first Tweet! ;)

I just hope some girls respond with "hey" and "finally!" and "a gazillion kisses" and "we all know you're the talented one!"

Maria is talking and I haven't heard a word. My eyes slip to the clock on the wall above her head. Is it really only 9.45? Why do my eyes hurt already? I bet Louisa is still in bed. Or maybe she's having breakfast with Alex Hunter, frothing up his milk so to speak... cracking his eggs... crisping his bacon #shutup #whatdoesthatevenmean?

Maria's question spears through my fog of thoughts. "Do you think you can turn him into a style icon?"

I blink at her, and without daring to examine Thijs's plain

t-shirt and wide- bottomed jeans with the horrible scraggy ends, I utter the answer she wants to hear.

"Yes, of course."

Then I pretend to make a note of something brilliant on my tablet, writing instead: *Look like you're writing something brilliant on your tablet,* which, all things considered, shows I work well under pressure.

I'm aware of Thijs protesting in a low voice.

"Don't worry. No one's going to make you wear a sarong," Maria snaps.

He might have the talent but it's clear Maria wears the trousers.

"So I've really got to do this?" Thijs says.

"It'll be really good for you," I say, shooting him my most sympathetic and encouraging smile, "and don't worry, if you change your mind, you can terminate the contract with immediate effect."

In theory this is true. In practice I'm not sure it would work too well. Sudden radio silence from an active celebrity on social media would be very suspicious. Of course we could come up with an explanation.

THIJSVANBRO @THIJSVANBRO

I'm sorry to leave you all. I've got to concentrate on my music. I hope my notes will be enough. Love you all. T

Great. I'm already composing Thijs's final tweet in my head. This feels promising.

"Okay," he says, smiling for the first time since he shook my hand. "I'm going to trust you."

"You won't regret it, Thijs," I say, cheerfully. "It just means you can focus entirely on your music while I make sure you're looking wonderful while you do it. What can possibly go wrong?"

Why did I just say that? Loads of things could go wrong. I could mix up my accounts again and tweet about the war novel he's not writing, or the cat he doesn't have, or that he's feeling

BOOOOOYAAAAA when he's never said BOOOOOYAAAA in his life...

"Nothing can go wrong," I say firmly. "Nothing at all."

I'm not sure how much more responsibility I can take and I've still got Angel Butler to look forward to.

Chapter 15

I get home to find that the flat has been taken over. Alex Hunter is in my kitchen looking like he owns the place. He's brought company. There's a young man with his hands on his hips, looking up at the ceiling, chewing gum. Beside him a pale-faced woman is sketching in a moleskin notebook. Jacob is leaning over the table, his garish Hawaiian shirt hanging loose at his chest.

Alex is first to see me. He gives me this big smile.

"Hi, May, how are you?"

The others turn and stare at me, which makes me feel self-conscious. I've just been on a packed Tube and must look a bedraggled wreck. The carriage was steaming.

"A bit tired," I say.

"We're just doing a reckie, we won't be long."

I worry they're going to think I'm the unfriendly flatmate and try to improve first impressions by offering them tea. They all decline. The toilet flushes and Louisa steps out of the bathroom into the corridor. She's wearing a red jumpsuit, which seems a bit much for a Monday afternoon at home.

"Hi, May! This is Diana, the set designer, and Neil, the cameraman. They're doing a reckie for the film."

"Yeah, I just heard," I say brightly. "So, set-wise, will there be many changes?"

"Don't worry," Diana says. "It'll all be put back to how it was."

"No, I don't mind about that, I'm just curious to know what you're going to do," I say, feeling eager to please.

"I can show you the script if you like," Louisa says.

"Careful, she might say one of her clients wrote it," Alex says.

Louisa cackles, "Don't be mean."

The remark hurts more than it should and I want to tell them both to piss off. Instead I count to five and announce I'm going to do some work in my room.

"We're having a beer after if you want one!" Louisa calls after me.

"I'm fine, thanks," I say, trying to keep my voice light.

I don't feel fine, though. The headache I've been battling with is back. I need to have an early night. Tiredness, that's all it is. I shouldn't have taken the comment so seriously. It just felt like they'd been talking about me behind my back and when I'm tired, I get sensitive. Doesn't everyone?

I sit on my bed and pull my tablet onto my lap. If I send off some tweets now I know I'll feel better because it'll mean less pressure in the morning. What I would love is a healthy, morning routine. To get up early, do half an hour of yoga and then sit with a cup of coffee and think about what I want to do with the rest of my life. Twenty minutes, that's all I need to get my creative juices flowing. Ten minutes, even.

How can I expect to get a good idea if I don't leave space in my head for one to enter?

I suppose I could just close my eyes and let my mind roam right this very minute. I slide down and rest my head on my pillow. My head pulsates as if my heart has taken up residence there. My mind automatically goes back over the day. I remember things I was going to tweet and tweets I forgot to reply to. I breathe out, breathe in and tell myself to let go. But I feel so restless.

I've got used to instant gratification. Everything I do always gets an immediate reaction, and when it doesn't, I delete it. Sitting here waiting for a life plan to maybe, or maybe not, take shape in my mind suddenly seems excruciating.

I force myself not to move. To take five minutes to have a thought deeper than what I'm going to tweet next.

Is social media diminishing the number of deep thoughts we're all having? Are we getting stupider? If so, what does that mean for the future of humanity? Judging from all the wars going on around the world, it seems as if we've learnt nothing from our history, that we are set on making the same mistakes over and over... It feels as though we are living in a world with less and less time for self-reflection, for contemplation, for stillness, and I've noticed it in myself, that each day it feels harder and harder to locate the peace at my centre.

Should I be setting up a website inviting deeper thoughts? I could invite spiritual leaders from around the world to collaborate... because they won't be busy at all! Who would advertise on my site? Meditation centres?

Oh God. Meditation and advertising... what a horrible combination.

I check the time on my watch and feel dismayed to see only one minute has passed. A moment later I sit up. It's no good. Taking time out to think is only making me aware of how much my head hurts and how lacking my content has been today.

I check what's trending.

#FirstWord

At a guess, Bernard's #FirstWord was "bastard". Mine was "No". It was forced out of me by my sister, who was hitting me over the head with a pillow at the time.

#ThingsNotToDoAtAFuneral

Well not tweeting would be a good start.

#TheTaste

I've actually seen snippets of the food show and Damian did mention he was learning to cook, so there is that connection. Contestants have to create a dish that fits onto a spoon and then famous chefs judge it.

DAMIAN DANCE @DAMIANDANCE
How much scrambled egg do you think I can fit on a spoon?
That's all I can make! #TheTaste

Oh it's pathetic. I should just delete it.

One notification. I feel nervous as I click on it. There's a lot of people who don't realise his account was hacked and now think he's a monster.

BELLALJ @BELLELAINE
@DamianDance LOL. I'd prefer scrambled eggs to whatever
that brown mush was!

What a relief! At the same time, how ridiculous to have such a strong reaction to something so banal. It's as though I was waiting for some scary hospital test results not a response about scrambled eggs.

There's a knock on my door. I lower my knees and brush out the creases in my skirt.

"They just need to take a quick look in here," Louisa says, holding the door open.

The others file in and stand there looking around. I feel exposed.

"Do you get much sun in the morning?" Alex says, his eyes running over the windowsill.

"No. Last I checked we live in England."

I meant for it to come out light-hearted not grumpy.

"It's been alright recently, hasn't it?" the cameraman says.

"It gets a bit of light, I suppose," I say.

Alex rubs a hand along his jaw, where a light stubble is starting to cast a shadow. He's looking more like a film director every day, with the black glasses and artfully dishevelled hair and this moody staring into space. Does he know Louisa will run a mile if he grows his beard back?

"We don't have to use this room, do we Alex?" Jacob says.

"Louisa's is the same sort of thing."

"I like this room," Alex says. I think it's very Cassie."

"Who's Cassie? I thought it was a film about a comatose male swimmer."

"The nurse..." Louisa says.

"Oh right," I say, and as casually as I can, "so who's playing her?"

"We're having auditions tomorrow," Jacob says.

I try to catch Louisa's eye, but she doesn't look at me.

Alex moves around my bed, his eyes roaming over my chest of drawers. I've got nothing to hide, but it feels so intrusive. His eyes linger on a photograph of my family. I'm only five in the picture. I'm wearing pink dungarees and probably have a matchbox in my pocket with a three-legged ant in it. It occurs to me that I've never had anyone to tell that to. I mean, I've never sat in this bed with a guy, post making love, and chatted about the stupid stuff I have in my room. I swallow back a lump in my throat and look down at my tablet.

"Alright, let's think about it," Alex says. "Thanks, May, we'll leave you to tweet in peace now."'

How does he manage to sound so patronising? Ten minutes later and I'm still trying to think of a comeback.

The front door slams shut and I strain my ears, wondering if they've all left. Were they having that beer here or out? Suddenly I really want one. It's not only that. I want the last word. It irritates me that Alex thinks I just sit around all day tweeting. In reality I'm a branding strategist, a marketing guru and a life coach. It's not even about that. I don't want him to think of me as one of those people who document the minutiae of their lives. Just because my clients need that sort of service doesn't make me one of them. If he followed @SparkyMay he would see the real me. Someone with a sense of irony, someone who is aware of the absurdity of the social media culture while being a part of it. Well, he *would* if he'd followed me a few weeks ago. I've been a bit quiet lately.

I get up and change into denim shorts and a clean chocolate-brown t-shirt. I'm too vain to wear trackies while there are potentially people in the house. Touching up my makeup is probably going too far, but I'm also stalling while I try to hear him in the living room. It does sound like everyone's gone and I feel a niggle of disappointment. "Oh... hello..."

I'm surprised to find Alex alone on our sofa with no sign of Louisa or the others.

"They've gone to get beer," Alex says, putting his notepad down. "They won't be long."

I sit down on the other end of the sofa and rest my phone by my side.

"I really fancy that beer now," I say with a smile.

"Busy day?"

As if on cue my phone vibrates by my side.

"Oh wait, you told me you're always busy," he says, pursing his lips into a knowing smile. "You see, I'm a good listener."

I wish I hadn't told him that.

"Yeah it's busy, but I don't mind," I say, with a shrug. "It's interesting."

"Yeah, you said."

He doesn't believe me and I feel myself blushing. I avoid his gaze by checking my phone. There's a direct message for Bernard.

"How did you get into it?"

It doesn't look like an automated message...

I glance up at Alex, aware he's asked me a question. "What?"

"How did you get into it?" he says again and nods at my phone. "Into tweeting for celebs?"

"It's a bit more than that, you know."

"So tell me about it."

I wanted the last word, didn't I? But really I should avoid the topic. The less people I talk about work to the better.

"We work for people who aren't very good at social media. They put their foot in things."

"Are they a bit racist?"

The question makes me squirm. A few of my clients have been quoted introducing their point of view with *I'm not racist but...* Of course they've all apologised, but once you've revealed how you think it's sort of too late.

"No...."

"Homophobic?"

I really hope not, but I wouldn't swear my life on it.

"No, nothing like that."

"Do they get drunk and post naked pictures?"

Yes, quite a few have attempted this. Luckily none of my clients are very good photographers.

"Unsuccessfully..." I concede.

He laughs. "Tell me more."

"I didn't think you were interested in celeb gossip."

"I'm not, I'm interested in what my neighbour does for a living."

"You're interested in taking the piss out of what your neighbour does for a living, more like."

He smiles. "I just want to know how they put their foot in things."

"It's not even that they do... some of them just don't like Facebook or Twitter."

He gasps in mock horror like I knew he would.

"So why do they have to do it?" he says, serious again.

This is why I hate talking about my job with people who evidently aren't fluent in social-media marketing.

"They aren't doing it. *I* am. I'm helping people who don't want to do what their job demands of them."

"Their job of being famous for being famous?"

"They're famous because they're talented!"

He raises a cynical eyebrow. "Are they?"

"Yes! They are singers, actors, writers..." His smirking face is so provocative. "Why am I even bothering to try to explain my job to you if you've already made your mind up?

"I'm sorry, I'm listening..."

"You're really judgmental, did you know that? You're one of those people who just assumes the worst of everyone, well I like to assume the best."

Talking to him so frankly has set my heart racing. I get up abruptly and go to the fridge. I retrieve a bottle of sparkling water, thinking I'll pop a vitamin C in a glass, but then I wonder how an effervescent tablet would react in sparkling water – would it double the fizz? That's a good speculative tweet. I'll store that for later.

"I don't assume the worst," he says. "I just see people for what they are."

"Oh, really, do you?"

"Look, any idiot can tweet. It's what people *do* that matters."

"I know that. Believe me, I know that."

"You just didn't strike me as someone who..."

"Who what?"

"This is going to sound harsh..."

"What?"

"From the little we've spoken, I got the impression you weren't the sort of person who would invest all her time and energy promoting people so devoid of personality or principles they have to pay someone to speak for them..."

My eyes widen at his honesty. But he hasn't finished.

"People who are so hungry for public adoration that they daren't type a word in case they write the wrong thing."

"It's not their fault..."

"I think, if they weren't so self-absorbed, if they looked beyond their miniscule existence, they'd find something worth having an opinion about and they might actually come across, if not intelligent, at least likeable human beings. I just think it's such a shame that instead of using your talent on social media for something original, or just something good, you're just churning out and encouraging all the rubbish..."

"Wow."

"No offence..." he adds, smiling.

I don't smile back. "I think it's amazing how you think you know me and what I do."

The key in the lock and Louisa's euphoric greeting abruptly ends the discussion, leaving a tension in the air, which my flat mate is clearly oblivious of.

"Yes! You aren't working! Quick, Jacob, give her a beer before she changes her mind!"

Jacob dumps the bag of beers onto the counter and hurriedly retrieves a bottle for me.

"Here," he says, grinning broadly. "Good to see you've come out of your room to play."

"Would everyone stop acting like I'm a workaholic!"

I'm still recovering from Alex's little speech and my voice comes out a bit hysterical.

"I didn't mean it like that," Jacob says. "It's just nice to see you, that's all."

"Good! Thank you! It's nice to see you too."

"Has she been off her phone all this time?" Louisa says, flashing her eyelashes at Alex.

"No," he says.

"Yes, I have!"

"Sorry, but you were checking it a minute ago!"

He laughs like he hasn't just put me in my place, like he hasn't looked inside my soul and shone a light on the doubts etched there.

"I was checking the time."

"On Twitter?"

That direct message. I didn't even get around to reading it.

"You're such a grass!" I snap. "I bet you were *really* popular at school!"

"Well, I'm a grass, but you know what you are?"

"Guys? You sound like little children!" Louisa cuts in.

"Leave them, they love it," Jacob says.

I ignore them. I'm too busy challenging Alex to say what he thinks I am with my ferocious stare.

160

"You're one of those people who's never quite there, even if you're not checking it, you're thinking about checking it," he says.

How dare he come in here and insult me like this? I take a swig of my beer in an attempt to cool down. It doesn't work. I can't stop myself.

"You know, you're right," I say. "So I'm going to my room to have my beer so I can check my phone to my heart's content and not annoy anyone in the process."

"No, don't go," Alex says, with laughter in his eyes. He thinks I'm joking. "Sorry, I take it back. I overstepped the mark."

"Stay!" Jacob protests. "Alex can go and sit on his own!"

"Yes, I'll go. I'm the rude one!"

"I don't get what's just happened," Louisa murmurs.

"I'm sorry!" Alex says, looking like he means it now. "I'm an outspoken, judgmental bastard! Ban me to your room and you stay and have a nice time!"

There's a choice there and then, between laughing it off and holding on to the feeling of indignation.

I regret my decision almost instantly. Alone on my bed I rest my beer on my stomach and blink away tears. By storming off, I'm only going to make them think they're right about me. That I am all wound up about my job. That I'm taking all the stuff I used to think nonsense more seriously than the celebrities themselves.

You're just tired. The kind inner voice makes me choke. I wipe my nose with the back of my hand, look at the tissues over on my chest of drawers and feel defeated by the distance.

What do they know about me? Or my goals?

What do they know about growing up with parents in a permanent state of anxiety? Louisa's idea of being broke is not being able to eat out three times a week. I just want to save some money. I just want to get to a place where I feel secure. Then I will make steps towards getting a job that makes me feel good inside.

Perhaps that's what I should have told Alex. But why should I have to give him an explanation?

When no one comes to find me I feel so miserable.

Their voices are barely audible so I imagine they must be whispering about me.

I pick up my phone and finally check that direct message. It's from @merlottijoie. The handle is familiar.

MERLOTTI @MERLOTTIJOIE

@bthomskinner you and Baxter seem close! Remember lilies poisonous to cats, though you haven't bought flowers in 20 years! Best to be safe

Oh my God, it's her! Bernard's wife! She's made contact. I feel a rush of adrenalin that sweeps the wretchedness away with the power of an avalanche.

I consider ringing Bernard, but decide against it. I want to prove to the grumpy bastard that I'm far more capable than he thinks. My fingers hover above the keyboard. My heart is beating fast. I'm holding a love story in my hands and I feel responsible for not letting it slip through. In the end it surprises me how easy it is to write back to Joyce.

BTHOMSKINNER @BTHOMSKINNER

@merlottijoie thank you for thinking of us. I'll avoid lilies. I bought some gladioli yesterday. They reminded me of you.

I take a sip of beer and sink back into my life, where there is no love story to get excited about.

I strain to hear Alex's voice in the other room. I wish I could go back, but pride stops me.

There are thousands of people I could be talking to right now under other names, but as myself, it feels like there's no one.

Chapter 16

I'm in a bad mood. The memory of my little strop is the first thing I think of. Louisa had a go at me for being so sensitive. Like I needed to be told. I'm so embarrassed I'm going to have to move flats to avoid bumping into Alex.

After that, I checked my phone to find over 20 scrambled-egg-related replies to Damian, three tweets in Dutch for Thijs, no reply from Bernard's wife and 42 emails. I told myself I should be celebrating the increase in interaction, but all I could think about was how on earth I was going to muster the enthusiasm to reply to everyone.

Now it's all just about to get much worse.

"What sort of quotes?" Angel says, looking up from the questionnaire she received from me as if it were the corpse of a long-perished rodent.

She has needed an explanation for every one of my suggestions so far.

"Motivational quotes, sayings to inspire your followers..." I reach for a pastel- coloured little book from my growing library of self-help. "Let me give you an example... '*Angels fly because they take themselves lightly*'..."

She doesn't react, but that may be because of all the Botox in her forehead. She's plumped her lips up too and painted them with glossy nude lipstick. They look like mini frankfurters coated in grease.

"Oh, I like that one, it's got my name in it... and it's true, ain'it? You've got to believe you can fly."

Do you? Really? Wouldn't it be better to have attainable goals and let the airlines do the flying?

I swallow and turn over the page.

"*Aim for the moon and if you fall, you'll fall among the stars...*"

She nods. "That's sweet."

"*Remember if people talk behind your back, it only means you are two steps ahead...*"

She tries to frown. "Who's talking behind my back?"

"No, it's another quote."

"I don't like it."

"But it's saying, if people are talking about you then you're ahead of them."

"I don't care where I am. If they're talking about me they can fuck well off."

I close the book. In the end I'll quote what I like.

"So, you're interested in fashion?"

I had a meeting with Craig this morning. He didn't seem in a very good mood either. He said I needed to be pushing much harder with everyone's profile. He said he needed some concrete evidence I was really making a difference before he could even contemplate that pay rise he'd promised. It made me feel angry and then flat, and then reckless. Angel is my chance to prove what I can do.

"I want to set up my own brand," she says.

Well it's her lucky day. She may not have studied fashion or even know how to sew on a button, but no one cares about those details any more. As long as she's got Twitter followers and some hot photos on Instagram...

#deepbreaths.

#KeepCalmandCarrytheFuckOn

"That's great. So we need to show that you're interested in fashion first, don't we?" I say. "That you know what's hot and what's not?"

I never did get around to telling Alex how I'd got into this job. How I was an intern for a fashion magazine called *Belle Femme,* working in their online marketing team. How I brought them into the 21st century. Craig was one of their columnists and we got talking at their Christmas party. I'd had a bit too much to drink and was bragging about how many new followers we'd got on Twitter thanks to me. He had asked a few pointed questions about what I'd achieved and I'd slightly exaggerated the answers. A week later he took me out to lunch and laid the plans out for his exciting new project. He said I was exactly who he'd been looking for. I suppose he saw someone young and hardworking, someone who understood the business, and would be grateful for more than a sandwich and train fare as payment. *What's Hot and What's Not* was a regular blog post that I set up for the magazine. That's why I'm thinking about it now.

"I've always been into fashion," Angel says. She holds up her wrist for me to take a look at her gaudy watch. "What do you think?"

"It's beautiful," I say, to humour her.

She squeals in delight. "Got you! It's a fake!" and then she looks sulky. "I'm going to get the real one, though. This one makes me feel cheap."

I think of Ola then and her HappyHeart brand I forgot to look up. Her beautiful orange-and-black dress had been a real stunner.

"What about ethical brands? Do you think that could be something you could be interested in?"

"You mean like African?"

"I mean, responsibly made."

I can see I've lost her. But I'm not worried. I'm suddenly aware of the freedom I have, and the power. I can make something of Angel Butler.

"Do you like animals?"

"Not in the house."

"But you think rabbits are cute."

She lets out a giggle, "I like Easter bunnies if they're chocolate."

I persevere. "You wouldn't want to wear one around your neck, right?"

Despite the Botox she manages a convincing look of disgust.

#Sorted. She can be a voice of support for ethical fashion, a campaigner for animal rights, a down-to-earth but motivational speaker inspiring young women to aim higher.

"Mink, though," she says. "As soon as I make some money I'm getting a pink one like Paris had. Well, she just had a bolero, I want the whole thing."

I smile at her, my head buzzing with my own thoughts. In a minute she'll sign the contract and what she thinks she wants will pale into significance. I'm not the kind of person who just tweets fluffy news for celebs and I'm not going to be looked down at by people like Alex Hunter.

Chapter 17

It's my old university friend, Jo Morris's, birthday and I've made it to the party only an hour late. It's been ages since I last saw her, but that's not my fault. Her Facebook activity suggests she's spent the last two years on holiday. I squeeze through the crowds to get to her so I can show my face. She screams and hugs me and I feel one of her diamante studs pull a thread in my cardigan. I offer to buy her drink, but a girl wearing a tiara has just arrived at her side with two cocktails. So that's why the Facebook event was entitled *Sparkles*. I'm obviously supposed to be wearing some.

"You can get me the next one!" she says, and I'm relieved because the queue at the bar looks like the rush-hour train I just jumped out of.

I spot Emma and Clare perched on some bar stools, deep in conversation. I feel a small glimmer of triumph because I'm there and they didn't think I'd make it.

"Hello, ladies!"

Their smiles are delayed. I sense I've interrupted a serious conversation.

"I was just telling Clare the latest on this bloody hen party," Emma groans.

"Ah, yes, you were all going to Scotland, right? To a cabin."

We spent a good chunk of time on this hen party last time we met. I feel like I know the non-confrontational bride, and Maya the bossy *money-isn't-an-issue* best friend, and the *best-things-in-life-are-free* hippy cousin, even though I've never met any of them in my life.

"Not any more. Scotland isn't hot enough," Clare fills me in.

"And they've only just worked that out?"

She giggles into her glass. Her cheeks are pink. They must be on their second glass already.

"It's not funny," Emma says. "Now we all have to fork out for a week in Mallorca!"

"A week?" I cry. "For a hen do?"

"Yes, because Helen *deserves it.*"

She's mimicking Maya now, with her American twang.

"What does everyone else say?"

"To her face, they're saying how wonderful, behind her back they're fuming because it's going to cost a fortune."

"That's stupid," I say. "They should just tell her."

My phone vibrates in my pocket. I'm hoping it's another fashion blogger following Angel on Twitter. I've done a brilliant job of attracting the right kind of followers for her today and I'm feeling good about myself.

Emma downs the dregs of her wine. "That's not all... but I need another drink first."

"I'll get us a bottle," I say.

"Thanks, May," Emma says. "I'm so glad you made it."

I'm going to get the wine via the toilet. I just need a space to check some of these notifications. It's a big evening for my clients and I need to be on the ball to retweet any news about them. Bernard is doing a reading in Oxford, DJ Buzzya is playing at a special night in Fabric, Damian is making an appearance on a TV programme about the birth of reality TV and the other two, well, they just need to show the world they are at the centre of what's happening.

"Finally!" Emma cries, when I get back. "I was just about to send a search party."

"The people in front of me ordered about ten mojitos!"

Okay, two gin and tonics, but I have been behind a mass order of mojitos before and it wasn't fun. My phone is buzzing in my pocket with all the responses from the tweets I sent off in the loo. I control the urge to reply to them all and focus on my friends.

"So what did I miss?"

The wine is delicious and I'm feeling positive. I can make this work. I can be good at my job and have a social life. Maybe even a love life. I scan the bar for cute faces.

"Clare moving house," Emma says, sounding a touch grumpy.

"Oh, yeah, where to again?"

"Battersea."

"One-bedroom, right?"

Clare gives me a tense smile. "Yeah, but we've been talking about it for ages... before you got here and on the phone... I'm bored of my own move now!"

I feel a little offended, but I push the feeling away.

"Okay," I say brightly. "So did you sort out the hen party?"

Emma sighs. "What do you think is a reasonable amount to spend on one?"

"I'd want afternoon tea at the Ritz," Clare says looking dreamy. "It would be so pretty."

"Maya wanted to do that too. A pre-Mallorca treat, would you believe," Emma says. "Fifty pounds each for a few sandwiches and cakes."

"Get her to treat you all if she has so much money," I say. "I'd just want to chill out with my friends... on a beach..." I laugh. "What's the problem with Mallorca again?"

"It's different if you're all real friends, but this is the most random hen party. No one knows each other that well."

My phone is going berserk. I feel like a big fish might have retweeted something I've posted. Perhaps a big celebrity. That would be great. I make an excuse about drinking too much coffee and having a weak bladder and head to the ladies. Jo is just coming out, her cheeks flushed and her lips freshly painted bright pink. She grips my arm.

"It's been so long, it's so good to see you," she gushes, her breath sticky-sweet from whatever she's just drunk. "We have to catch up more!"

"Yeah, definitely," I say.

"Next week?'"

"I'll check my diary."

There is no space in the diary, but I've learnt from past reactions that it's better to sound open and optimistic than to say you're too busy. Maybe life offline isn't so different from life online. Maybe it's all make-believe too. I just need to decide what my story is.

Emma has turned up behind me, "I need the loo too," she says. "I broke the seal!"

I can't stand around tweeting now so I go inside a cubicle and take my phone out. Away from the noise of the bar, my phone vibrations sound like minor earthquakes. I hurriedly go to settings to turn it to mute.

"Are you tweeting from the loo?" Emma cries.

"You better not be!" a stranger calls. "We're waiting out here!"

Oh, for God's sake. It was empty a second ago and now a really important blogger has just asked Angel a question. I can't let hours pass before I reply. I flush pointlessly and unlock the door.

"No, I'm not tweeting in the loo," I announce to the strangers waiting.

The next place I try tweeting is behind a coat stand. It's in a corner and has more umbrellas on it than coats, so I'm not as concealed as I'd like. I type as quickly as I can, feeling a little rush as I send off each response. I'm getting better at my different voices, more confident, and it's not just the wine.

A flash of turquoise in my periphery vision makes me look up. Emma is heading towards the bar. She'll be getting tap water. She always does that. Red wine makes her sleepy if she doesn't hydrate. That'll give me a few minutes; there seems to be only one barman on at the moment.

Head down, I scroll through my notifications. DJ Buzzya seems to be dividing the crowds, with some people saying they'll be back when the DJ changes. As for Bernard, his audience are evidently not of the Twitter generation because there's not one tweet about his reading.

One more tweet and I'll head back over. Everything is going great. I'm on top of things for a change. I can be offline for a bit now and review all the interactions on the way home. I'll get the bus instead of the Tube, it takes longer, but at least I'll have reception.

Emma is already back at her seat when I return. They're both looking at me strangely and I sense a change in the atmosphere.

"Have you finished?" she says.

"What?"

"Or do you want to take your wine over to your work corner?"

Heat prickles at my neck. I feel embarrassed for being spotted, but I'm annoyed too.

"I was just texting my mum!"

"Why couldn't you text her here?" Emma says.

"What does it matter? It was a quiet spot."

"You were hiding behind a coat stand!"

Clare is looking so uncomfortable. She hates our spats. Emma and I have always been able to speak our mind because we've always known our friendship is strong enough to take it.

"I wasn't hiding!"

Emma looks at me, wanting to believe me. "So you were really just texting your mum?"

It's the hesitation. I guess it shows a shred of honesty. But I still say yes and she knows it's a lie.

"My sister is coming over from Brazil," I explain. "She was telling me the dates."

"Okay," Emma says. She sips her wine. "What are they?"

"What are what?"

"The dates!" Clare cries.

I feel backed into a corner. If they weren't always nagging me, I wouldn't be worried about answering my phone! I wouldn't have to lie to them and cover up for what is a completely acceptable situation of needing to be on standby for my clients. I'm not the one with the problem, it's *them*.

"Wow," I say. "All I did was reply to some text messages and now I feel like I'm getting told off. Shall I just go?"

"Don't be stupid," Emma says. "Just don't keep disappearing to tweet!"

Last time I went off in a strop, I found myself all alone and regretting it.

"You always used to take the piss out of those people," Clare says gently.

"Yeah, what happened to Sparky May?" Emma says. "My twitter feed is boring without her."

I roll my eyes at her, but the anger has subsided, and now I just feel flat.

"I don't know. I just can't seem to think of anything to say as Sparky May."

"Because you don't have the headspace. You really need to set some boundaries. We know what Craig is like. You've told us he's obsessive, but don't let him drag you along with him."

I've never been good at saying no to bosses. I like to please people. Even horrible people like Bernard Thompson-Skinner. Maybe I need therapy. Who doesn't need therapy?

"Alright..." I say. "I'll sort out my work-life balance. I really will. It's just so hard because social media doesn't fit between nine and five."

"You have two phones don't you?" Emma says. "Turn the work one off when you get home. Simples."

"Yeah, I guess so."

It's not *Simples*. The Platinum package states we will take over our clients' social media 24/7.

Clare fills up my glass. "Here."

"Yes, a toast," Emma says, raising hers. "To life *offline*!"

"I wish..." I say.

"Say it!" she says.

"To life offline."

It won't be a life offline for very long and I know it. As soon as I'm on the bus, my phone will be coming out. I won't be able to resist.

For a minute, I'd thought I was a multi-tasking genius. I got that wrong. I've just proved to my friends I'm not only a workaholic and a phone addict, I'm now also a compulsive liar.

Chapter 18

Google Search:

How to turn an ordinary boy into a style icon

If Google was a real man, he'd be on a lot of antidepressants.

Abigail pops her head around the door, looking worried.

"Hi, I've got Mr..."

But if she knows his surname she doesn't have time to say it before Damian steps around her into my office wearing a big smile that sends a bolt of panic and excitement down my spine. I get to my feet, my hands hurriedly pushing my loose hair up into the clip that has been clawing at my scalp.

"I thought I'd surprise you!"

My heart is racing. Abigail is hovering at the door, her eyes peeled on me while she waits for instructions. Has she worked out who he is yet? Will she tell her friends about this?

"Thanks, Abigail."

She closes the door behind her, leaving me and Damian alone. His smile widens. His eyes are sparkling and his cheeks are flushed, like he's excited about something.

Me?

#getoveryourself.

"I wasn't expecting you. Is everything alright?"

"I know, I'm sorry. I'm just feeling so high right now."

A cold bucket of dread washes over me.

"High on life!" he adds.

My stomach shifts back into place. Thank God.

"You can tweet that if you like. I've been at the recording studio."

He flops onto the seat in front of me. I sit down at mine. In all the time I've worked here I've never had an impromptu meeting with a client. I hate the feeling of being unprepared. What is my hair doing right now?

I open his account, wanting to impress him with my efficiency.

DAMIANDANCE @DAMIANDANCE
Feeling high on life after the session in the recording studio!

"Done. Anything else I can do while you're here?"

His playful green eyes are searching mine so intently I'm starting to feel really self-conscious. It doesn't help that he looks so handsome in that khaki-green t-shirt that fits snugly over his toned chest. He's ditched the rosary and the trucker hat, and he looks like a man, not an overgrown boy from a pop group.

"May, what are you doing to me?"

My heart does a little lurch.

"You're so smart... You can see through all the bullshit..."

My voice comes out a little breathless. "I'm just doing my job."

"I know you are," he says, his teeth tugging at his bottom lip as he looks away. "You're so in control."

It's clear to me that I'm not as in control as I'd like. That the professionalism in this room is fading fast. The atmosphere is completely charged and I have no idea how to diffuse it, or even know if I want to.

"I can't stand it," he says abruptly. Then he gets to his feet, comes around my desk, rests his hand on it and leans down over me.

It's the sexiest thing to have happened to me in months. I don't want to stop him. But I know I've got to. I'm aware of the beep of notifications as he leans forward and kisses me. My lips submit without the barest struggle. We're going to do it right here, right now. A shiver of sexual desire ripples through me. This is what I need, to lose myself completely in this ridiculously hot moment. I've never broken the rules at work. Never. Ever. But I'm going to. This is it.

The tentative knock on the door makes me cry out.

"Go over there!" I hiss, waving at the chair in front of my desk.

Damian laughs and without any sense of urgency moves back to his place, but not before the door opens.

What does Gabe see? Me standing behind my desk, with pink cheeks and wild eyes, looking like I've been caught nicking from petty cash. And Damian. Not sitting down, but standing too near to me, his eyes twinkling with mischief. I feel so mortified I can't get my words out. It doesn't escape my attention that Gabe has forgotten whatever he was going to say too. He's just staring at me, his brow twitching, like he wants me to confirm his suspicions telepathically.

"We were just doing some role play," I stammer.

Damian bursts out laughing.

"For social media!" I say, hurriedly.

"I've never heard of social media role play," Gabe says, deadpan. "How does it work?"

"It's a bit like that word association game, lots of back and forth... but standing up."

#StopTalking

Damian is having a silent giggling fit and my cheeks are burning. "Right."

"I'll tell you about it later, it's really quite productive." I nod at Damian, who has twisted in his seat to get a good look at my colleague. "I'm a bit busy now. Did you want something?"

"I'm sorry, I didn't realise you were busy," Gabe says, his voice laden with sarcasm, "it's not urgent. We can speak later."

He lets the door go and it closes slowly as he retreats back to his office.

"Shit."

That was horrible. Gabe and I have always felt mutual respect for each other. What's he going to think of me now? What if he mentions something to Craig?

Damian is smiling. He gets up off his chair and starts to come over. I hold up my hand to stop him.

"Are you alright?"

"No."

I don't want him coming any further forward. What just happened was completely unprofessional. What's more, this stupid hair clip is making my head itch. In a wave of frustration I unclip the blasted thing and throw it across my desk.

"I'm sorry, it's just got these vicious claws. I think they've over-filed it or something."

"Don't be sorry. You look gorgeous with your hair down."

"I feel more professional with it up, although it clearly doesn't make me more professional!"

"You should get a lock on your door."

I raise an eyebrow and he laughs.

"What?" he shrugs. "Look at you... you're so sexy..."

"Shsss, stop it please. Do you want me to lose my job?"

"No, I need you."

"You should go."

He presses a hand against his chest and feigns pain, "Will I see you later?"

I daydreamed about this, about having a little fling with my famous client, whizzing off to top restaurants, getting VIP treatment. But it was just a dream. It's unacceptable as a reality. He's Damian Dance, for God's sake.

He throws me a bewildered smile, "I'm not asking you to marry me, May, just to go for a drink."

New notifications buzz in. It's like my computer reminding me of my duty.

"I don't think it's a good idea," I say, hating myself even as I say it. Have I always been this responsible? But I've got my future to think about, the one where I reap the rewards for working around the clock.

"Alright..." he says, getting to his feet.

He looks disappointed. The feeling is mutual. I don't want to be alone any more and I have this awful sensation that I'll be alone forever if I let him out of the door. It's like one of those irrational mind games where you have to step between the lines of a pavement or buy an even number of tomatoes.

But I just can't.

"I'll call you, then," he says, "or Andy will."

I don't want to be called by his agent. I want him to call me, and not to talk about work either. His hand is on the door handle. I still have time to say yes to that drink. It's like he knows it too the way he walks so slowly out of that door.

Then he's gone and I'm alone, and it's like that crazy scene didn't just happen, that my fantasy didn't just manifest in my office, and I didn't just wake up at the wrong moment and blink it away.

The wretchedness tugs at my gut. I turn to my computer. The internet doesn't stop for personal dramas. It feels weird clicking open Damian's twitter account but not as weird as it might have if I'd run off with him. I breathe out. I did the right thing.

I scan down the replies to Damian's tweet, favouriting the positive answers and then I spot this one.

TINTINO @TINTINO
Aw. 'Life'. That's a cute little euphemism. RT @DamianDance feeling high on life after the session in the recording studio!

The comment stops me in my tracks.

The truth is he had seemed a little altered.

I push the thought away. Just because this cynical loser never feels high on life, doesn't mean other people can't.

Who is he to make snide little remarks anyway? Has he ever

178

even met Damian?

I check out Tintino's profile. His biog runs *I like stuff, you like stuff. Let's do this.* His profile picture is of a cartoon Ninja. It doesn't tell me much. He has 6,003 followers, not bad considering he's only following 224. He hasn't got a blue tick but he's got klout, that's for sure. I'm not going to block him. I'm not going to reply to him either, because I think he would love a reply. He's a shit stirrer. He probably loves arguing on Twitter. I hate it as much as I hate arguing off Twitter. I don't know why people dedicate so much time to it. I guess the joke's on me, because I'm getting worked up just imagining the arguments.

A tweet about the maltreatment of rabbits in the manufacture of angora comes up in a search I've been doing for Angel Butler and I pluck it out for a RT, adding a sad face and a *Say no to angora girls!!* There, now if that raises just one person's awareness of the cruel practice that's good work.

The retweets are good, but they don't make me feel significantly better. I pick up my phone and scroll down my contacts, until I reach Damian. I stare at it until the office phone makes me jump.

"Bernard Thompson Skinner for you."

"Thanks, Abi."

I clear my throat. "Hello, May Sparks."

"Has my wife replied?"

"No, but I think the fact she contacted you must mean something, though."

She must be out of her mind if she misses him.

"It was only because she thought I'd kill Baxter."

It's a strong possibility.

"Perhaps you should write something else. Can you send her a picture of some gladioli perhaps?" he says.

"Okay. Any particular colour?"

"You decide. You're the woman. Just let me know if she replies."

As soon as I replace the handset, my mobile starts ringing. It's Maria Kuebler. I wince, realising I'd been about to tweet for my youngest client when Damian came in. I'm really going to have to step up my game if I'm going to justify a pay rise.

The next time I look at the clock, it's gone half past nine. I'll have to tell Louisa I went out for a drink with a friend. Three nights in a row, she'll be really impressed with me. Shame it won't be the truth.

I realise with a sinking feeling that Gabe didn't even bother to say goodbye. I'd almost convinced myself that we hadn't looked that suspicious after all, but now I know for sure we had. The stupid thing is we didn't even do anything. Not really. If Gabe's going to be all judgmental it should have been for something more than a peck on the lips. We may as well have had wild sex across my desk. I feel a twinge between my legs and cross them. Thinking about it now, I wish we had.

Chapter 19

It's six o'clock in the morning and I'm wide awake. My body feels hyper-alert. It feels like fear. Intense fear. I try to calm myself down by breathing deeply. After a moment, I push myself up and reach over the side of my bed to grab my tablet, which I dropped to the floor moments before drifting off.

There's nothing unexpected posted across the networks of my Platinum customers. Why would there be? I only had that one glass of wine last night. Louisa wasn't home and I drank it standing by the kitchen window looking out into the darkness, thinking about what had happened with Damian. I felt a mixture of regret and longing. I simultaneously wished it had never happened and at the same time, found myself hoping he would try to kiss me again.

I push away the memory and continue to scroll through all the likes and retweets and banal comments. I have come to depend on these interactions to prove how good I am. Resentment bubbles up my throat. It's assumed that while I'm awake so are my clients. But it wouldn't even be realistic to tweet now. Everyone will either be asleep or getting back from a late night out.

I sit at the edge of my bed and look over at my battered grey trainers poking out from under my chest of drawers. In another life, before I made the adventurous move to Craig's startup, I used to run. It was *my* time, where I could explore the city at my pace, listening to my music. It used to feel so good. I used to feel fit and healthy. I want that feeling back. I need to reclaim some time for me.

Ten minutes later I'm closing the front door quietly behind me. I've got my Lycra leggings on and fluorescent orange running tee. My phone is strapped to my arm, for music mainly, but also just in case...

Outside I'm met by a beautiful blue sky and my heart soars because for once I'm savouring the sunshine. I set off at an ambitious pace, thinking to myself that I should have done this months ago. The tug at my ribs makes me slow down two roads later to a pace more suited to Johnny Cash.

Everyone should be doing this, getting outside, doing some exercise. This is life. THIS. IS. LIFE. Not all that stuff on our screens. That's just a poor translation. I can smell freshly cut grass and tar and possibly dog shit. I can hear the faint sounds of jazz coming out of someone's window and the screech of a bus breaking and someone swearing at the top of their voice. My skin is tingling at the touch of the fresh breeze and my feet are connecting with these paving stones that might have well been here before I was born.

I glance down at my feet and I can't help visualising a neat, square Instagram photo. Grey Trainers with a dash of a brightest blue against a sunlit pavement, perhaps with an X-PRO II filter. Oh fuck, just one little photo.

I stop and take my phone out. Angel Butler, this is going to be the new you!

As I'm focusing the camera, it occurs to me that she would have trendier, newer trainers than these ancient Decathlons. But isn't that another thing worth advocating? The new Angel Butler doesn't need diamond-studded designer trainers to do exercise. She's the girl next door. Everyone can be like her. Nobody will be accusing Angel Butler of influencing young girls to max out their credit cards to keep up with the celebrity lifestyle. People are going to commend her for going against the stereotype. She'll advocate #fashionwithaheart, a lifestyle which won't break the bank. She'll encourage young women to be more conscientious of their environment, of their influence on the world around them.

In fact I could really grow to like Angel Butler.

ANGELBUTLERXF @ANGELBUTLER
You don't need new shoes to go for a run! Get up and go girls! #recycle #fitness #instahealth #feelinggood #practicalgirl

Stopping like that has cut into my running time. It's also drained me of some of the good energy I was feeling. I won't stop again. This is *my* time.

I turn the music up and increase my pace. Ahead of me is a small gated park where an old lady in a pink fleece is waiting for a little white dog to finish sniffing a bush and do his business. I breathe in the smell of soil and pine as I run along the small pathway. Nature is a healer. I could a hug a tree right now. That one up ahead.

What a tree. It looks so old, like an Ent out of *Lord of the Rings*. I bet it's seen some history. I think of Bernard and slow down. I know he likes trees because there were three whole pages of description in *Backstage* dedicated to an old oak tree in his grandmother's garden.

I take a shot of the tree, lopping half of it off. The light isn't right so I run over to the other side and try it from a new angle. An argument rattles on in my head between the two sides; the one that thinks I should have taken pleasure from seeing the tree but carried on running, and the one who reasons that by photographing it I'm taking the time to notice my surroundings.

It's while I'm taking the photo that I become aware of a runner approaching out of the corner of my eye. I look up to see how far away he is, because I don't fancy being caught distracted by a "pretty tree" mid-run, which is what it's going to look like. My eyes focus and I feel a jolt of alarm when I recognise Alex. He's on the path, running in my direction. And he's running fast.

My heart is clamouring in my chest as I hide behind the tree, pressing my back against the bark. The last thing I want to do this morning is talk to Alex. Especially looking as though I've just rolled out of bed.

I turn my music off and hold my breath as I listen out for his feet pounding a rhythm along the path. That brief glimpse gave me enough evidence that he's a seasoned runner. For a start, he's wearing a FINISHER t-shirt, which means he's completed at least one marathon. I also couldn't help noticing the blue short shorts, the long brown legs, the strong, upright running style, and the focus of his look.

Did he run when he had the beard too? Wouldn't it have been too hot and sweaty? The good thing is he's wearing earphones, which means he won't be able to hear me, which also means I could probably breathe normally now.

I peer out from behind the tree just in time to see him disappearing around the corner. It's ridiculous, but I feel a bit disappointed. It wouldn't have been such a bad thing for Alex to see me outside in the fresh air, doing something other than checking my phone. It would have shown him that I've got a life.

I decide I've done enough running for one morning. He can see me run another time, when I've brushed my hair. I switch from Johnny Cash to Daft Punk and run as fast as I can to the gate. A stitch forces me to slow down, and then to walk. I rub at my side, but the pain doesn't go. I half-walk, half-jog the rest of the way home.

Outside the front door I notice the mud on my shoes and bend down to untie my laces. My phone is bleeping with notifications and that feeling of stress has come back to torture my insides. It's my fault for tweeting too early. This could have been my time, but I made it my clients'. I hover outside the door with my shoes off, and check the responses.

GABRIELLASTORMLEY @SPORTYGABS
@angelbutler Knackered trainers aren't good for your ankles!
Be careful out there!

Oh piss off.

MAMAGIRL @MAMAGIRRL1
@angelbutler I'm impressed you got up. I'm still in bed burping
up that kebab! LOL!!!

Shit. Obviously they were out together. It's a good job Angel didn't
crash on her sofa last night. It reminds me just how easy it would
for people to find out that it's not my clients tweeting.

I scroll down to find the picture of the tree and upload it to
Bernard's account.

BTHOMSKINNER @BTHOMSKINNER
I wonder what this tree would say if it could talk?

Downstairs there's a bang of a door closing. It must be the neighbours leaving for work. I read over the tweet before pressing send.
It's not a magnificent tweet, but I've got a whole day to write
something better.

"Hey good morning!"

I look up in alarm. Alex has appeared on the landing, his face
red, his chest still heaving from what must have been a grand
finale sprint. I didn't hear him come up. He gives me a big smile,
which I'm not sure how to react to. The last time we saw each
other I retreated to my room in a hump.

"Good morning," I say.

"I didn't know you ran."

"I don't. It's the first time in ages."

"Nice t-shirt."

I glance doubtfully at my fluorescent top. "Thanks, it's about five years old."

"Well, it still works..." He's pushes a hand through his hair, seems to be considering something, "Look, I'm sorry about the other day."

I wasn't expecting an apology. "I'm sorry too, I overreacted."

"No, I was rude… I mean, we hardly know each other."

I let out a little laugh, "So it's okay to be rude if you know the person?"

"It's okay to be *honest…*" he says, suppressing a smile.

"Look, I have issues with my job too..."

I'm about to launch into an explanation, but he cuts me off.

"It's none of my business, May."

No it's not, but his conclusion feels unsatisfactory. He's basically telling me he doesn't care.

"It's just something I need to do now..." I say.

He nods at my hands, which are gripping my phone as if it were trying to escape. "You run with your phone?"

I feel frustrated that he's caught me with it. "It's just for music."

"Oh yeah of course... is it heavy?" he shows me his shuffle mini clipped to the top of his shorts. I get a glimpse of his toned stomach. "This is a bit lighter."

"I don't really notice the weight."

He nods. "Well, I suppose I better get going."

My phone buzzes with a new notification.

He lets out a little laugh. "That's the other bonus of a shuffle, it leaves you in peace."

I wish you'd leave me in peace, I think half-heartedly.

"I meant to put it on aeroplane mode," I lie.

"That's a good idea."

He hovers there a moment longer and I find myself searching manically for something witty to say.

"Well, see you later, then," he says. "Hope you have a productive day!"

Was that a last little poke at my job?

"Thanks. Good luck with whatever advert you're filming today."

"Thanks! It's a freebie for Save the Children. Should be good."

It *was* a poke! How I wish I'd just gone straight inside and not hovered on the landing sending those pointless bloody tweets.

Alex starts up the second flight of stairs, taking two at a time. The gorgeous scent of his aftershave lingers in the air. He must have been using it so long, it's become his natural smell. I bend down to pick up my shoes and turn to the door.

"Oh, May," he calls, coming back down a couple of steps. "Did Louisa tell you she got the part?"

That explains why she was out so late. Louisa believes in celebrating small steps. I prefer to commemorate big steps. The downside is big steps take longer to come around.

"I didn't see her last night."

"Oh, did she stay out?" he says, and then adds quickly. "Not that it's any of my business."

He's embarrassed. His red cheeks are from the run, but they'd probably be red at this point anyway. It's obvious he fancies Louisa.

"No, she didn't stay out, I heard her come in."

"Cool... I hope she didn't wake you."

"That's how I knew she came in."

He slaps his head and does a Homer Simpson, "D'oh."

I grin, "Go have some coffee."

"Yep, I obviously need it."

"Have a good day."

"Thanks May, you too!"

He hurries back up the stairs and I turn to the door, a frown battling with my smile. There's something about him that makes me feel compelled to engage. I'm trying to pinpoint what it is about him, when I read the tweet.

JOEHIGGS @JOEHIGGS101

@bthomskinner Stop photographing me you perv...

The shock knocks the breath out of me and I stare at the screen with my mouth open, my head uncomprehending. And then sense creeps in and I hurriedly scroll up to see what the tweet is in answer to.

BTHOMSKINNER @BTHOMSKINNER
I wonder what this tree would say if it could talk?

I press my hand against my chest and breathe out with relief. I've got to get a grip. I've got to calm down or I'll burn myself out. At least Miss Inky Toes doesn't sound so naughty this morning.

MISSINKYTOES @MISSINKYTOES
Don't get so distracted by talking trees and forget your reading!
We're looking forward to having you in Winchester next week!

She's said "we" rather than "I". If she'd written "I'm looking forward to having you" then I'd be worried. More worried that I already am. The sooner the Winchester gig is over, the better. There's a lot at stake. Joyce could be watching his interactions closely, looking for affirmations she did the right think leaving Bernard.

I rub my aching eyes and head for the bathroom. I know I shouldn't be popping Ibuprofens like Vitamin C, but I can feel a headache coming on again.

As the water warms up in the shower, I work on my responses. I have to answer these strangers. Not later, but now. Twitter requires immediacy. A few minutes later steam fills the bathroom, the water pumps hot, and still I'm working on them. I just don't know what to say about a talking tree. I'm aware it's a ridiculous predicament, but it's a predicament that paralyses me on the spot.

Chapter 20

The secret of getting ahead is getting started.

You don't have to be great to start, but you have to start to be great.

Stop wishing. Start doing.

As much as I hate being quoted at all day, some of them do make a lot of sense. Today I'm focusing on Angel promoting HappyHeart.

ANGELBUTLERXF @ANGELBUTLER
I've fallen in LOVE with new ethical designer @HappyHeart! Do you think the pink maxi will suit me? #loveit #fashion-withaheart

I've researched the company and I'm in love with their style and their values. Their clothes are bold and bright, their accessories eclectic and enticing. The website has interviews and pictures of the artisans, who are based in Kenya and South Africa. I felt a burst of joy when I saw the picture of Ola. She has no idea about the publicity I'm going to throw her way.

I just need to get some pictures of Angel wearing some of these clothes. If only I could get some free samples. Or someone else to model for them. No, of course I can't do that. I click onto my own Facebook account and scroll through a list of my friends, hoping to find Angel's identical twin among them. I end up scrolling through my newsfeed instead.

"Shit," I cry, when I see what time it is. A whole hour has slipped by while I've been nosing about on my own Facebook account.

Feeling panicky I turn to my to-do list.

THIJS - makeover?

I've been toying with the idea of asking Thijs to do a photoshoot and fire off an email to Craig asking his opinion. If Thijs wants to be a style icon then he needs to get some pictures of him looking like one. We need a whole new wardrobe, but I'm not sure how that's going to happen. A moment later the phone starts ringing.

"May, it's me."

Craig sounds out of breath. From the whir in the background I'm guessing it's because he's at the gym on a treadmill. Clearly neither of us are very good at turning off our phones when we run.

"I just saw your mail."

"That was quick."

"Go ahead, book the shoot."

It's very easy to say "go ahead" but what do I know about booking shoots?

"Don't I need to ask Thijs first? He's the one who'll be paying for it, right? In fact, maybe Maria will want to organise it..."

"You can do this, May. This is the bit extra we promise our Platinum customers. We've got to show them our worth. Just sort it out and give them the date to come in. They can use our conference room for it."

"What about his wardrobe? He'll need to get a stylist and probably a makeup person and what about a photographer?"

I hear the whining tone in my voice and trail off.

"Where's your *can-do* attitude today, May?"

I feel irritated, both at the question and at myself for involving him at all. I should have just gone ahead and done it, then he would've seen that my *can-do* attitude is perfectly intact.

"Alright, I'll sort it," I say.

"Get Abigail to help you shop."

I swallow back the swell of doubt. "Fine."

"Any other problems?"

"No, everything's under control."

"Good. I'll be in later."

I replace the receiver and stare ahead at the wall, grinding my teeth.

Action will remove the doubt that theory cannot solve.

I call Maria and tell her the plan. She's thrilled. I ask her for Thijs's measurements and let her imagine we're getting in a stylist and clothes made to measure. In reality I'm going to buy them off the high street, get Thijs to mix and match them for the shoot and then I'm going to return them all. Oh, what fun this is going to be. I hate shopping for myself, let alone for someone else. What I'm not going to do is go out into the wilds of Oxford Street hoping for the best. I need to know what I'm looking for. What should an 18-year-old in a boy band look like?

I think of Damian in his torn jeans and expensive designer t-shirts. He makes his backpacker chic look work because he's got the hair and the physique. I've noticed his strong upper arms and the muscles outlined beneath his t-shirt. He's got the healthy golden tan that blondes get too. Thijs is as white as a bap and as doughy. I also can't imagine him approving of shredded jeans. I think he needs a more classic look.

Alex Hunter comes to mind. I have to admit he does have a certain style that Thijs might appreciate. He's got that smart-casual thing going on, with the quality leather shoes and the shirts and cardigans. But maybe Alex pulls it off because he's also got a manly face; the chiselled cheekbones and strong angular nose, the two-day stubble and the dimpled chin. The glasses give him that sophisticated edge.

Could I get Thijs to try on a pair of glasses?

I dismiss the thought with a shudder.

SPARKYMAY @SPARKYMAY

Have you got 20/20 vision? Are you wearing glasses just because they're fashionable? Would you like a fashion hearing aid to match? #Idiots

I let the problem of Thijs style stew for a moment and turn back to my tablet. I'm pleased to see HappyHeart has retweeted Angel's tweet and responded. If Craig is happy to spend hundreds of pounds on a photoshoot for Thijs, surely he won't mind me spending £60 on a dress for Angel.

ANGELBUTLERXF @ANGELBUTLER

Just bought the pink maxi @HappyHeart! Photo soon! #fashionwithaheart #summerstyle

HappyHeart favourites and retweets it. Angel might just be their first "celeb" customer. I bet they can't believe their luck. I smile as her followers start engaging with her tweet, giving their opinion on the dress. It's quite amazing how interested people can be and I get caught up replying to her followers for quite some time. I'm careful not to preach at them. I know Angel's followers are going to need some convincing about a label they don't recognise. They're the type of people who, if they've got the cash, want to splash it on logo-splattered designer bags, the ethics behind their fashion choices being the least of their concerns.

After I've engaged for long enough on Angel's account, I spend an hour trawling through pages of handsome men staring moodily into the camera. It occurs to me that a younger woman might have a different view of what is attractive in an 18-year-old man. I get up and head out to reception.

Abigail quickly hides her mobile under her desk, like I care if she's checking her text messages.

"How do you feel about going shopping for Thijs?"

She shoots me an uncertain smile. "What do you mean?"

"We need to get him some outfits for a photo shoot. I need your help deciding what an 18-year-old boy-band member should wear. He can't be the same as the others, obviously, he needs his own style."

"Isn't he coming?"

"No."

She's confused.

"He's not very interested in clothes," I explain, "but he needs to sort out his image."

"It's going to be quite hard to buy clothes for him without him being there, isn't it?"

I smile wryly, "Come on, Abigail, where's your *can-do* attitude?"

It doesn't come out as playfully as I meant and she nods her head, looking all serious.

"I used to help my brother shop," she says, "I'm sure it can't be that hard."

"Excellent. I don't have a brother, so you can be in charge."

She smiles tentatively, "Alright, then. I think I know what will suit him."

I raise my eyebrows. "Oh yeah?"

"Maybe," she says dismissively, and turns to get her handbag, but not before I notice the spots of pink appear at her cheeks. It looks like I'm not the only one with a crush on a client.

Chapter 21

I'm on the phone in the middle of Zara Menswear getting an earful from Bernard. He's arrived at Winchester too early, so he's decided to use the spare time to have a moan about me. His main issue is with his wife, who I have failed to win back. Then there's my productivity rate. He's counted my tweets and he doesn't think the pay is justified. He's not bowled away by his 200 new followers, even though they are all genuine. I could point out that I could easily buy him a few thousand, but that fake followers don't buy books.

Nearby Abigail is fingering a tailored leather jacket in dark chocolate. I blank out Bernard's rant as I try to imagine what Thijs would look like in it. We started too cautiously, deliberating for ages over every item.

"Are you even listening?" Bernard barks.

"My original brief was to promote your book," I say, trying not to raise my voice, "and I've been doing that successfully so far. This other mission…" is one I should never have agreed to, "…is more delicate and will take a bit more time."

"I don't have *a bit more time*! I've got to write my World War Two novel and I can't write if I'm not in France!"

Then sell your London flat and move there, I think irritably, and talk to your wife face to face like a normal person!

There's a gentle tap on my back and I move aside, thinking it's someone trying to get past me. But the person just hovers there and when I glance up it's to see Alex Hunter looking down at me with a quizzical grin. My eyes widen in surprise and I hold up a finger to indicate I'll be one minute. I bet if I'd bumped into anyone else I would not have been on the phone. He shakes his head dismissively, to say not to worry about him. Abigail comes back holding the leather jacket. I want to wrap up this phone call as quickly as I can.

"Isn't there anyone else in France you can stay with?"

"Are you mad? I can't write in someone else's house! I need to be in my own space, my own zone..."

Who did he vent to before he had me? His wife, I suppose. She'd be a mad woman to go back to him. But then, how can I be sure she's so wonderful herself? Perhaps they deserve each other.

I'm aware of Alex and Abigail talking behind my back and feel a sudden panic that Abigail is going to tell him who we're shopping for.

"Look, I've got to go, I'll come up with a plan tonight. I really am doing my best."

I breathe out and drop my phone back in my handbag. My smile is tense as I turn around to my assistant and my neighbour, who is now modelling the coat.

"Hello, what a coincidence."

"My office is down the road," he replies.

"Really? So is ours. Strange we've never seen each other on the Tube."

"My timetable's all over the place."

"It looks good, doesn't it?" Abigail jumps in.

Alex does a little twirl for us, then lowers his glasses to look over the rim with mock sexiness. The irony being that he does look sexy. The jacket fits him perfectly across the shoulders, as though it was made for him. I can't help thinking it won't look half as good on our younger client.

"So, what am I helping you with?" Alex says.

"We're being personal shoppers for the day."

Abigail glances at me to check that her explanation is correct.

"Yep," I nod, "for a busy client."

"It must be hard getting it right when he's not here," he says.

"I know!" Abigail gushes, "So hard!"

"We might not have got it right either," I say, flatly. "What about you? What are you doing shopping in the middle of the day?"

"Pretty much the same. I'm after a neon headband for a client. I could have got a runner to do it, but I wanted to get outside the studio. I've got a horrible shoot coming up tonight." His face crumples at the thought, but he recovers quickly. "But you know, I love what I do, so I can't complain."

It's so familiar what he's done. Catching himself sounding negative and switching over. I do it all the time. He's trying to convince himself it's all fine when he's obviously pissed off.

"I thought you were taking a holiday?"

His expression darkens again. "I was, but you know... I couldn't say no to this job..."

"I know the feeling."

Abigail looks as though she's bursting to say something, "Is it a photo shoot you're doing? Aren't we looking for a photographer?"

"No it's a music video, but I know plenty of photographers," Alex says. He looks at me with renewed interest. "I can mail you their contact details if you like."

I'm trying to think of a reason why I should say no to the offer, something along the lines of wanting to keep my work life separate from everything else.

"Yeah, that would be great."

He takes out his phone, which I notice is the latest Samsung. I thought he'd have something old school. He looks up, his fingers poised and I dictate my email.

"Okay then, I better get going," he says.

"Good luck with the shoot."

"Thanks, and you with yours."

He gives us a smile and a little wave and starts to head off towards the escalators.

"Are you planning on pinching the jacket?" I call after him.

He blushes when he realises he's still got it on. Abigail hurries towards him with the hanger and takes it off him. She's grinning from ear to ear when she comes back to me.

"Oh my God, who was that? He's gorgeous!"

"My next-door neighbour."

Her mouth drops open. "And how many times have you popped over for some sugar?"

She winks and I raise an eyebrow in reply. She's let her guard down.

"What? He's lovely!" she cries.

"He was only being nice today to make up for being so rude on all the other days."

Abigail looks shocked.

"He's very judgmental," I clarify, and in my head I add that I'm a bit sensitive when I'm tired.

"About what?"

"He doesn't approve of my job."

"Why not?"

I forget that Abigail doesn't know everything we do.

"He doesn't think much of social media."

She frowns. "What does he do?"

"He's a director of music videos and adverts."

"Like that industry doesn't depend on our work, right?"

"Exactly."

"Weird."

"Anyway, my flatmate's after him. Louisa. *She* doesn't like my job, either. Nor does my mum, come to think of it."

I think I must be having a delayed reaction to Bernard's yelling. I feel deflated. Abigail senses my mood change and gives my arm a squeeze.

"My mum doesn't approve of me being in a band, if that makes

197

you feel any better."

"Not really. Now I feel sorry for you too."

She laughs. "Why don't we get a coffee? I think we're flagging."

How can we stop for coffee? My inbox must be overflowing and we still haven't got this photo shoot sorted.

"Or a proper drink..." Abigail says, absently, "shopping is much easier when you're tipsy."

I'm quite surprised at the suggestion. Abigail has been nothing but the well-behaved assistant. Is this her rebellious streak coming out? And why am I still standing here considering the suggestion? I lick my lips. I can almost taste the cold glass of white wine.

"Oh God, why not?" I say. "Let's do it. It'll be good to stop and review the situation."

We pay for the jacket and then we head around the back of Oxford Circus. Despite it being a lovely day I insist on us sitting inside the pub in a far corner. I don't want Craig to catch us out. I order a large glass of wine for me and a pint of beer for Abigail, who gets out her notebook and starts making a list.

"I guessed you were in a band, you know," I say.

She smiles.

"What do you do?"

"I sing and play the keyboard."

"What do you think of Thijs's music?"

She laughs and those little spots of pink come back to her cheeks. "I would love to jam with him without the other guys."

"Really?"

"Yeah, we were chatting the other day and he seems really cool."

"Yeah he does... mature... balanced..."

"So you're doing his marketing right?"

I nod, but decide that's where this strand of the conversation is going to end.

"Right, have a think what we've seen and what we might need. I'm going to answer some emails."

I reach for my phone as it starts to buzz. I pray it's going to be someone easy to deal with.

"May, it's Damian."

His voice brings our last encounter flooding back and my cheeks redden. I've tried to put it out of my mind these last couple of days, but I knew we'd have to talk eventually.

"Oh, hello, you probably tried the office didn't you? Everyone's out at the moment, sorry about that," I ramble.

"No, I didn't call the office."

Abigail glances at me. I give her a guilty look and then get up off the table and head outside for some privacy.

"Okay, well... how can I help?"

Keep calm and be professional.

"Meet me," he says. "Let's go somewhere."

This is really happening. The realisation is both thrilling and also cause for concern. I know I should say that I'm working, that I'm very busy, that what happened can't happen again. Instead I utter one word:

"Where?"

"My friend has a canal boat in Little Venice. Meet me there. It'll be just me and you."

In my mind I picture a painted narrow boat moored along a cobble-stone tow path, pots of flowers spilling pinks and greens across its bow. My heart is beating fast. I've always been practical. I've always made good decisions. But now I'm standing here, torn. Louisa would tell me to go. She'd tell me that life was passing me by.

Enjoy life today. Yesterday is gone and tomorrow might never come.

"I'm working," I say weakly. "I've got so much to do."

"Getting to know me will make your job easier," he says, a smile in his voice.

"I wish it was just you I needed to get to know."

In the silence, my words gain so much more meaning. Without

uttering the word, I've said yes.

"Get a taxi," he says. "Please."

"I'll be there as soon as I can."

"It's blue... the boat's blue... you'll see me... call me when you're near..."

"I shouldn't be doing this."

"You worry too much."

"If you had my job you'd worry too."

"We're wasting time. Hurry up, May."

I suppress a smile, "See you soon."

Then I go back inside to see Abigail and I tell her something urgent has come up and I have to go. She looks momentarily daunted by the task of finishing off the shop, but after I've apologised ten times and reassured her that whatever she buys will be better than nothing, she perks up.

"I've got an idea," she says.

"Great," I say encouragingly.

It's only once I'm in the taxi that I realise what her idea is. My phone bleeps with a notification for Thijs's Twitter account.

BANDGIRLABI @BANDGIRL

@ThijsVanBro Hi there! Question from a fan, if you have to describe your style what would you call it?

Great. Do I really have to pretend to be Thijs and tweet back to my own colleague? It's that or tell her the truth, and Craig hasn't given me permission for that. I click on Abigail's Twitter profile picture. It's a blurry snap of her thrashing it out on a keyboard with neon lights flashing brightly behind her. You can't see her face properly because she's looking down. I check out her biog. *I'm in a band called The Rocking Roosters, check out our Facebook page for our next gig!*

The Rocking Roosters? Do they play the banjo and chew tobacco? God, I'd love to give her some social media pointers,

but then she's not my client, and she can't know what we do.
Well, here goes.

THIJS @THIJSVANBRO
@bandgirl That's a tough question! I'm all about my music and not what I'm wearing! I didn't know people cared about that stuff!

Right then, @bandgirl, it's back to you. She replies instantly.

BANDGIRLABI @BANDGIRL
I don't care about that stuff either! To me it's all about the music too, but just some people having a debate over here!

I'll reply one more time because I'm sure Thijs would.

THIJS @THIJSVANBRO
Cool, let me know what the conclusion is! ;)

I drop my phone back in my bag. My stomach is churning with nerves and excitement. Soon I'll be with Damian, hiding from everyone in a barge on the canal. How naughty, how completely not me to bunk off work and run off with my client…

Maybe I should tell the taxi driver to turn back.

Am I really going to risk my job over a little bit of passion?

But perhaps I'm being overdramatic. I'll take pictures of the boat. I'll make use of this time. If Craig ever found out, I'd say I was doing research. My body tingles at the thought of the research we're going to do. I haven't done this kind of research in a very long time and my body is aching with anticipation.

Chapter 22

I spot him immediately, waving at me from the back of a narrow boat, which is painted royal blue. There's a cigarette in his hand. He takes a last drag then flicks the stub into the canal.

He's wearing faded camel shorts and a vest that shows off his three faded black tribal bands. His sandy blonde hair is flopping out beneath his green-and-white trucker hat. Seeing him so summery makes me appreciate what a beautiful day it is. I wish I was in shorts and not my funereal outfit of black skirt and buttoned-up shirt. He jumps off the boat onto the tow path to greet me.

"Hey, you came!" he cries. His smile is triumphant.

He leans in and kisses my cheek, and I catch a whiff of cigarette and beer on his breath.

"Ergh, smoker breath," I say, waving away the smell.

"Shit, sorry," he says. "Come on, let me get you a drink."

He jumps back onto the boat and disappears inside, returning shortly with a cold bottle of Moët.

"I thought you'd want something a bit posher than lager," he says, grinning.

To think I wasn't going to come! This is perfect!

I consider my heels for a second and decide to take them off.

"Do you need a hand?"

"I'm fine."

I've abseiled down cliffs, I've rock-climbed, I've walked over logs across rivers, maybe a lifetime ago, but still, I don't need help getting onto a little narrow boat. On the other hand, I didn't do any of these things in a tight skirt. My enthusiastic foot up is accompanied with a horrible ripping sound as my seam splits right up the middle.

"Shit!" I hiss, quickly getting my other foot on board. I twist my head to check out the damage.

"Let me see," Damian says laughing.

The split has stopped an inch below my bum. As long as I keep my legs together...

"Just take it off," Damian says.

"Very funny!"

"What's the difference between knickers and a bikini anyway?

"I don't walk around in the middle of London in either."

And also, my knickers are sheer.

"Prude," he says.

He hands me the bottle, apologises for not having any nice glasses. Drinking Moët straight out of the bottle doesn't feel quite as special. He takes my other hand, leads me down into the boat. I feel the ripple of butterflies in my stomach, the tightening knot of anticipation. I'm aware of the feel of his skin on mine, cold from holding the chilled champagne.

"Look at this place..." he says. "From the outside you'd never think it would fit all this, would you?"

The interior is fully customised to the narrow space and feels like a caravan. There's a compact kitchen area with a half-moon table and a curved bench around it upholstered in dark-green velour. Further along there's a sofa covered in an orange throw, and beyond that, a partition behind which the bedroom must be.

"Whose is it?" I ask.

He sits down on the sofa and pulls me down with him. I sink into the extra-soft cushions, which push me towards him so our legs touch. The light coming through the small windows picks out the blonde hairs on his legs.

"It's my friend's. He's away on holiday so I'm looking after it. Do you like it?"

"Yeah, it's cute."

I take a gulp of champagne. In the ensuing silence I hear the buzz of my phone.

"That could be one of your fans," I say.

He shrugs. "Well, I'm busy... I'm with a girl."

A stupid smile tugs at my lips. "Oh yeah? How's it going?"

"To be honest I felt more confident last time I saw her."

"When you stormed her office you mean and got her into trouble?"

He looks amused. "Did I?"

"I don't think so. I haven't seen Gabe and he wouldn't have told Craig."

"Told him what?"

"Exactly."

He reaches out a hand and gently pushes back the strands of hair that have fallen over my cheek. I unclipped it in the taxi, remembering how he said he'd like it down.

"You're beautiful," he says.

I'm not very good at taking compliments, but I don't want to ruin this moment by protesting or babbling over him. My teeth press against my bottom lip and I wait for him to go on. But he doesn't. He leans forward. There's an intake of breath, mine, and then my mouth is on his. This time I don't feel any holding back. All that reasoning flies out of my mind. There's no fear of being caught now and what's left is a throbbing, sexual desire that makes me kiss him so hungrily. His masculinity turns me on, his strong arms moving to hold me, the toned muscles under his t-shirt responding as I rise.

I push him back against the cushions and bring my leg over him, straddling him. He cups my buttocks and pulls me towards him, sending a rush of pleasure to my centre. I run my hands through his gorgeous mess of hair and press my lips deeper against his, losing myself in the hot wetness of his tongue.

These past six months everything feels like it has happened in my head, my thoughts have felt like writhing snakes, hissing headaches at every turn. It feels so good to escape that prison, to feel my body so alive again. I don't care about the notifications on my phone, whether Bernard gets his wife back, or what Thijs is going to wear. I don't give a damn about Angel's views on fashion or if Craig thinks I'm doing enough. I want every thought to be obliterated and all my senses to be on fire. I want Damian inside me, driving a rhythm until there is nothing but white light and mind-numbing pleasure.

He's pulling back, his chest rising and falling. "Wow... May..."

I feel a trickle of alarm. Is there something wrong? I sit back, sweeping my hair behind my shoulders, my pulse racing. Am I coming on too strong?

"Just maybe... slower?" he says, reaching for my face. "But wow... you're so hot."

"Sorry... I'm just..."

Really horny because I haven't had sex in two years?

"No, don't say sorry."

I kiss him more gently. His hand brushes past my hips and slide up under my shirt. They can't go further because my shirt is so fitted. I help him with my buttons, and we smile at each other, and I feel a moment of shyness.

"It's been a while..." I say, and immediately feel embarrassed. Why did I say that? I didn't need to show him I'm anything other than confident.

"We can go as slow as you like."

I let out a little laugh.

"What?" he says.

I just never imagined I'd be on a narrow boat kissing a reality TV star.

I never imagined Damian Dance would be someone I'd want

to kiss.

"Nothing," I say. "Just... this. I never imagined this."

He opens the last button of my shirt, pushing it over my shoulders and I shrug out of it and it drops to the floor. He runs his hand down the straps of my lacy black bra, and follows the silky band to my back. His fingers fiddle with the butterfly hooks and I raise my eyebrows teasingly. But he's got it now and he pulls it off. I breathe in softly.

"You're incredible," he whispers.

He caresses my breast and I close my eyes as he leans forward and runs his tongue over each nipple, making my body ache for him to touch me. He lifts me up, his biceps tensing, and rests me on my back. He runs his finger down my chest, circles my belly button and stops at the waist of my skirt.

"Take your t-shirt off..." I whisper.

He hesitates and his jaw twitches. It's his tattoo. I sit up on my elbows, wanting to say something to reassure him, that I'll find him beautiful no matter what, but that doesn't sound quite right. While I'm trying to formulate my feelings, he slips it over his head.

Our eyes connect and it feels like we're recognising something in each other; that we understand each other. I can't see his tattoo but I don't care what it looks like, I care what it's done to him, the hurt that he's gone through. In that moment I feel certain I know Damian Dance more than any of his fans.

After so long, it hurts. But we take our time and he inches his way in, holding me tight, kissing my neck, until the pain subsides and we find our rhythm, our breaths rising to a pant and a moan as all my thoughts and all my worries disappear and in their place a sense of exhilaration and joy and relief.

Our bodies sticky with sweat, we hold each other on the sofa, not saying anything. And I feel like I could cry, because I've been wanting to be with someone for so very long.

"Is that yours?" he says, as a phone vibrates against the floor.

My heart sinks. Fucking phones. I want him to leave it alone but I don't say so. He reaches for his shorts and takes it out of his pocket, checks the screen. Then he holds it up.

"Selfie?" he says, grinning.

The suggestion horrifies me. "No!"

I try to reach for it before he takes the picture, but I'm too late. He laughs and lowers the phone to show me it. He's sliced our heads off, and all you can see is his chest and the bottom half of my face, my mouth open in protest.

"Not good enough for Twitter?" he jokes. "Hashtag just got naked with a beautiful girl?"

"Hashtag if you put that on Twitter I'll kill you."

"Hashtag would it be so bad?"

I glare at him. "You're joking, right?"

"Not naked pictures, I wouldn't do that... I'm just talking about you. How bad would it be if we had a picture on my Twitter?"

I feel a sense of panic rising in my chest. Isn't it obvious why that's a terrible idea? Can he not see why we can't risk any specu-lation? Why I mustn't be identified?

"No Damian, we can't have people wondering who I am. It's essential that we're discreet."

He sighs, "Yeah, you're right... I'm being stupid..."

"Anyway, it's better if your fans think you're free and single..." Oh God, that came out wrong. My cheeks burn as I try to clarify that I don't mean we're suddenly an item. "I mean, you *are* free and single, I'm just saying why make it look anything else?"

He nods, pensive, and lets his phone fall back on top of the pile of clothes on the floor.

"Yeah, you're right. I'll leave it to you. You're in charge."

I nuzzle back into the crook of his neck, his arm settling around me.

"It must have been your phone before," he says.

"It always is."

I don't want to check it. I just want to steal one more hour away from my life.

"I'm DJing tonight... do you want to come?"

I kiss his chest, happy to be asked. "Maybe another time."

"Next time, then," he says.

I close my eyes and feel his chest rise and fall. If I did just this for the rest of the week I'd be so happy.

Chapter 23

Two days after that idyllic afternoon with Damian and I still feel like I'm playing catch-up at work. But if I had the chance, I'd do it all over again. It's renewed my energy and increased my appetite for my job. There's this bubble of happiness inside me leaking doses of positive energy to cope with every setback. Even Bernard's offload isn't going to get me down. A calm inner voice tells me that any minute now he'll lose phone reception because he's on a train on his way back to London.

"Bernard I can't hear you... You're breaking up..."

Eventually I hang up and instruct Abigail to tell him I'm on a conference call if he phones back.

I switch to Damian's Twitter account and smile at his sexy profile picture. He's leaning against a wall covered in bright graffiti, one foot up pressed against it, his hands relaxed at his pockets. He's looking up at a blue sky with a knowing smile on his face. Okay, it's totally poser, but he looks good.

DAMIANDANCE @DAMIANDANCE
Someone once said to me, 'Look after your body or you'll have nowhere to live' – OK magic mat, let's do this. #yoga #fitness

I get a kick of satisfaction as the tweet gets instantly retweeted several times. I'm encouraging people to get fit and look after themselves. That can only be a good thing. I move on to my other clients, tweeting, sharing, liking.

THIJS @THIJSVANBRO
Teeth or no teeth? What's your best photo face? :)

The selfies start pouring in from female teenagers around the world, many showing more cleavage than teeth. I roll my eyes, but I'm pleased with myself. Ten points to me for getting his fans engaging with him. My mission is to make Thijs more popular than shiny Jake Helms.

I click back on Damian's profile again, unable to resist checking every notification. The yoga tweet went down well and I feel a hunger for proof of overall progress so I check the search column where any tweet mentioning Damian Dance, whether directed to him or not, will come up. That's when I spot @tintino and my good temper fizzles out.

TINTINO @TINTINO
Damian Dance is promoting yoga today. Surprised he's got the energy after he nailed the dead dog pose last night.

I feel tense as I click on the picture attached. What I see makes me breathe in sharply. It's a picture of Damian splayed out across a pavement, looking very much the worse for wear. His eyes are half closed and his mouth is hanging open, drool caught between his teeth. There are signs of people going towards him, an elbow, the back of a head.

I can't even pretend this is an old photo. He's wearing what he changed into before I left the narrow boat; a red t-shirt, black cargo shorts and a grey trilby, which has fallen off his head. This must have happened the night after we got together. When I'd left him, he'd looked great and seemed really together. I barely recognise this destroyed rag doll dribbling on the pavement.

"He got wasted, so what?" I snap, annoyed at myself for the judgmental thoughts that have just poured in.

I don't know how his night of DJ-ing had gone. For all I know someone spiked his drink. I'm not disgusted with Damian. It's @tintino I'm pissed off at. He thinks he's being funny, but he's just another vulture feeding on the vulnerable, like all the bloody paparazzi. I start composing tweets in anger.

DAMIANDANCE @DAMIANDANCE
@tintino I bet you've looked like this before but there isn't a photo of it on Twitter because no one cares about you.

DELETE.

DAMIANDANCE @DAMIANDANCE
@tintino You could have helped me get up you prick.

DELETE.

DAMIANDANCE @DAMIANDANCE
@tintino What's your point? Have I ever said I was anything other than an ordinary human being?

I swallow. I'm going to send it. No, don't send it. I'm going to send it. People need to hear it.

"Bastard," I say, exhaling.

Of course, I can't tweet as Damian. He wouldn't even have seen the tweet. But that's not the only account I control.

SPARKYMAY @SPARKYMAY
@tintino Have you got a new job at Heat magazine? Next you're going to tweet that he's put on weight.

The last thing I need is coffee, but I get up and go in search of some because otherwise I'll know I'll just waste half an hour clicking refresh.

On reception, Abigail looks like a deer caught in the headlights: wide-eyed and nervous.

"Are you alright?" I say. "No one has arrived yet, have they?"

I still feel a bit guilty for leaving her to finish off the shop. She did a decent job, though her taste for black and purple may have got the better of her towards the end.

"Yes, he's in the bathroom."

"The photographer?"

Alex never got around to sending his list. It had probably just been one of those things you say to sound helpful. Luckily Craig had a friend who could fit us in at short notice and he negotiated a good price.

"No, not the photographer. *Thijs.*"

"Already?"

"Better early than late, right?"

"Not always."

I was hoping to have a private word with the photographer about my thoughts on how I want Thijs to be presented.

"I really hope he likes the clothes..." Abigail says, looking anxious.

"I don't think he'll be too fussy."

From the other end of the corridor we hear a lock turn. A moment later Thijs appears. His cheeks colour when he finds us waiting for him so expectantly.

"Hey, so great to see you," I gush. "I'm so grateful you were fine about coming in today. Getting your image right is so important."

"So Maria keeps telling me."

Oh come on, I think, lighten up. Some people would love to do this. To be fair, I'm not one of those people either. Having to fix your face in the perfect smile over and over, how tedious is that?

"Let's go into the conference room and we can show you some

possible outfits."

He looks uncomfortable but resigned to his fate. I'm thinking how good it would be if there was a masculine influence around when Craig turns up. He acts delighted to see Thijs, shaking his hand and telling him he's just been listening to Five Oars at the gym. Knowing Craig's cheesy taste, he's probably not even lying.

"Everything alright?" Craig says to me.

I don't think his look is significant and yet suddenly I'm thinking about my reply to @tintino. It's now glaringly obvious that I shouldn't have reacted. I took it too personally. I have now linked myself to Damian, however tenuously.

"Yeah, I'm fine, can you just oversee things for one second..." I say, smiling tightly.

Craig is already following Thijs into the conference room so I don't wait for a reply. I hurry back to my office and turn on my tablet. I feel a stab of apprehension when I see Tintino has replied.

TINTINO @TINTINO
@SparkyMay he will put on weight if he carries on with that kind of yoga!

I let out an involuntary snort of laughter.

"Smartarse!"

I should leave it at that. What's the point in replying? But I can't help myself.

SPARKYMAY @SPARKYMAY
@tintino I don't think he's doing yoga to get a body you approve of. Have you heard of inner peace?

TINTINO @TINTINO
@SparkyMay Yes I have heard of it, I just didn't know it came free with a bottle of vodka! Off to buy some.

@tintino drinking vodka in the morning? Now who has the problem?

"Uh, May?"

I look up startled to find Abigail standing at the entrance of my office. I hadn't even closed the door. I quickly log out of my account.

"Are you ready? The photographer has arrived."

I blink away a hundred thoughts. "Yep, I'm coming. Any reaction to the clothes?"

Her pursed butterfly lips break into a smile, "He's changing right now."

"Oh God, Abigail, you're going to have to hide that crush of yours a bit better in front of Craig."

She blushes a deeper shade of red, but doesn't begin to deny it.

Chapter 24

"No way," Louisa says, her mouth dropping to the floor, "No fucking way."

I point a warning finger at her, "This is not to leave this room, okay?"

"I can't believe it."

She's curled up on my bed opposite me. I've just told her everything. I couldn't help it after she came into my room and started moaning about how I work too much and don't have a life.

"But wait... let me get this straight..."

I can see all the questions buzzing in her head. I should be offended she's so shocked at my secret. It's like she's forgotten I always used to be the last to leave the party.

"OKAY?"

"Yes. Got it. I won't tell anyone. But what does this mean?"

I know what she means by that question, but I try to play it cool. "What do you mean, *what does it mean?* It was just an incredibly hot encounter on a barge. My first time in two years. Exciting. That's all."

She shakes her head. "No, that's not all. Do you like him? Do you see this going anywhere? I mean this is serious. Do you know what it's like to go out with a celebrity?"

"Do *you*?"

"They'll be all over you. They'll want to know where you popped out from. They'll be putting their noses in our bins and it'll only take them half an hour to find out what your job is. Oh, they'll love it when they find out *you're* actually the one tweeting for *him*... oh my God, can you imagine?"

"Yeah alright, you're kind of jumping ahead a bit."

It's not like I've not thought about this. Every time Damian pops into my head, it's followed by these exact thoughts. *Every* time. I'm tired of thinking about it.

"I'm not going out with him."

She narrows her eyes. Sceptical. "So it was just a one-off shag in the middle of the day with your client?"

"Yes."

Not exactly. We've been texting each other non-stop. Not about work stuff. Not about what's being said on Twitter or how I lost my cool and responded to that distant critic @tintino. It's just been lots of flirty texts.

"What's he like, then? What's the real Damian Dance like?"

Our time on the narrow boat comes winging its way to the forefront of my mind. After cuddling on the sofa for half an hour we'd gone on deck and finished the champagne in the sunshine. We'd chatted easily about all sorts of things – from our families to pets we'd had as kids. His story of leaving a hamster in his cousin's crib had made me wince, and the language he'd used to describe half his family hadn't been all that poetic, but he'd made me laugh too.

"He's a funny guy... easy-going..."

"And you're sure it's not a cry for help?"

"What?"

"Because your job is getting on top of you and a part of you secretly wants to get fired?"

"You're the only one who wants me to get fired!"

"That's not true..." and then she shrugs, "I'd like you to be made redundant so you get a nice severance package."

216

"Thanks."

"I'm just giving you the chance to speak your mind."

This isn't fair. She has turned my exciting bit of news into a cry for help. She must read the outrage on my face because she leans forward and squeezes my arm.

"Just joking," she says.

"No, you weren't."

"I just worry about you."

"I know I've been a loser lately, but now you know that I'm not always working."

She grins, "and I'm pleased to hear it."

I muster a smile and try to change the subject to her life, which isn't hard because Louisa loves talking about herself.

"The film's been postponed, annoyingly. Alex got some studio job he couldn't get out of," she says. "Jacob's furious because he'd booked a week off and now he has to see if he can get it back."

I look at her pointedly. "So how *is* Alex?"

"How do you mean?"

"You know what I mean... he likes you, you like him... is anything going to happen?"

She wrinkles her nose in a feeble attempt to hide her delight at being told she's got an admirer.

"You don't know that he likes me."

"Oh come on, it's obvious. He's always dropping by and then the other morning he seemed very anxious to know if you'd stayed out partying or if you'd come home."

"Really? He asked you that?"

"Yes. Then he blushed a million times."

She breaks into a grin. "Really?"

"I thought this was all very obvious."

"No. It's mostly been the three of us."

Whose fault is that? She keeps inviting me to join them for drinks. She could have gone on the picnic with him on her own.

"Well, I'll try to keep out of the way."

"I didn't mean you. Jacob's been around a lot too."

"Oh right... we'll have to get rid of him, then."

She laughs. "Aw. He's so lovely, though."

My phone buzzes and instead of rolling her eyes, Louisa flops back against my pillow and smiles dreamily. I risk picking it up, hoping it's a message from Damian and wondering how I'm going to compose my face if it is. But I've mixed up the notifications and it's actually an email. I'm surprised to find it's from Alex apologising for the delay and including a list of photographers with their mini biographies and estimated costs. The time shows he sent it half an hour ago. As I'm skimming through it, feeling a little guilty that he spent time on this when I no longer need it, the doorbell buzzes.

I give Louisa a knowing look. "Go on, then, he's standing outside the door, fingers crossed, hoping you're going to open and not me."

I don't think that's entirely true. We don't dislike each other. In fact I think he enjoys the banter we have, and when I'm not being oversensitive I'm happy to give as good as I get. Louisa doesn't need any more encouragement, though. With a big grin still plastered across her face she jumps out of bed and stomps down the corridor to open up.

It is him. I can hear the deep tone of his voice.

I give them ten minutes to greet each other before I sidle into the living room to thank him for the email. Louisa is standing by a boiling kettle, Alex has pulled out a chair and is sitting facing her. He looks tired, but he arranges his face into a bright smile when he sees me.

"Hey, May, how are you doing?"

He half gets up and I half bend down to meet him, and we exchange an awkward kiss on the cheek. I'm not really sure where it came from. We haven't greeted each other with a kiss before. I don't think we'll be doing it again, either.

"I just came over to... uh... update Louisa on the status of the film..."

It's kind of sweet he feels the need to make up these little excuses to come over to see her.

"And what is it?" I say, unable to resist.

He looks uncomfortable. "Pending."

Louisa groans. I bite my lip to stop myself laughing out loud, because it's such a lame excuse.

"Thanks for the email, by the way," I say. "We did actually find one for this shoot, but for the future it will be handy."

"What email? What shoot?" Louisa says.

She hates to be out of the loop.

"I needed a photographer and Alex sent me some contacts. Didn't I tell you we bumped into each other on Oxford Street?"

Her eyes widen. "That's amazing."

"Well, not really... we both work in Soho..." he looks at me for reassurance. "You said you worked around there, right?"

I nod. The kettle comes to the boil, mirroring Louisa's excitement.

"That's so cool, guys! You can have lunch together!"

Alex laughs drily. "Lunch break? What a cute idea."

It makes me smile because that's exactly what I was thinking. What surprises me is that he said it, not me.

"Yuk. You sound like May," Louisa says, casting a disapproving eye over him.

I laugh and his cheeks redden slightly. "I meant, what a brilliant idea. I love my five-minute lunch breaks. They are so invigorating."

"Five minutes? That's terrible," Louisa scolds him. "You two need to take a proper lunch break. Why don't you have lunch tomorrow together?"

#NotGoingtoHappen. I look at Alex expecting to find the same sentiment written across his face, but instead find he's looking at me, as if he's considering it. Oh, he *is* considering it. What is Louisa doing? She's useless at this. She's supposed to be arranging a lunch date with him, not me with him. Unless it's because she wants me to find out what he thinks of her. That's probably why he's thinking about it too. For grownups, they're pretty pathetic at this whole getting-together thing.

"I guess we could grab a sandwich together one day," I say.

"Yeah..." he says, shrugging. "We could. The weather's nice for it. We could go to that little garden bit."

"See, you don't have to be workaholics, do you?" Louisa says abruptly.

I check her expression. I don't know if I detect a trace of regret in her voice, as if she's realised she has just set up her friend with the guy she fancies. Well, she doesn't have to worry about me.

"We can email or something," I say. "I'll leave you two to discuss your pending film."

"You don't have to leave. It's not top secret like your job."

I stick my tongue out at him and he laughs.

"By the way, did you ever..."

Louisa hands him a mug of tea and we both look at him.

"What?" I say.

"I was just wondering if any of your clients, you know... are supporting guerrilla gardening these days?"

There's a twinkle in his eyes and he looks as if he's trying to hold back a smile.

Louisa looks at me warily, "Don't get annoyed, May."

But I'm not annoyed at all. I think we've put that little confrontation behind us.

"No, I haven't. But you might be pleased to know that one of my clients is now supporting a small ethical fashion brand."

"That's good of them," Alex says, grinning.

"Well, *I* think so. See, I *can* make a difference."

"I never doubted it."

I narrow my eyes, "yes, you did."

"I said you weren't, not that you couldn't."

"Oh, piss off," I say, laughing.

"What brand?" Louisa asks.

"What brand?" I echo stupidly. Obviously I'm not going to

name the client in front of Alex, but surely I can name the brand. "HappyHeart. They've got some nice stuff. I just need to get my client modelling some outfits."

"I've never heard of them."

Louisa now seems to be waiting for me to leave, so I do her a favour and take my mug into the bedroom. I plump my cushions up and rest my tablet on my legs, logging into my Facebook page to check up on my friends before I set to work as my clients.

Clare Willis: *Forgot to label the boxes! Smelling each one to see where the cinnamon is! Lol :))))*

Anna Jamison: *I just found my phone in the fridge. That's how tired I am.*

Joe Mathers: *WHALE FOUND WITH 40 KG OF PLASTIC INSIDE ITS BELLY! SAY NO TO PLASTIC! SIGN THE PETITION.*

Emma Priestly: *Looking forward to Clare Willis' flat-warming tomorrow! :)*

That stops me in my tracks. I check my Facebook events to see if I've overlooked my invite. But there's nothing but random invitations to gigs from people I barely know. I feel like a door has just been slammed in my face and my friends are giggling together on the other side. It's easy to miss out people by accident on Facebook invites, but it horrifies me that I've become one of those forgettables.

It's not fair, I had tried to talk to Clare about the move, but she hadn't wanted to. She said she'd talked about it enough. Well not to me.

I feel uneasy as I remember how late I've been arriving to events. Perhaps they had always discussed it first thing... perhaps they couldn't face recapping everything for me. Is Clare annoyed with me? She's the sweetest, most patient person I know, but even she has her limits. Maybe not inviting me to her house-warming is her way of showing me that she's fed up.

I feel horrible now. Hurt and excluded. I have been trying to be a good friend.

Unable to shake the feeling, I pick up the phone and call my mum. She does all the talking, but I don't mind. It's comforting to listen to her. She stops halfway through a sentence.

"You're alright are you, May?"

I feel my throat tightening and tears welling up.

"I'm great..." I say. "Really good."

"You'd tell me if you weren't, wouldn't you?"

"Yes, of course."

After we hang up, I log on to Bernard's Twitter account. I hate feeling negative. I hate feeling sad and sluggish. Everything is going to work out. I'm doing much better than I think I am. I just need to shock myself out of this melancholy.

I click open the private message thread with Bernard's wife. She never replied to his last message. I take a breath and type the words I'd want to hear if I were his wife.

BTHOMSKINNER @BTHOMSKINNER

@merlottijoie I miss you. Without you nothing has any meaning.

After I've posted it I feel horrified at myself. I switch off my tablet and my phone and try not to think about it. It's impossible, though, so I get up and head into the living room. Alex has already left and I end up watching a terrible film with Louisa and drinking half a bottle of wine. She thinks the old me is back. She has no idea. I'm too ashamed to tell her what I've done.

Chapter 25

It's one of those mornings when you wake up wishing it were bedtime. I could have had an early night, but once we'd watched the film, I'd switched my phone back on, curious to see if Joyce had replied on Twitter. With each refresh I'd felt this momentary thrill, followed by a pang of disappointment, and then a little voice would whisper in my ear that the next refresh would be the one. I imagined her reply in capital letters. Something to put him in his place and show Bernard that using social media to patch up a broken marriage is not the answer.

It's almost noon and Joyce still hasn't replied. I'm relieved. Mostly, I wish I hadn't sent the message in the first place. It looks as if Joyce is not going to fall for him again and I'm dreading having a conversation with Bernard about terminating this particular part of the job. Hounding a woman who has made up her mind to stay clear of her cheating husband is definitely above and beyond my call of duty, and more importantly, against my principles. If I were her friend, I would be encouraging her to stick to her guns.

I've still got to work for him, though, so I spend some time hunting for some piece of quirky news he might comment on. It's always with a feeling of impending doom that I tweet his opinions, expecting the phone to start ringing the second after I've posted them.

I switch to Thijs's account and sit up as I note the unusually high number of notifications. The photographer sent me a selection of photos last night and I immediately updated his Twitter profile picture and tweeted a few chirpy tweets about what it had been like to have a photo shoot, and how he had renewed respect for models. I'm blinking the sleep from my eyes and trying to work out what it is everyone's getting so excited about when Craig bursts into my office.

"Have you replied to her?" he says, his eyes wild with excitement. "Oh my God, May, this is fantastic!"

I look up at him, then back at my screen, knowing that the key to everything making sense is right in front of me.

"It's incredible, Ankara Davies... Ankara fucking Davies..."

Before he's finished uttering her name, I see it. The tweet from the top model is sandwiched between inarticulate, adoring fans.

ANKARA DAVIES @ANKARADAVIES
Wow. I love @ThijsVanBro's new look. Gorgeous and talented.
I hope I get to meet him at Glastonbury! ;)

I swallow back the alarm that comes rushing at me and coolly click on Ankara's Twitter handle. My eyes widen as I see she has 102.8K followers and is only following 127. Why would I expect any less? Everyone knows who Ankara Davies is. She's a regular in the gossip magazines, posing with a champagne flute wherever she goes, her golden hair pinned in complex braids, her eyes twinkling, her bee-stung lips pouting playfully for the cameras that are always following her. Ankara has the reputation of being both intelligent and beautiful, and if she thinks Thijs is also talented and beautiful, then I know why Craig is standing in front of me barely able to contain his excitement.

"I'll favourite it," I say.

"Hang on, before you do that, we've got to think this through." The phone is ringing and Craig eyes it warily, "That could be

Maria."

It *is* Maria and she's as concerned as Craig that we deal with this "great opportunity" very wisely. She feels strongly that this is Thijs's chance to leap to the top of the celebrity food chain. Craig takes the phone off me and I swallow back the swell of indignation, the feeling that when it comes to the crunch he doesn't trust me.

"Yes, of course we've got to engineer a meeting," Craig says. "Where will he be staying in Glastonbury? ... Yes... alright... well, of course they have to get together... it shouldn't be tricky... yes, music is magic, you don't need to tell me that, I lost my virginity because I could play three bars of 'Voodoo Child' ... no he shouldn't have to talk too much..."

Are they aware how ridiculous this is? It sounds like they're arranging a marriage. Poor Thijs doesn't have clue, nor, for that matter, does our young receptionist, who I notice has retweeted and liked all his photo-shoot-related comments. She's also made some joke about the purple tie he didn't want to wear. It would be a good time to ask Craig whether we should tell Abigail what's going on. It doesn't feel right replying to her chirpy tweets and giving her hope.

"Okay, then," Craig says, with a note of finality. "Will do... thank you... yes... I'll let her know... bye now... bye... bye."

He replaces the phone and claps his hands.

"Well, she's very pleased with you, May... which means I'm very pleased, which means..."

I straighten up in my chair, thinking of that promised salary.

"Really well done," he finishes lamely.

A feeling of disappointment trickles down my spine.

"Shall I reply to Ankara now?"

"Favourite her tweet and say thank you, and that you're looking forward to meeting her..."

"What about, looking forward to comparing wellies?"

Does being humorous make what we're doing any better?

"Wellies..." Craig echoes, rubbing his chin pensively.

The forecast for Glastonbury is a solid week of rain, meaning, as usual, it will be welly heaven, as everyone marches through the mud to watch their favourite bands.

Is what we're doing so bad? When they meet, they can decide if they like each other or not.

"Or, looking forward to meeting you. What do you think of my wellies? And then I can attach a funny picture of them... something which will make her laugh and she won't be able to resist sending him a picture back..."

Craig is nodding energetically, "Yes! Excellent idea!"

I lap up the praise with a smile.

"At this rate she'll be in love with him before they've even met," Craig says, getting up out of his chair. "Someone had better make sure Thijs knows who Ankara Davies is and fill him in on their conversation. It'll be very awkward otherwise."

My smile falters as I think of my young client. Perhaps we should talk to him before we reply as him. But then I check myself. What 18-year-old wouldn't want help chatting up someone like Ankara Davies? If we pull this off, it'll be like all his Christmases rolled into one.

"One more thing before you go, should I tell Abigail I'm tweeting for Thijs?"

Craig frowns. "Do we need to?"

"Well, she's been tweeting to me... I mean *him*. It's a bit awkward."

He looks amused. "I think we'll wait a bit longer. She hasn't been here very long. I'm undecided whether we'll keep her or not."

I feel a tug of sympathy for Abigail. She may still have some learning to do, and she does need to be more confident on the phone, but she's very willing, and prepared to go out of her way to help.

"She did a great job of the shop," I say. "I had to leave her to finish it off and she was very good."

"Really? Where did you have to go?" he says, raising an eyebrow.

I feel a prickle of heat creep up my neck. Well, Craig, I had to go and have sex on a narrow boat with one of our clients.

"I had so much to do."

He accepts my excuse and nods towards the computer. "You'd better get on with that tweet. You've got to nail this, May, it's very important."

He leaves me googling "outrageous wellies" and I have to push back the mocking voice in my head questioning how important my job really is.

Chapter 26

It's eight o'clock and I'm still in the office when my phone breaks into a tinny rendition of Electric Six's "Danger! High Voltage!" It's like I'm a teenager again and my mum has just told me Rob Baker is on the phone. "Fire in the Disco!" You'd think I'd be too busy to assign a special ringtone.

"Hello you," I say casually. "What can I do for you? Do you need me to tweet something super-exciting?"

"Yes, tweet that I'm missing a beautiful girl called May and that I haven't seen her since she came on my narrow boat... literally..."

I let out a snort of laugher.

"Ask all my followers to please retweet it because it's urgent," he adds, solemnly. "I need to find her by tonight."

"Why's that?"

"Because I need to take her out."

I lean back in my chair and look over at the window. The long summer evenings are deceptive. Judging by the light it could be four in the afternoon. How I know it's not is how tired I feel, and the fact I'm the only one left in the office.

It's Friday evening. At Clare's flat-warming everyone will have started picking at the carrot batons and hummus and crunching on the Kettle crisps. I don't like to admit it but I was still half hanging around for that invitation, that last-minute text from her.

I even brought a change of top and shoes, just in case.

"Where do you want to go?" I say.

"We could go for cocktails in the Oxo Tower. I love the view from there."

Craig loves the view from there too and there's a chance we could run into him wining and dining with his gossipy entourage.

"Or the Groucho Club."

I think of what Louisa said and sigh. "People will wonder who I am, and the next minute they'll be looking through my bins."

He laughs. "How famous do you think I am?"

Not famous enough, according to Craig. That's what I'm working on.

"Maybe if I got on this bloody jungle show... but right now everyone has forgotten about me."

"Is there still a chance you could get on it, then?"

"They're undecided."

This is big news. This is the sort of thing I should know about. The decisions taking place about him are the kind I could influence with a bit of cunning social media skills.

"But your agent said that it was off... that whatshername had a grudge against you..."

I should be starting a campaign, coming up with a hashtag. I don't know, something like:

#GetDamianOnTheJungleShowSoICanGetAPayrisePay-
OffMyCreditCardDebtThenGetAJobMyMumAndMyCon-
scienceApproveOf

Too long?

"You mean Melanie Walters?" Damian says. "My agent is always trying to blame someone else for his incompetence."

"So she doesn't have a grudge?"

"She thinks I'm unpredictable."

"That makes for good TV, doesn't it?"

229

He laughs. "Exactly!"

"#WhyIWantDamianInTheJungle," I say, with a sudden rush of clarity. "That's what we need trending."

I'm going to need some celebrity endorsement but that shouldn't be too hard. Tweets can be bought. No one can resist a bit of easy money. It's cheating, but it's cheating at a game that carries little weight in the real world. It's not like I'm rigging an election.

I realise he hasn't replied and wonder if he's worrying about the trolls.

"It doesn't matter what people say as long as it's trending."

I hear him breathe out. "Yes, let's do it. But first we need to meet up. Tonight. No excuses."

I smile, the excitement growing in the pit of my stomach. I had expected him to play it cool but he doesn't seem to be putting up any barriers.

"Alright, if you insist..."

"I do."

"I know a place," I say. It's my turn to take some initiative and choose a venue. "A dark, secretive place..."

"I like the sound of that," he says, and I can hear the smile in his voice.

Clare's flat-warming floats out of my mind as I remove my silky handkerchief top from my desk drawer. It's a loose off-the-shoulder number, with a watercolour of big flowers splashed over it in bright colours. I'd bought it at the first sign of summer. It slips deliciously over my skin. I kick off my flats and put on my wedges, and let my hair down, pushing one side up with a flower pin in bright red.

Forty minutes later I'm waiting outside Gordon's Wine Bar, the oldest wine bar in the city. I'm keen to get inside. Downstairs, in the dimly lit cellar, the stone ceiling arches over wooden tables lit by candles in wine bottles, their necks dripping with wax. In my memory it's an intimate venue, a place to share secrets and get to know each other in the moody light. I've only ever been there with friends, but I always thought I'd take a boyfriend one day. I have an archive of places I'd like to go with someone special, and although I don't think Damian is *the one*, he's the closest thing I've had to it for a long time.

Outside the air smells of hog-roast barbecue and my mouth waters. I haven't eaten anything since the limp salad at lunch. I wasn't trying to be healthy; it was all that was left in the cafeteria by the time I took a lunch break.

Damian arrives ten minutes late, looking pristine with his hair blow-dried and tossed to the side. He's wearing a pale-blue linen blazer with three-quarter-length sleeves over a white v-neck t-shirt and stonewash jeans. We kiss on the cheek and I breathe in his fresh scent, feeling a little rush of pleasure at the thought that he'll be all mine later.

"You look gorgeous," he says, "all summery."

He touches the flower in my hair and smiles.

"Come on," I say, heading down the stairs, "I love this place."

At the bar, I notice the discomfort on Damian's face as he flicks through the wine menu. It's pretty obvious he's not a connoisseur and is feeling a little insecure. I like a man who knows his wines, but it's a hardly a make-or-break point.

"The Montepulciano is good, let's do that," I say.

I get the impression he would have agreed to anything. He insists on carrying the bottle and glasses and follows me into the seating area under the arches. It's even darker than I remembered. It's also quite busy. One big table has only two people on it so we sit at the other end and I suggest we move when something becomes free. We've barely said a word to each other yet and there are little knots in my stomach. Perhaps I should have let him choose where to meet after all. He's probably so used to going to the best places, that this must feel like slumming it.

I pour out the wine and we clink glasses. It's full-bodied, peppery and dry. I savour it on my tongue and feel the taste of my workday slip away. I don't know much about wines but I'd love to learn. Damian looks pensive after he swallows his first gulp, sucking on his tongue, his brow furrowed.

"What do you think?" I ask.

He shoots me a guilty smile. "It tastes a bit like carpet."

I think he wants me to laugh, but I just feel disappointed.

"I mean, it's not very refreshing is it?" he says, leaning forward into the candlelight, his nostrils flaring as he smiles.

What was he expecting? It was never going to be like cold lemonade.

"Haven't you ever had red wine before?"

He takes another sip. "I just don't think wine is all that."

How can he put every wine in one big category of mediocrity? It's like saying you don't think cheese is all that.

"Why didn't you say you didn't like it? We could have gone somewhere else."

"I don't mind it. I can drink it."

"It's not the same, though. Where's the fun in sharing a bottle of wine with someone who isn't enjoying it?"

He could have said something before we ordered a whole bottle.

"I wanted to see what you like," he says, smiling apologetically. He casts his eyes up at the low ceiling. "And now I know. You like medieval prisons."

He takes another sip of wine.

"I think it's growing on me," he says, licking his lips.

Shadows flicker over his face, the light picking out the flecks of gold in his green eyes.

"Liar."

"Honestly, I can taste the... uh..."

I raise my eyebrows, challenging him to come up with something credible.

"...subtle hint of... uh... Lynx Africa, the traditional fragrance worn by Italian winemakers..."

I can't help laughing.

"You can tweet that," he adds, posing with his glass.

Another stab of disappointment. The last thing I feel like doing is tweeting, but he's my client so I haven't got my choice. I dig around in my bag for my phone, but I can't see a thing.

"Do you want me to ask them to turn the lights on?" he says.

I muster weak smile.

"You *are* May, right?" he says, reaching out uncertainly and trying to touch my face.

I catch his hand and push it away. "I bet you like disco lights and cocktails the colour of hubba bubba, don't you?"

It sounds a bit bitchy, but he doesn't seem offended. He cocks his head in mock reflection, and then nods enthusiastically. "Yep. You've pretty much nailed the kind of person I am."

"Pina Colada or Strawberry Daiquiri?"

"Whichever matches my glow sticks on the night. It took all my self-restraint not to wear some out tonight."

I'm being a snob again. He's allowed to not like wine. He's being honest.

"I'm glad. You look good... I like the blazer, very tasteful."

I make a mental note to suggest a similar outfit to Thijs.

"Thanks. I'm trying to make it up to you after the trucker hat faux pas the other time."

I smile, pleased he cares. "You don't have to impress me."

"Yes I do."

He tops his glass up and takes a big gulp. "Oh yes, I can really taste the crush of cherries now."

He's read that description off the label.

I put my nose in my glass and breathe in deeply. It's time to lighten up.

"Oh yes, I'm getting it too... crushed cherries with a dash of vanilla..."

"Really? You're getting vanilla?" He breathes in deeper. "I'm getting oak."

"Mmm."

"With a hint of furniture polish."

"What kind?"

"Mr Sheen. I recognise his aftershave."

I burst out laughing and the woman on the other end of the table throws us a disapproving look. I lower my voice.

"And tobacco," I whisper. "They always throw in a bit of tobacco, don't they?"

"Camel Lights or Marlboro Reds?"

"You tell me, you're the dirty smoker!"

He looks hurt. "I've given up. I haven't smoked since I saw you last. You called me a dirty smoker then too."

The admission takes me by surprise. I hadn't realised my insult had been taken so seriously.

"Really?"

"I don't want you not wanting to kiss me, do I?"

He holds my gaze and I feel this burst of hope. I had assumed he would lose interest after that afternoon on the narrow boat, but the way he's looking at me, so earnestly, it makes me feel like he wants more than that. Perhaps, despite our differences, we can make something of this.

"Well, good," I say, and lift my glass. "Let's toast to your lungs."

"My lungs!"

We drink deeply, maintaining eye contact, because we both know that if we don't that'll mean seven years of bad sex. Although after our narrow boat encounter it seems unlikely.

"Good," I say, blinking away a steamy image and feeling my cheeks flush. "I'll now feel less of a hypocrite when I tweet anything health-related on your behalf."

I'm thinking of Tintino.

Damian looks wary. "What do you mean?"

I should have kept my mouth shut. It's easy to forget that while this is a job to me, it's very personal to him.

"Oh nothing. Just people not believing you get up early and do yoga, that sort of stuff."

He frowns. "Well I do."

"Yeah, but obviously not after you've been DJ-ing. I didn't factor that in. I mean you probably got drunk so wouldn't be doing yoga the next day... even though I tweeted quite late so... anyway."

"I don't get drunk when I play."

I frown at him. I've got that image in my head, of him lying on the pavement looking like he can barely open his eyes he's so wasted.

"I might have a couple of beers, but I still get up and do my yoga, do my breathing and my visualisation..."

If I had ended up looking like he had, the only thing I'd be visualising would have been a tombstone signifying the end to my pain. I can't function at all when I'm hung over, which is why I try to keep on top of what I drink. Right now, I'm drinking too much and too fast. I also haven't eaten, which is rule number one.

"What are you thinking?" he says, his eyes narrowing. "Don't you believe me? Why would I lie to you?"

"No, of course... I just thought you might drink more. *I* would, I'd be scared to DJ in front of so many people."

"It wasn't that many... but, yeah, it can be scary."

Who am I going to believe? Damian or some random off Twitter?

It's very possible that Damian has worn the same outfit to DJ before. He's not some megastar who can't be seen wearing the same thing twice. DJ Buzzya has a lucky sweatband he wears at every gig, so it's not impossible that Damian has a set of clothes he feels particularly good in when he's working.

"Anyone in particular being a dick?" he asks.

I can feel the tension coming off him in waves. I don't want him to be tempted to go online to track down Tintino. Especially since he would come across me being all chatty with him and having a pretty good laugh about things.

"No," I say. "No one in particular."

I pour myself another glass and decide to change the conversation.

"So, reasons Damian Dance should be in the jungle?"

He looks confused.

"We can only talk about Twitter if it's productive talk," I clarify.

"Fine by me."

"Who do you know who could help get this trending? What famous people?" I say, getting to the point.

"I know a few radio DJs who might help."

Instinctively I take out my tablet. Damian glances at it warily.

"Isn't it interfering with the atmospheric lighting?"

I notice the woman at the far end of our table glaring at me. I put the tablet back in my bag feeling stupid.

"Sorry, that was really boring of me."

"We can brainstorm, but we can also have some fun, can't we?"

Yes, we can. Why do I have to turn everything into work? Is it because I'm a workaholic? Or am I boring? Or is because the man I'm on a date with is my client and therefore makes me think of work?

Despite the wine, I'm now feeling inexplicably tense and rather emotional. I'm not sure going out for a drink was such a good idea after all.

"Sorry, I wish I hadn't done that... you know, brought my tablet out, like we're in some meeting... we aren't, are we?"

It's such a little thing, but for some reason it's really niggling me.

He gathers my hands up in his. "No, May, this a date."

I smile, feeling tears well up. I'm tired, that's what my mum would say right now.

"You know what you need," he says. "You need one of those glow-in-the-dark drinks."

"Poison?"

"Sugar," he adds. "You need a sugar rush."

I drink the wine. "I'm alright... just need to unwind a bit more..."

"After this, I'll take you to the best hidden cocktail bar in town."

"The best, is it?"

"It's private members only and there's only one member."

I shoot him a quizzical look. "Is this your flat we're talking about?"

He laughs and in the dim light I see his cheeks colour. "Will you come if it is?"

I lean forward, feeling a ripple of sexual desire rush over me, "Well, I hope so."

It doesn't take us long to finish the wine after that. Next we're in the back of a black cab, our hands teasing each other, as we head for his bachelor pad in south London.

Chapter 27

"One margarita coming up," Damian says, reaching for the chrome cocktail shaker.

The chill-out music is on. It's a slow electronic melody with a woman singing in hushed Portuguese over the whoosh of waves, supposedly from Copacabana beach. He's dimmed the spotlights and switched on an ambience lamp. It's currently projecting a huge shadow of the palm plant on the wall in slowly changing colours.

It's endearing the way he's so proud of his flat, especially his kitchen bar. The granite island is better stocked than a hotel, with an impressive variety of rums, tequilas and vodkas. He's got a crushed-ice dispenser on the outside of his fridge and sliced limes and oranges waiting on a shiny black chopping board. He's even got straws in black and red, and a mini holder for little black serviettes.

The flat is open-plan, with the kitchen joined onto the living room. It's all very tidy and I'm guessing he has a cleaner. There's a big red sofa, a chaise longue attached to one end, where I imagine him stretched out watching films on his 50-inch flat screen. He's got all the paraphernalia of a gamer; the X-box, handsets and boxes of video games. We haven't made it to the bedroom yet.

"Make yourself comfortable," he calls.

I sink into the sofa and my eyes scan over the coffee table. I'm surprised at the pile of celebrity gossip magazines, and have to push away a critical little voice.

I reason that he reads them for work purposes, the same as a shopkeeper might read a trade magazine. I'd just assumed he'd want to avoid the negativity.

On top of a TV guide, there's a glass ashtray with roll-up butts and a ripped-up Rizla packet. If I'd given up smoking, I'd definitely have put the ashtray out of sight.

He brings over my drink and I'm impressed with the margarita glass rimmed with salt.

"Thank you."

"It should have a kick to it."

He goes back to his worktop and prepares an Old Fashioned for himself. I smile as I watch his concentration, his nostrils flared, his brow tense. For a moment he's like a small boy at a chemistry set, and then he glances up and gives me this flirty little wink. All that matters right now is that I really fancy him. That's reason enough to be here.

"How is it?" he asks.

"Delicious. Definitely deserves a photo."

I may as well embrace my job while there's no one about to criticise it.

"How about...#WhyIWantDamianIntheJungle *Because he makes the best cocktails?"*

He looks pleased with himself.

"I doubt I'll be able to recreate this with rat testicles and parrot shit."

"Details shmeetails."

"Won't I sound like a nob if I tweet that myself?"

"That's why we'll get some friends to do it."

"What friends?"

"Don't you worry."

On Craig's instruction I've set up some Twitter accounts posing as Damian's friends. Not that they say that explicitly in the biog. Their biogs are pretty mundane, and their faces are randoms which Gabe Photoshopped for me. For obvious reasons they aren't being followed by millions; there's only so much time I can spend on fake accounts. The point is, they can tweet about Damian and he can just retweet it to his followers, and so begins the campaign.

"Cheers," I say, and take a deep gulp of my drink. It's zingy and fresh and perfectly complements my sudden rush of optimism.

Damian settles onto the sofa beside me, takes a sip of his drink and smacks his lips together. "Oh, yeah, that's what I'm talking about. Try that."

Mixing drinks. That's also a big "no no" in my book. That comes after rule number one of "always eat something before a night out".

"Now tell me that's not better than wine," he says.

His cocktail is also delicious, with the sweetness of the cherry and whisky mixed with the bitterness of the orange.

"It's good," I say, chasing the taste along my lips with my tongue. "Better than in a bar... they always make cocktails too watery in bars..."

"Yes! That's what I always say!"

He sets his glass down on the coffee table. "Excuse me a sec."

While he's absent I take the opportunity to check the notifications coming in. Damian's retweet has already provoked some pointless replies, smiley faces and lols, but nothing to further the hashtag. I obviously need to give it more than five minutes but I'm impatient. I just want to keep refreshing. Refresh. Tweet Favourited. Refresh. Tweet Favourited. *Seriously, you don't think you're an addict?* My inner voice scoffs.

"Hey," he says, leaning over the back of the sofa and kissing my neck. "You're not working again, are you?"

I tip my neck back for another kiss. His hands run over my shoulders, caress the top of my arms.

"I just want to get you in that jungle."

But he's not interested in the jungle right now. Beside me on the sofa again, he leans in to kiss me. His lips taste as good as his drink. I feel his hand finding my waist, slipping under my blouse. I run my hand through his thick blonde hair, thinking how I could get used to having a man in my life.

He pulls back, drops his hand to his lap, his attention on something in his hand.

"Do you want a line?"

"Sorry?"

I've heard him, but it takes a second to sink in. He holds up the tiny bag of white powder and I get this knot in my throat. I'm a bit stunned. It doesn't really feel like the time or the place. I thought we were having a chilled evening with a few drinks and working on where we left off.

"I'm okay, thanks."

"Oh..." he looks as if he's not sure what to do next.

"I don't."

He waits for me to finish the sentence.

"I don't take it," I clarify. "I never have."

I feel as though I should add that I'm not judging him, that he should go ahead if he wants to. But I don't. The truth is I don't really want to watch him snort a line of coke in front of me.

"That's cool," he says, pushing a hand through his hair. "Sorry, I don't really either."

I frown at him. "Well, that's not true, is it?"

He tosses the bag dismissively onto the coffee table. "It's just my friends always expect it so... I don't know... so, you've never even tried it?"

I pick up my drink and take a sip, then another. The atmosphere feels a little uncomfortable. Actually, it's not the atmosphere, it's me. *I* feel uncomfortable.

"I've never felt like it..."

"Wow, that's crazy."

That little ripple of doubt has come back, and a little voice is trying to make this out to be a bigger deal than it really is. And now I sound really cagey about it all.

"I watched this documentary about the effect of cocaine in Bolivia... about the farmers being forced to grow it..." It comes out much heavier than I intended but I keep going, flashbacks popping into my head of the dead body they'd shown of the young gang member and the leathery-faced prostitutes flapping the flies from their faces. It had been inappropriate viewing for an eight-year-old, but my parents had fallen asleep and left the television on. "I'm not sure you can separate the two aspects. If you take it, then you're supporting all the horrific stuff that goes with it, aren't you?"

His face is twitching somewhere between a smile and a frown. "I don't know about that, May."

"But if there wasn't such a demand for it, they'd be growing potatoes."

"They wouldn't earn as much from potatoes."

"But their sons wouldn't be getting killed in gangs."

"O-kay..." he says, scratching the back of his head.

"Oh God," I sigh. "Sorry. I feel like a vegan at a butcher's convention."

He laughs. "It's good you're sensitive, but I think you might be taking it a little bit far. You could look at it the other way," he continues, "if we didn't buy, they'd be out of a job."

I feel a half-hearted urge to argue with him, to regurgitate some horrible statistics and throw them at him to untangle. However my job is to stay calm and collected when faced with differing opinions. And isn't this all it is? A difference of opinions?

"Alright..." he says, getting up off the table and picking up the little bag of powder that has managed to put a spanner in the works of our smooth evening. "I'm going to flush it down the toilet."

I laugh in surprise. "What?"

"Yep."

"No, you don't have to."

"You've got to understand, May, I'm a bit rough around the edges. I'm still working through stuff... but, you know, I don't need this. But no one has ever pointed that out till you... so that's that. My mind's made up. When I make my mind up, that's that."

"Don't do it because of me."

"No, I'll do it because of me."

Those few words restore my good feeling. He heads to the toilet and I lean back into the sofa, my heart beat drumming with exhilaration. I feel like whatever is happening between us is escalating fast. It's both alarming and wonderful to have someone respond in this way, to have someone listen and care about what I'm saying.

There's the sound of the flush, and then a bang, presumably of the toilet lid, and he comes back in, looking cheerful. He picks up his glass and takes a deep sip and then seems to consider me for a moment, obviously toying with something.

"What is it?"

"No, nothing..."

I reach out for him and pull him towards me. "Where were we?"

We start kissing, that whisky-and-cherry flavour making me want to lick his lips. I can taste the citrus on his warm skin. My hands slide up under his t-shirt and run over his back. I think of his tattoo and marvel how my fingers are blind to it.

"I never showed you the bedroom," he says, in my ear.

"That was very rude of you."

He gets up, reaches out for my hand and leads me down the corridor to his room. His bed is a beauty, a king size with fresh white sheets that feel so good beneath my skin. We can't get enough of each other now, the moment of awkwardness truly left behind. He orgasms quickly, pushes his head into my neck, moaning.

"Sorry," he whispers.

"Don't."

He rolls over and gathers me up in his arms. I lie against his beating chest, the lounge music reduced to a faint beat. I sense him thinking about something and I wonder what it is. But I'm not going to ask. I know that question is the one guy's hate most. In fact that question has been responsible for most of Louisa's breakups. She always wants to get inside their heads and have a thorough look around. I'm sure there are things in Damian's head I'd rather not know, and likewise I wouldn't want anyone to hear the goings-on in mine.

He shifts and then returns to the same position.

"Are you alright?" I ask.

"Yeah, yeah, I'm fine."

But after a while, he's twitching again.

"You sure?"

He leans back and looks at me, frowning, "You don't mind me having a fag do you?"

He asks it like it's such a serious question. I almost feel sorry for him.

"I thought you'd given up?"

"I know, I know... but after throwing the coke out... well, I think maybe... you know..."

"Have a cigarette if you want a cigarette!" I say.

He smiles with such relief. "Thanks. I just need to have a little relax before part two..."

I smile back. He's still embarrassed because he came too fast. Damian Dance wants me to think the best of him, is chasing my approval. It feels pretty good.

"I'll go get our drinks too..."

He pulls on his tight grey boxers and heads out, giving me

the full view of his massive, blotchy tattoo. Even the second time around it's still a bit of a shock. I want to ask him when he's going to get the cover-up done, but I don't want to sound insensitive.

Alone in his tidy bedroom of blues and greys, I think about the evening so far. It's not like it's that easy to give up smoking. As for the drugs, sometimes it seems like more of my friends are taking them than who aren't. Is it any worse than drinking? Just because something isn't illegal doesn't mean it's any better than something that is. It's just someone's decision. Some people would argue sugar is worse than cocaine, but all around the world parents are using it to reward their kids.

I don't know, maybe it's my idealism that has stopped me getting a boyfriend in the past. Being idealistic would blind me to Damian's good qualities. He's easy to talk to, funny, caring, attentive. He doesn't have a boring nine-to-five job I have to pretend to be interested in and he sounds like he's up for a life of adventure. Though it doesn't look like it now, I also plan to have an adventurous life, one that exists beyond a computer screen.

Damian comes back, with a cigarette between his lips, and our two glasses.

"Thanks," I say, taking my drink.

"I'll open the window and drink loads of mouthwash after so you don't call me a dirty smoker."

I smile at him and feel a rush of affection. Nobody's perfect after all.

Chapter 28

MERLOTTI @MERLOTTIJOIE
@bthomskinner You've made me look so stupid

BTHOMSKINNER @BTHOMSKINNER
@merlottijoie No my love, I'm the only one who looks bad.

Would he say "my love"? My heart is pounding. I'm holding a marriage in my hands and it feels as delicate as butterfly wings. How could I not have replied? How could I have tricked her into replying and then left her message unanswered?

MERLOTTI @MERLOTTIJOIE
@bthomskinner I wish you had talked to me. I wish you had told me what you were feeling, what you thought you were missing.

BTHOMSKINNER @BTHOMSKINNER
@merlottijoie I was a fool. I'll never stop regretting it.

I wait for a reply.
Nothing.
With every minute, I feel my stomach clench a little tighter.

Does she want me to keep writing? Or has she clocked on that this Bernard who's replying doesn't sound like her husband?

MERLOTTI @MERLOTTIJOIE
@bthomskinner Sorry. Postman.

I breathe out heavily and rub my hand over my face. Thank God. The tension in my shoulders is killing me. It serves me right. I should stop this now. I should phone Bernard and insist he log on and be himself.

But I don't.

Do I want his approval? Is that it? Am I trying to earn a pat on the back for getting his wife back? This is not a game to her. This is her marriage.

She wants him back, though. I can tell. Perhaps she's messed up in the past, too? Perhaps she slept with the postman in revenge when she first found out. Who knows? Maybe that was her telling the postman that it's over. I mean, how long does it normally take to sign for a package?

Maybe they both need forgiveness.

BTHOMSKINNER @BTHOMSKINNER
@merlottijoie Sorry for shutting you out and being an obnoxious bastard. Maybe I should retire from spotlight and become electrician?

Each time I press SEND MESSAGE I feel this sickening sensation rush through me. It's like standing on the edge of a precipice with a bungee rope attached to me knowing that any minute now someone is going to push me off. When will I fall? Which tweet will catch me out?

MERLOTTI @MERLOTTIJOIE
@bthomskinner Don't even think of giving it all up. We both

know presenting is the only thing that keeps you bearable.

That's a surprise. I would have thought it was what inflated his ego. But perhaps without the responsibility he loses balance. If he got axed from the show, maybe his drinking would start even earlier. More reason to make sure he stays on it then.

BTHOMSKINNER @BTHOMSKINNER
@merlottijoie You know me so well.

MERLOTTI @MERLOTTIJOIE
@bthomskinner I know. That's why I can't let you go.

I cover my mouth, my eyes welling up. Oh my God. It's happening. Now that I've done it, I want to retreat from my computer with my hands up. But I can't possibly leave it like this. She's just opened her heart. It would be so cruel not to reply, not to tell her that I want her back, that I'm grateful, that I love her.

I swallow back the lump of misgivings in my throat.

BTHOMSKINNER @BTHOMSKINNER
@merlottijoie I love you so much.

MERLOTTI @MERLOTTIJOIE
@bthomskinner Do you?

BTHOMSKINNER @BTHOMSKINNER
@merlottijoie Of course.

How did I end up here, wooing someone else's wife back over social media?

BTHOMSKINNER @BTHOMSKINNER
@merlottijoie I can't believe we're having this conversation on Twitter.

MERLOTTI @MERLOTTIJOIE

@bthomskinner We don't have to be. Do you want to talk in person?

#JobDone. Bernard is going back to France. That's the end of my involvement.

BTHOMSKINNER @BTHOMSKINNER

@merlottijoie I'd love to. I'll look at flights.

MERLOTTI @MERLOTTIJOIE

@bthomskinner You don't need to. I'm here in London. I can be home in half an hour.

My eyes snap open wide. The panic punches the air from my chest, leaving me gasping in horror. Joyce is in London? She's on her way over? What if he's not home? What if he's drunk? Or watching porn?

I grab my mobile and hit Bernard's number.

"Shit, shit, shit..." I hiss, as I wait to hear the ringtone.

Hello, Bernard here, please leave a message...

"SHIT!"

I don't know what to do, so I just dial again.

Hello, Bernard here, please leave me a message...

Should I leave a message? Is it wise to leave my voice on his answer phone? It might be evidence against him in a bloody court of divorce law. Oh, fuck it, it's not like he's killed anyone!

"Hi, it's me... May..."

Oh shit. It's evidence that could go against *me* in a court of law, isn't it? Am I committing fraud? Why has this only just occurred to me?

"Your wife is in London," I say, trying to sound calm. "She wants to see you tonight. Now. She's on her way. Call me, it's urgent."

This can't be his only number. There must be a landline.

"May?"

I look up to find Craig at the door holding up a bottle of champagne, a Cheshire grin plastered across his overly orange face. It strikes me in the same moment, that a) he must have had the sun bed on the wrong setting and b) he must be spying on everything I do if he knows what I've just done for Bernard.

"I thought a congratulations was in order for the trending hashtag!"

So, I may have been wrong about b).

"What's wrong? You look like you've seen a ghost."

"I need to get hold of Bernard now. I've done something terrible. I've made up with his wife but his wife doesn't know that it's me. She thinks it's Bernard. Bernard doesn't know anything. She's not in France. She's in London and she's half an hour away."

"Wait, slow down."

"I can't slow down! I need to talk to him now. He must have a landline."

I throw open my filing cabinet and start rummaging through files. I've never bothered with saving landlines on my phone. Mobile numbers have always felt like the only sure way of getting hold of someone.

"Can you stall her?" Craig says, quick to understand the emergency.

I stop flapping and turn back to my computer. "Yes, I think so."

I pull the keyboard towards me and start typing.

BTHOMSKINNER @BTHOMSKINNER

@merlottijoie I can't believe it! That's incredible! I can't believe you're here! Half an hour? Can you give me more time?

There are probably more exclamation marks in that message than there was in both his biographies, however I'm not really in a state to analyse grammar right now. I think if I leant over a toilet, I'd throw up the contents of my day without any effort.

@bthomskinner Really? Do you think I care about your dirty dishes at this point?

"I've got the landline," Craig says.

Now that I need to save myself, it seems lying comes even more naturally to me. I feel ashamed of myself but type on regardless. There's a chance he's not home. I really need Joyce to give us at least an hour.

BTHOMSKINNER @BTHOMSKINNER
@merlottijoie I know and I love you more for it. But give me an hour. I don't want you changing your mind.

I turn around to grab the paper with the number on, but Craig has anticipated me and starts dictating it. I love him in that moment. I feel like we're really in this together.

"It's ringing," I say.

I wait, my body rigid with nervous anticipation. And then I hear a divine crackle.

"Yes?"

I've never been so glad to hear Bernard's grumpy voice.

"Bernard! You're home!"

I lean against the desk as if the puppeteer has just let go of my strings.

"This is not a good time. I'm in the middle of something."

I spring to attention.

"You'll be in the middle of divorce if you don't listen to me. Your wife is in London. She's on her way. She thinks you've made up. I'm emailing you the interaction you've just had."

"What? She's in London?"

"I won her back! Over Twitter Direct Messages!"

After all the abuse I've had to put up with, I want him to know that he underestimated me. Craig looks at me, nodding. His hands are clapping softly and there's newfound respect in his eyes.

"Fuck!" Bernard cries.

"A thank you would be nice. Now hurry up and read the messages. And wash up any dishes."

"Dishes? Oh, right, shit, I've got to go..."

He sounds much more panicked than excited. I'm thinking his flat must be in a terrible state when I hear the voice. My finger is already on the cancel button so I cut it short. So short I wonder if I really did just hear a voice or not.

"I think I just..." I begin.

No, it can't have been.

"You think what?" Craig says.

My mind is buzzing with horrible thoughts.

Craig reaches out for the bottle of champagne; the smile is back on his face. As far as he's concerned the crisis is over.

"Can we take a break and celebrate now?" he says.

I think I'm in shock.

"Celebrate what?"

"You don't even know, do you?" he says, "Your hashtag #WhyIWantDamianInTheJungle has been trending since last night!"

"Oh my God," I say, finally breaking into a weak smile. "That's great."

In the end I keep it to myself. I swallow it down and feel the weight of it lying on the top of my stomach. I smile through it. I pretend I'm thrilled by what I've achieved.

I don't tell Craig that I think I just heard a female voice in Bernard's house, that I think it might have been another lover. I don't tell him that I'm worried I've just seduced an innocent wife back into the hands of her cheating bastard of a husband.

"You sure you're okay?"

"Yeah, yeah... just a lot of drama this morning."

I mustn't assume the worst of Bernard. He's grumpy, but he's not evil. Maybe I'm just jumping to conclusions. If I did hear a woman, and I might not have, how can I be sure it wasn't a friend? Or a relative? Or a cleaner? Or a neighbour? For Joyce's sake, I really hope it's the cleaner. Please be the cleaner. Please let me have done a good thing. Please don't let me have broken someone's heart for money.

Chapter 29

Damian goes to the bathroom and I turn to look out of the restaurant window, the smile falling from my lips. This is a celebration lunch, but I'm not in the mood. I can't stop thinking about that Twitter conversation with Bernard's wife. It seems so outrageously bold now. I can't believe I instigated it. Every time I think about that woman's voice, the doubt curls around my chest and squeezes tight.

I dig out my phone and stare absently at the screen. I'm not going to compose another tweet as Bernard until I know what happened. Instead I review my other clients' social media accounts. Thijs is heading to Glastonbury on the weekend.

BANDGIRLABI @BANDGIRL
@ThijsVanBro Jealous! Wish I was going! Don't forget your waterproofs!

I favourite it. What else can I do? I feel sorry for Abigail. She's been in a funny mood ever since Ankara started tweeting our youngest client. Or should I say, since Ankara started tweeting to *me*, pretending to be him.

I've never flirted with a woman on Twitter before. If Abigail ever finds out, it's going to be awful. We should have told her from the beginning. I hate carrying around these secrets. It felt like acting before, acting for a good cause. Now I feel like a two-faced bitch.

What if Thijs and Ankara did fall in love, though? I could add "Cupid" to my job description, and how could that be a bad thing?

Alex makes me jump. I don't know how long he's been looking through the glass, trying to catch my attention. He smiles when he gets it. I straighten up, stuffing my phone back in my bag and scrunching my hair to get a bit of volume back. We never did make lunch. Is he hoping to join me for some now? I glance towards the toilets, feeling a little anxious. Why is Damian taking so long in there?

I get this image of him in my head, leaning over the lid of a toilet, a finger pressing down on his nostril as he goes in for the snort. I have to blink it away. Maybe he's just got an upset stomach. He's obviously hung over. He hasn't taken his sunglasses off since we met. There's a popular quote going around on Facebook for people who wear sunnies indoors. It goes:

The only people who wear sunglasses inside are blind people and arseholes.

Alex is coming inside. I get up to greet him.

"Oh, wow, I've caught you having a proper lunch," he says, "I feel like I should be taking a picture and tweeting it!"

I smile. "Except you're not on Twitter."

We hover in front of each other.

"Are you with someone?" he says.

"Yes..."

"Of course you are, stupid question. The food here is amazing, isn't it?"

I wish I wasn't with someone. It's Damian's energy. Despite looking like he should be in bed, he's all hyper and agitated. Meanwhile I'm feeling so knotted. I can't get it off my chest either. I can't spill one client's secret to another.

A waiter approaches, "Will you be eating, sir?"

"No, I'm good thanks," he says. The waiter retreats, unimpressed.

"I saw you and thought I'd say hello... we should have that lunch..." Alex says. "Although I wasn't thinking somewhere this nice. You've set the bar high!"

"It's a client lunch..."

Will he recognise Damian? It would probably be best if he didn't see my client.

"So you're not on holiday yet?" I say. "Louisa must be getting impatient."

I watch his face carefully to see what reaction her name triggers.

"I know," he says, wrinkling his nose. "I'm getting impatient too. It's just hard to turn down this work. The money I'm getting can help with the film. It's worth waiting if I can get the funds to make it better. It's pointless making a rubbish short film, it's hard enough getting them into festivals when they're brilliant."

"Yeah, I bet."

"Anyway, you don't want to hear all this," he says. "I should leave you to it."

If I can get Bernard back with his wife, I think grimly, I can definitely get Louisa and Alex together. I just need a little more time.

"Let's get lunch this week sometime."

"I don't actually have your number," he says, taking out his phone.

It feels like a big deal swapping numbers. I guess this means we're no longer two people who bump into each other when we're putting the rubbish out. We're friends.

"I think your friend, sorry, client, is back," he says, nodding behind me. There's a tiny glimmer of surprise in his eyes, but it passes before I can be sure. "Enjoy your lunch, I'll see you around."

By the time I've turned back from looking over at Damian, Alex has already stepped back outside onto the busy Soho streets.

"Who was that?" Damian says, sounding grumpy. "He looked familiar."

He sits down heavily in his seat and drains his glass of still water, immediately looking over for a waiter to order some more. It might be easier to catch their eye if he took those silly sunglasses off. My eyes glance to his nose. There's no incriminating powder at the end of it, so that's good. He's definitely hung over, though.

"My neighbour."

"Your neighbour? And you just gave him your number?"

I frown at the tone in his voice. "Yeah, he works around here. We thought we could meet up for lunch."

"Why?"

"Why not?"

He sighs and looks over at the waiter again, finally gets his attention and points at his empty glass.

"Are you okay?" I say. "You seem a bit on edge."

"I leave for one second and you're planning a date with another bloke."

I start to laugh. He doesn't join in. "You're joking, right?"

He looks out of the window, sulking.

"Please tell me you're joking."

Does he want to hear a quote on jealousy? It has the word "insecurity" in it.

"I just don't have that sort of relationship with my neighbour," he says.

"Damian," I reach over and take his fidgeting hand. "Don't be a dick."

He pulls back his hand sharply, his cheeks reddening, and turns back to the window. Is he not talking to me now? Funny how I could paint a different picture for the whole world. I'm so tempted to whip out my phone and compose a little tweet.

DAMIANDANCE @DAMIANDANCE
HAVING SO MUCH FUN RIGHT NOW! #BESTLUNCHEVER

One look at his stony expression tells me he's not going to find anything amusing anytime soon.

How did we get here?

I'd forgotten how this felt, this swollen silence, pregnant with blame. I've been here before, of course. Everyone who's ever been in a relationship must have. My last boyfriend, Stewart, and I were breaking up for three months. It was so hard to let go, even though we were making each other so miserable.

But Damian isn't a boyfriend. We're just going with the flow, seeing what happens. I think of the narrow boat and feel resigned to the fact that it might have just been a one-off. Shame, because it had been fun. I really don't have enough fun.

"Don't ever call me a dick again," he says in a low voice.

I look at him and suppress a nervous smile. I'm getting told off. "I'm sorry."

He nods. Apology accepted. Sex on a narrow boat is back on the menu. #LetsMoveOn.

"I'm just under a lot of stress," he says, turning back to me.

He's not the only one, but I'm not about to start a "who is more stressed?" contest.

A phone is vibrating. Is it mine? I decide not to answer it. Damian leans back in his chair and slides his phone out from his tight jeans. Oh. It's his.

"Hello?"

The waiter arrives with our meals. I've gone for salmon linguine because I like to order things I don't usually make. Damian has gone for spaghetti Bolognese. I suppose that's a good meal for a hangover.

"Yeah, yeah... tell me..."

I pick up my cutlery and glance over at him, wondering if he's going to tell whoever it is to ring back afterwards since our food has arrived.

"No, go on, I'm not busy..."

He's not busy?

I pick at a piece of linguine because I'm starving and I like my food hot.

Damian's face breaks into a big smile. At least it's good news. I didn't much like the trailer for his grumpy side.

The salmon falls apart in my mouth. Delicious.

"That's amazing... so, what did she say exactly?"

Is this what I do? I very rarely miss a call and I always respond to my text messages. I deal with my clients' social-media notifications wherever I am, with the exception of the cinema.

Actually, I did once leave the cinema for ten minutes to deal with some Twitter interactions. It was an important day for DJ Buzzya. He'd just released a single. One of the main characters in the film got kidnapped while I was tweeting. Sitting in the cinema, confused, with Emma fuming at my side, should have been a wake-up call. That's when I should have checked myself. Because, in hindsight, it wouldn't have made any difference if I'd tweeted an hour or two later.

Am I having a wakeup call now about how I've changed? I don't want to eat with someone who talks on the phone during their meal.

"That's amazing, mate... I'm proper stoked... I can't believe you pulled this off..."

Does he not realise how rude this is?

I dig into my linguine and start to eat hungrily. It strikes me that this would not be happening if I was having lunch with Alex. The thought almost makes me laugh. What would he do? Probably pluck the phone off me and ask the waiter to store it in some hot soup where I can't get at it. I smile to myself. He's alright, really. Alex Hunter. Even when he's being argumentative and judgmental, I can see where he's coming from.

I wonder what they'll be like together. Louisa and Alex. I wish I knew what he thought of her. I guess I'll find out soon enough.

"Yep, yep... alright... bye for now...."

Damian rests his phone at the side of his plate. He doesn't excuse himself, but he does at least push his sunglasses up onto his head.

"So, that was Andy," he says.

He's excited. Talk of jealousy. I can't help feeling a tug of the stupid emotion just thinking his agent might have done something more impressive than I have with that hashtag.

"Oh yeah?"

"You're not going to believe this. I'm in! I'm going to be on *Sing Me Out of the Jungle!*"

My mouth drops open. Well, I'll be damned! The power of a little hashtag.

"Fuck yes! Fuck those twats online that tried to put me down!"

"Don't you dare say that on Twitter," I say quickly.

"Of course not. *You* can say it."

I glare at him.

"I'm joking!" he laughs. "I'm not logging in, I've promised you that!"

"Good," I say. I pick up my glass of water and take a large gulp. I've a feeling we'll be ordering something stronger in a minute.

"Congratulations," I say. "This is huge."

Huge, if being on trashy TV eating kangaroo testicles is your thing. I don't think my mum would rate it. Or Alex, for that matter.

"I can't believe it. That was great, May. What you did. It really helped."

I smile. At least I earned this result without lying. If you don't count the fake Twitter accounts, anyway.

"We should celebrate, you should come back to mine," he says. "Yes, you should definitely do that."

"I've got to go back to work."

He winks at me, "Let's go to the narrow boat. You can be back at work in a couple of hours."

I raise my eyebrows. "Oh, I see, you only want me for a couple of hours?"

Isn't that what I wanted? God, I'm a hypocrite.

He looks genuinely shocked. "Of course not! I want you for much more than that! I want you to spend the night with me!

Not just the night, the day, the week, the month, the year..." he pauses, breathless. "May, you're my lucky star."

His lucky star?

"You know what that means?" he says.

"That I'm good at my job?" I say, trying to bring a bit of cool into the equation. Right now it means I'm feeling a little over-whelmed. I'm thinking he's a little bit up and down. His forehead is shiny with sweat. Can't he feel it?

"That I can't let you go!" he says.

#Shit. I thought it might.

"In fact, I've got you something."

"For me?"

"Yeah, a thank you."

He pushes back in his seat, hoists his pelvis up to retrieve a little velvet box from his pocket.

He's not going to propose is he?

"Open it," he says grinning.

I do. Inside is a shiny, gold, Star of David. I stare at it, speechless.

"Well? Do you like it?"

"Uh... I'm not Jewish."

He frowns. "What's that got to do with anything?"

"It's the Star of David... a Jewish symbol. I'm agnostic."

"It's a fucking star! A religion can't own a fucking star!"

His voice has risen to an uncomfortable volume. People are turning to look. The waiters are looking shifty. This is not the publicity Damian needs. I need to defuse the situation carefully and quickly.

"It's beautiful," I say. "You shouldn't have."

He really shouldn't have. What kind of moron buys someone a necklace with a religious symbol on it that isn't their religion?

"So you're going to wear it?" he says, sounding stroppy.

Do I have any choice?

I pluck it out of the box and it glimmers in the light.

"It will go with anything," he says.

I feel a bubble of laughter rise up my throat. I swallow it back. "It really will."

"You can tweet a picture!" he says, looking chuffed. "Go on, a present for my lucky star... no one need know it's you."

Oh, Tintino would have a field day. He'd know straight away that Damian didn't realise what he'd given me.

"We've discussed this," I say, gently. "You know you've got to stay a single man, otherwise the girls won't vote for you."

"Fuck 'em," he says, but I can tell my words have hit home.

"Alright," he says. "It'll be our secret."

He downs his second glass of water and then excuses himself to go to the bathroom again. Maybe it's just an upset stomach. Maybe I should go back to his flat and look after him; play girl-friend for a bit. Ha! Is that where this is heading? My life might be completely out of balance, but I'm still connected enough to hear my instincts screaming out that he's not the man for me.

Chapter 30

The suspense is over. Bernard has finally decided to pick up the phone. I've asked him how he is, which was a mistake. Now he's talking about the crick in his neck and his late-blossoming hay fever.

"So what's the situation?" I cut in. "Are you back together?"

"Why ask how I am if you don't care?"

"You've got a wife to care for you now, right?"

Just give me the bloody low-down, you difficult man.

"What about you, May? Do you think you'll be someone's wife one day?" He lets out a little laugh. "What a terrifying thought, I bet."

I roll my eyes. "I haven't really got time to chat. I really need to know the facts."

"The facts are these. Joyce and I are back together. Better yet, Joyce is giving an interview right now about forgiving me."

"An interview with who?"

"*The Daily Mail.*"

He sounds very smug.

I think about the woman's voice and wonder how I'm going to phrase the question I really want to ask.

Should she forgive you? Is your affair really over?

In the end I don't ask. My office phone is ringing, reminding me of all the other things I need to attend to. The match-making between Bernard and Joyce is over, they can take things from here.

"I hope you and Joyce are very happy," I say. "Keep me in the loop."

Maria Kuebler is on the other line.

"Where are the photos from Glastonbury?" she cries.

The panic in her voice is contagious. I hurriedly click onto Thijs's Twitter account. In the back of my mind I knew it had been too quiet for comfort. I asked him to mail any selfies to me so I could upload them for him but he just laughed and said the day he took a selfie was the day he sold his soul, which struck me as something I might have said six months ago.

"It's a bit tricky as I'm not there," I admit. I squint at the ceiling, waiting to be shouted at.

I was hoping other people would be doing his publicity by tagging him in their posts. Ankara Davies has been very busy on Instagram and so far has documented:

a) *her outfit of the day #ootd*
b) *everything she has eaten and drunk in the last two days #nomnomnom*
c) *her friends having the greatest time of their lives #bffs*
d) *the sunset #nofilter*

Frustratingly for me, there's no Thijs Vandroogenbroek #mynewboyfriend

"Can't you get someone down there for the weekend? He's paying a lot of money for your services! A social media blackout is unacceptable!"

Get someone down there? Who exactly? It's not like I'm in charge of a small army of assistants.

"I'll see what I can do."

"No," she snaps. "That's not good enough. That's what people say when they have no intention of doing anything."

It's her bossy voice. It pushes my buttons. It's like when Craig says *where's your can-do attitude today?* I'm not just an office drone. I'm a miracle worker.

"Not people like me. In fact, just consider it done."

That shuts her up for a few seconds. "Really?"

I just keep talking like I'm in control while my brain goes into meltdown.

"Yes, there will be full coverage this weekend."

"Good. With Ankara Davies?"

I grit my teeth. "If they are hanging out together, then, yes."

"Can you organise that too?"

"I'm doing his social media, Maria. I can't organise his love life too."

She puffs into the receiver. "When it comes to Thijs, don't you think they are related?"

We end the call a few moments later. I'm trembling. It's the coffee and also the adrenalin that comes from uttering the words, *consider it done.*

I'm about to ring Craig to explain my predicament, but then change my mind. At the moment I'm high up in his favour and I want to keep it that way.

I ring through to reception and Abigail answers in that nervous voice that always sounds like she's suspicious of the phone, or hasn't worked out what it is yet.

"Abigail. It's me. Will you come into my office, please, I've got a little mission for you."

Her mission is to go to Glastonbury. She's the perfect person. Thijs knows her, so it won't be awkward, plus she actually knows about music and the art of tweeting.

"You're paying me to go to the festival I've been dying to go to? Why?"

She's all wide eyes and flushed cheeks. She looks like she wants to throw her arms around my neck and kiss me. Now to break the bad news to her.

"I need you to be in charge of Thijs's Twitter account," I say.

"What do you mean?"

"He's not very good at it so he needs your help."

She frowns. "He seems alright to me... he's funny and friendly... he's following me back, you know."

"Yeah, about that..."

She stares at me, waiting. She has no idea.

"It's not him."

"What do you mean it's not him?"

Maybe Craig is right. Maybe Abigail isn't exactly the right fit for this company. Lucky her, that means she's a nice person.

"You know how we're a social-media marketing company..."

"Yes..." she says, drawing the word out as if she's working out the answer as she says it.

"Well, we do his social media."

I wait for the penny to drop. My phone is buzzing with new notifications.

The penny is not dropping fast enough.

"I do his tweets," I say abruptly.

She frowns. "But he's been replying to me."

I rub my neck. #Awks.

"What? He has. I can prove it!"

Poor thing. It's harsh to be told you've been getting excited over the replies of your 28-year-old female boss instead of the famous boy-band member you have a serious crush on. A part of me is tempted to lie right now. I could tell her that those particular replies were from him.

"Oh my God! You were the one replying," she murmurs, her cheeks burning pink. I watch the look of dismay transforming into one of anger. "Why didn't you tell me?"

"I wanted to, but Craig was worried you'd tell people."

"I feel so humiliated right now."

"No, don't," I say, firmly. "I'm the only one who should be embarrassed. You've said absolutely nothing humiliating at all.

266

Actually, you're going to be perfect for this job... if you still want to work here..."

She looks doubtful. "So, let me get this straight, you want to send me to Glastonbury to tweet for Thijs?"

"Tweet *as* Thijs."

The lure of the festival has stemmed her outrage, but will she go through with it?

"It'll be easy if you're near him," I say.

"I'll be near him?"

"Absolutely. You'll be hanging out with the lot of them."

The thought of meeting Five Oars has rendered her speechless. It's a pretty big deal, but I can't let her think it is. She's got to remain calm and collected... and just a little bit invisible.

"Of course, you're probably really annoyed with me right now. If you don't think you're up to the job..." I'm hoping she'll insist she is, because I have no plan B.

She breathes out, shakes her head. "What do you want me to tweet about?"

"Oh you know, the music, the atmosphere, the people he's hanging around with..."

Should I drop another bombshell now or later?

"Especially Ankara Davies... if you can get a picture of them together..."

I didn't think it was possible for her big brown eyes to open even wider.

"Oh my God, *you* were the one tweeting to her?"

Finally, the penny has dropped. From the horrified look on her face, I'm guessing she doesn't agree with Craig that it was a stroke of genius. He thought me very witty, as did Ankara. I don't know what Thijs thought as he probably didn't read what he said.

"I know it sounds bad..."

She's shaking her head. "I can't believe it..."

Disgust is written across her face and it's horrible to watch her struggling to keep her emotions at bay. I'm regretting telling her. Cold sweat pricks at my skin as it dawns on me that she hasn't signed a confidentiality agreement. That she could just blurt the truth out to the whole world right this minute without any consequence. She's got 432 Twitter followers. That's all you need to get something started, for something to go viral. I feel my throat constrict and I swallow. I'm about to open my mouth to invent a story.

She moves towards the door.

"Where are you going?" I ask, my voice coming out hoarse.

She turns to looks at me, her face composed now, "Time is running out and I've got to track down a ticket."

"I can help you get the ticket. But you're saying you're up for the task?"

She nods. "I'm not the world's best photographer, but then again Ankara Davies is very photogenic."

She lets out a weak laugh and closes the door behind her.

I take a deep breath and wonder whether I've just made a massive mistake. Some people need to be given responsibility to make them feel part of a company. Maybe she'll stop seeing this job as a means to an end and start enjoying it. If I train her up, I won't feel so bad about leaving. Abigail could be the key to getting the rest of my life back on track. This is an excellent development. So why do feel like I'm going to throw up?

Chapter 31

I should be in bed but I can't muster the energy to move off the sofa. I'd quite like to talk to a friendly face. I'm scrolling through Facebook, wishing I could reach out to someone.

Clare Willis: *Caramel for breakfast! #100HappyDays*

The happiness is not contagious. It only reminds me that she forgot to invite me to her house-warming. It was all a mistake. She texted me after, asked me why I hadn't come. I should have swallowed my pride and called her when I'd found out about it, but it's a hurtful thing for one of your best friends to turn you into a Facebook forgettable.

Anna Jamison: *Just when you think you might do a Sylvia Plath, bubba smiles and it's all worth it!*

Sylvia Plath stuck her head in the oven... is this a cry for help? If I was feeling *that* bad, I don't think a dribbly smile would sort me out. I notice a few other new mothers have commented on it with smiles and *Aws*. I know they are new mothers because all their profile pictures are of babies. I suddenly don't feel qualified to comment.

Emma Priestly: *I've got a free ticket for the party in the park happening this weekend at Hyde Park! Message me! :)*

Why don't I go? I click on her profile to message her, but then find myself scrolling through her photos instead. Either she's with a group of beautiful girls, holding a cocktail, or with her arm around a male friend with a glimmer of hope in his eyes. Who are these friends? People from work, I suppose. Her smile is big and practiced and her blonde hair cascades over one shoulder in perfect, ironed curls. She used to do mine before I finally cracked it myself. She's probably already had loads of people messaging her about that ticket.

Louisa has arrived home. I hear her feet thumping up the stairs well before she's even put her key in the lock. I don't want the first thing for my flatmate to see is me staring predictably at a screen, so I push my phone away under a cushion and delay my decision about contacting Emma for now.

"Hello!" she calls, as she bangs the door shut. "Anyone home?"

I wait for her to find me. She swears a few times before she makes it, tripping up on something, then stopping halfway along the corridor to take off her sandals. Finally she bursts into the living room.

"Hey! You're here!"

She's dressed in a yellow playsuit, which I think makes her look like an overgrown child, but which I know she adores and wears to impress. The question is, who has she been trying to impress? Her cheeks are flushed. Wine was involved.

"Hi, where have you been?"

I've been craving company ever since I got home three hours ago.

"With the boys," she says, with a little shrug, and a twinkly smile that undermines her attempt at being casual.

I never expected Alex and Jacob to become "the boys" so quickly.

"Both of them?"

Her smile dips. "Yeah."

"You need to get him on his own."

She looks at me, her mind elsewhere. "Mm, I know."

This is ridiculous. "Can't you just text each other and arrange something?"

I move over and she plonks herself down on the sofa.

"I don't mind, really."

Of course she minds. How is she supposed to make a move on Alex with Jacob hanging around all the time?

"I bet he's dying to be on his own with you. If you never suggest it he'll start to doubt..." A thought occurs to me and I let out a little laugh, "he might even think you fancy Jacob."

She doesn't laugh. She's obviously frustrated with herself. I didn't think Alex would be the shy type. As for Louisa, how can she go from stroking his clean-shaven jaw and exclaiming "sexy" to being shy about texting him to meet up for a drink?

"I'm fine, May, I just had a nice time," she says, getting up again and going straight for the kettle. "What about you? How are things coming along with Damian?"

I'm too embarrassed to tell her about his present.

"If you really like him, I'm sure you could hand him over to Craig," Louisa says, thinking my hesitation is because he's a client.

I let out a snort. "Craig seems to be passing on all his clients to me, so I doubt it."

"Is there really no one else?"

I think of Abigail. Her ticket for the festival is secured. Thijs has been informed. She was flushed with pleasure after she came off the phone to him, had to go and wash her face. It's going to be hard for her taking photos of him with Ankara Davies, but she's going to have to. If she proves she's got what it takes at Glastonbury, why couldn't she take on Damian?

"If you had to choose between love and work?" Louisa says, sounding dreamy.

"Believe me, I don't love Damian."

Louisa groans and gives me a shove. I flop onto my side, laughing a little.

"You're no fun," she says.

"My work isn't everything, you know. I've got a plan. I'm nearly there."

"Yeah, yeah... you're going to pay off your credit cards... bla bla bla... what's the hurry? The whole country's in debt and it seems to be doing fine."

I feel suddenly annoyed. What does she know about money troubles? She grew up in a five-bedroom house in Hampshire. She did horse-riding and ballet and went skiing in the Alps. For her 18th birthday her grandmother gave her five thousand pounds.

"It's hanging over me. How am I supposed to even think about buying my own flat when I'm in debt?"

"No one can afford to buy a flat in London. The answer is not to think about it."

"You can.'"

"Sorry?"

"Oh nothing."

"I'm working in a coffee shop," she says.

As if that income was paying for all those outfits. I know she gets money from her parents still, but what's the point in arguing?

"It's not a great job, but it gives me the flexibility to pursue the career I want... isn't that more important?"

"This job is going to help me get the career I want. I'm getting a massive pay rise soon, which will help me pay off a chunk of money. I just need to hold out for six months, a year max... It will be well worth it."

"Are you sure you can trust Craig? I'm beginning to think he's all mouth."

"We've built the business up from scratch! You can't just pour money out of it before it's up and running."

She shakes her head, suddenly exasperated, "But is it just about the money? If he couldn't double your salary, would you stay?"

Would I? *Could* I keep up this pace? Would I have the energy if there was no financial incentive?

I feel mentally drained. It's the constant noise from all those interactions between strangers, every minute of the day. I can't switch off. I have to engage to turn fans into super fans, so they then become my clients' marketeers, retweeting all that content I'm responsible for creating each day.

"I don't know," I admit. "What else would I do?"

"You could do anything," Louisa says.

SPARKYMAY @SPARKYMAY
Find a job you love and you will never have to work a day –
Confucius

TINTINO @TINTINO
@SparkyMay Did you just tweet a quote?

SPARKYMAY @SPARKYMAY
@tintino I know, but it's a good one!

TINTINO @TINTINO
@SparkyMay I didn't have you down as a quoter.

SPARKYMAY @SPARKYMAY
@tintino I'm not a quoter.

TINTINO @TINTINO
@SparkyMay was it scheduled?

SPARKYMAY @SPARKYMAY
@tintino yeah, a few months ago.

TINTINO @TINTINO
@SparkyMay I think I'm going to have to unfollow you.

SPARKYMAY @SPARKYMAY

@tintino how will I cope? Bye bye!

....

SPARKYMAY @SPARKYMAY

@tintino you're still following me.

TINTINO @TINTINO

@SparkyMay I thought I'd give you another chance.

SPARKYMAY @SPARKYMAY

@tintino "Sometimes life gives you a second chance, because maybe the first time you just weren't ready" – unknown.

TINTINO @TINTINO

@SparkyMay I regret my decision.

Chapter 32

Friday morning begins with a direct message from Happy Heart for Angel.

HAPPYHEART @HAPPYHEART
@angelbutler Hi! Thank you so much for your supportive tweets and your arty photographs!

"Arty" is a kind way of putting it. "Shit" would have been more accurate. Angel didn't want to pose wearing any of the clothes I'd bought so I had to improvise. I stuffed some cushions up my skirt, looked away from the camera and blurred and discoloured the hell out of it with Photoshop.

Your voice is really important to us, especially as you're such an influential woman and ordinary people see you as one of them.

I let out a little sigh at the faux pas. Angel does not enjoy people telling her she's ordinary. *I* might be going for the girl-next-door angle, but as far as she's concerned she'd only be happy with that description if she was living in Beverley Hills and she was the girl next door to Ryan Gosling. Luckily for HappyHeart, I'm on the other end of Angel's Twitter account and I'm very sympathetic.

I'd love to get your email so I could propose an idea that you might like? Thank you again, Ola.

I think of the lovely Ola in her gorgeous maxi dress, her solemn face breaking into the sunniest of smiles. She must be running her company almost single-handedly. The thought makes me feel wistful. She's working hard, but at least it's for her own business, a business that's she's passionate about, that's making a difference. However hard I work here, I'll never feel like it's mine, and with the nature of the business it'll never feel like I've actually created something.

"Shut up," I mutter, irritated at that negative inner voice that has been getting the better of me lately.

If it wasn't for my work, HappyHeart wouldn't be contacting me. There, that's proof I'm doing something right.

I give Ola an address of an account Angel won't be looking at. Then I spend five minutes staring into space wondering, not for the first time, where I might be able to get an Angel look-alike because I've got a feeling this proposal might require her making an appearance at some point.

My eyes dart up to the clock when the phone starts ringing. I'm expecting it to jog my memory about some meeting or other I should or shouldn't be having. But no, today should be a quiet one at my screen.

"May, is that you?"

No *Good Morning*, no *How are you?* No *Thank you for getting my wife back.*

"Good morning, Bernard, how are you?"

"I want to close my Twitter account."

The request stops me in my tracks. The relief is quickly over-powered by panic. If I lose a client, my salary could drop rather than rise. I remind myself that Bernard always does this. First he says what he wants, and then I persuade him that's not what he wants, because what he wants is stupid.

"You have over 10,000 followers. That's years of work. Why would you want to throw all that away?"

"I think it's getting in the way."

"Getting in the way?" I echo. "Of what, exactly?"

This feeling of dread running down my spine is an overreaction. Everything is going to be fine.

"Of my life. Of who I am. I'm a bolshy, opinionated TV presenter. I'm Marmite. You either love me or you hate me. I don't need a Twitter account to try to change that or prove that, or whatever it is you've been doing."

"But…"

"I've just had enough of it. It complicates things."

"But you're not even on it."

"I know, which suddenly seems odd."

I pull out my hair clip and rub my hand up the back of my head, kneading my scalp.

"I don't understand. Where has this come from?"

I can hear him exhale and start to move around his flat. What did he do before cordless phones? He can never keep still when he's talking, which is rubbish for keeping a steady reception. I bet he wrote letters of complaints in the old days; long, indulgent letters to neighbours, newspapers, TV channels, the government…

"I think it was the Twitter conversation with Joyce… it made me feel a bit uncomfortable."

"It made *you* feel uncomfortable? How do you think it made me feel?"

If I'm fishing for sympathy. I should know I'm not going to get it from Bernard.

"Look, why don't we just delete that conversation?" I say. "I can shut down direct messages even. We can simplify your account."

"She'll still see my timeline, though. She'll get involved."

"Then maybe you'll have to tell her someone else is tweeting for you."

"Christ. No. She'll think I'm pathetic."

I need his business. I can't let him go, even though I think the quality of my life would be dramatically improved if I didn't have to deal with him.

"Why don't you think about it for a few days? It's a great marketing tool and it's helping you sell books and promote the show. That's the most important thing, isn't it?"

He's deliberating, sucking the air into those sticky tobacco-filled lungs. Hopefully the freshly oxygenated blood to his brain will give him an inspired thought, and he'll realise he's once again acting irrationally. I mean, he is, isn't he?

"Maybe you can tell Joyce you'd rather she didn't follow you."

As often is the case during conversations with Bernard, I wish I could pop the words back into my mouth.

"How can I do that?" he snaps. "She thinks Twitter saved our marriage, for God's sake! Don't you think she'll be a bit suspicious if I tell her to piss off?"

"If you used those exact words, then, yes, probably," I reply, unable to stop myself.

I glance up as my office door opens after a half-hearted knock. Gabe is standing there, looking extremely agitated. I get that sinking feeling. This isn't going to be good news. I cover the receiver.

"What is it?"

"Damian's account," he says.

Shit. Not again.

I'm already logging into it.

"May, I've made up my mind," Bernard says. "I want you to delete it. I can't risk Joyce finding out."

"Bernard, just take a minute to think about it," I say, my voice rising a few octaves as I take in the damage on Damian's account. "I won't tweet anything in the meantime. I've got to go now."

"May!" he says. "You have to do what I say."

"I've got to do what's best for you."

I'm vaguely aware I sound hysterical and that Gabe is still in the room witnessing me being hysterical. His respect for me must have dissolved some time ago.

"I'm coming in to see you," Bernard barks. "I'm not happy about this!"

"Bernard, it's all going to be fine! You don't need to come in!"

"I'm on my way now!"

"Alright, I'll delete it! I'll delete it!"

There's no way I'm deleting it. I just can't face him storming in right now.

"Really?"

"Yes, in a sec, I need to go now! Talk later!"

I've got an avalanche coming at me right now, and I have no idea how I'm going to dig myself out of it. Correction: I have no idea how I'm going to dig Damian out of it.

"How can he be hacked again?" I cry, slamming down the phone.

Gabe looks at me, one eyebrow raised, "It's very weird... he hasn't got his password by any chance, has he?"

Typical. I feel defensive on Damian's behalf. "You can't seriously think he's doing this to himself!"

"Just wondering, that's all. Well, I'll leave you to it."

Yes, leave me to sort out this massacre of character! Thank you very much!

As I'm sitting there, wondering how the hell I'm going to clear this up, it occurs to me that it's also very strange that Gabe should always be the one to inform me when Damian is going AWOL. As if he were watching. As if he knew exactly when it was going to happen.

Chapter 33

I can't sleep. I'm in Damian's big comfortable bed and he's snoring softly at my side. My body is on hyper-alert again. I'm trying to breathe through the feeling, but I haven't got the concentration. My mind keeps veering back to the events of the day and to all those nasty little responses on Twitter.

DAMIANDANCE @DAMIANDANCE
@JoMyars67 No I'm not scared of poisonous frogs. Gonna get high on them.

DAMIANDANCE @DAMIANDANCE
@GFHardy1 You look like a frog. I think you need some bitch to kiss you. #nevergoingtohappen

DAMIANDANCE @DAMIANDANCE
@greggerr Are you a man or a woman? Can't tell.

DAMIANDANCE @DAMIANDANCE
@lewisfind24 Jokes on you. I'm the one making the money.

DAMIANDANCE @DAMIANDANCE
@lewisfind24 shut up poor person

My tweet had been too little too late.

I didn't plan to end up here tonight. It's been an exhausting evening. We had a spectacular argument. He blamed me for leaving his account exposed. When I mentioned my suspicions about Gabe, I thought he was going to come over to the office wielding a cricket bat.

After I changed his password yet again, I logged off my computer and got a taxi straight over to his flat. He was sitting on his sofa, chugging on a cigarette, half a bottle of vodka open on the coffee table. It took me a while to soothe him, to reassure him that his reputation wasn't in tatters. He said he didn't want me doing his social media any more. I was about to say I didn't want to do it either, but then I thought of Bernard, and my salary, and Louisa mocking my lifeplan.

My mind keeps slipping back to Tintino's mocking tweet.

TINTINO @TINTINO
Want to insult people on Twitter without them hating u?
Simple! Just say your account was hacked after you've done it!
#TheDamianDanceWay

It's had over 1,000 retweets already. To be honest, if Damian hadn't been my client, I might have retweeted it myself. Or at least, laughed at it. It does seem horribly suspicious that Damian's account keeps getting hacked and that the insults sound very similar to how he once was ten years ago.

But that's just it. Someone is mimicking an old version of him. His distress was so real. I told him I'd emailed Twitter to find out the IP address of the computer these tweets were coming from. That calmed him down a bit. They could take days to reply, though. Weeks even. I've got to get to the bottom of this. I'm feeling so paranoid now. I'll have to log in and log out for every tiny tweet as if I had loads of time to spare.

Was Gabe capable of doing something like this?

I think of him standing in the doorway the day Damian kissed me. He hadn't been impressed. I think of the sarcasm in his voice. Why would it have bothered him, unless...?

Gabe has always been super-complimentary to me. I just assumed that's how he was, but what if all this time he's actually had a bit of a crush on me? He's asked me out for a drink several times and, except that once, when we overdid it and I had the worst hangover for two days, I've brushed him off. I brushed him off specifically because of the memory of that bloody awful hangover. Too much work has been my excuse ever since. Then Damian waltzes in with his money, fame and fancy hair, and I leap straight into his arms, and suddenly all that work I had to do pales into significance. What if Gabe got jealous of Damian and decided to sabotage his reputation?

I push myself up and lean against the padded leather headboard. Damian stirs and I worry he's waking up, but then he starts snoring again.

No. Surely Gabe isn't a closet psychopath. Although he is a bit too thin and the strain has been showing on his face lately, in the grey bags under his eyes and the flaky skin along his sideburns. I can't ask him, that's for sure. If I ask him, and I'm wrong, our relationship will be irreparable. What I need is proof. I need to get that IP address.

In the silence, another thought occurs to me, that while I'm here I may as well get Damian's IP address too. I feel a twinge of guilt at the thought. But it's not him I'm accusing, but anyone who could have had access to his account. After all, I was lying to Gabe when I said Damian didn't have his password. He does still have it and if he left Twitter open, any one of his friends could have played a trick on him. I know from stag- do stories, that guys can have a warped idea about what constitutes a funny prank.

I slip out of bed and pad quietly down the hallway. Damian's laptop is in the living room on the coffee table and my heart starts drumming rapidly as I sit on the edge of the sofa and reach over for it. It should only take a few seconds.

It whirs reluctantly into action and I quickly dim the screen. There's no pop-up window asking for a password, which I might suggest he changes, although right now I'm relieved I'll be able to get his IP address without any complications. The desktop opens with a background picture of him on his decks and I click on the Internet browser and search *My IP Address*. It comes up immediately and I realise I don't have any paper or pen to write it down.

I go over to the kitchen and open and close a few drawers, wincing as the cutlery clatters against my hand. I was hoping for one of those miscellaneous drawers where I might find a pen.

I freeze in the silence, thinking I've just heard a noise coming from the bedroom. But the only sound I can hear is the ticking of the oven clock.

I'll have to memorise it if I can't find a pen. It's only nine numbers. Less than a mobile. I can do this. I head back to the sofa and sit back down in front of the screen.

82.47.239.12

I try to think of things I can associate the numbers with. I haven't got very far when I'm startled by the definite sound of a duvet being pushed away. I hurry to exit the page and close the laptop, my heart pounding.

I get to my feet and head over to the kitchen sink. I can hear his bare feet on the wooden floor. I grab a glass from the dryer.

"May?"

I turn around. He's standing by the sofa in his boxer shorts, one hand kneading his neck, which, judging from the way he's moving it, must be stiff.

"I'm just getting some water," I say.

He wipes the sleep from his eyes and looks around at the living room. I glance over at the laptop, worried I've left some evidence.

"Can you get me some too?"

I smile. "Yeah, of course..."

He doesn't wait for me. He pads back to his room and I open the cold-water tap, breathing out as it rushes over my hands.

"82.47... 239... 12..." I whisper to myself. I read somewhere that if you say a stranger's name three times you will remember it. I repeat the numbers to myself until the glasses have filled. Then over again in my head, until I know I won't forget it.

Chapter 34

I'm standing outside my office, half-watching a couple of smokers swap gossip. They lean into each other, their smoking hand tilted back, smoke swirling on the breeze. I'm thinking how I wish I could exchange places with one of them when someone touches my arm and whispers in my ear:

"Lunch?"

I turn around in alarm to find Alex looking back at me, bright-eyed and smiling.

"You scared me!"

He holds up his watch. It has a sleek metallic blue face and stylish mesh strap. It would make a nice little Instagram picture for Damian #ootd #accessories #amwearing. But then Alex always looks good. Today in his plain black v-neck and dark-blue jeans, with his laughter lines and tussled hair, he could be a male model from a perfume ad, jumping out of a helicopter and running across rooftops without breaking a sweat.

My headache is throbbing again. I don't know if it's better than the numbness I was feeling half an hour ago when I discovered the news about Damian.

"It's one o' clock, the ideal luncheon hour," he says.

He's so cheerful, so oblivious to the chaos going on inside my brain.

"I can't," I say.

"Why not? Are you waiting for someone?"

He looks around for a likely candidate. Everyone is hurrying around us, but no one is coming for me. My shoulders sag.

"No..."

I pull out my phone and look at my screen, which is full of little icons indicating the billions of responses required of me. My stomach twists. I can't face any of them. Oh God, I feel like I'm going to cry. I push the phone back in my pocket and sniff back the tears.

"Are you alright?"

I don't trust myself to speak, so I just nod. He looks uncertain about what to do. I don't blame him. I'm a mess.

"You really look like you could do with some lunch," he says. "Are you sure I can't persuade you?"

"I suppose I should eat."

"You should. Eating is good."

"Where?"

If he says "wherever you want" I might actually lie down on the pavement and close my eyes.

"I know a little sandwich place... they also make some amazing lasagne... two- minute walk... I know it's not as swanky as where you usually go."

"Sounds good, I don't feel like swanky today."

"Good... right, then."

He walks at a speedy London pace, which suits me perfectly. I'm allowed to have a half-an-hour meltdown, but I can't let it go on too much longer than that.

A meltdown. It sounds simultaneously dramatic and reminds me of ice cream. It's Damian's Twitter abuse. The hacking. It made it into the Metro newspaper today. A little snide piece about how the "troubled" ex-reality star was getting a bit wild ahead of his entry into the jungle. It said Damian had claimed his account had been hacked, but it had ended quoting @tintino's tweet, the author of the article blatantly in favour of the *"popular and entertaining twitter aficionado"* over my client. Now it's up to me to clear Damian's name and the responsibility is making me feel a little sick.

"It's just here..."

I'm glad Alex doesn't ask for my opinion on the ordinary-looking café. I'm glad we can just plonk ourselves down at the last-remaining free table near the window. What a relief the plasticised menu is straightforward and there's not going to be any annoying querying of pretentious-sounding ingredients.

The waiter comes over with a scrappy pad and a tea towel over his shoulder.

"Usual?" he says to Alex.

"Yeah, and a sparkling water with a bit of lemon."

I glance up at him. He took the words right out of my mouth. "Yeah, me too. Sparkling water and a bit of lemon... and the lasagne."

"That was easy," Alex says. "So... why were you standing outside your office looking like a zombie?"

"Are you insulting my makeup?"

He laughs. "No. You had dead eyes."

"Ah, well, I was reflecting."

"On the meaning of life?"

"Yes... and work issues..."

"Are you allowed to expand?"

"Don't tease me today," I say. "I can't take it."

He looks taken aback. "I wasn't going to tease you. I never mean to."

For a brief moment I consider avoiding the subject altogether.

"Hacking," I say, because I really need to offload on someone.

He looks intrigued. "Your account or someone else's?"

"Well, they're all technically my accounts, aren't they?"

"Oh yeah, I forgot about that."

"Don't smile. It's not funny."

"I wasn't going to!"

It's not like I can talk to Damian about it because he just gets so angry. Not Craig, or he'll think I'm crap at my job. Or Gabe, because I'll end up accusing him. Or Louisa, because I don't know if I trust her not to leak it to everyone she meets immediately afterwards.

"What are you going to do about it?"

The water arrives and I take a deep gulp. It's so refreshing after all the coffees of this morning. My headache dulls a little.

"I'm trying to investigate who did it."

"With the police?"

"No, just me..."

"So the client who got hacked," he starts, then stops, "it was a client, right?"

"Yep."

"It's not that *Big Brother* star who was in the paper, was it?"

I take too long to deny it.

"It was!" he says, a glimmer of triumph in his eyes. "They were suggesting he'd done it himself."

"It's not true and it's so annoying! That was just one bloody tweet by some random called Tintino. They just love a scandal."

"Tintino?"

"The Mr Popular of the moment."

Alex looks amused.

"He's very..."

Infuriatingly witty.

"... mean," I finish lamely.

A lot of people take the piss out of my clients, but the problem is that when Tintino does it, his tweets get embedded in blogs and shared widely. I wouldn't care if my job wasn't to make the same people he's laughing at look good.

Alex looks confused, "So he's a troll?"

I wrinkle my nose. "No, not really. He's not vicious. But he just can't let my clients tweet anything without undermining them."

"When you say your 'clients', you mean *you* pretending to be them, right?"

I bristle, hearing the familiar judgement in his voice. If he starts preaching at me, I'm leaving.

"Sorry, I'm just trying to get the facts straight," he says, raising his palms in a gesture of peace.

"Tintino doesn't know it's me behind the tweets," I say, "so it's my clients he's being horrible to. For instance, anything I tweet as Damian..." I cover my mouth, horrified at my slip.

"You already admitted he was in the paper," Alex says, with a shrug. "It's the Dance guy."

"Shit..."

"I'm not going to tell anyone."

"Good. So, yeah, basically this guy takes the piss out of Damian whenever he tweets..."

"But he's not a troll?"

I squirm. "The thing is, he doesn't tweet to him directly. He just writes about him on his timeline."

"So he just tweets about your client, but doesn't insult him to his face?"

I can hear how ridiculous it sounds. Everyone's allowed to tweet their personal opinion on their own timeline. He's not attacking anyone directly.

"Yeah, I know, it's not that bad, it just makes my job harder. I just don't know why he has to focus on Damian. Why can't he piss off and talk about politicians? Well, actually, he does too. He's like Mr Current Affairs. He knows everything and he's really witty and satirical and seems to have an opinion on everything."

Alex laughs, "Sounds like you like him."

I let out a groan. "I do. That's the thing. We have banter on Twitter."

"You tweet with him? From a client's account?"

I blush. "No... my own."

He raises his eyebrows. "And your clients don't know you're friends with their troll?"

"He's not a troll... not at all. In fact I agree with most of what he tweets. That's the trouble. I try so hard to see the best side of my clients, but most of them..." I break off with a sigh. "It's not very professional of me to moan about my clients, is it?

"Go for it. I won't tell anyone."

It's nice to have someone really listening. I open up to him. I forget confidentiality clauses and I tell him about Bernard's strops and Angel's total disinterest in the identity I'm moulding out for her. I tell him about feeling guilty, about the headaches.

"A job shouldn't make you ill," he says.

"I know... I keep telling myself I just need to work harder to get on top of everything... but now I'm not so sure..."

Now I'm thinking of Damian and last night's disastrous evening. Why did he have to be so volatile? Why couldn't he just talk things through without resorting to wanting to punch someone? I push the thought away. Of course Damian was furious. So would I have been if my reputation was being questioned and my career was on the line. But is his career on the line or is this hacker doing him a favour? You don't have to be liked to be famous. You can also be famous for being hated... although who in their right mind would want that? I guess if you're desperate enough for fame you don't care what it's for.

The lasagne arrives. My appetite has gone again and I wish I could reduce the meal to the size of a pill and swallow it with another gulp of water.

"It's stupid. I'm stupid. It's addictive."

"You're not stupid," he says. "The fact you're observing yourself getting caught up is proof you can get yourself out of it."

I breathe out. I have no clear plan to get myself out, though.

"Wouldn't it be stupider if you thought what you were doing was brilliant? If you didn't feel guilty about pretending to be other people?"

I let out a weak laugh. "You're not making me feel better."

"Sorry. I just think how you're feeling demonstrates that you do have principles..."

"It's lovely to hear you say that. I thought you thought I was a monster."

"Hang on a minute, *I'm* the monster. I'm the one who keeps having a go at you every time I see you."

It was a good idea to have lunch. The lasagne is delicious. With every mouthful I feel a part of me being coloured in.

"I have wondered why you care much..." I say.

"What do you mean?"

"About me doing this job or not..."

He looks uncomfortable. "I care about a lot of things."

It's not much of an answer. What did I want him to say?

In the ensuing moment of silence I think of Louisa and the real reason why he wanted to have lunch with me. I was going to wait for him to bring the subject up, but maybe he needs help.

"So... Alex..."

Alex smiles uncertainly. "Yes, May?"

"You've been hanging around a lot with Louisa..."

He frowns and spears a piece of cucumber. "Yeah, I suppose I have... She's nice."

"A drama queen, though..."

I'm supposed to be helping her, so why is my impulse to put him off?

"Drama queen, but really lovely," I add quickly. "I guess all actors are a bit dramatic anyway," I bumble on. "Part of their charm."

He shrugs. "I don't live with her, so I guess I haven't seen much of that side, like you must have..."

I think of the time she threw a cactus out of the window to silence a bird, and the time she cried for three hours because she tore a sequined top, and the time she cut up a pile of old photos because she didn't want the baggage of memories.

"She's not really a drama queen. I don't know why I said that, really. She's a good friend."

"You sound like you have a volatile friendship."

291

"Did she say that?"

"It's just the impression I got."

"I don't think you should trust your impressions. You thought I was alright in the first five seconds of meeting me..."

I stick my tongue out at him, then worry I'm flirting.

"I still think you're 'alright'. I also think if you're talented at engaging on social media, why don't you do something for yourself? I mean, you could be the star..."

Just like that, he's changed the conversation.

"And be famous for being famous?" I say, going along with it. "No thank you."

"No, be famous for saying something that matters."

"I'm no Tintino."

"Good. You're not supposed to be anyone but yourself."

Oh I know that, I've got all the quotes.

Be yourself, because an original is worth much more than a copy.

Never change who you are so people will like you. Just be yourself and the right people will love you for being you.

Courage is being yourself every day in a world telling you to be someone else.

It makes me cringe to think I've tweeted these quotes for my client.

"I have to be honest, though," he says, slanting his head to one side, "I really thought you'd be one of those people who leave their phones out on the table."

I made a conscious decision not to because I knew he'd hate it.

"You must love that about Louisa," I say, having another stab at helping my friend.

"What?"

"Just how she doesn't like phones, you don't like phones, she hates the internet, you hate Facebook... you're perfect for each other."

He laughs and scratches the side of his neck. "Is that all it takes to be perfect for each other?"

"Well, no... but that's not all, is it? You're also both interested in film, acting, directing..." I want to add *you're both good-looking*, but think I'll blush if I do. "They are massive subjects."

He pushes his black frames up his nose and looks straight at me. You both have beautiful blue eyes, I think, and suddenly I feel embarrassed.

"Sorry, I'll shut up."

"Why?" he says, letting out another awkward laugh. "We do sound pretty perfect."

"See," I say. "I knew it."

#JobDone.

But like all my successful jobs lately, it feels bittersweet. Because, well, it feels manufactured and as we start to talk, I begin to doubt. There's something so considered about Alex, so grown up. It's not just his smart-casual clothes that are a world apart from Louisa's fancy-dress wardrobe, it's also the way he talks about things.

After the lasagne, I order a mint tea and he gets a coffee, and we talk about films we've seen and books and current affairs and things I've picked up in the news which I haven't got my head around. Things I want to care about but haven't had time. And I can't help thinking, as an another half an hour slips by, that I couldn't imagine Louisa patiently talking through these issues, without wanting to sing and dance and conclude with something easy and unsatisfactory like, *well, that's life isn't it?* Even though she'd be right. This is life. My life. And after our intense and lovely lunch I find myself really questioning what I'm doing with it.

Chapter 35

It's Saturday afternoon and I'm in bed. My bedside table is over-flowing with tissues, medicine and empty mugs. I'm so blocked up I hardly slept last night. My head is fuzzy and my eyes ache. I've got my tablet beside me tuned into Thijs's Twitter timeline although it hurts my eyes even to look at it.

Abigail is in position. I spoke to her this morning; let her do all the talking because my throat hurt. She promised she'd start to take some shots of Thijs with his band mates. He's told everyone that she's his cousin, so they're feeling very comfortable with her in their midst. I got the sense she'd have rather been just a friend, but I think the plan is genius. If she's his cousin, she's not going to let her guard down and try to snog him, which was one of my fears.

I close my eyes and rest my head back into my pillows. At least it's the weekend. I should be better by Monday. Glastonbury will also be over by Monday and Abigail will be back behind her desk. It would be amazing if she did manage to get a snap of Thijs and Ankara together, but it's probably unlikely.

"Another lemon and ginger?" Louisa asks, poking her head around the door.

I open my eyes and stare groggily at her, "have we got anything stronger?"

She comes over and sits at the end of my bed. "You've already had three Lemsips. What your body needs is time to be sick and time to heal."

I groan. "Can I have a cup of time, then?"

She squeezes my foot. "I'll get you the lemon and ginger."

Outside wind and rain lash against the window, all sign of summer obliterated for the day.

"Stupid English weather," I say, punctuating my lines with a sneeze.

"This has nothing to do with the weather and everything to do with your work- life balance," Louisa says sternly.

"I know."

I can tell she's surprised to hear me agree with her. But I'm not an idiot. I know that stress weakens the immune system. I know that if I had eaten more and taken some vitamins when I felt the first tug on my throat then the cold might not have arrived with such force. But I felt too anxious to eat, didn't want to leave my office to go to the chemist for vitamin C, so this is what I get. It's my own fault.

"I'm going out in a bit..." Louisa says. "Alex and I are going to watch that new French film."

I can't imagine anything worse than being stuck in a dark room with loads of people and having to read glary subtitles right now. But if that makes them happy...

"Are you going to kiss him?"

She laughs. "You sure *you* don't want to kiss him? You do talk about him a lot."

"Only to encourage you..." I say.

"You don't fancy him at all?"

"I don't fancy guys my friends have their eye on. I've got a very intelligent system for selecting people I fancy."

She frowns at me, but she's still smiling. I'm guessing she's feeling sorry for me, wishing I could find my own Mr Right. I think she's made up her mind that Damian was just a passing fling. I texted him to tell him I was sick, and he replied to say so was he, that he had a hangover of at least 50 on the Richter scale. I was going to reply that being hung over didn't count as being sick, and also that the Richter scale only went up to ten, but then the whole thing was so pointless and stupid and I felt too sick to bother.

Louisa leaves to make my tea and I close my eyes again, thinking that my answer wasn't entirely truthful. Alex keeps coming into my head and with him a complicated mix of emotions.

I try to drift off until a Twitter notification pulls me back. I move my tablet towards me and register the first photo from Abigail of Thijs with his arm around Jake Elms. I groan out loud when I see she hasn't included Jake's Twitter handle, diminishing the chances of him retweeting it. I grab my phone and start texting her to alert her to her mistake, but give up halfway through and decide ringing her would be easier. She doesn't pick up and I let out a whimper of despair. Why can't she just use her common sense? Why can no one do a decent job but me? Tears run down my face as I go back to texting her. I'm wiping them away when Louisa returns.

"Oh, May, what's the matter?"

The sympathy in her voice makes me cry. I cover my face and feel my body shake. I'm aware of her moving to my side, of her hand running up and down my arm.

"You need to rest," she says. "You need to switch off a bit. Tomorrow you'll feel better."

I nod my head, but I can't talk, the words are lodged in my chest like heartburn. I breathe out to stop the tears and wipe away my hot, sticky face. This feels much worse than a cold and I wish my mum was here.

"I'm going to take this and put it on the side," Louisa says, holding up my tablet.

I don't resist. I feel too awful to care. I just want to sleep now.

She puts the back of her palm against my forehead.

"You're a bit hot."

"I'll be okay," I say, between hiccups.

"Alright… well, I'll let you sleep now. You will sleep, won't you?"

I nod dumbly.

"Good. I'll check on you later."

She turns the light off on her way out and I turn over, rest my tear-stained cheek against my pillow and let myself sink finally into a deep sleep.

I don't know how long I'm out for. When I wake up it's dark outside. My throat feels parched and I drain the cold cup of herbal tea that Louisa left on my bedside table. I hear voices in the living room and my heart sinks. I feel vulnerable and I don't want anyone to see me like this, but if I want to go to the bathroom I haven't got much choice. How lovely an en suite would be right now. I slip out of bed and pull on my fleece dressing gown, which feels like a hug, and pull the hood up.

Alex and Jacob are with Louisa in the living room. There's a bottle of wine half empty on the coffee table. Jacob seems to be arguing some point, and Louisa and Alex are on the sofa, heckling him. It occurs to me that he really does not leave them be for five minutes.

"May! How are you feeling?" Louisa gushes.

"I'm contagious, don't look at me," I say, covering my face.

"You look all cuddly in that," my flatmate says, jumping off the sofa and coming over to give me a hug. I feel self-conscious with the two guys staring at me. I must look terrifying without makeup and with my unbrushed hair wrenched into a ridiculous lopsided ponytail.

"Have you got brandy?" Jacob says. "I've got a killer cure."

"I'm fine," I say.

"No, really, you should try his cure," Alex says. "You don't look great."

"Thanks. I know. Which is why I just wanted to sneak past you all without you noticing."

"He meant you don't look well," Louisa hurries to his defence.

297

"Not that you look ugly. You could never look ugly."

"Yeah, you just look sick," Alex says.

How sweet, I think miserably. They're like a little couple backing each other up. I feel the sneeze building up and turn away to let it go. Not once, but three times.

"Go on, I'll try the cure," I say, sniffing back my leaking nose.

I head to the bathroom, leaving them to discuss this magical cure. At the sink I splash cold water on my hot skin and stare at my puffy face in the mirror. My lips are sore, which has made them look all red and pump, which ironically improves them. I grab a brush and tidy up my hair a bit, draw the line at applying makeup. It's Saturday night, why don't they go out? Why are they all here? Why doesn't Jacob admit defeat and leave them alone?

They haven't finished making the cure, so I pad back to my room and hide under my covers. I think about checking my tablet, but I don't feel like moving. I lie there for what seems like ages before there's a polite little tap on the door. It fills me with dread because I know it's not Louisa. I sit up, pushing my hair out of the way. I was expecting to see Alex, as out of the two of them, he's the only one I could really call my friend now. But it's not; it's Jacob. He's holding a steaming mug of something and looking pleased with himself.

This is my chance to have a private word with him. To give him a hint. To stop him wasting his time. He's a lovely guy, after all. I barely know him, but he radiates a lot of warmth. He seems easy-going, happy all the time.

"Thank you," I say, taking it from him. "Dare I ask what's in it?"

"All good stuff... lemon, brandy, ginger, honey..."

He hovers there, waiting for me to try it, and when I do, warns me it's hot. I rest the mug on my chest, and the heat seeps quickly through the duvet cover. I haven't got much time to say what I want to say, so I'm going to have to be horribly direct.

"So, Jacob..."

He smiles. "It smells good, right?"

"Yeah, really good."

How to say it?

"I was thinking... We're never going to get those two together if we keep joining them..."

His smile withers and dies. "What?"

"Alex and Louisa... they like each other, but they're too shy to do anything about it."

"They've told you?"

He looks like he had absolutely no idea.

"Yeah, pretty much."

"Oh."

"Sorry, I didn't mean to offend you or anything... I didn't, did I? I just thought we needed to give them some space."

"You mean me," he says, with a hurt smile.

"No... I mean both of us..."

But he's already made up his mind about what I mean or don't mean.

"Enjoy your drink," he says, throwing me another forced smile, which makes me feel like the worst person in the world.

After he leaves the room I sit in the silence, full of cold and regret. A few moments later, I hear the front door shut. I didn't expect him to act on my advice so soon. Am I happy now? No, not a bit. I bury myself under the covers and wallow in self-pity, until, exhausted, I fall back into an uneasy sleep.

Chapter 36

Thijs and Ankara kissed last night and the whole world knows about it thanks to a well-played tweet by our dear receptionist. Abigail tweeted the photo from her own account, knowing that it would look a bit odd Thijs taking a photo of himself kissing.

I want to hug Abigail right now. The news has done more for me than any of the meds and special drinks put together. It's Sunday morning and although I'm still feeling blocked, I've got a bit of my energy back. The sun is out too. I'm sitting at the kitchen table basking in it while I skim through all the tweets about my youngest client, who just happens to be trending right now. YES! TRENDING! And with his name spelled correctly. The Thijs bit, at least, no one has bothered with his surname, he's *that* famous. Ankara is also trending, although that's partly to do with a protest happening right this minute in Turkey.

To: maysparks@smcb.com
From: craigbrown@smcb.com

Absolutely tremendous result re-Thijs. Great job of delegating. You really have proved yourself to be an essential part of this company. Soon we'll be working exclusively with A-listers, partly because we'll have turned all our C-listers into them!

Talking of which, what's the plan for Angel?
    C

It would have been a perfect email if he hadn't brought up Angel. I feel I deserved to bask in the success before moving on to the next job. But if he's looking for holes in my progress then he'll have to keep looking.

To: craigbrown@smcb.com
From: maysparks@smcb

I've been working on using her voice to promote ethical fashion. On Friday the emerging ethical clothing brand HappyHeart wrote to me asking if Angel would be their ambassador. They are being featured in next month's Marie Claire and also in Style magazine so HappyHeart just need some photos of her in the clothes and a few quotes.
    May x

To: maysparks@smcb.com
From: craigbrown@smcb.com

Superb work. I didn't take Angel for an ethical clothing sort of girl! I know she loves her glamour! Re quotes, perhaps you could compose them for her and email them ahead? We can't really trust Angel to say anything suitable. Also, you might need to prep her before any meeting. I wouldn't put it past her to turn up wearing crocodile skin.
Have a good rest of the weekend. Don't work too hard.
    C

Don't work too hard? What a joke. I notice I'm grinding my teeth and stop. If he didn't want me to be thinking about work, he wouldn't have mentioned Angel. For all my enthusiasm in that email, the truth is, my plan is severely flawed, because Angel has yet to respond to my phone calls. Angel has not agreed to be the face of HappyHeart, only I have, as Angel. I should have waited to talk to her, but I just got carried away. I love HappyHeart. I love their clothes, their values, their vibe.

It's going to be fine. Everything is going to be fine. Despite the little bumps along the way, I have a lot to be positive about.

1. Damian is going to be on a TV show
2. Bernard and Joyce are back together
3. Thijs is now Mr Popular
4. Angel will soon be face of HappyHeart and loved by all

So sod it, I'm going to take the rest of the Sunday off. I'm not going to worry about another thing.

Chapter 37

A direct message is waiting for me on Monday morning in Bernard's Twitter account:

MISSINKYTOES @MISSINKYTOES
@bthomskinner so wifey comes back and you pretend I don't exist? Didn't you like me sucking your cock in Winchester? YOU BASTARD!

My jaw drops as I read it. I push away the croissant I was about to tuck into. There's no way I can eat anything now. Even yesterday's supper isn't so sure it should have been eaten. I look over at my bin, my stomach churning, then back at that stinging revelation.

I knew it. I knew he had had a woman there with him. I knew there had been something suspicious about those endless winky emoticons. I'd almost managed to convince myself that everything I'd done, I'd done in the name of love, and that I deserved only thanks and champagne. Well, there's the truth. There it is, burning a hole in my retina.

My mobile is ringing and I'm about to let it go to answer-phone, but have a change of heart and grab it last minute without checking the screen.

"Yes?"

"It's Alex."

I feel relief that it's not a client, dismayed that he's calling me in the middle of this fresh disaster.

"Hi! Are you okay?"

"I need to talk to you. Are you free for coffee?"

I let out a groan. "No! I'm in the middle of a crisis! Another one!"

"Coffee might help you come up with a solution."

"I doubt it. It'll just make me more hyper."

"Please?"

Why is he so desperate to talk to me? I feel this sense of hope. This lightness. I can't explain it.

"It's about Louisa..." he adds.

The hope dissolves, replaced with inexplicable disappointment.

"You really should just talk to each other."

He breathes out. A sigh of an idiot in love?

"Okay, well, another time, then?"

"Another time..." I say, without conviction. I put down the phone, forgetting to even say goodbye.

For the millionth time this week I feel like crying.

As usual at a time of crisis, a voice that sounds like my mother's suggests I should start doing yoga. *Or running? You used to love running? Remember when you used to look after yourself...*

I look back at that awful message.

The weight of Bernard's lie is heavy on my shoulders. It's my lie too. I helped him trap a woman who had almost broken free of him. I cover my mouth and breathe heavily into it, as layer upon layer of dread wraps around me and mummifies me in that lie. Alone, the truth will crush me. But I'm not alone in this company.

Craig needs to know we have a serious problem. He might act like a cold-blooded businessman a lot of the time, but I know he'll understand when I explain the situation to him and tell him what we have to do. He won't like it, but he'll see it's the only way to move forward. It doesn't mean exposing SMCB, just revealing that there are companies that act on people's behalf and that unfortunately, this time, such a company made a judgement error.

The bottom line is this: there is no way I can continue to represent Bernard. And there is no way I can let his wife continue to believe it was him behind their Twitter reconciliation.

Chapter 38

"I need you to calm down," Craig says, leaning forward to squeeze my shoulders. "Take some breaths. This is not your fault."

"Of course it's my fault!"

I've told him the whole story. I've witnessed his full range of emotion in the stiff rise and fall of his plucked eyebrows. Two things have become clear to me a) he thinks I'm overreacting b) he has had Botox injections. Right now his reaction has cooled to a steady stare and eyebrows at half-mast.

"You only did what Bernard would have done himself," Craig says. "He told you to do it."

"I took the initiative."

"No," he replies firmly. "He asked you to do it."

"I should have said no."

"He's paying your salary."

"This isn't about money, this is about ethics! I trapped an innocent woman! I made her believe her cheating husband was dying of remorse."

"He would have made her believe that with or without you."

"You don't know that."

"Of course I do. She was already in London," Craig sneers, "she was probably on her way to see him to sort things out."

"If she was, then she would have caught him in the act with

306

Miss Inky Toes!"

He shoots me a pitying smile.

"I gave him an hour!" I cry, feeling another pang of guilt. "She would have found them and she would have realised that he was never going to change!"

"You don't know that. Some people are suckers for abusive relationships."

"But I don't want to be the person who encourages them!"

Craig takes a deep breath and crosses his arms.

"May," he says calmly. "You're not seeing the bigger picture."

I want to cry out that the problem is I am seeing the bigger picture and I'm not liking it one bit. But instead I swallow back my emotion. Craig's patience isn't infinite. He likes me because I don't have meltdowns. He likes me because, up until now I've been very accommodating.

"It will only be a matter of time before he slips up," Craig says, "personally I think she'll forgive him over and over, because her life is insignificant without him."

"Wow..."

"Let me finish."

The heat has poured into my cheeks at the insult to this poor woman. I feel so angry right now. How dare he say that about her? He doesn't even know her.

"Bernard will have his comeuppance in time, so there's no need to precipitate it by being rash and contacting his wife, and, more importantly, risking harm to this company, which I might add, could be paying you double what it's paying you now within the next year."

I'm shaking my head. He doesn't understand that this is unbearable for me. He wasn't the one typing *I love you* to someone else's wife. I'm so deeply ashamed, and I can't see how I'm going to cleanse myself if I let Joyce continue to believe his lie.

On the other hand, I'm not sure I could face her in person. Perhaps an email? But who would believe it? And what if Craig is right? Maybe it is only a matter of time.

"Bernard wanted me to delete his Twitter account the last time I spoke to him, but I didn't," I say. "Should I?"

Craig looks thoughtful.

"No," he says, at last. "I'm sure he knows you never intended to. Have a word with him, when you're feeling calmer."

"In a few months' time, then?"

He lets out a little laugh. "Come on, cheer up. Everything else is going brilliantly for you."

"Yeah, like the Damian hacking..."

His smile fades. "Have you found out anything more about that?"

"I'm still waiting for Twitter to get back to me."

He nods, "well, so what? Damian got the jungle gig, didn't he? That's the main thing."

His hand is back on my shoulder, squeezing encouragement into it.

"May, you were made for this job."

He means it as a compliment, but it doesn't feel like one. What does it mean? That I was made to pretend to be other people? That I was made so unoriginal and uninteresting that I had to inhabit the lives of everyone else?

I rub my eyes. The flu medicine must be wearing off. I can feel its grip on me tightening. My eyes are watering and my nose is running. I need to go the bathroom to splash my face with water, shock me out of these negative thoughts that are pulling me down. I cover my mouth, feeling the approach of a sneeze.

"Do you want to take the day off?" Craig says.

The sneeze doesn't arrive, morphs instead into a yawn. I wipe the corners of my eyes.

"Yes. I do."

He looks relieved. "Good. Go on. You'll feel so much better tomorrow."

I don't argue. My ego still wants to please him. I want him to think I'm so tough that this little saga will only shave half a day off my working year. Right now, the thought of tweeting on anyone's behalf is filling me with dread.

Chapter 39

The flat isn't Chubb-locked. Louisa is either home or she forgot to lock up behind her. I should know which days she works at the coffee shop by now, but I suppose I've never treated her job seriously enough to ask. That's going to change. Serving coffee is a decent job, unlike covering for cheating husbands. I close the door quietly behind me and slip off my pumps. She's not here, I think, and I feel relieved that no one is going to witness me collapse into a heap of regret and self-pity.

I pass her room and pause for a second, because it's so unusual for her door to be shut. Usually there's an object preventing it from closing: a bag or a shoe or that wooden doll's house she planned to fix up into a mini theatre set. I'm about to dismiss it as a random occurrence when I hear a squeak of bedsprings. My first instinct is to poke my head around the door to find out what my flatmate is doing in bed in the middle of the day. I'm glad I don't when the solitary squeak quickly becomes more rhythmic.

I smother my surprised cry with my hand and hurry down the corridor on tiptoes to hide in my room. On my bed I sit in stunned silence, my mouth wide open. I can't believe it. I think of Alex's phone call earlier and feel baffled. What on earth could have been so important? Had he just wanted to double check I was at work?

I suppose I should feel happy that they finally got it together. But I don't feel happy, I just feel shocked.

What am I going to do? Pretend I didn't hear them? I lie down on my bed and pull one side of the duvet over me. Those springs need a squirt of WD40. I don't remember them being this bad.

I think of Alex running in the park in his FINISHER t-shirt. I think of his toned body and the steely focus in his eyes. I feel yet another pang of disappointment and hate myself for it. Isn't it bad enough I'm lying for everyone? Am I really going to lust over Louisa's future boyfriend too?

I guess in the back of my mind, I'd started thinking it was significant that my job wound him up. I'd started to believe he cared I wasn't fulfilling my potential because he cared about me. We've argued, granted, but we've also laughed a lot. We had banter. Louisa and Alex don't have banter. Even when they're talking about film, they don't seem to be on the same page. They're formal with each other.

The springs have stopped and I breathe a sigh of relief.

I wait to hear voices. Instead I hear the hum of electrics, the fridge, perhaps, or a light bulb. It's a hum that I've tried to locate during my insomniac nights and have concluded is the sound of city living, impossible to escape.

A door opens. I hold my breath. Footsteps pad across the corridor then the bathroom door closes. I'm not sure when I should reveal myself, if ever. Maybe I should just try to fall asleep. That's why I'm home, after all, to get rid of this cold once and for all. But then the bathroom door opens and a male voice calls out:

"Which towel shall I use?"

My mouth drops open again, because it's not the voice I expected to hear. It's not Alex's voice. It's Jacob's.

I've never felt so relieved in my life.

Chapter 40

"I'm so happy," Louisa gushes, her cheeks pink from pleasure and the homemade beer Jacob left behind.

Lover boy has left the building. He couldn't stay as he has to prep food for a busy shift at the restaurant tomorrow. I didn't hear this first hand. I actually couldn't bear to leave my room until he'd gone. I kept thinking of what I'd said to him. I must have encouraged him rather than put him off. Louisa hasn't mentioned anything, so I'm assuming Jacob never told her about my words of advice. Thank God for that.

"When did you know you liked him?"

She shoots me a big smile. "I think it was from the first moment I saw him."

I look at her suspiciously. "Really?"

"Yes... there was so much chemistry between us in the park."

Really? I'd been too busy arguing with Alex to notice.

Who's going to tell him he's no longer in with a chance? That his enthusiastic friend has pushed him out of the running? Despite their close friendship, they clearly haven't been communicating that well. Jacob is too nice to have gone ahead if he knew his best friend liked her.

Alex could turn up here any moment, persuaded by my conclusion that they're perfect for each other. Maybe he was ringing up to run an idea by me of their first date? The thought brings a new sinking feeling and I reach out for Louisa's beer.

"You shouldn't be drinking," she chides, but lets me have it anyway.

"You'd be drinking if you'd had the morning I have."

I wouldn't have been able to taste a weaker beer because of my blocked nose, but this stuff is potent. It's not strong enough to make me forget Miss Inky Toes's message, though. It keeps coming back, like a mosquito looking for some exposed skin. I shudder at the image I've been trying to ban from my mind; Bernard in a poky bathroom with his trousers around his ankles. If it wasn't all so awful, I might have laughed at the fact that in my head Miss Inky Toes is the spitting image of her cartoon profile. One thought of Joyce, though, and the whiff of humour vanishes.

"I don't think I should do this job any more," I say.

Louisa refrains from breaking out into a song and dance. She wants to, though. It must be like when a friend suddenly realises that her horrible boyfriend really is horrible and she's finally had enough. She'll be disappointed in a minute, because despite my announcement I can't see how I'm going to escape, how I can afford to.

"You could do anything you put your mind to. You have so many transferable skills," Louisa says. "That's what Alex was saying the other day."

I frown at her. "Why were you talking about me?"

"Just because you were sick and stressed," she waves a hand dismissively. "Just because we all care about you."

I think of Alex sitting on this sofa analysing my transferable skills. He was probably trying to demonstrate to Louisa what a caring person he was.

"He's lovely, really," I say. "Alex."

"Yeah, he is. You hated him at first."

"Because he was patronising and rude about my job."

"Your job does divide opinion."

"Which is why it was supposed to be kept a secret!" I say. But there's no point digging that argument up again, so I move swiftly on. "Is Jacob going to tell Alex the news about you two?"

313

Louisa's face crumples with concern.

"I just didn't see it," she says. "Me and Alex. I feel sort of stupid when I'm around him, too ditsy... I don't feel like that with Jacob, I feel like I can be *me* with Jacob."

"That's what being with the right person should feel like," I say, mustering a smile out of the wreckage of my day.

My phone is ringing. "Sorry, I've got to take this."

Louisa doesn't seem to mind. I've a feeling that nothing is going to dampen her spirits today.

"May?"

I get up and head towards my bedroom, wanting to take the call in private.

"Thijs? Why are you whispering?" I ask, finding myself whispering too. His voice has an echo. "Where are you?"

"I'm not... I'm..."

"What's wrong?"

"It's Ankara. She's annoyed with me for not answering her on Twitter."

"Oh, I'm sorry, I'll get on it."

"It's too weird," he interrupts.

"What is?"

"Why do we need to talk on Twitter? I mean, why is she telling me to reply to her on Twitter when we're together?"

I frown. "You're together right now?"

"Right now I'm in the bathroom of the restaurant we're in."

I've logged onto his Twitter account and can see she's posted a picture of herself cheering with a champagne flute, a majestic lobster nestled on a bed of dark-green leaves in front of her. She's mentioned him in the picture.

ANKARA DAVIES @ANKARADAVIES
Lobster Lunch with @ThijsVanBro! Smile! :) #nomnomnom

"Okay, so she's tagged you in a photo," I say.

"That's the other thing, taking pictures of food... why would you do that on a date?" He's so unimpressed. "There's a window in the bathroom. I'm seriously thinking of..."

"Thijs! Don't you dare leave Ankara in the middle of a meal! Are you crazy?"

"Taking pictures of your food is crazy, asking the person you're eating with to retweet the picture of the food you're eating is crazy."

"Is that all she wants?"

I retweet the picture immediately. Okay, so a bit weird that he's done it from the toilet. Not an ideal image for Ankara to have when she notices he's done what she wanted, because she will notice, because of course she'll have her phone out on the table.

"She wanted me to take a photo of us together and tweet it," he says.

"She's obviously proud she's having lunch with you."

"I don't know. I feel very uncomfortable."

"Relax. It's a massive compliment. She's a gorgeous girl."

"I wouldn't know how to tweet a photo if I wanted to."

It still surprises me that he's this disconnected from social media.

"Make an excuse..." I say. "Hold her hand, look into her eyes and tell her, this moment is your own special private moment."

He makes a sort of spluttering sound. "I'm not some kind of lothario, who can just turn it on like that."

The heat seeps into my cheeks. He's right. What am I playing at?

"But you like her, right?"

"I don't know. She's pretty but she's full-on, like really, really enthusiastic about everything...."

"That's nice, right? That she isn't playing games?"

Unlike the rest of us, I think.

"You need to get back out there," I say. "She'll lose her enthusiasm pretty quickly if she starts imagining you've got diarrhoea."

"Shall I just tell her the truth?"

"NO!"

I hear him sigh. "Alright... I'll make an excuse."

"Yes, say your battery has run out, better throw the battery down the loo now!"

"No way, that costs money!"

"You're on your way to being a millionaire."

He laughs. "Okay..."

A millionaire. No wonder Ankara is so desperate to get a snap of herself with him. Maybe someone should warn him of what happens to young millionaires. I hope there's someone guiding him. I think of Maria Kuebler and feel myself deflate. What he needs is someone who has his best interests at heart. Sadly that person isn't me or Maria, and yet we seem to be the ones with the most control over his life.

"Just go with your gut," I say.

Too little, too late, my inner voice scoffs. I'm not even sure he heard me.

Chapter 41

Alex is ringing me. I feel torn as I watch his name on the screen of my phone. I want to talk to him, but I don't want to be the one to tell him about Louisa. I feel guilty for letting him believe she was interested. If only I'd kept my mouth shut and not tried to meddle. Not just with his life, either. There's a lot of meddling I wish I could undo.

The ringing stops. I've got a meeting to go to but I decide to quickly text back.

Sorry! Have meeting. Zzzz. You okay?

Craig is checking up on me. He must have spent most of yesterday worrying I'd get in touch with Joyce. Meanwhile I was worrying Thijs might confess to Ankara that he has never tweeted in his life. In the end it would seem that neither of us needed to worry.

"So you're fine about everything?" Craig says.

"No, I'm not fine about everything."

I'm not fine about my role in helping a cheat get his duped wife back. I'm not fine that I'm covering for his adultery.

Craig stiffens. "But you understand the contract?"

He's spent the last ten minutes dictating the legal reasons why I can't talk to Joyce. I was too busy trying to dilute my fury to listen to the particulars. But I know what the crux of it is. If I tell Joyce that Bernard's Twitter account is false, then I will have to pay a fine of £10,000 in damages. It's almost funny, really, that by opening my mouth and uttering a few words I could double my debt, that all those months of work could suddenly amount to nothing. I guess that means my voice matters after all.

"Yes, I understand perfectly."

"Good. So things need to proceed as normal."

"Craig, you must see that I can't continue tweeting as Bernard." My phone is buzzing. I pull it out. It's a message from Alex.

I'll take you somewhere really swanky for lunch if you get out of that meeting!

I smile sadly. *I don't care about swanky, I care about you,* I think. I wish I could get out to meet him. But it will be horrible if he's just meeting me to find out about Louisa.

"May," Craig says, his voice brusque. "Did you hear what I just said?"

No, I was miles away. I was imagining Alex's gorgeous smile crumbling at the news his best friend is sleeping with his crush.

"You will continue to tweet for Bernard for the time being," he says. "I did speak to him about his request to delete his account and he realises he was overreacting."

Frankly, it's probably the first time he wasn't overreacting. He obviously knew Miss Inky Toes was going to get in touch sooner or later and he didn't want me finding out his dirty little secret. Craig must have convinced him I was trustworthy.

I meet his gaze and breathe in deeply. This is only going to be temporary, until I've got a new plan.

"Alright, then, since you're not giving me a choice," I say, smiling tightly.

He doesn't smile back. The bond between us has weakened over this, and I sense his loyalty to me is waning. Our meeting is over and I head back to my office.

I'm in a bad mood and distracted as I log on to my computer. In the moments I'm waiting for it to load, I look at Alex's message again. I feel torn. I do want to meet him for lunch, but I know we won't be meeting for the right reasons. He wants to know about Louisa and I... well.

I close my eyes and roll my neck. Now that I know Louisa doesn't fancy him, I've let myself think about him. That day he came to our door, I thought he was handsome, but I'd assumed he and Louisa had more of a connection, with their acting interests and all that, so I'd just shut those thoughts off. It had been easier when he started being judgmental. And yet, even then, a tiny part of me couldn't help thinking he had a point.

It's like Tintino. I get annoyed with him for making my job more difficult, at the same time I respect him, and I sort of envy him, speaking his mind and making everyone laugh with his satirical tweets.

Going to lunch with Alex doesn't seem like the right thing to do when I'm feeling like this, especially with Damian still in the picture. He's been texting me a lot recently; obviously feels bad for shouting at me so much the other night...

Angel.

Her name pops into my head and I scroll through to her phone number. Ola has emailed twice since my first enthusiastic reply, desperate to set up a meeting.

A groggy voice answers the phone, "Hello? Who is it?"

"It's May Sparks. I've been trying to get in touch with you for ages," I say, my voice cheerful. "I've got great news."

"What is it?"

She sounds suspicious.

"The owner of HappyHeart, an amazing up-and-coming ethical designer, wants you to be the company's ambassador."

There's a long pause. I'm about to elaborate on the concept of being an "ambassador" when she pipes up again.

"How much?"

I feared she might ask that.

"At the moment, it would be a case of just getting free clothes and positive publicity..."

Ola made it pretty clear they didn't have funds to pay for a big campaign. After so many enthusiastic tweets, she thought Angel might just be happy to get free clothes from her "favourite" brand and promote a cause she felt so passionate about.

"I've never heard of them," Angel says. "I was thinking more Chanel."

I almost laugh out loud.

"Do you know anyone in Chanel you can set up a meeting with?" she continues.

"I think Chanel have already picked their team."

She clicks her teeth, annoyed. I want to shout at her that working with HappyHeart would be the perfect opportunity to improve her image. I'd get involved with them myself if they wanted me. Unfortunately the only thing people want me for is to amplify other people's voices.

"What about Prada?"

"Those top designers only use top models, Angel."

"What about those tweets you've been saying about following your dreams?"

"You can't make yourself taller, though, Angel."

I feel like I've got to tread very carefully if I don't want to upset her.

"I can wear heels. I can go on a diet."

"No one wants you to go a diet."

"You've been running for me..." she says. "I definitely feel fitter."

This is useless. Unless I can get her to a meeting there are going to be no drastic changes to Angel's reputation or image.

"Angel," I say cutting through her ramble about Vogue cover shoots. "This gig with HappyHeart could be the beginning of something brilliant. Do you think those top models started at the top of their game? No, they began small and worked their way up."

She's fallen quiet. Is what I'm saying getting through?

"Why don't you just go to one little meeting?" I beg. "You might fall in love with their brand. They are going to be big. I just know it."

"Does anyone famous wear them?"

"Yeah," I say, "All the eco lot, Gwyneth Paltrow and uh... Jennifer Aniston has one of their handbags, I think..."

This is a load of rubbish, but out of all the things I've lied about over the last month, it's definitely going to be the one I'll least regret.

"Alright, I'll go to a meeting..." she says, reluctantly.

"Great! Brilliant..."

Now for the next problem. Her mouth. HappyHeart are obviously happy to have a plus-sized model and aren't holding her background or her history against her. But that's only because she has been advertising herself as someone who cares about the environment, fashion with a heart and animal rights. What comes out of her mouth need to be carefully tailored.

"When do you think you'll have a moment to pop over to my office? We'll need to discuss your stance on ethical clothing."

"My what?"

"You just need to give the impression that you care about where your clothes come from, that's all. I don't mean the shop, I mean the process. How they are made. I thought if you came in, I could give you a quick overview."

She lets out a sigh. "Can't you just do all the talking for me?"

Alex was right about some of my clients. They don't care what opinions they're given, as long as it puts them in the spotlight. Perhaps as long as Angel just nods at the right places, we could pull it off. There's no reason she needs to be an expert in ethical fashion. That's Ola's job. All she needs to do is to look like she cares. It would feel better if she did care, but I've got to think about the bigger picture. If she acts like she cares, it will make her fans care, and that will benefit everyone.

"Alright. I'll do the talking," I say. "You just act like you're enthusiastic."

"I'd be really enthusiastic if they were paying me."

"Stepping stones, Angel, stepping stones."

"I want an escalator."

That makes me laugh. I hang up the phone and manage a small smile of relief. And then a moment later, the memory of Miss Inky Toes comes back, bringing back that guilty feeling I'm having such trouble trying to shake.

Chapter 42

I didn't want to go home. I didn't want to find Louisa and Jacob entwined on the sofa and feel my loneliness magnified in their cosy silence. I didn't want to bump into Alex and talk about the weather or recycling boxes when there's so much else I want to say.

So I'm at Damian's with a large glass of red wine in my hand. I brought the wine with me. As soon as I walked in, I knew I shouldn't have come. It would have been better to have spent five minutes on the staircase in the company of my lovely neighbour than an evening with my self-obsessed fling.

Damian's got me watching the interview he had earlier in the week. It's a special preview. All the contestants from *Sing Me Out of the Jungle* are on it. He's sitting in between a 50-year-old female journalist called Rose, and 23-year-old singer of a one-hit wonder called Elize. For the show, he's wearing green ripped jeans and a yellow shirt with a v-neck plunging low down his chest.

"It's for the gay vote," he says, laughing. "I've got to get everyone voting for me."

"Please don't wear that when you're with me."

"What does it matter? No one sees me with you, do they?"

I look up to see what expression he's wearing, but he's turned away, grating cheese onto a piece of toast. He says he's given up on learning to cook. With the money from the show, he says he's going to be eating out more. He still wants me to post tweets of great dishes, though, to make him look good.

He pops his plate under the grill and comes over to the sofa. He looks so excited to see himself on television. He says he's already watched it three times. His only regret is that he didn't sit up straighter.

He points his beer at the screen.

"This is where they ask us what we're most scared of."

There's a ripple of laughter as Elize confesses she's afraid of spiders. I watch as Damian puts a casual arm around her bronzed shoulders.

"I'll make sure they stay away from you," he says.

The camera zooms in on her blushing, giggling face. The audience in the studio is whistling.

"What?" Damian says, shrugging. *"I'm a gentlemen."*

"Damian will keep the spiders away," Rose says, rolling her eyes, *"but who will keep Damian away?"*

More peals of laughter from the other contestants, while the presenter winks at the camera.

"She was a bit of a bitch," Damian says, flopping down beside me. "I was just being friendly."

"You were flirting."

He laughs. "I don't fancy her. She looks alright on TV, but up close her skin is horrible."

Now it's Damian's turn to tell everyone what he's scared of. His arm has moved off Elize now and his hands are clasped between his legs. He leans forward as he talks, which makes him seem eager and sincere.

"Well, as you know Johnny..." he begins, talking to the presenter as if they had already had this very conversation. And they probably have, because it's not live, they could have stopped and started 20 times already. I'm about to ask him if they did, but he shushes me and points at the screen. *"I've had a lot of people attacking me lately..."*

"Are you referring to Twitter?"

"Yeah, that's right. People have been really trying to make me out to be this bad person, but I'd never say the words those hackers put into my mouth..."

"Offline you would!" I snort.

He doesn't reply. I glance at him and notice that he's smiling at the screen, enjoying every minute.

"So already I feel like I'm at a disadvantage... like everyone hates me... which is scary, I suppose..."

"Do you really think that?" the presenter says, turning on his faux concern look. "Surely not?"

"Yeah, of course, I know there are people who think I did it myself. The hacker insulted everyone and anyone who thinks that was me is going to think I'm a bastard, excuse me... but they swore at everyone, swore at people's mums... I'd never ever do that. Mums are special."

Some of the audience let out a sympathetic "awww", seduced by this hunk saying sweet things about his mum.

"Mum vote," he says, nodding. "Good, right?"

I frown at him, my lips curling into a half-hearted smile. Is that what he was thinking in that moment?

"So I know it's going to be difficult for me to change people's opinions... but I hope they do... coz I'm a nice guy..."

He breaks into a big cheeky grin and actually winks at the camera. I'm simultaneously shocked and impressed at how well he's playing it. I don't think his big head needs another compliment, though, and I'm about to point out instead that he hasn't answered the question when the presenter gets there before me.

"So what are you saying you're scared of, though? ... in the jungle I mean..."

Damian takes a deep breath. "Well, Johnny, I'm saying that after everything I've been through, I'm not scared of some little animal biting me, am I? And I'm not scared of eating something horrible... it'll make me feel a bit sick, but I'm not scared of it. In fact, I'm really looking forward to getting into the jungle to get away from *the stuff I'm actually scared of, people taking over my identity and invading my privacy...*"

That gets a round of applause. He's already got a whole bunch of new people on his side.

"*Is there anybody you're going to miss?*" the presenter asks.

It's stupid, but I feel this little flicker of excitement. My overactive imagination is waiting for him to look out, into the camera and say with a smile, "yeah, and she knows who she is".

"*My little dog, I'll miss him...*"

I look at Damian, who is biting the bottom of his lip, laughing.

"I didn't know you had a dog," I say.

"I don't," he laughs, "I just want the dog-lover vote!"

"Wow."

I want to ask him, is anything about you real? But the presenter is talking again and I find myself mesmerised by the drama unfolding, as Elize fixes her big, smoky eyes on him.

"*So there's no one special then in Damian Dance's life, right now?*" the presenter says, his eyes twinkling.

Damian shakes his head. "*No, Johnny, not in mine, I'm afraid.*"

I told him he needed to say he was single for the show, but he didn't need to be so convincing!

What's wrong with me?

I don't want to be Damian's "someone special". If I did, I'd be wearing a Star of David around my neck...

"Yeah, that's me done... it gets boring now," Damian says. He lowers the volume with the remote and takes a swig of his beer. Then he lifts the magazine balancing on the wicker bowl and grabs a half-empty packet of cigarettes. He doesn't make a ton of excuses this time when he lights up.

I'm aware I've gone quiet. I might even look like I'm seething. I shouldn't be taking it personally. If anything I should be celebrating his acting skills. This is exactly what reality TV is about, wooing the crowds, melting girls' hearts, making them dream. I can imagine Tintino having great fun with that interview.

"You should be tweeting about it," Damian says, frowning at me. "Are you alright? Didn't you like it?

Didn't I like the feeling of the man I've been sleeping with telling the whole world there's no one special in his life? What about his lucky star speech?

"It's just weird, I suppose... the whole... I don't know ..."

I can either sit here feeling hurt or I can spit it out. Seeing as I spit it out for everyone who isn't me all day, it might be an idea to use my voice at least when I'm offline.

"What's weird?" he says, sounding defensive. "I thought it was good. Andy thought it was fucking genius. So what's the matter?"

His words press a button. I feel irritated by him, but I still feel hurt.

"It's just the *I've got no one special in my life* thing..."

I watch the words register on his face, the alarm in the subtle widening of his eyes. I feel my cheeks redden, embarrassed that I've shared my feelings, and they are so bloody pathetic. Would I have wanted him to mention me? Of course not. But a tiny acknowledgement of *something*...

"But you said..."

"I know, I know! It's just hearing it made me feel funny, like I don't exist."

He digs the butt of his cigarette into the glass ashtray and turns to me. I don't react to the smell as he leans in to kiss me. His hands reach up for the buttons of my shirt and start to undo them. I feel my body resist.

He pulls back. I'm glad, but also confused.

"I just want to check something..." he says.

He reaches for the remote and presses rewind.

"You're not going to watch it again, are you?"

He doesn't answer. Right now he's on a planet where he's the only one who matters. I reach for my phone. I've got 22 new emails.

To: maysparkes@smcb.com
From: craigbrown@smcb.com

Hi May

I just thought you should know that I'm letting Abigail go. She's still not getting the simple things right, like getting people's names.
C

"You idiot," I mutter, quickly composing a reply.

From: craigbrown@smcb.com
To: maysparkes@smcb.com

Don't think this is a very good idea. Abigail has been really supportive to me. Also, she knows everything we do, so it seems risky to send her off with that knowledge. Can we discuss?
May

I should have praised her more in front of him. I should have made more of a fuss about how she helped me with the photo shoot. What about Glastonbury? She had acted professionally and responsibly. She had swallowed her instincts to get drunk and throw herself at Thijs. That takes willpower. I can't let Craig just get rid of her. She deserves to stay and prove herself.

I'm feeling worked up as I click through to the next email. I start reading it without understanding it and then I stop and refocus and start reading it again. My eyes widen as I realise what this is. It's from Twitter and they've got an IP address for me. As I read the formal reply from Kevin at Twitter, my stomach tightens in anticipation as I think of Gabe and what I'm going to say to him.

"Oh my God..."

My eyes have jumped down to the numbers. I was worried I

might forget them, but now they are burning a hole in my mind.

82.47.239.12

I feel my skin crawl. Damian shifts to the edge of the sofa, leaning forward, the corners of his lips creeping into a smile as he watches himself make love to the camera.

"People have been really trying to make me out to be this bad person, but I'd never say the words those hackers put into my mouth..."

"You fucking liar."

The smile is wiped off his face and the shock is quickly replaced with anger, "What did you call me?"

My heart is pounding in my chest and I feel this wave of fury that makes me want to start beating my fists against him.

"A liar! You're the hacker, aren't you?"

He clicks his teeth, his face reddening, "Don't be stupid."

"Twitter have sent me the hacker's IP address and it's yours."

"They've got it wrong. Hackers must've made it look like it was me. They do that all the time."

I glare at him in disbelief. Is this really the line he's going to take?

"Damian. You kept your password."

"You said it could have been your colleague."

"And now I know it wasn't!"

"But you could have left my account open at the office and he could have logged on it."

I look at the tension in his jaw, the anxious biting, and I know everything I need to know. He's hungry for this fame. He doesn't care what he has to do for it. Perhaps it was all plotted out perfectly, for him to gain sympathy for being a victim of those awful hackers.

"You said yourself you suspected him," he says.

"Because I didn't want to believe it was you!"

He presses his head into his hands and lets out a growl of frustration. In the background, his cockier self continues to talk to the presenter.

"*Well, Johnny, I'm saying that after everything I've been through, I'm not scared of some little animal biting me, am I?*"

I get up abruptly and grab my bag. I can't stand to be here a second longer. I should have trusted my instincts.

"Where are you going?" Damian cries.

"Home."

"You can't just go."

I reach for the door handle and he gets up and rushes to stop me. He holds my arm, squeezes it until it hurts.

"What are you going to say?" he says, his eyes wild. "What are you going to tell everyone?"

My bubble of calm bursts.

"How could you do this to me?" I cry. "Don't you realise what I went through? I thought it was my fault! I had sleepless nights from worrying! I had to spend my weekends apologising when I should have been spending time with my family! I've lost a stone from just pure worry! I wanted to believe you were better than everyone made out you were! But you're not! You've turned my job into a complete farce!"

He drops my arm as if it's suddenly too hot to touch and he looks at me warily. Is he going to carry on denying the truth?

"You don't understand what it's like for me..." he begins cautiously.

"What? Being hacked by YOURSELF? I bet it's very traumatic!"

"People keep bitching at me... what am I supposed to do? Lie down and take it like a pussy?"

"You need help!" I spit. "You need serious help!"

"May, it doesn't even matter now. We got what we wanted!"

"This is not what I wanted. I didn't want someone like you to walk into my life, seduce me and then lie to me to the point I'm playing detective to help you."

"Okay, I admit I should have told you earlier. But you won!" he says, his face cracking into a crazy smile. "I'm famous right now. I'm everywhere. That means you did a brilliant job!"

I stare at him and it dawns on me that, yes, he's right. I did do a brilliant job. I have a choice to take the credit, to put the unpleasantness behind me and to move on. But what about us? What happened between us makes this truth so much harder to swallow. I feel like I can't breathe.

"I've got to go..." I say.

"Don't go. Let's talk about it. Stay the night with me."

I shake my head in disbelief and point at him and then at me, "That part is over."

"Don't be like that."

I open the door and he reaches for me again.

"You won't tell anyone?" he says.

I feel sick to my gut. He doesn't care one bit about me walking out of his life. There's only space for one person in his, and it's him.

"Your secret is safe with me. I signed a contract," I say coldly.

I don't get the satisfaction of slamming the door behind me because he's holding the door open. The only thing I can do is not look back.

Chapter 43

It's six forty-five in the morning and I'm running. There's no phone attached to my arm. I'm alone. Just me and my battered grey trainers taking on the streets of London. I'm fighting every thought about Damian, wrestling with my guilt about Bernard and trying not to think about Alex. I just need to get a bit of balance and perspective back. So I'm running until I get it. I might have to run all the way to France before I do.

What if I did? What if I kept running forever, like Forrest Gump? And how could I prove it if I can't even grow a beard? My lungs are already hurting and I've only been running ten minutes. I slow down as I reach the small park. A familiar old lady in a pink fleece is waiting for her dog to do his business. I breathe in the smell of pine and keep on going.

It's over with Damian. After an evening dwelling on it, my main emotion is still disgust that I went along with it in the first place. It was lust and it was fun, but it was never going to grow into something meaningful. If there is a part to him that is real, then I haven't seen it yet. He'll go off into the jungle, no doubt cause a stir and a scandal, shagging one contestant in the bushes and telling another he fancies her. He'll divide the public. Some will vote for entertainment factor and want him to stay on, others will take it all too seriously and flock to their Twitter feeds to moan about him.

The hardest part is accepting I'm not going to be able to get away from my current clients until there's someone good enough to take over. With Abigail out of the picture, the hope of having someone to share the workload has faded into thin air.

My feet begin to drag and I force myself to pick up pace to escape the thoughts pulling me down. Just run. That's all I've got to do. But I suddenly feel so utterly miserable that I just stop in the middle of the path and put my hands on my hips, and I seriously consider lying down on the path and never getting up.

The thought comes so loudly and so clearly it's like being bulldozed:

I can't do this job any more.

Behind me, I hear a runner's footstep. So I bend down to pretend I'm tying my laces to disguise my morning meltdown, and then, just as I'm about to set off again, I hear him calling me.

"May!"

It's Alex. I know it's him, but I pretend I haven't heard and I keep on running.

"May!" his voice breaks into baffled laughter. "Wait! Don't run off! May, what are you doing?"

How can I pretend I can't hear him? I'm not even wearing earphones. I slow down to a halt and turn around, feeling that familiar stirring in my stomach. He catches up with me, not a bit out of breath. He's not wearing his glasses and his blue eyes are sparkling and clear.

"Hi..." I say, feeling awkward.

He pushes a hand through his silky hair and rubs the back of his neck.

"Hi..." he says, "I've been trying to catch you..."

"I didn't think I ran that fast."

"No, I know, I mean..."

He means the text messages, the phone calls I've missed.

"I'm sorry, I've been too busy for lunch..." I say, looking back up the road I should be running down, away from all these feelings that are pouring in.

"I thought you might be avoiding me."

I feel embarrassed. "No, it's just..."

"Is it because of Louisa?"

Does he know?

"I know she's with Jacob."

"I'm sorry."

"That's what I thought you'd say and I don't know why you're sorry. I never fancied Louisa."

"But... but... you kept popping over with such lame excuses?" I stammer.

He's looking at me so closely.

"It's always been you," he says.

My voice comes out hoarse. "What?"

"I like you, May..."

Me? My eyes start welling up. I can't seem to control them. I had this tight knot in my chest. I was readying myself for it to tighten even more, until I could hardly breathe, but instead it's melting. I cover my mouth and turn away, because I'm so embarrassed, but I'm actually going to cry.

"May?"

I shake my head, unable to speak, and cover my face as my shoulders start to tremble. I'm helpless to stop it. I can feel his hand on my shoulder.

"Shit... is it that bad?" he says. "I mean, you don't have to do anything about it... I mean, it's not compulsory to go out with me... in fact if you feel you'd rather I start looking for another place to live...."

I stop crying and start to laugh and hiccup at the same time. Encouraged by my reaction, he goes on.

"It's because I'm interrupting your run and you were about to break a record, isn't it? God, I'm annoying. I mean, you were stopped in the middle of the path, so I thought it'd be alright, but that was probably your technique, psyching yourself into a grand sprint... I'm so sorry..."

I wipe away the tears. "Shut up!"

"I'm going to. Promise."

"I feel such an idiot now I really want to run away from you."

"*You* feel like an idiot?" he says, in mock shock. "I told you I liked you and you started crying, how do you think that makes me feel?"

I laugh. "I'm sorry... it's just..." I run a hand over my hair, flattening it down. "I feel like such a scruff..."

He waits for me to go on. It's not much of an answer. We're both standing there, crimson-cheeked, talking about everything but his admission. I don't know what to say, or do. If he was ever going to attempt a film kiss, my running eyes and nose have put him off.

"Are you with someone?" he says, suddenly looking pained.

I think of Damian and shudder. "No, thank God... I was but..."

"Was it that guy you were with in the restaurant? The famous one?"

"The one who hacked his own account?" I blurt out, feeling bitter again. "Yep."

"Shit. So it was true."

"I shouldn't have said... oh God, I'm just..." I breathe out. "Not really in a good place right now."

"Yeah, I can see that."

The way he says it makes me feel anxious that he's changing his mind. I don't want him to see me like this, in this mess, tied to my job like this. I can get balance back. I can.

"You probably need some space... I shouldn't have stopped you running..."

"No, you should have," I say. I want to rewind the moment. I want to go back to the bit before I burst into tears, so I can react differently. I could have kissed him. We could be kissing right now, in the middle of a park, with a Scottish terrier doing his business under nearby tree.

"Shall we run?" he says.

I stare at him. Is that another way of saying shall we forget this happened?

"Okay..." I say uncertainly. "But I'm probably much slower than you."

"I don't want to go too fast... I didn't even want to go running this morning... I just heard you leave and thought this would be my only moment."

I break into a smile. "Really?"

He looks embarrassed. "Yep."

"That's dedication..."

He laughs, "Come on..."

So we start running. We don't even talk. We just run side by side, enjoying the light breeze of another summer's day, as London wakes up and construction workers shout across the rooftops. I keep breaking into a smile and I notice so does he. To passersby we must look like a pair of smug idiots, grinning all the way through our workout. There's no kiss at the end of our run. But at my door he says we should start again and suggests a place for dinner.

Chapter 44

Abigail has gone. In her place we have a fierce blonde called Joanne. There's something so familiar about her features, but it's only while I'm sipping my third coffee of the morning that it hits me. She looks like Craig.

It doesn't take me long to discover she's Craig's cousin and knows all the ins and outs of what his company really does. I can't shake the feeling that she's got her sights set a lot higher than being our receptionist. There's something about the way she asked me how I was feeling which made me realise she must know all about my issues with Bernard. I'm guessing she has told Craig that she wouldn't have such issues. Or perhaps, all the coffee is making me paranoid.

"Damian Dance for you," Joanne says.

"Thank you."

I wait for the transfer, feeling a strange indifference at the prospect of talking to this man I once thought might just be the answer.

"May, it's me. Are you still angry with me? Look, I'm sorry. I was an idiot. Okay, worse than that, I went a bit insane."

"Insane," I echo. "Yes, I'd agree with that."

"Can you forgive me?"

He wants my approval. He wants the whole world's approval and he can't have it, so he'll never be happy. The thought strikes me there and then, and I actually manage to feel a tiny bit sorry for him. But no, I don't forgive him.

"I'm not happy about it, but I'm employed by you so I'm going to have to stick it, aren't I?"

"I don't want you to be angry with me."

"I'm a professional. I won't let it interfere with my job."

"May, don't be like that."

I want to leave, but how can I without another job on the horizon?

"I'll be in the jungle soon, where I won't be able to tweet anyway," he says cheerfully. "

"I know. I'm looking forward to it. I won't have to worry about your account being hacked."

I open the top button on my shirt, feeling flushed. I shouldn't have had that third coffee. It tasted like tobacco.

"Don't be like that, May."

There's a knock on the door. It's Gabe. He comes inside, his hand running over his cropped hair. His shirt is undone, revealing a red South Park t-shirt beneath it.

"Code red," he hisses. "Code fucking red."

A second later, Craig comes bursting into the room and says something that makes my world go up in flames.

"May Sparks... why are you trending on Twitter?"

Chapter 45

There I am, sandwiched between #TalkLikeAPirateDay and the vice-president of Turkey. I'm trending on Twitter.

"Why did he give my name?" I say, for the millionth time. "He didn't need to do that."

Thijs broke up with Ankara, admitted that he hadn't composed any of those cute little tweets. Ankara responded by going public with a bitter blog post entitled *Love in the Times of Twitter*.

"They weren't even together five minutes... How did it get to this?"

Craig is outside in the corridor on the phone to Thijs. Apparently our young client is stuck in his house, paparazzi waiting outside, eager for his confirmation. A small, mocking voice in my head tells me that I've succeeded because isn't having paparazzi outside your door the very proof of fame? They'd be outside the office too if they had tracked me down.

"She wants to protect other women from you," Gabe says, not looking up. He's sat in the chair opposite me, scrolling on his tablet, his eyes flickering. "That's what she's said on Twitter."

"Oh come on!" I cry.

"*#MaySparks is playing with people's lives, tricking them into opening their hearts. Who else has she lied to?*'"

I press my face into my hands, colours fizzing in the back of my eyes. I push away the thought of Joyce. I can't think of that now.

"Why does she have to share every little thing that happens in her life?" I cry, feeling another surge of anger and frustration. "She got dumped. She should have just had a fucking drink like the rest of us."

"You can see why she'd be angry, though. It's all pretty fucked up."

"Gabe! Whose side are you on?"

"I don't feel good about it, that's all."

"Nor do I. But what am I supposed to do now? Deny it? Change my name? How many May Sparks are there in England? Can you Google that please?"

Gabe opens a new tab, starts a fresh search. I bet all the May Sparks on Twitter are gagging to know why their name is trending. It would be a dream come true to most of them. To all of them, perhaps, except for me.

Craig comes back into the office. He looks tense, his cheeks drawn as he grinds his teeth.

"What's Thijs going to say?" I ask.

"He wants to go for honesty. He's going to say he's embarrassed and very sorry. He's also going to say he was misled... he's already fired Maria Kuebler."

"Fuck!"

He looks grave. "Indeed. She wants to sue us."

"On what grounds? These were her ideas!"

"Yes..."

I wait for him to go on, but he doesn't. He just looks pensively at the space behind my head.

"What are we going to do?" I ask.

The phone starts ringing and I look at it warily. I can't think of anyone who might be friendly at the other end.

"Take it," Craig says.

I can't bring myself to say my own name. "Hello?"

"May, what's going on?" Bernard hisses. "Everyone is talking

340

about the woman being paid to stand in for celebrities. My wife, miss fucking Twitter addict, has just been telling me about it. She even jokingly asked me if that's what *I've* been doing."

"Don't shout at me, Bernard," I say, trying to keep cool. "Remember that I only did what you asked me to. I shouldn't have, but I did."

"I thought you were a fucking professional. I didn't think you were going to be telling everyone."

"I am a professional and I didn't tell anyone!"

Gabe and Craig are staring at me. What do they want me to say? I feel a pressure building in my chest, the air being sucked out of it. I rub my fingers along my collarbone, try to regulate my breath. Why do I bother to keep calm? A panic attack would come in handy right now. Why can't I faint and knock myself out? That seems like the only way of escaping. But for how long?

"Can they link you to me?" he barks.

"No."

"How can you be sure?"

"Why would they even try?" I say. "There's nothing suspicious about your online profile," and can't resist adding, "your offline life, however, sounds far more scandalous, judging by the last DM from Miss Inky Toes. I can't believe you made me confess your undying love for your wife while getting sucked off by another woman!"

I'm trembling. It's the adrenalin of telling him the truth, letting him know what I know. I'm furious I did what he wanted me to. I should have told him I wouldn't get involved in his personal relationships. Craig reaches for the phone, his nostrils flaring like a cartoon bull.

"I want to speak to your boss," Bernard says, as Craig grabs the phone off me.

Craig doesn't approve of my attitude or the emotion that I'm injecting into the situation.

"Hello, Bernard," he says, warmly. "I understand you must be concerned..."

He turns away, heads out of the office again. What happened? When I first started here, Craig talked to me as though I was his partner. He promised me high stakes in the company. I was to have one of those swish, high-paid jobs before I hit thirty. But now I'm realising it was all talk to keep me working like a dog for him, while he sat back sipping his designer espressos while congratulating himself at what a genius he was.

Gabe swears and looks up at me.

"What now?"

"You're fucked."

"No one knows who I am. I'm invisible!" I say.

He turns the tablet towards me. I wave my hand at it. I don't need to see every tweet people post. Everyone has an opinion. But not every opinion matters. Tintino pops into my head and I feel a twinge of curiosity. I wonder if he's had something clever to say about me. If anyone's going to successfully rip me apart in 140 characters, it'll be him.

"I don't want to see," I say.

I know what Twitter bile can do to people. Like hydrofluoric acid it can melt a backbone.

"I think you need to," he says.

"It's just one celebrity accusing me. Two if Thijs is going down the honest route. It'll blow over without anyone finding out who I am..."

Gabe coughs, "actually, it's just gone up to three people accusing you."

I narrow my eyes at him. "What do you mean?"

"Damian..." he says.

I feel my stomach constrict. What has Damian done now?

"He's just tweeted that you were responsible for hacking his account after a disagreement."

"WHAT?"

"How has he even got his password?" Gabe says, frowning.

A cold sweat washes over my skin. It's like being immersed in icy water, and yet I'm on fire with rage.

"He never gave it up," I shriek. "*He* was the hacker! He admitted it last night. It was him. He's made my life a fucking nightmare! How could he do this to me? No! This is not happening!"

"Calm down, May."

"No, I'm not calming down! I'm ordering a hit man!"

I grab my mobile and dial Damian's number. I expect it to ring and go to voicemail, because if I'd tweeted what he had, I'd be anticipating a furious May Sparks at the end of the phone. I'm dumbfounded when he answers in a cheerful voice.

"Hi, May, I know what you're thinking..."

It only takes me a second to overcome my shock and find my voice.

"What the fuck, Damian? What the fuck?"

"Don't swear at me, May. I'm your client. You need to respect me."

"You just accused me of being the person behind all that abuse!"

"But it's fine. No one knows who you are."

"What do you mean?" I explode.

"You don't have a reputation to think about it, do you? You're the behind-the-scenes-girl, taking one for the star. This is really good for me. People thought I'd lied about my account being hacked."

"You did lie!"

"Wait, hear me out... now I'm at the centre of things, in the middle of the conversation... I'm going to admit I made a mistake thinking I needed your services and when I terminated the contract, you were so angry, you tried to sabotage me. It's good, isn't it?"

"Are you insane?" I cry. "Can't you hear yourself?"

"May, don't shout at me. I hate it when people shout at me. That was my dad's problem."

"Don't talk to me about your dad! You're lying about me, trying to destroy my reputation, you... you..."

"But no one knows who you are," he says.

"I'm trending on fucking Twitter!"

He lets out a little laugh. "I know. That's what gave me the idea."

"I can tell everyone the truth!"

"But why?" he says, sounding genuinely baffled. "This isn't about you. This is about me getting into the limelight."

"You are the most self-centred prick I've ever met."

"I can't believe you just said that."

"I won't let you drag my name through the gutter like this."

"What name? No one knows who you are."

"Stop saying that!"

"Anyway, you can't do that. It's in the contract."

Gabe leans forward, swiping a hand at his neck. I swing my chair around, away from him. The blood pumping through my veins. I have never been so angry in all my life.

"Fuck the contract!" I shout. "You're the shit who's going to come out looking like a complete fucking arsehole!"

"May!" Craig's voice booms across the room. I turn back around, my heart pounding

Craig has come back into the room. He is standing there, red-faced.

"Give me the phone," he says. "Now."

"He's accusing me of being the one to hack his account!"

"Give me the phone."

I reluctantly hand it over.

"Mr Dance..."

"Mr Fuckwit," I hiss under my breath. Gabe purses his lips. I think it's a smile of condolence.

"No, there won't be any breach of contract," Craig is saying coolly. He gives me a warning look and I crumple back into my seat.

"Yes, she is feeling very sensitive, understandably. A little bit of transparency would have been preferable... yes, I understand... and yes, I'm delighted we've been able to help you..." My jaw drops open. He glances over at me, his nostrils flaring. "No, she's very

344

fiery when she's angry. But she won't say anything. "

"Yes, I fucking will," I mutter under my breath.

"#MayDay is trending," Gabe whispers. "And #WhereIsMaySparks."

I reach over for his tablet to see the evidence.

"Oh my God..." I gasp, as my eyes roam over the growing list of celebrities reassuring their fans they aren't being duped by May Sparks. Then there are the thousands of others who just want to get involved in another pointless conversation.

CANDYMILLS @CANDYMILLS

Just to confirm. I'm tweeting this not May Sparks!!! LOL! #whereisMaySparks

ALFIETV @ALFIEMONS

You can tell I'm not paying for my tweets, right? Coz they're shit. I know it, you know it, May Sparks probably even knows it.

ELLISTURNER @ELLISTURNER

Who cares where Wally is now? #WhereIsMaySparks

JODIEFANGIRLJUNE @JODIEJUNE

I'm so glad that @DamianDance didn't say those horrible things! #crushbackontrack #WhereIsMaySparks

What did I expect? Of course people will believe Damian. I swear under my breath as I scan over the tweets of relief from his fans.

Craig gets off the phone.

"What's he going to do?" I say. "He's a lunatic!"

"It won't go further. No one needs to know it's you."

He sounds just like Damian.

"I can't believe I'm hearing this."

"Denial," he says. "Don't mention this to anyone. It will die down if we keep quiet."

"How can we trust Thijs not to give me away?" I cry. "Where I work?"

"He won't," Craig says, firmly. "That said, I think it's time to..." he hesitates, looks over at Gabe, and then back at me, "to take a step back. I think you're no longer in an emotional place to deal with the work we do here."

I stare at him. What has just happened? I feel like I'm being punished! Does he need to be reminded that it was Ankara who let the cat out of the bag? That it was Damian who sent all those nasty tweets?

"What are you saying?"

"I think you need a break."

"A break?" I cry, my voice rising an octave.

"You're in a state. Look, you're trembling."

"It's not her fault, though," Gabe says.

I'm grateful that he seems annoyed on my behalf, because we all know it's not a break. Craig is buckling under the pressure. He wants to get rid of the problem so he can relax. In the end he's turned out to be as ruthless as my clients.

The phone again. Of course. It never stops. I reach for it, but Craig intercepts.

"Hello?"

I fold my arms across my chest. Who does he have to sweet-talk this time?

"Abigail..." Craig says, the colour draining from his face. "How are you?"

Gabe and I share a tense look. It can't be a coincidence that she's ringing in the middle of this crisis.

"Wait, let's talk about this... you must have a price... please, surely there's something we can do..." I've never heard his voice so high before. I've never seen that look, either, of Craig losing control. "What have you done?"

A few moments later we're staring at exactly what she's done.

346

I know. I used to work with her. So glad I left. #WhereIsMaySparks

"Left!" Craig spits, outraged. "She got fired!"

"You pissed her off," I say, feeling a fresh bout of fear. "She's going to spill her guts."

A moment later she does just that.

BANDGIRLABI @BANDGIRL

You can hear it from me... OR just ask @ThijsVanBro @DamianDance @bthomskinner @angelbutler. Go on, ask them to reply to you now and see what they say!

"I think you'd better go home," Craig says. "Before she leaks the address."

The energy seeps out of me. My head is a battleground. Thoughts slice and cut and tear into each other.

"Get a taxi..." Craig says, and I nod, suddenly on autopilot, and grab my coat.

As I descend to ground level, one thought creeps to the forefront of my mind. It's not even a thought but an overwhelming wish, a desire that tears at my heart. That if only my outrage was because I was being wrongly accused. Because I'm not innocent in all this. Not even a little. I'm guilty, guilty as a hell.

Chapter 46

I push through the revolving doors and step outside onto the pavement. A light wind whips at my hair, makes my eyes water. A taxi whizzes past, but the light is off. I start to walk, thinking some fresh air might untangle some of the knots in my chest. From somewhere near by a man's voice shouts out my name and I glance around me in alarm.

"MAY SPARKS!"

My eyes land on a slim, bald man with a heavy, black camera with a zoom lens. He lifts it to his face and I turn back, my heart thudding and pick up my pace. They've found me already. Who did Abigail tell? Should I stop and confront him? Instinct tells me to keep going. I don't want to give him the opportunity for some ugly close-up, my face frozen and twisted in an expression that they'll gleefully interpret as GUILTY.

I glance back to see if he's following me, gasp when I catch sight of him advancing past a group in suits, fast on my heels. He's all dressed in black: black anorak, black cargo trousers, and yet he stands out a mile.

A taxi turns the corner and I throw up my arm to hail it. The driver halts abruptly, unfazed by the fury of the cyclist behind, who skids into the curb. I get in, call out my address and then lower myself down into the back seat. Next I get out my phone to warn Craig that my cover has been blown.

"Don't give them anything. Don't talk to anyone. Don't even think of coming in for a while," he says. "You're off the job, for your own sake."

Home at last, I stand in my empty living room and I feel the fear creeping up my legs like the cursed scarabs from a disturbed Egyptian tomb. I don't want to be alone. I must talk to someone.

I think of Alex. His confession in the park plays in my head, makes my heart start beating with hope again. Not everyone is hunting me down for the kill.

I head up to his flat, anticipation growing in my chest. #Pleasebehome. I knock tentatively on the door, and then harder. There's a scrape of a chair, the sound of muffled footsteps and a moment later Alex opens the door, in a soft grey t-shirt and pyjama bottoms.

"May!" he says, his face lighting up in an instant, and falling, when he looks down to check, that, yes, he is wearing pyjamas.

"Sorry, did I wake you?"

"No, I had a night shoot last night so..." he peters off, looks at me closely, "are you alright?"

The concern in his voice sets the tears off. The reality of what has happened comes charging over me.

"No," I admit. I wipe at my eyes, aware that this is the second time in a row that I've burst into tears with him. "This is the worst day of my life."

He leads me into a messy living room, where tall white book-shelves line the walls, swollen with paperbacks and hard-backed comic books. He clears Sunday newspaper supplements off the sagging leather sofa so I can sit. There's a patchwork quilt crumpled on one end, which he picks up, starts to fold badly, then chucks onto the cream Ikea recliner on the other side of the room.

"I'm trending on Twitter," I say. "One of my clients exposed me to that model, Ankara Davies. Damian Dance jumped on the bandwagon, decided to blame me for the hacking..."

His brow crumples and I worry he doesn't understand anything I've just said.

"But no one knows what you look like?" he says. "Who you really are?"

I think of the man with the camera and feel sick to my stomach.

"There was a paparazzi outside my office. I think he got a snap of me. Our receptionist wanted revenge for Craig firing her and leaked our address."

"What? She gave out your address on Twitter?"

I nod. He looks shocked. "That's horrible."

"I think I've just been fired."

He pushes his fingers through his hair. I expected sympathy, but he looks as anxious as I feel.

"Are you okay for money?"

I'd hoped he'd be practical. Had Louisa been home she would have treated it all like some exciting scandal and not my life falling apart.

"Yeah... I'm fine... I'm just..."

"In shock," he finishes. "I don't blame you. It's crazy."

He reaches for my hand, squeezes it.

"I'm going to make you some chamomile while I think what you should do."

"Thank you... I'm sorry to burst in like this, you can tell me to go if you like."

He gives me a quizzical smile, "don't you remember this morning in the park? When I said I liked you?"

I find myself blushing. "I like you too."

What are we? Primary school kids? Are we going to swap stickers now and throw things at each other in the playground?

His eyes are on my lips, as though he's thinking about kissing me. But then it must kick in that this isn't the time for romance and he heads off to the kitchen. I lean back into the sofa cushions, look around me at his habitat. There are film posters on the wall mounted in thin, black, wooden frames. *Life Aquatic, O*

Brother Where Out There, ET, The Adventures of Tintin. There's also that famous picture of Tarantino holding an old-fashioned video camera to his eye.

I get up, suddenly needing the toilet. I find it without asking, in the corridor, like ours is. It's got the same beige lino and white cabinets. The only difference is he's gone for wooden drawers whereas we went for white wicker. I wash my hands in the sink, my eyes scanning over all the grooming products that I always suspected he had. He's into his boy toys too. There's a giant white Lego storm trooper, three space raiders in a row, and a little plastic figurine of a popular comic-book star I've just seen in the living room. I find myself picking up the familiar plastic toy. Ginger hair in a quiff, a beige gabardine and short brown trousers, Tintin is frozen mid-walk. His black pin-prick eyes are punctuated with eyebrows that have left him with a look of permanent surprise.

A feeling of unease creeps over me. It makes the little hairs on my arms stand on end. I think of those hard-backed comic books on the shelf.

Tintin... Tintino...

It has to be a coincidence. Alex isn't even on Twitter.

Is he? Has he ever actually said that? Haven't I just assumed he isn't? My mind scrambles to past conversations. I think of him coming into the restaurant that day and seeing Damian. Hadn't Damian said Alex looked familiar?

I hadn't thought anything of it, because I'd been pissed off with Damian for wearing those silly sunglasses inside. But what if he was familiar because Alex had been the one to take that photo of him, drunk and lying across the pavement?

No, I'm jumping to conclusions. I'm being paranoid. Damian might have just seen Alex in a Soho recording studio. The thought doesn't reassure me. I remember that first mocking tweet:

TINTINO @TINTINO
Aw. "Life". That's a cute little euphemism. RT @DamianDance

Hadn't it sounded personal? Like Tintino had seen for himself the real high he meant? I had. That day he'd come in and kissed me, Damian hadn't been himself. I just hadn't wanted to acknowledge it, so desperate was I to think the best of him.

I step out into the corridor. Alex is coming towards me with a steaming cup, but stops when he sees my expression.

"What is it?" he says.

My voice comes out shaky. "Tell me you're not Tintino."

His eyes widen in alarm and he opens his mouth to speak. I can see the indecision in his eyes, whether to deny it or admit the truth. I feel winded.

"Oh my God, how could you? ... you knew... you said..."

It's too awful for words. I head for the front door, a thought occurring to me that the only way to escape it all now would be to get the hell out of the country.

"Wait! You don't understand!" he calls after me. "I was Tintino long before I met you! I only said what needed to be said!"

"Leave me alone!" I cry, without turning back. "I hate you!"

He must know that whatever flicker of feeling between us has just been snuffed out. That's why he doesn't chase me and bang on my apartment door, begging me to let him in so he can explain. How could I ever look at him in the same way again? I don't even know who he is. All I know is that I never want to see him again.

Chapter 47

By the time I've reached my parents' house, I've decided that fleeing the country might be a bit dramatic. My mind has been manically editing what I'm going to say to them instead. That I'm "trending" will only draw a blank look, at most a sympathetic pat on the back and an offer of a cup of tea. I could tell them about my two-faced clients, but then I'd have to confess I played along. The hacking, then? I could tell them about Damian. Yet, without admitting to the sex they wouldn't be able to appreciate the full extent of my hurt and rage and incomprehension.

Then there's Alex, aka Tintino, who I'm having real difficulties banishing from my brain. I just can't believe all this time, he, who acted as though he hated social media, was the Twitter king, effortlessly entertaining the masses 140 characters at a time.

No, my parents wouldn't be able to get their heads around that last kick in the teeth. The man I'd fallen for being the man laughing the hardest behind my back.

The front door swings open as I'm battling a fresh burst of emotion. There's a shriek of surprise and, before I can say anything, or take in the bronzed figure standing there, I'm being smothered in my sister's embrace.

Behind her I hear my mum cry out in delight.

"May! You made it! I thought you never read my emails!"

I'd forgotten all about Katie coming and I must have put off my mum's emails to read them later, and as usual with emails, out of sight out of mind.

"Of course I read your emails," I say, my voice cracking.

I bury my head in Katie's shoulder, drawing comfort from her familiar honey smell. My eyes well up. The final plan had been to just blurt it out: *Mum I've lost my job*. But to do that now would be to take the focus away from the happy reunion and I won't do that.

Katie lets me go and a big toothy smile fills her freckled face as she looks over me. She's put on weight and has the curves we used to dream about when we were teenagers.

"Oh, I did the same," Mum says, flapping at her face. "Balled my eyes out when she arrived. Come in! Come in! You've got to meet Lucas!"

Lucas? Oh God! I'd completely forgotten about him too. I brush away a runaway tear.

"You'll love him," Katie says, linking her arm in mine and pulling me through the living room to the kitchen.

I push away the dread and arrange my face in the sunniest of smile. No, there's no way I can offload my horrible news now.

Lucas is on the patio, sharing a beer with Dad and they're laughing at something. He has one hand in the pocket of his baggy jeans, which makes him slouch forward. He doesn't look much taller than Katie. He's broad-shouldered, with a visible paunch and soft brown arms. I take instant affection towards his easy smile, which lands on me as we walk outside.

"Look, she made it," Mum calls out from behind me.

I give my dad a hug and then turn to Lucas, and there's a split second where I'm not sure if we're going for one kiss or two, and then he envelopes me in a bear hug as if we were long-lost friends. To be honest, I almost start crying again.

"This is my sister, May," Katie says.

"It's so good to meet you," he says, in a thick Brazilian accent. "I really wanted to meet all of Katie's family."

354

"And we wanted to meet you," I say, feeling ashamed at my moment of dread.

Dad eyes me with interest. "They let you off work, then?"

"That's one way of putting it."

"Oh?" He's waiting for an explanation because I couldn't just be straightforward and say "yes".

"I thought I'd take a few days off..." My cheeks feel as if they're burning up and I glance around, avoiding eye contact with both parents. "I was wondering if I could stay over tonight?"

Katie's answer is another big hug. "It's been so long!"

"You don't have to ask!" Mum cries. "I'll put clean sheets on your bed."

"You don't have to do it now."

She looks so happy. Everyone does. There's no way I can admit to the real reason I'm here.

I think of all the frantic activity online and wonder how Craig has decided to deal with it. Has he stepped in under different guises to fend off Abigail's accusations? Or has he told each client it's up to them now to fight their own corner? Who will be left after all this? I think of the meeting scheduled for HappyHeart and my heart sinks. I have a lot of emails to write.

Mum's voice breaks through my thoughts. "Where's your bag? Didn't you bring an overnight bag?"

"No... I... it was very last-minute."

She frowns and I know she's onto me.

"I only need pyjamas."

"Well, you can borrow some..." she says. "Right, who wants wine? Red or white?"

"Lucas only drinks red," Katie says.

"If it's okay..." Lucas adds, looking apologetic.

My dad gives his shoulder a friendly squeeze. "You can have any colour you like!"

Lucas gets the best treatment a boyfriend has ever had in our house that afternoon. My parents want to know everything about him. They laugh at his jokes, beam at his stories and offer him something to eat every half an hour. Katie doesn't want to leave his side, so we don't go off into the other room to discuss our lives.

I sip my wine quietly in the corner, preferring to do the listening, because I know that if I open my mouth it will all come out. Mum's attention moves from Lucas to Katie. She wants a full update of her life. I watch Lucas slide a phone out of his pocket and start to scroll. I give in to the same impulse and get my own phone from my handbag in the living room.

The anxiety is immediate as I unlock it to have a look. Ten missed calls. I check them and the disappointment at seeing that Alex hasn't even bothered trying to call with an explanation makes me sink deeper into the sofa. Bastard, bastard, bastard. I simultaneously hate him so much and don't hate him at all.

There are voicemails and Twitter notifications in double figures, 25 new emails and five new text messages. I feel an urge to check my trending status, but what good will it do to see what a bunch of strangers thinks of me? Do I really want to get burned by all the inevitable vitriol?

I overhear Lucas ask after me and feel guilty that I'm in the living room checking my phone instead of finding out more about my potential brother-in-law. It doesn't have to be like this any more. If I'm fired, I could start a life without this phone dependency. But what would I do?

I feel an ache in my chest. I'm not ready for change. I just want to hide under a duvet for a week and wake up as a younger version of myself. I want to be back at *La Belle Femme* learning the ropes. If I could go back in time, I wouldn't say yes to Craig. Instead I'd be flattered by the offer, decline it and develop my own idea on the side. I'd probably still end up building a platform for other people's voices, but they would be voices that inspired me, voices that had something valuable to say. I'd invite guest bloggers to this creative hub, arrange interviews, attract advertisers, promote brands I believe in.

Why am I daydreaming about this now? It's over. My name is being dragged through the gutter. I'm a lying, home-wrecking, two-faced, unscrupulous bitch. The only place I'm heading is offline.

"May, come look at this!" Katie calls.

"What is it?"

"Just come look."

My stomach starts churning and I tell myself I'm being paranoid, that it's not going to be anything bad.

But when I step into the kitchen, my heart sinks. Mum and Katie are standing behind Lucas looking down at his phone. Dad is leaning towards them, his chin reaching up, his glasses slipping down his nose.

"Yes?" I say, tentatively. They're just looking at pictures. That's all.

Lucas looks up, an uncertain smile hovering on his lips.

"You are on trending on Twitter," he says.

Katie laughs. "Do we know any celebrities called May Sparks?"

If I tell them, then this whole drama will last much longer. If it blows over with only a handful of people ever knowing, I'll be able to just get on with my life a whole lot easier. I don't even have to say I got fired. When I'm ready, I'll tell them I quit on moral grounds. They'll love that. They'll look at me the way they look at Katie, with pride and affection.

"No," I say, with a shrug, and then look at Mum. "I thought we weren't allowed phones at the table."

"Oh, good point!" Mum says, backing away from the spectacle. "Put it away, Lucas. We're all going to be offline today."

"Why?" Katie protests, but she doesn't really mind.

"My parents say the same," Lucas laughs, and seems happy to oblige.

Mum winks at me. "Well done, May!"

I smile weakly. She wouldn't be giving me that approving look if she knew the truth.

Chapter 48

I don't go back home the next day either. Halfway through dinner I announce I can't face the train journey.

"And how often is Katie here, anyway?" I add, polishing off another glass of wine.

"It's not like you to miss work?" Dad says. "Won't you get into trouble?"

I let out a high-pitched giggle. It's a bit late to worry about that.

"I've done so much overtime, I feel like I shouldn't have to go back for a year!"

"Well, that's true," Mum says, but she's looking at me with concern.

My phone is upstairs, switched off. I held it above the toilet for a while, tempted to drop it in the bowl.

Bernard's lie was leaked yesterday. Miss Inky Toes finally decided to get her revenge. It was only ever a matter of time.

MISSINKYTOES @MISSINKYTOES
.@bthomskinner Now I know why you were so Jekyll & Hyde! You and #MaySparks deserve each other!

The newspapers didn't become aware of the scandal until it was too late. The *Daily Mail* went ahead and published the interview with Joyce about forgiving Bernard that had been written up days earlier. When I read it I cried into my pillow.

Afterwards I spent ages trying to find Joyce's personal email. I wanted to prove to her that I wasn't a cold-hearted bitch without a moral compass, who would say anything if the price was right. Later, trying to get to sleep, I told myself I was still being selfish, trying to alleviate my own inner turmoil instead of really understanding hers.

Did it make any difference that I hadn't known he was having an affair? I still pretended to be him. I still lied to her. Would it make her feel any better if she knew I wasn't paid the vast sums people were quoting on Twitter? No, of course not.

Interviewer: *You say you've forgiven him, has it been a difficult decision?*

Joyce Thompson-Skinner: *Of course it's been difficult. He broke my heart. You put on a brave face for the neighbours and try to look like you're getting on fine, but all the while, it's like you have terrible indigestion. To be honest, I wasn't entirely sure I would ever forgive him.*

Interviewer: *What changed?*

Joyce Thompson-Skinner: *He said he was sorry and I believed him. There was something so humble in his apology, in his reaching out to me. In the past he's never been good at admitting his mistakes. It has felt romantic getting back together and I'm optimistic about our future.*

Twitter exploded as people put two and two together and tweeted the news. On the one hand, Joyce was forgiving him in an interview, on the other side, it was being revealed that Bernard's Twitter account had been run by the elusive May Sparks, and that it had been her that had wooed back his wife.

I should have looked away because what good did it do to read the comments? But it was like I was possessed. I couldn't take my eyes off the screen, but just kept scrolling, as if I felt I should be punished, as if I wanted to hurt.

Joyce announced her presence on Twitter that night. Her followers went from 10 to 210 in the space of an hour. She tweeted that she felt ridiculed and embarrassed, but was determined to learn from her horrible experience. Her egg profile picture was soon swapped for a professional photograph, my guess from over ten years ago. As for her biog, she updated it to: *Not just Bernard Thompson Skinner's wife. Soon, not even his wife. Hurrah.*

While thousands of strangers ganged up against me, others focused on doling out their support to Joyce, which I hope must have helped her a little bit.

JAMELIAFOND TV @JAMMYFOND
@melottijoie everyone is so angry on your behalf and we're all supporting you! Be strong!

MHKING @KING234
@merlottijoie don't let that bitch and bastard get you down! We will find them and kill them (metaphorically speaking, at least!)

ANKARADAVIES @ANKARADAVIES
IMHO women should support each other, not conspire with men to deceive them. #MaySparks should come forward and apologise.

"May?"

I look up to find my mum staring at me. It's the third time I've been caught miles away this evening. She points her big silver serving spoon at the bowl of creamy, raspberry trifle.

"Dessert?"

"Just give her some, she looks like she needs fattening up," Katie says. "Seriously, sis, you look too thin. You're alright, aren't you?"

My shoulders sag and I feel my resolve to keep everything to myself weaken. There's nothing worse than a bit of well-meant concern. It makes you feel okay to be vulnerable because you're in safe hands. These are the people I trust most in the world. Well, all of them, except Lucas, but he does have one of those kind smiles, so maybe I could trust him too.

"It's stress..." I say, and I swallow back a lump in my throat.

"At work?" Katie asks, gently.

I can't bring myself to speak, so I just nod. I take my bowl from Mum and focus on filling my spoonful with a bit of each layer of trifle. If they move on to a different topic, I'll be fine, but if they ask me about work...

"You were stressed last time, too, weren't you?" Mum says. "You had a bit of a crisis on your hands."

"Oh yes," Dad chips in, "There was someone hacking your client on the Twitter thing, wasn't there?"

"Yeah, but it turned out he was hacking himself."

"What do you mean?" Katie says, her jaw dropping.

"He blamed all his nasty tweets on a hacker, but it was him all along."

I think of Damian watching himself on television with this self-satisfied grin on his face.

"Wow," Katie says. "He sounds like he needs therapy."

"He's not your client any more, is he?" Mum says.

I shake my head.

"That's good."

"Well..."

I'm about to tell them everything, but then the doorbell rings. Mum looks confused. She glances at Dad, who is looking back at her, equally baffled.

"What have we forgotten?" she says.

"It could be a neighbour dropping off a parcel?"

"But we've been in all day."

In spite of the money troubles and the mess, my parents' home has always felt like a safe place. It's where I want to be when I feel sick or when I'm feeling flat. That's why I don't even consider that the person on the other side of our front door could be after me.

But did I really think that that cameraman outside our office would give up so easily? Did I really think I could disappear without a trace only an hour away from my flat?

"May?" I hear my mum's loud voice say. "Yes, she is. Who are you?"

I leap out of my chair and run in the living room, but don't go out to the front door.

"Shut the door!" I hiss. "Don't let him in!"

Katie hurries out to see what's happening. "What is it, May?"

I stare at her, my heart pounding. "Lucas was right... I am trending. It's me. And it's for a horrible reason."

Katie registers my panic in seconds and hurries to the door to help Mum get rid of the cameraman, who is trying to push himself into our home, into the space I no longer feel safe in.

"We just want her comment!" a deep voice barks. "Doesn't she want to tell her side of the story?"

I cower in the living room, praying he'll just disappear.

"I'm sorry, she's not here," my mum says, in a shrill voice.

"That's funny because you said she was a minute ago," replies a mocking voice.

Katie comes to the rescue. "If you don't get off our property right this minute, I'll call the police."

He protests that she's overreacting, that he's doing May Sparks a favour giving her the chance to stand up for herself. But Katie is unmoved and eventually he gets the message and retreats reluctantly from the house.

Chapter 49

When the doorbell sounds at ten o'clock next morning, I think it must be the paparazzi again. My body tenses. I'm still in bed, though I've been awake for hours. I am completely lacking the motivation and the guts to face the day.

It's not fair. Why are they hounding *me*? There are wars breaking out and epidemics and plane crashes and human rights violations, but none of *that* is trending.

I hear my dad shout gruffly at the door. "Who is it?"

It could be Katie and Lucas. They left half an hour ago to see the sights, but perhaps they forgot something. It seems unlikely, though.

I can't hear the reply, just the clunk of the lock being turned. I sit up in my bed, alarmed because it sounds as if he's letting someone in. I strain my ears to hear the low voices in conversation. Is some sly journalist lying his way into our house? I feel the approach of panic and consider screaming down the stairs, GET OUT! In the end I keep my mouth shut. I don't want to blow my cover.

The door closes and there's no more talking. I lean back into my pillow, relieved. Last night was awful. I hated the look on my parents' faces as I confessed the whole story. They couldn't get their heads around me pretending to be all those other people. The way Katie had kept saying, over and over, that it was the clients'

363

fault, not mine, only made it feel like she was trying to convince herself. I just felt so ashamed to have let them all down so badly.

The stairs creak as someone climbs them slowly. There's a pause and then a quiet knock on the door.

"May?" my dad says.

"Yes?"

He comes in, looking uncomfortable. "There's someone at the door for you."

The dread washes over me and I shake my head. "I don't want to talk to any journalists. If I don't feed the story it will die. No one trends forever."

"He says he's your friend. He says he's called Alex Hunter."

My heartbeat quickens. What on earth is he doing here?

"Do you know him?"

"He's my neighbour... what does he want?"

My dad looks relieved. "I was worried I was being tricked. I'll go let him in, poor man."

"But I'm in my pyjamas!"

"I can't leave him outside, can I? It's drizzling. You get changed while I make him a cup of tea."

I can hardly ask my dad to tell him to piss off instead. He heads towards the door, not needing my answer, but then stalls and turns around.

"Are you two...?"

I stare at him, my eyes widening. Is my dad going to ask me what I think he is?

He changes his mind. "It's very sweet of him to come all this way."

I'm about to say appearances can be deceptive, but hold myself back. I don't want my dad to side against him.

While my dad lets him in I hurry to get ready. I've been borrowing Katie's clothes, which are all too big. I put my outfit on from my first day, which, being a skirt-and-shirt number, seems ridiculously formal. Then I put on some mascara and brush my hair.

Fifteen minutes later, with a knot in my stomach, I go downstairs. I don't know what I'm going to feel when I see him. I felt so angry, so betrayed. The worst thing was not getting an explanation or an apology.

I find him in the kitchen, leaning on one of the chairs, turned towards the window. He's wearing a plain grey t-shirt and worn jeans, a watch with a khaki wrist strap that brings out the tan on his arms. His unruly hair is drying and he pushes it back as he stands there, unaware I'm watching him.

My dad glances up as he pours water into the cafetière.

"Hello, love..." he says.

Alex snaps to attention, taking his hand off the chair, like he's been caught doing something naughty.

"May!" His voice breaks as if he hasn't used it for a while. "Hi, sorry to barge in on you like this so early in the morning."

My dad shakes his head, "you should have seen the other guy last night, now that was barging in."

Alex looks startled by the revelation. "Who was it?"

"Just some guy wanting my photo..." I say.

I suppose Dad must be waiting for me to give this "friend" a hug. That would be the normal thing to do. But it's complicated.

"I'll do that," I say, getting the cups from the cupboard.

I can sense Alex's eyes on me.

"Alright, love," he says, "I'll leave you to it."

I'm grateful that he understands without me needing to spell it out. He heads into the dining room and I hear him switching on the radio.

With just the two of us now, the atmosphere grows tense. I pour out the coffee and hold out a mug to him.

"Here."

I can barely meet his eyes.

"May, look at me," he says.

His voice is so firm, I instinctively obey. I find myself locked

365

in a blue kaleidoscope of emotions. He's trying to say how sorry he is just by looking at me. He's pleading with me, he's asking me to forgive him without uttering a word.

"What?" I say, glancing away. He's not going to win me over that easily.

He sighs.

"How are you holding up?"

"Fine."

How annoyed should I be? I'm not even sure. He undermined my clients, but it wasn't him who blew my cover. And he didn't have to come all this way.

It's not like he's one of the people hounding me on Twitter. I fixated on one of his tweets for a while yesterday. I know he wrote it thinking of me, and not of his following. It soon got buried in his feed.

TINTINO @TINTINO
Think we should leave #MaySparks alone and go back to looking for Wally! #oldschool

He pulls out a chair and sits down.

"Did Louisa give you the address, then?"

"Yes. She's really worried about you. She wanted to come down too, but she couldn't change her shift."

I wonder how far we can go with just small-talk. There's always the weather. How it looks like the best of summer might be over. I pull out a chair and sit down next to him. I've so many questions still unanswered.

"Did you know they were all my clients?"

He winces, runs a hand through his hair. "Yeah, I worked it out... Louisa isn't very good at keeping secrets, is she?"

"So you were taking the piss knowing it was me on the other end."

"I was annoyed with what you were doing. I was working in the studio with Damian and he was a complete wanker to everyone, and yet you were making him out to be this wonderful, holistic, friendly guy. I couldn't take it."

"You should have told me."

"Would it have made a difference? You were being paid to tweet for him, nothing you would have tweeted would ever have been true."

I swallow the urge to argue. I thought I'd had a choice in the company, but I hadn't. Craig wouldn't have let me drop Damian, like he hadn't let me opt out of working with Bernard.

"You said yourself I wasn't a troll," Alex says, his expression pained. "You only found my tweets because you were looking for them... as for that tweet that got into the paper, I could never have anticipated that."

But that doesn't explain why he's here now.

"Why did you want to meet me for lunch if you hated what I was doing?"

"I don't know..." he lets out a little laugh. "There's something about you. Even when we were arguing I just felt like I wanted to kiss you."

I can feel myself blushing. "It doesn't make any sense."

"Does it have to?"

I don't know.

"What do you want, Alex?"

He gives me a weak smile. "I want to take you away from it all."

If only it was that simple.

"I know it's a bit rash, but I've hired a car. I thought I could whisk you off to Wales."

I start to laugh. He can't be serious.

"I've got a tent. It's only a single, but I thought maybe your parents could lend you one... or not, I mean, I don't mind if you want to share my tent."

"You're joking, right?"

He shakes his head. "No. I know it's mad, but why not?"

"Because I'm angry with you!"

"I know... and you can still shout at me, but by the seaside."

I cover my mouth because my face is cracking into a smile, and I feel I should be angry a little longer yet.

"It will be fun. You'll get away from it all," he says.

Get away from it all? I think about all the people who I've hurt. Joyce can't get away from it all. Ankara still feels used. Thijs will always be known as the one who tried to buy the public's affection.

My face falls. Alex reaches forward and squeezes my shoulders.

"Trust me. Everything is going to be fine. You and everyone else are going to get past this."

I shake my head. "I don't deserve to get away from it all. I need to say sorry to all these people. I need to email them now."

"Come to Wales. Give yourself some time to breathe, to find your voice, to know what you've got to say."

I breathe out. "I can't... I've got no clothes."

Why is he grinning at me? I'm not joking. There is no way I'm going to a blustery coast wearing my office angel clothes.

"Yes you do," he says.

"No. I don't."

"Trust me. You do."

"Where?"

"In the hire car. Louisa packed everything you could ever need."

Why am I not surprised Louisa was involved? I can just imagine her writing lists and getting excited about it all. She's probably dying to know how I'm reacting. She would be so disappointed if I didn't give him a chance.

"Well?" he says. "Will you come to Wales with me?"

I hear the key in the front door. My mum starts talking before she's even made it inside. My dad thinks he's whispering, but we both hear him clearly telling her that "a young man" has come around to see me. Mum whispers loudly back that, oh, she had no idea there was a "young man on the scene".

My cheeks redden and I look at Alex.

368

"Aren't you afraid to tell my parents you're whisking me away to Wales without any warning? They might be really protective," I say, raising an eyebrow.

My mum, who can't stand suspense, rushes into the kitchen with a load of shopping bags.

"Hello," she says, smiling brightly. "Who are you, then?"

"Alex," I say. "He's a friend."

She drops her bags and offers him her hand. He gets to his feet and she looks him up and down, her eyes sparkling with excitement, and I make up my mind there and then.

"He's come to pick me up. We're going to Wales."

My mum's eyes widen. "Wales?"

"Yes, until it all dies down," Alex says. "I thought it would be good for May to have a break from all the virtual noise."

Mum nods her head. "I totally agree. That's a fabulous idea, Alex."

Oh God, that means she really likes the looks of him.

"But you've got to eat something before you go!" she says, pointing at his chair, "sit down, I'll make you a sandwich."

She wants to ask him a 101 questions. I witnessed Lucas's interrogation on the first day. It wasn't gentle.

"It's already quite late," I say.

"Well, you get ready," Mum says, "and I'll make Alex a sandwich."

Alex grins at me. "Sounds good to me. I left your stuff in the living room."

I roll my eyes at him when my mum's back is turned. He looks like he's in his comfort zone now and it gives me this warm feeling seeing him so at ease in the place I call home. I leave them chatting amicably behind and head upstairs to have a shower. I forgot to mention that no one in this house owns a tent, which means we're going to have to share the single.

I may have my own clothes now, but I'm still missing decent pyjamas. I cast my eyes over the big baggy pink ones borrowed from my mum. I may still harbour some resentment towards

Alex, but it's certainly not enough to submit him to an image of me in those.

A little shiver of excitement runs down my spine at the thought of being alone with him.

I grab my dressing gown off my bed and notice my phone lying on my pillow. Should I leave it behind? I might need it in an emergency. I just won't turn it on. It'll be easier to keep it off while Alex is close by.

Chapter 50

We don't get to the coast until gone three o'clock and in the four-hour drive we find out a lot about each other. After being so discreet about his Twitter account, I'm surprised that Alex is so open about everything else. It turns out the short film he wanted to make was based on the story of his father, who was a keen footballer and was on his way to hear the good news that he'd been selected to play for the first team, third division, when he was hit by a car. Alex was only three, but he can remember being taken to the hospital to "say hello to Daddy". He remembers being held near this pale man covered in tubes and feeling afraid. His dad was on a life-support machine, and a month later his mum took him back to "say goodbye to Daddy". Apparently he'd thrown a tantrum in the hospital corridor and refused to go into the room. The guilt caught up with him, still makes him cry sometimes. The film was a way of making himself feel better, imagining that his father was in a dream, where he could live out the life he had wanted.

Alex has decided to postpone it for a while, until he's sure it's a good film and not just a cathartic experience. I tell him not to think so much, that it won't be the last film he ever makes, and maybe he needs to get this one out before he can move on to making others.

After that we spend a while just talking about films. I tell him about the moment I realised he was Tintino. He says his dad used to read him the comic books at bedtime, putting on all these funny voices. He says he opened his Twitter account in 2006 one late night and, scrabbling for a username, just looked around his flat and his eye landed on those comic books. He bought the Tintin figurine in a charity shop a few years later.

"It didn't occur to me to think of branding," he laughs. "I probably should have used my name and tied it into my website and everything. But I usually act first, think later."

"Your tweet made it into a national newspaper. You must be doing something right," I say.

The road is narrow now and all around is lush and green. Spots of sunlight fall between the leaves, leaving a pattern on the tarmac. I wind down the window and breathe in the sea air. We pass picturesque houses with gardens bursting with flowers and twee garden decorations, and pubs with hanging baskets and sandwich boards announcing the fish of the day.

I feel excited. We pay for our stay and drive down the bumpy road to the field where we are going to camp. Alex has done all the driving and only when we stop, does he lean back, let out a sigh and admit he didn't sleep a wink the night before.

"I kept going over it in my head," he says. "What I was going to say, what you might say. I didn't know if you would come."

I smile. "I'm glad you had the guts."

"Ditto."

When I frown at him, he shrugs. "You don't know me that well. It takes guts to be spontaneous."

I open the car door and get out. We left the drizzle in London. It's windy but the air is warm and the sun is about to break out from behind the clouds.

"Come on," I say, feeling another surge of excitement. "Let's get a blanket and lie in the sand dunes. You need a nap."

"I need a beer."

"A beer and a nap?"

He sighs again. "It sounds like heaven."

Thanks to Louisa's forethought we have everything we need. Jacob has supplied us with more of his beer, though Alex admits he's actually finding the last batch too bitter and goes up to the small corner shop to get some cans of Red Stripe. A minute up the sandy path, we remove our shoes and, laughing, we slip and slide up to the dunes.

At the top, we take in the stunning view of the sea and of the cliffs rising up in the distance covered in bright-green grass. The beach stretches out for some distance before meeting the grey-blue sea. Surfers in wetsuits take on the choppy waves or watch each other from the shore.

Alex flaps the blanket out and tries to bring it down flat, the ends rebelling at the last minute and folding back on themselves. I help spread it out and rest a shoe on each corner. He passes me one of the beers and we sit with our knees up and grin at each other. I crack open mine and the releasing hiss seems to reflect all my stresses being let off into the summer air.

"This is perfect."

We sit in silence, sipping our beers. Gulls cry in the distance, voices of other people looking for a private dune rise and fall around us.

"Normally I'd have taken at least five photos by now," I say. "My mind would be buzzing with which hashtags would get the most shares and I'd be composing a dozen captions at a time... I'd either be stressing because the coverage is bad, or stressing because I'd managed to send out the tweets but feeling they could have been better, then I'd be debating whether to delete them, but wondering if I sent out a practically repeated tweet a second later, would it look desperate? And then, of course, if no one replied, I'd feel like I tweeted something really dumb, and then have to check what I said..."

"Oh my God, stop!" Alex laughs.

"I couldn't.... I can't. I'm thinking now whether I should be tweeting something, or at least sharing this on my own Facebook, and proving I do have a life away from work after all. We could do a selfie right now, actually. You look gorgeous, so it will get loads of likes and smiley faces and..."

My face has gone red because I've just called him "gorgeous", but I'm ploughing on in case he notices. But it seems he's too busy digging his can into the sand. Then he takes mine straight out of my grasp and pushes it in the sand next to his.

"I was enjoying that," I say, mock-grumpily.

He's sitting up now, and he turns to me, smiling.

"Come here," he says. He reaches for my hand and draws me towards him. We are sitting face to face, and I'm thinking of making a joke about having a blinking match. But it's only because I'm feeling nervous and excited, because the atmosphere between us is suddenly so charged. He puts his hand on my neck and I feel this flutter of butterflies, and then he leans forward and kisses me.

It doesn't feel like a kiss between two people who have spent their brief history bickering. It's tender and sexy and our lips gel as though they belong to each other. We get into a more comfortable position, lying on our blanket, him on his back, me resting on his chest. I breathe in the spice and sandalwood scent of his aftershave and kiss him again. Of all the people I know, I didn't think it would be Alex Hunter coming to my rescue with a hire car and a tent.

"This is our moment," Alex says, stroking my hair behind my ear. "We don't have to take pictures to prove it happened."

"It's going to take me a while to retrain my brain."

"Close your eyes..."

I rest my cheek against his chest and close my eyes.

"Listen to the sea..."

I breathe in deeply and let my senses float out beyond our bubble on top of the sand dune. I can smell salt and seaweed and charcoal, and a hint of beer. The breeze rustles the leaves in the bushes around us. Beyond that sound I can hear the rush of water like an amplified whisper, of the waves dragging the sand back and forward along the shore. I can feel the sun on my hand, my nose, my cheek. I feel my body relaxing, my eyelids feel heavy. I am falling asleep. Judging from his breath, Alex is falling asleep too. We are falling asleep together on the beach. It feels intimate, it feels right.

A weird vibration in my pocket pulls me back from the oblivion I was seconds from finding. An annoying beat gathers momentum, triggering a familiar jolt of panic. Alex groans.

How many moments has that ringtone ruined? I swear and scrabble to get it out of my pocket. It's Craig. I get to my feet, wanting to spare Alex the interruption and hurry over to the furthest edge of our mound in the sand dune.

"Hello?"

My voice is so tentative. Was there ever a time I answered my phone without this feeling of dread?

"May? Thank God you're there! I think your phone is broken, I've been trying to get through to you for ages!" Craig cries.

I open my mouth to tell him that I've actually had it switched off a lot of the time, but he keeps on talking.

"Now I know I said you should take some time off, but now I'm thinking we should be striking while the iron's hot, taking advantage of all this publicity you're getting..."

"What are you talking about? It's bad publicity! It's over! I'll never get a client ever again."

There's a smile in Craig's voice, "Well, that's what you would have thought, but we're getting a lot of phone calls, actually... a lot of people think it was all an elaborate stunt to get our clients' names out there, and they are out there now, aren't they? Right now everyone knows who Thijs is, and Bernard, and Damian..."

"Yes, but it was all a lie. How can anyone think that lying to their fans is the way to go after what's happened?"

"It wasn't lying exactly..."

I glance behind me to see if Alex is listening. He's resting on his elbows looking at me with a sad smile. He's disappointed. He thought he could take me away from it all, but he's thinking that he can't take myself away from me. That *I'm* the problem, not the job.

Craig is babbling in my ear at turbo-speed. The good feeling I had is fading. I'm being dragged back to that drama and I don't want to go.

"Craig," I say. "I don't want to do it any more."

"You can do it! You're brilliant at this, you're the real star in this company! Gabe and me are just your minions, really..."

"You misheard me, I didn't say I can't do it, I said I don't want to do it."

"I know you've wanted a salary increase and now I'll be able to do that! How far away are you? Can you come in now so we can talk about it?"

The tide is coming in. A girl is in a race against it to reach her bag. Too late, the water sloshes over it and she shrieks in dismay. An elderly couple nearby say something to her. Behind them, two surfers balance in parallel. The slightest wrong twist and one slips and falls, disappearing for a moment beneath the grey. That's what it would feel like to go back, like falling into the dark.

"No," I say again.

"You need a bit of time, I understand that, but hear me out..."

"No, you don't understand. I'm ashamed of what I did. I'm never going to be someone else's voice again."

The surfer's head pushes through the water, mouth open, gasping for breath.

We all deserve a second chance.

"From now on, I'm only using my voice."

"But, May, listen to me..."

I reach my arm back behind my head, the phone still in my hand, and with all my energy I lob it into the air.

My heart pounds with exhilaration as I watch it sailing far away from it. It lands somewhere, without a sound.

Silence.

"Shit," Alex says. "You could have killed someone."

I turn around, suddenly guilty. "I didn't think of that."

"And it's littering."

"Damn. You're right."

Alex breaks into a smile. "I'm still glad you did it. It makes me feel like you're going to be alright"

I smile back at him. "I am going to be alright. I know that now."

I head back to the blanket and resume my position beside Alex. I nuzzle my head into his neck and close my eyes again. The noise in my head fades for the first time in months, and an overwhelming sense of peace pervades me. In that moment, not looking ahead, not looking back, not wanting to freeze it, not wanting to share it, or track it or analyse it, or have other people validate it.... just being, there, in the moment, I find happiness.

Epilogue

It's time. I breathe into my cupped hands to settle the nerves.

Alex is adjusting the tripod. It's a pretty impressive camera to record a little YouTube video with, but it seems silly not to take advantage while we've got it. Ten minutes ago Alex declared *Shadow Man* a wrap. It took three days in total to film and I was there every minute of it, helping out with the food and making teas for everyone when they were flagging.

Louisa was a great nurse, although with her patient in a coma the whole time, she didn't have as many lines as she would have liked. Jacob says her expressions spoke louder than words, which means he's besotted. He's spending a lot of time here, and they're very intense, but intensity is what Louisa loves. Luckily I've been able to escape to the flat upstairs. I'm determined not to make staying there every day a habit. I don't want to rush things. What we've got going, Alex and I, I want it to work.

The motley film crew has gone ahead to the local pub for wrap drinks, leaving Alex and I alone. We have to do it now so we can return the camera, another day's hire is another eight hundred pounds. My video might make a stir, but I can't afford that.

"Ready?" Alex says, peering through the camera lens.

"I think so."

I've gone for a plain green t-shirt and a simple silver necklace.

I'm wearing subtle makeup and I've curled the ends of my hair to boost my confidence. I want to appear humble, not defeated.

"I'm going to count you in..." Alex says. "Are you ready?"

"Oh God..."

"Just be yourself."

I might not be trending on Twitter any more, but I haven't been forgotten either, like I hoped I would. There are vile blog posts about me, and outpourings of hate, and rude cartoons. No one has any facts, so I've basically turned into this evil caricature.

A lot of people think I'm mad doing this. They think I should stay in the shadows, safe and out of trouble. But there are things I need to say. It's just taken me a little while to formulate it all. I've been so busy developing other people's voices, I forgot for a moment what it's like to have my own – my own voice and my own audience.

Alex hold up his thumb and I nod.

Three, two, one ...

"Hello, my name is May Sparks. I know a few people have been wondering where I've been. I'm sorry it's taken me so long to show up, but when you do something you're not proud of, it takes time to come to terms with it. But I'm here with an apology, and I hope the people I've hurt will be able to forgive me..."

I do my utmost not to well up when I direct my message to Joyce, telling her how despicable my actions were. The last thing I need is people criticising me for acting like the victim. It will happen, though. You can't please everyone, and I shouldn't try to. I've seen what it's like to constantly seek approval. No happiness comes of it.

To Damian, I wish him all the best in finding what he's looking for. I don't mention that he hacked himself. He has enough issues to deal with.

To Angel, I tell her I was wrong, that she should go after what she loves. HappyHeart was never her first choice, it was always mine. Luckily, that door hasn't closed. After I admitted to Ola what had happened there was silence for a week. Then last night she sent me an email saying she still wanted a meeting, but with me. She wants to know if I'll help her with HappyHeart's social media profile. She said she had time for anyone passionate about her company, and despite everything, she senses I am. So there might be a part-time job in there somewhere, which will be good. I'm not ready to jump into anything full-time just yet. I need to take a bit more time for myself.

Tomorrow I'm catching up with the old gang. It'll be at Clare's new flat and Emma will be there too. I'll give them my full attention and I'll not spend one minute tapping on my phone. Not just because my phone is busted, either. Turns out sand isn't so soft after all. Alex has leant me an old Nokia from the days before internet. Right now, I'm in no hurry to change it.

"... from now on I'll only be using my own voice and only supporting causes I believe in. I've learned that integrity is everything and you can't buy fans or love or approval..."

There was never going to be a pay rise. If I'd been a mathematician I might have worked that out sooner. The numbers would never have added up. Would I have carried on being a professional liar if my cover hadn't been blown and the salary had been delivered? I'm glad I wasn't put to that test. I like to think I would have done the right thing, but money has corrupted stronger people than me. Eventually the noise and emptiness would have forced me to re-evaluate my life, and I'm sure I would have chosen a different path in the end. I'm just glad it's been sooner rather than later.

"There are hundreds of opinions about what I've done and what I haven't done. Most likely you've already made up your mind about me. Well, in that case, thank you for stopping by and listening to this video to the end. All I can say is, this is my voice, and it's the only one that belongs to me. I'm not evil, I never meant to hurt anyone, I'm just an ordinary girl who lost her way for a while. Now I'm on a new path, and it feels right, and I'd love your support so we can leave the past and head together into the future... It took a while to

find my voice again, but I've found it now. My name's May Sparks, thank you for listening to my side."

Alex switches off the camera and we stay in silence for a moment, the atmosphere heavy with my apology. I feel torn between crying and laughing. It feels like one life ending, another beginning. Alex gets his computer to upload the video. I lie back on my bed, the weight I've been carrying a little lighter now.

I listen to his fingers tap over the keyboard. To think Alex pretended he was low-tech and a social media beginner. I look over at him and feel a burst of affection.

"I hope Tintino has something nice to say about me."

He doesn't look up, but a smile plays at the corners of his lip.

"You know Tintino doesn't do soppy."

He's booked a table for dinner, somewhere posh, he said, to mark this moment.

"He does offline," I point out.

"But no one needs to know that."

No, no one does. Just because something isn't documented, doesn't mean it doesn't exist.

I slide down beside him and kiss his neck.

"I'm going to take forever if you're going to start that..." he says, nudging me off.

I lean my head on his shoulder and smile. Just because you don't write what you're feeling in your status update, doesn't mean you don't feel. I don't think any emoticon could describe this feeling of hope and fear and love.

"Okay, May Sparks," Alex says. "You're live."

I glance up at the video, my face frozen behind the play arrow. A few weeks ago I would have insisted on staying in the whole night to spend the evening clicking refresh.

"Thank you," I say, and then I reach over and close the laptop softly shut.

Acknowledgements

Thank YOU. Yes, YOU. I'm absolutely thrilled that you bought my book. There are moments on this writing journey where you feel like you're climbing up a rocky mountain carrying a grand piano. A niggling voice tells you that you're being ridiculous, you'll never make it, no one will be up there to hear you play, and why couldn't you have chosen a lighter instrument, like the triangle? Thank you for making the climb worth it.

I may tease our social media addicted society, but I'm so grateful to all those people on Twitter and Facebook who encourage me, engage with me, laugh with me, educate me, and don't immediately unfollow me when I tweet nonsense. Thank you to all the readers, writers and book bloggers who have shared my work with so much enthusiasm - thank you @StephenCandy, @KimCooper, @debrabrown_ @beccasboooks @fhayesmccoy @Rosie_Canning @LindsayBamfield @Scarlettelling @JacquelenePye - to name just a few!

Thanks to my wonderful agent, Laura Longrigg, for her insight and for pushing me to make the book the best it could be. This is just the beginning!

To my husband, who, with a roll of the eyes, stopped me succumbing to the selfie craze - thank you for being such a positive influence in my life. To my wonderful family in Wales, England, Spain and Colombia, thank you for your continuing enthusiasm for what I do.

Finally, back to YOU. If you loved #PleaseRetweet please help me spread the word! Tell the postman, tell your grandma, tell your cat, tell your friends – every tweet, every status update, every post about my book helps me on my next literary climb! And do come over and say hello on Twitter @EmilyBenet – I'm sure we'll get along just fine!